SHADOWS OF ATLANTIS

GOLDEN AGE SERIES: BOOK 2

DD ADAIR

To Alexis,
Even in the darkest of times,
there is always a light to be found.

Love,
Diana Adair

Spiral Path
PRESS

Copyright © 2018 by Spiral Path Press
First Edition

Published by Spiral Path Press
PO Box 1183 Divide, CO 80814.

Cover design by Susan Krupp at yuneekpix.com
Maps drawn by Dr. Jason Grundhauser.

For information about special pricing for bulk sales, please contact Spiral Path Press at ddadair2@gmail.com

ISBN: 978-1-7328055-6-9 (paperback)
ISBN: 978-1-7328055-7-6 (ebook)
ISBN: 978-1-7328055-8-3 (audiobook)

Library of Congress Control Number:

Please visit the author's website at www.ddadair.com

To my Siblings, my Parents, my Friends and my Lovers

Two things—maybe three;
When you wonder if I'm writing about you. I am.
When I disappear into this writing addiction, assume I still love you. I do.
And thank you, for helping me become.

Placement of Atlantis in the Atlantic Ocean

Bourne of lightning and fire,
One shows the way. Mark
the hour of early birth with
crimson flower.
Darkness flayed in breast of men,
given now the way to mend.
Heed the two, follow one and
light prevails before
end.

One to come and turn
the tides, clear destruction
of evil minds.
Change the course and move
our race to fearless ground
on higher plane.
Be it so on mountains high
midst scouring wind and clouds
that fly.

Courses etched among the stars,
mirrored on earth in blood and flowers.
Salvation wove as dark and light
work together, ignite

a spark of endings to begin.
Birth causes death
and in between,
triumphs of time and sadness wing
to end unholy reign.

-Atlantis Book of Prophecies: Vol. Six

RUINS AND SPIRITS

9,971 BCE. CRYSTAL CITY, ATLANTIS

"... he is to instruct them about all the periods of history for eternity ... and in the statutes of the truth. Anticipating the time, dominion passes from Belial and returns to the Sons of Light."

— "THE COMING OF MELCHIZEDEK", FRAGMENT OF
THE DEAD SEA SCROLLS

AHNA

"Why would there be a door three hundred feet above the ground?" Aiela's exotic, angular face squinted with incredulity, straining to peer skyward on this relentlessly sunny morning. One hand swept back strands of blackberry-colored hair, escaped from her mass of braids.

Wind gushed and stilled in a rhythm only the mountain folds understood.

"I'm not sure it's *three* hundred feet. Ziel will know." Ahna's gaze roamed the valley below, trying to spot Ziel and Auntie Sage in this deserted ruin, overtaken by high mountain forest.

She could see faint movement of spirits as they bustled to and fro in their own time, unaware of visitors. Unaware that their city had become a monument, an uninhabitable place where the veil was too thin to fully separate time dimensions. Like catching movement from the periphery, they were here and gone before her brain could translate what exactly it saw.

Her teeth chattered, not just from the cold. "What's taking them so long?"

Aiela shrugged and turned, thin sunlight catching the pale blue tattoo, a double spiral running along the left side of her long neck. "Auntie Sage has never been here. Ziel's likely showing off. His colors sure get brighter when she's around."

"And she... softens." Ahna added. They smiled knowingly.

No one had lived here since the third Epoch. For one thing, the energetic frequency was too fast to stay more than a few hours. The four of them had prepared themselves all week; eating special foods, meditating for hours, applying essential oils, and tuning their chakras with crystals twice a day. Even so, they'd stay here only a short time.

Originally, Crystal City was Atlantis' treasure vault. Their entire collection of knowledge had been stored and maintained here. For it wasn't metals or jewels, not beautiful art nor any rare substance that Atlantis valued most. It was knowledge. The accumulation of all that had been experienced and learned in millions of lifetimes, since souls first began inhabiting human form on planet Earth.

Here, midst a mountain range of quartz, the Ancients had built an entire city from crystals—some left whole, most ground into a cement that could be cast in molds or friezes, designed and embellished in endless ways. Such high frequency had been all the protection needed. It was rumored those of low frequency could not physically see the city, and few could enter without intense illness or mental distress.

Ahna and Aiela, one light, one dark, waited on a worn flat spot, perhaps a balcony once, hewn into the mountainside. Bare, jagged peaks jutted out in all directions. Crumbling remnants of this once holy City, littered a bowl-shaped valley below with broken walls and toppled columns.

"If only we could fly like our ancestors!" Ziel panted as he and Sage appeared in the arched stone doorway, gasping from their climb. Dressed alike in creamy linen tunic and pants, with light-reflecting cloaks of gold thread streaming behind them, they looked a perfectly contrasted pair. Shoulder-length silver hair blew across his fine-boned face, the color of burnt sugar. Light cerulean eyes gave him an almost alien look. Auntie Sage's skin was as pale and welcoming as butter. Her features were soft, almost blunt, topped by long hair turning from gold to cream and currently piled into a messy bun.

"There you are, we wanted to ask you about that." Aiela pointed to the curious round door, glinting high above where they stood.

"How's everyone feeling? Alright so far?" Ziel glanced at each in turn, concerned they not stay too long in this high ancient place.

"Symptoms are comparable to oxygen deprivation at extreme altitudes", he'd explained to them over and over. "You may feel light-headed, or hyper-focused as your brain works overtime in an environment that uses more of it. You will tire quickly because your body struggles continuously to adapt."

"We're fine." Aiela answered.

Ziel tipped his head back, gazing at the weathered door. "That was for the Priests and Priestesses of this original Temple of Knowledge. You had to be able to levitate to enter. It was once Atlantis' most sacred place—where the wisdom of the universe was kept—both a vault and a test that contained the understanding of where we all began. Some of it was brought to us by visitors from the stars."

"I thought *everybody* could fly back then." Ahna puzzled.

"Not everybody. There were those who carried the ability, the innate understanding of levitation—unbinding gravity's force—and also plenty who didn't. It's the same today; we have natural talents and abilities that differ widely from each other. Such as the ability to draw a perfect likeness of what we see, or the ability to flourish fields of plants, or engineer complex technologies based on mathematics. It only *seemed* that everyone could fly, because those that could, helped transport those that couldn't, by touching them, or levitating simple objects. A carpet often carried those people and objects gravity-bound on their own. It's said the energy used was the same frequency as a child playing. That sort of joy and pure imaginative state the brain enters when involved in play. We are all capable of it—even still today —if only we tuned in to the exact frequency."

"At the time this city was constructed, Atlanteans believed those with such powers were holier than others. So they were named Priestesses and Priests and became regarded as set apart—a higher or more advanced sect. This ability of flight was gradually lost, like many psychic powers after the third epoch's calamities destroyed much of humanity. Fewer and fewer of the remaining gifted ones procreated— so it was not passed down in DNA structures."

"And that door was for those who could fly." Aiela squinted at its faded gold luster. "What's inside now?"

Ziel shook his head. "Nothing. Everything was relocated. No doubt we've lost a bit. What's left is in the Hall of Records. Our 'Book of the Dead' was written here you know, along with some of the books and prophecies from the first two epochs."

Atlantis' 'Book of the Dead' was said to have been written by souls who'd passed on, returned to converse with the living. They assured humanity that death was not to be feared, describing in great detail the process of leaving a physical body, crossing to the "other side", and deciding what came next.

Ziel continued, "This was also home to the 'Seers', those who could see forward and backward in time as easily as you and I see the present. The Seers searched through future possibilities until they found what seemed the best outcome and Atlantis followed their suggestions. As humanity has fallen in frequency, those abilities disappeared. Snippets are all we have left; visions and dreams "

"Does the sun seem incredibly bright here, or is it just me?" Ahna's eyes hurt.

"It is bright at this altitude—stronger. But definitely not warmer!" Auntie Sage shivered and pulled her shimmering gold cloak around her, the breezes playing with her hair.

Ziel took Sage's hand. "Let's go inside. I will show you the things we came to see."

"It feels strange to see people alive in another time, doing daily things in the same space we're walking through now. I can't quite wrap my mind around it." Ahna spoke in hushed tones inside the crumbling building. It looked like the air itself took shape and moved. *What might they think,* Ahna wondered, *of being observed thousands of years after their time.*

Auntie Sage's eyes followed traces of movement around the room too, even in mid-air above. "The Space/Time continuum gets tangled in our understanding." She murmured. "Time seems a sequential straight line, because that is its movement from inside; A perspective quite different from the reality seen from without. Really, it's all happening at once in a spiral-like movement. Ascending rings of events take up the same space, separated only by time dimension. It's like time is really an infinity of space... or multiple spaces layered by time in the same space..."

She stopped with a small laugh, "My mind understands it but when I use words, it sounds confusing!"

Pausing to think, she squatted in the gloomy dust, drawing a line the length of two hands. "Space makes time possible." She crossed it with an equal line. "And time is what multiplies space, or makes it infinite. Where the two meet, is the hallowed place." Her fingertip dimpled the center of the equidistant cross. "Herein lies the present moment—which is all we really ever have."

She straightened, eyes tracking the ghostly movements again. "The energy is so special here—a much higher frequency—so the dimension membrane that normally separates time rings is thin. That's why we catch glimpses and echoes. Scents are the strongest. Can you smell the people walking by? The incense they burn here?"

Ahna stood still and closed her eyes, inhaling. "Sweetgrass, rose, pine resin, myrrh, and something else... it's familiar but I don't know what."

The four of them wandered, dream-like and abstruse, examining large interior halls with deteriorating walls. Centuries of mountain trees and grasses slowly digested the rubble humanity left behind. Each step they took grated with broken crystal shards, ground to a loud dust. Interior surfaces had been glazed with plasters made from powdered quartz, and the ruins still sparkled beneath earth's reclamations, when light passed by.

They gathered by a bank of hollow windows where sunbeams

touched the floor, turning its forgotten carpet of grit to flashing stardust.

"It may have been this very spot where our ancestors first conceived The Order of Melchizedek." Ziel began as they huddled in the scant warmth of the sun. All four of them gazed across the picturesque valley.

"There had always been a Melchizedek; One of great personal righteousness who devoted his or her lifetime to gathering, organizing and protecting humanity's knowledge. As you know, the experience of each and every lifetime is significant, sacred to our collective path. Each serves as mile cairns, maps, caution signs and 'place of interest' markers to those coming after.

Because knowledge of all our truths begats abiding peace, male Melchizedeks were called the King of Peace. Understanding and living according to our vast experiences begats a rightness or wisdom, so female Melchizedeks were called the Queen of Righteousness.

Portions of texts are missing that might have told what event or events caused the Melchizedek to become an Order. What we do know is, at some point, someone realized a time was coming when all knowledge must needs gradually be lost. That Someone wrote;

To enter the shadow is humanity's fate. To journey in darkness, our greatest hope. This choice shall wear the mask of doom, shall burn all truth. But ignorance begins our winding path home, to glory."

Ziel finished quoting, and glanced at the shivering forms around him. "Come, let's hydrate and warm up. We've perhaps an hour left, and there's more I want you to see."

He continued the story as they picked their way down stone steps, decaying in damp semi-gloom. "The Melchizedek who led this city at the end of the third epoch, was faced with a riddle; she knew that humanity would eventually destroy, change, lose, or reject every bit of truth they possessed, yet they would need to regain it once the lessons of darkness were learned."

"What lessons of darkness? I don't understand." Aiela asked, as they stepped into sunshine again and headed towards the shiny, triangular aero they had piloted here.

Ziel quirked an eyebrow. "I don't fully understand either. Perhaps it speaks of times past; those long descending cycles away from the Source of all that is." He sounded doubtful. "More likely, it is the long darkness still to come. Because we are born of Divine Source, we already know the light—indeed we are the light. It is the darkness that holds our greatest lessons."

Aiela nodded. "And spiritual darkness, by definition, would have to be void of truth."

"Yes." Ziel paused to study her, a gaze both affectionate and sad. "You are very like your mother, Aiela. So very like her..." His eyes were moist when he shook himself into motion again.

Auntie Sage passed out thermoses in the plush warmth of the aero.

They drank spiced plum tea, fragrant and steaming, while Ziel finished his tale.

"The Melchizedek who conceived the Order was female, but her plan depended on a male. She selected her successor, trained him with explicit instructions, then tricked him into taking her life, binding him into the duties and powers of the Melchizedek.

Following their plan, he encoded Atlantis' knowledge—the entire collective story of humanity—into his very DNA. For the first time, the knowledge became biologic, known as 'Body-gnosis'. It had been kept in many forms: written texts, symbols and images carved in stone, even geometrics and mathematical equations communicated through architecture of buildings. Eventually of course, it was encoded in crystals, as it is to this day.

Over a span of many and more years, hundreds of women from all over Atlantis came here to literally birth the Order. They were known as the 'Divine Feminine'. They came here, to the great Crystal Pyramid of all knowledge, to be impregnated with Melchizedek's seed. A process known as 'immaculate conception', because there was no mating or sexuality involved. It was all done clinically and spiritually.

As per the agreement, the Divine Feminine spread across the world, and the resulting 'virgin-birthed' babies grew into women who carried our universal knowledge, and passed it to their own daughters. On and on it went, down through generations. The Order of Melchizedek was established in the very bloodlines of we who must walk through a great 'era of wickedness'."

Ahna squinted in the over-bright afternoon as they emerged from the aero. City ruins flashed around them but the spot they stood on was empty. "I don't see Crystal Pyramid ruins, what happened to it?"

"I was wondering the same thing." Auntie Sage agreed. "You'd think it would have partially survived, as structurally sound as pyramids are."

"You tell me." Ziel looked intently at Ahna. "I think if you concentrate and ask the question, you could discover the answer. Try. See with your inner eye, listen with your ear of knowing."

Ahna and Aiela both closed their eyes, opening awareness to this strange place, as high mountain winds played sonatas through a thousand empty tree branches.

Nature's melodies rushed frantically to and fro, as if there were only this one moment of life. Arrhythmic and overlong pauses, highlighted bird voices singing odes to utter freedom, and arias to nature's bliss.

"I see it!" Ahna turned in slow circles, eyes shut tight, smiling in wonder. "We're standing inside... it was here on this very spot!"

"Yes! Yes it was!" Ziel clapped his hands together. "Describe what you see."

"It's huge! Just... enormous... made entirely of crystals. The pyramid walls are not smooth but formed from thousands of crystal clusters that spike out like fur standing on end. Both the exterior and interior surface in fact! It sparkles in the sun, so bright I can barely look. Most of the inside is filled with crystals, but there is a small chamber where about a dozen people could fit. It's in the upper third of the pyramid. Clear panes are laid as a floor. Other than that, there is only crystals... there must be millions!

El, you're here... I see you here with me!" She reached in Aiela's direction, catching her sister's hand like they had as little girls, facing their large, strange world together.

Aiela laughed with delight, "I *am* here with you. Look at this place!

It's incredible, and the altar! There are crystals forming all the moon phases."

"I wonder what it was for?" Ahna mused.

"I think it's used for the 'initiates'—what they call the women who come to form the Order. They go through an initiation called 'The Welcoming'. It's basically the process of impregnating them on a waxing moon night. They return on the next full moon to bless the conception and go through a ritual which attunes the mother's frequency to that of the embryo, so the DNA coding is less altered by her own." Aiela laughed again. "I don't even know how I know all this! I just feel it…"

But Ahna knew. They were born of this line—through Mama. Standing here in this thin place, the spirals of time overlapped, and she felt oddly split between realities.

"What else do you know… or see?" Auntie Sage asked.

"Only women were involved in the entire process, from beginning to end. Melchizedek's priestesses take the mothers through the initiation… because the divine feminine is to carry the knowledge… and the masculine is to protect it… because it will not be safe for a long, long time."

"What do you mean, the knowledge will not be safe?"

"It will be used by those negatively oriented, those addicted to power, those who seek to destroy beauty, or what is innocent and expansive. The knowledge will become weapons that control…" Aiela's voice lapsed into tones of horror.

Ahna had felt the rush of knowledge downloading into her awareness, saw the images her sister had spoken. There was more coming in so fast she could only focus on bits and pieces. But it was enough to complete the story. "Ohhhh. This pyramid, all these Crystals held the knowledge. This chamber was built specifically so Melchizedek could encode his own DNA within it."

Aiela was walking around in their luminous, fog-like dimension, examining things. "There is a beautiful, jeweled dagger on the altar, used to draw blood. After the conception, a tiny thimble of blood is taken from the initiate and poured into the earth… but I don't understand the significance…"

And then a moment later, "Of course! It's a covenant. A trinity of trinities, see? Crystal, blood, and feminine. The earth crystals correspond to the crystal matrix of the human body, which is a microcosm of the crystalline universe. The moon cycles correlate to feminine cycles which tell the story of universal cycles. Women bleed. Blood carries iron which interacts with earth iron, binding them like magnets, one to the other, signifying the covenant between humanity and this planet. A trinity is the strongest number there is and this particular trinity, this pact, ensured the DNA would be carried a long, long, looong time. They knew some bloodlines will end and others will be tampered with, diluted, but some must remain strong and pure to the end."

"To the end of what?" Sage asked.

"To the end of the 'Era of Wickedness'. They used the trinity of elements and energies to ensure the Order of Melchizedek will endure until humanity needs its knowledge back. Until those that live, perhaps, millennia in the future, are ready to have their history returned. Only then can they step from the shadow, made stronger by surviving their darkness." Aiela paused.

Ahna opened her eyes to see if Ziel and Sage understood. "It's the truths of Source. The Light of wholeness. We have to *understand* the light. We have to experience all possible darkness, before we can enter the higher realms of wholeness." She finished.

The four of them stood silent, each absorbing, what had just transpired.

Aiela, ever the inquisitive one, thought of one more question. "But where did it go? There should be remnants, a mountain of shards at least. It was so big! Why's there nothing here?"

Ziel looked pointedly at her. "How should I know? Get your own answers."

PIECE BY PIECE *the crystal pyramid was taken apart. A crowd of men and women worked feverishly, some using their minds to disassemble, the rest packing it into large wooden crates. The sky was dark. Menacing. And the*

earth itself moved, seeming to breathe and rumble. Ferocious winds tried to blow the workers off their feet and lightning grabbed at trees, rendering them to splinters spouting smoke and fire. But the workers kept on, ignoring the obstinate weather. A jolt shook her...

Ahna woke as the aero bounced in an air pocket.

"It's alright." Auntie Sage assured her from the co-pilot seat. "Just a spot of wind. We're nearly home." She looked tired. The visit, short as it was, had worn them all out.

Ahna and Aiela had curled up in the seats, falling asleep before the aero even reached traveling altitude.

"I dreamt of the Crystal Pyramid." Aiela sat up beside her, yawning. "It's in a land to the west. Somewhere on Merika. I saw priestesses re-assembling it and I saw the earth was rearranged around it like a mountain. It's inside a bare, beautiful Peak, part of a long chain of mountains that winds from north to south."

Ahna smiled. "I dreamt of it being packed up in a storm..."

2

NOT ENOUGH

9,971 HIGH CITY, ATLANTIS

"I have heard of certain words that have all the force in them, of the most powerful charms."

— SOCRATES

AIELA

*A*iela crunched on fat green snap-peas as she wrote, pausing to consult notes now and again. Her stomach felt empty enough to echo, not appeased with the handful of vegetables. She hadn't stopped to eat a meal since breaking her fast this morning—almost sixteen hours ago.

Ridiculous! Her mind joined the complaining. How had she gotten herself into this?

Most people worked an average of twenty hours in a week, choosing between four-hour shifts five days a week, or three seven-hour days. Apprentices, of course, had classes and studying that totaled more like thirty hours a week.

She wasn't most people though. Longingly, she pondered what it might be like to actually have free time again. Or even just time to enjoy proper meals.

Standing to stretch loudly, she set about heating water in her small, private room in the top-level of Poseidon's Palace; an unheard of luxury for a first year apprentice.

Impressive recommendations from the Ireland trip leaders—and of course the private influence of Ruler Ziel—had landed her a direct apprentice to Ruler Kenna, whose House was Justice. All of the first-level staff for the High Seven were housed in the top level of the Palace. "My cozy little room", she tried to convince herself, noting its raggedy carpet beneath still unpacked bags heaped in the window-less space. Judging by its size, it had probably been a closet once. But the convenience of no commute through a congested city made up for it.

While tea brewed, Aiela plucked the last of four knowledge crystals, borrowed from the World Library, out of a cracked mug. If a librarian saw this crude storage, she'd be banned from taking them out of the building. But it had been Mama's favorite mug and though it wouldn't hold liquid anymore, she couldn't bear to throw it out.

Connecting to the crystal, she listened, as its knowledge flowed into her mind. Six facets of the point indicated it held six separate programs. Or in this case, six treatises on hostage negotiation.

Rolling her head to ease neck tension, she paced, chanting "almost done, almost done," in an effort to stave off sleepiness.

THE COMMON PATH for an apprentice would have had her studying leadership and government, history of war, economics, and all areas of philosophy for a minimum of two years. Then perhaps apprenticing a Councilor, town or city Governor, Judge or Lawmaker. Once she had learned all that she could from a position, she would move on to apprentice another leader in another area.

But Ruler Kenna had a position vacated on her small council when one of her five was asked to serve as a town Governor.

Ruler Ziel had pulled quiet strings and slipped Aiela into the vacancy, with Ruler Kenna's candid relief that she wouldn't have to waste time in the exhausting game of filling such a coveted position.

"Evade the questions of how long you've been apprenticing and where you've served." Ziel had cautioned Aiela when he'd explained her placement. "Don't weave lies you have to keep track of, simply redirect the conversation. You're already a master at these things, I've no doubt they will serve you well."

Aiela had decided to take that as a compliment. "And if I'm pressed by those who think they've a right to know, such as a teacher perhaps, then what?"

"Then tell the truth: That you were forbidden to talk about your preparation and background as it relates to this position. I hereby forbid you." Ziel smiled.

The whole package would have made any other first year apprentice wild with envy—until they understood the reality of the days and nights that exhausted her, physically and mentally.

Already, two moons had passed since she and Ahna arrived in High City with their little boxes of mementos and a few bags containing uncomplicated wardrobes. Both of them heartbroken after their parent's deaths.

Since she was six, Aiela had planned to apprentice in the Healing Temple. Everything was set. She'd even assuaged her grief a little by reminding herself of all that she would learn and experience in the one field that held her passion.

But then, the very day they'd arrived with Auntie Sage at their side, Ziel had explained how Mama was—had been—his Keeper of the Crystals. And now he needed them to be; her and Ahna both. He didn't trust very many people. Not because they were bad, but because they didn't have "the character for it", he'd said, "and certainly not the abilities either."

So she'd agreed to it, believing it was what Mama and Papa would have wanted, understanding instinctively that she had a giftedness, some unnameable strength beyond her healing abilities. Meant for something she didn't yet understand—but Ziel seemed to, and if Mama had trusted him, had quietly served him, then she would too.

She still yearned for the Healing Temple with its compassionate sciences, its endless variety of people and problems needing solutions, its daily miracles of healing. Her sacrifice grew more difficult, as her days were stuffed to bulging, attending council meetings, listening to people debate things that felt a million miles over her head, going to classes like any normal apprentice, and spending evenings late into the night with her tutor.

Ziel had hired a teacher to cram years of knowledge into her as fast as possible. To academically catch her up to the position she was filling.

"You could probably fake your way through it, between the common sense you inherited from your parents and the charm you were born with, but I don't want you to have to fake it. I want you to have the education, same as the rest. It'll just be accelerated, quite, ahhh, condensed, that's all." Ziel had said, confident in her.

So HERE SHE WAS, preparing to give Ruler Kenna a recommendation on how to deal with a particularly savage people group near China, who had taken a party of traveling Atlanteans hostage and were demanding payment from Atlantis to release them. The Rulers had received the message a day ago and would make a decision in the morning.

In addition to running all manner of errands, small councilors did research to help their Ruler see all sides of an issue, giving recommendations and arguments, so decisions could be made quicker.

Aiela had managed to stay quiet until now. She'd been the first to volunteer for the most mundane duties, uncharacteristically silent unless spoken to, not wanting to reveal her inexperience or ineptitude.

But this time, Ruler Kenna requested a recommendation and notes from each of her five councilors and Aiela had dropped all else. Spending the entire day in the World Library she studied history on hostage situations, methods of manipulation and the fine art of negotiating conflicts. She'd changed her mind countless times on what might be the best answer. Her final decision, and supportive summary, felt cobbled together. Horribly amatuer. But it was the best she had.

If nothing else, I fully understand how important this education is, that Ziel is insisting I need. I do—desperately!

She carried a steaming mug of spicy chai tea the few steps between her only two pieces of furniture: a rickety bamboo table, stacked with hot pot, two tea tins and three mismatched cups—one cracked—and a mattress on the floor. Abandoned items. Someday she'd have time to furnish her room properly, actually go shopping and pick out interesting, attractive things. But that day continually moved further and further away.

She sat cross-legged again, adding notes to overcrowded pages. As the knowledge crystal played, she gulped tea and rubbed tired eyes that kept blurring the pages strewn across the bed, spilling over the prettily carpeted floor. "Just a little more and then sleep. Keep going girl, we can do this!"

"Talkin' ta yerself I see... perhaps ya need ta make some friends... or be gettin' a roommate... no' that there's room fer another." An amused male voice with a heavy Irish accent spoke and she startled, then leapt across the room at him.

"Turner! You're back already? I thought it'd be days yet. You have *no idea* how glad I am to see you!" This last bit was muffled into his considerable bulk of shoulder as she clung to him, almost weeping at the instant relief from the drain of constantly missing him, missing familiarity itself. Missing all that her life had been until two moons ago.

He held her, smoothing back long hair that needed washing, outlining her arms, meeting her unexpressed emotions with his own.

"Aye, we'd a breeze at our backs much o' the crossing, an' the sea smooth as a loch on midsummer eve. I feared I would'na remember the way ta yer room, but I had ta try—though it's so late I'd not thought ya'd be waking still." He pulled back to look at her with questioning eyes but didn't wait for an answer. Finding her lips with his, soft kisses turned quickly passionate and greedy.

Turner had been their local guide and leader on a student trip to Ireland last summer; thirty days that had challenged the twins—

grown them—brought love and loss in equal measure. He'd given up his lifelong dream of apprenticing his uncles in Greece, agreeing instead to work for his merchant father, just to be with Aiela. He'd chosen to begin a life with her, even though it would be sporadic for awhile.

Aiela's hands burrowed beneath his tunic, fingers tracing the firm belly up to mountainous muscles winging his ribs. She broke their kiss to push the worn fabric over his head. Registering briefly its sea-tossed scent, she dropped the tunic behind him, fingers returning to push the springy brown curls back from his face.

His curls, grown longer over the two moons since she'd seen him, were streaked with light from long days of sailing. "You've the body of a god", she whispered appreciatively, on her way back to his lips.

Tenderness tempered the raw hunger of their lovemaking, but only by fractions. Her notes rustled protest, crushed beneath straining bodies as they sought solace and majesty equally, in the bewildering immensity of desire.

Laying a bit dazed, on his back, Turner heaved a great huffing sigh, clutching Aiela to his chest. "I didna hurt ya? Sorry fer the haste, I needed ya so much…"

Aiela lifted her head to look at him, drily arching an eyebrow, "Of the two of us, I was both rougher and hastier. I'm no delicate thing my love. If you hurt me, you'll know it."

His laughter escaped. A warm, booming appreciation, which she squashed with her hand.

"Shhh! Everyone's sleeping!" But she felt balance trickle back as she giggled at him, as they recognized a new sort of individual completion in their union.

"What've we done ta yer papers? I hope ya hadn't need o' them… intact." Turner looked around at the slight carnage.

"It's just notes, preparation for my morning meeting." Aiela sat up, gathering and smoothing them, handing the lukewarm tea to Turner. "I'm finished with preparing. They're just going to have to take me as I am and if it's not enough, well, that'll be Ziel's problem I guess. He put me here anyway."

She shoved the stack of ruined notes under her rickety table as

Turner drained the mug. Her muttering wasn't meant to be heard, "If it's wisdom he wanted, he should have made Ahna the Ruler, not me."

"Sure an' maybe yer so used ta the roles you an' Ahna play, ya've started believin' them." Turner argued gently.

Aiela stared at him with tired eyes, before kneeling beside the mattress to sort out her mismatched heap of blankets.

Turner helped her spread and smooth the fleecy softness, returning her pillow to its rightful place. "I've only that one," Aiela said, eyeing it, "You can have it, I'll make something else work…" Spying her meditation cushion, she pressed it into service as they settled and she waved off the lights.

"Thank you for saying that." She whispered, cuddling close. "I'm just overwhelmed by all that I don't know… and need to. A lot is being asked of me and it's only the beginning… "

Turner listened to her, caressing her neck, tracing her collarbone, encouraging and accepting as she spoke her confusion and doubts into the night. She was almost asleep when he whispered, "Yer enough, my Moon Goddess. Brave, imperfect, glorious… much more'n enough."

3

MARDU'S NEED

FIFTY-SOME YEARS AGO, DESERT NEAR GREECE

"I saw the world from the stars' point of view, and it looked unbearably lonely."

— SHAUN DAVID HUTCHINSON, WE ARE THE ANTS

MARDU

"*I*t isn't that he's bad—he's always underfoot. My little mistake." Mitera said, followed by a laugh that turned the chilly air shrill.

Four-year-old Mady shrank back into the shadow he was supposed to be asleep in. His rag pallet on the floor hid behind a cracked chest that held everything he and Mitera owned.

The cold had woken him. Thinking those in the bed were asleep, he'd been planning to creep towards the little peat fire in the corner and warm up, when his mother's voice sounded from the depths of her rush bed.

He saw the mound of wool blankets begin to move, like a monster slowly rocking in the dim fire shadows. Male grunts and moans grew louder as the monster rocked faster and Mitera's little answering sounds brought Mady shame. She didn't want him. Being underfoot was worse than being bad. And what is "mistake"?

He curled back into a tight, shivering ball under his blanket, and focused on the hot tears that warmed his cheeks. He cried harder, because it made him warmer and he knew he'd be tired after, stuffing the blanket against his mouth, careful to mask any sound.

This wasn't the first time he'd sobbed while Mitera worked.

"Your Pater? Do you *see* a pater here Mady?" Mitera was cranky today, beating their threadbare rug with a green branch cut from one of the shrubby little trees that dotted the rocks and dirt. Clouds of ash puffed away every time she smacked.

Mady looked around as if a father might have magically appeared in response to his great longing for one. Seeing only their stone hut, crouched in heaps of powdery dust with patches of sharp grass grown tall against its scoured stone walls, he shook his head.

Their current town was a short walk away, just over the ridge and down the cliff. A cloud of dust hung perpetually in the air above it from people, ox carts and horses moving through its parched streets.

He was looking the wrong way when the green branch caught him on the back. It didn't really hurt but he hated to be struck.

"Didn't I tell you to fetch water? Do not stand there being useless! We need to wash the bedding in time for it to dry before the sun sets. Hurry up!"

"Don't. Hit. Me." Fists knotted at his sides, Mady bellowed with all the loud his six-year-old voice could muster, before running away fast so she couldn't do it again.

"You will not eat today!" She shouted after him. "Get the water or you'll not eat tomorrow either!"

Tears made wet tracks down his cheeks as he trudged down the cliffside with two leaky buckets. He didn't stop the tears. At least they washed the dust away that tried to cake in his perpetually itchy eyes. Anyway, the anger making him cry felt good. When Mitera struck him to get his attention, a giant hot feeling exploded inside and made him shout or sometimes even strike out.

He'd been hit a lot. Usually by men that came to visit Mitera in the tents, hovels and huts they lived in. Always outside villages.

They never stayed in one place long. After walking for days, sometimes even weeks, Mitera would pick a place and there would be a lot of different men visiting her at first. Many days would pass like that, and then fewer came. Sometimes, the same man would come often, and Mitera would turn the others away.

Not too long ago, they lived for a whole autumn and winter in a nice little earth-block cottage with a thatch roof that didn't leak. Only one man came to see Mitera the whole time, and he didn't come very often. Mitera had seemed happy there and the man was kind to Mady.

Mady had been hoping that man was his Pater and they could maybe go home to him soon. Wiping his eyes with gritty hands, Mady determined to ask Mitera again.

He would be very good and help her do the washing. He would rub her feet, and ask her while she sighed and smiled, and told him how pretty his thick black hair was. Even though her hair was much longer and just as black.

4

THE JOURNAL

9,971 BCE. HIGH CITY, ATLANTIS

"Words begin and end wars. They create and destroy families. They break hearts. They heal them. If you have the right words, there's nothing on earth you can't do."

— LORI HANDELAND

AHNA

*T*he middle-age lady worked in the Palace kitchens. In a pause between morning and midday meals, she came asking for an Oracle who might help her understand the meaning of a strange dream.

"I'm sorry but there are no appointments available with a dream interpreter until tomorrow. Would you like to see someone just after midday?" Ahna asked politely. Today she was working in the receiving room; a sort of greeting and scheduling area for those seeking help from the Oracles.

"No. I won't... I don't need a full appointment. Anyone will do... how about you? Do you have a few moments?" The lady's large eyes were earnest and kind. Her spirit felt nurturing. Hazel-colored hair was partly piled on her head, the rest hanging in waves that reached past her waist.

There were two other apprentices on duty. "Yes, but I'm only a first-year apprentice and new to dream interpretation so I may not be the best—"

"Thank you, you'll do just fine." The lady cut her off, looking around. "Where are we to sit?"

"This way." Ahna led her to a consulting room, tiny spaces furnished with two comfortable chairs and a round table barely large enough for two teacups.

They lady began before they sat. "I dreamt of a crowd of people, some that I know, some strangers. Someone brushed against me and I felt a prick in my leg that I noticed but thought nothing of as I continued moving through the crowd, greeting others, enjoying the celebration—or whatever it was we were all doing. Later, while undressing in my room, I looked down to find a huge, gaping hole in my leg where I had been pricked. It was as if something had eaten away the flesh and muscle. I could see streaks of white bone showing at the depths of the wound! Quite disturbing! It seemed as if there is a significance I am intended to understand and apply, but I can't quite grasp it. What do you think?"

Ahna leaned forward into wafts of bread yeast and rosemary floating from the lady. "Who brushed against you when you felt the prick?"

The lady's thin eyebrows pressed down, "I don't think it was anyone I know—one of the strangers around me."

"Alright. We'll take that to represent your contact with other people in general, who sometimes poke or prick you. What were the emotions of your dream?"

"I was... just going along with what was happening. Pretty comfortable really, no strong emotions until I saw the gaping hole in my leg. Then I felt horror and wondered how in the world it could have gotten that bad without noticing. I worried about infection and the time and effort it would take to heal."

Ahna nodded, "Which leg and where on the leg was the prick and the wound?"

"Right here." The lady splayed a hand on her left thigh, partially on the front and partially on the inner thigh, midway between her knee and groin. She was wearing the lemon yellow, simple pants and blouse of those who prepared food. More than cooks, they were artisans who crafted flavors, mixing nutrition, colors and textures, using produce in season.

"Alright, it sounds like your strongest emotion was about the wound itself. The left leg ties to your past—right is present—and the thigh location would indicate something impacting your personal strength. Your muscle being eaten away reinforces the message being about power that helps you stand strong or move forward, metaphorically of course. It could also be somewhat sexual in nature, as the inner thigh connects with sexuality.

So what is happening in your life that seemed an insignificant small pain, perhaps, but is eating away your personal strength in some way?"

The lady blinked a few times, mind processing what felt to Ahna like restrained or tamped down things.

Finally, she spoke. "There's someone whom I've had disagreements with lately. I discounted her little 'attacks' as just who she is, but I haven't stopped thinking about the things she accuses me of, and analyzing myself to see if they're true. I suppose I have lost some confidence in who I am... haven't been my usual strong self with others since then. I'm having doubts about my own goodness... "

Tears welled in the lady's eyes.

Ahna nodded compassionately, saying nothing, offering the lady a silent opening for understanding to enter, and a space to process emotions she had been ignoring.

Letting tears fall for a few moments, the lady sniffed and smiled at Ahna. "I guess it's a sort of warning then. Something I thought small is potentially harmful, and could create quite a wound if I don't take care of it. It's nothing sexual in nature... nor really tied to my past..."

"Well, the left side also represents the feminine." Ahna said, thankful for all she had absorbed from Aiela's knowledge in healing.

"Perhaps that was the indication, something with femininity, instead of the past?"

The lady nodded, "The person who 'pricked' me is female. You're good at this, what was your name? I'd like to come see you again when I need to. I appreciate that you don't talk constantly or ask a hundred irrelevant questions. You're very calming."

Ahna smiled with relief, "My name is Ahna and thank you. I'm glad you found understanding. Sometimes just speaking it aloud makes a difference. Sort of like looking in a mirror, seeing ourselves in ways we can't without the reflection."

RUMINATING ON THE ENCOUNTER, Ahna walked through winding hallways in Poseidon's Palace, with newfound confidence.

This had been her first consultation with someone who wasn't another apprentice in the House of Oracles.

The students practiced on each other every day—whatever the topic or skill of the day was. Almost all Oracle learning was experiential. Sure they were expected to read books packed with ancient knowledge and watch holograms outlining endless and dizzying modern discoveries—all on their own time—but practice was the fastest way to learn, and the only way to hone abilities or develop skills.

"The metaphysical world is infinite." Ziel had lectured on their first day of orientation to the House of Oracles. "All other fields of study have some sort of container, obvious boundaries. If you need to work within a finite container, or prefer to navigate using a map of known roads rather than trusting your own knowing, you may be uncomfortable in this work. It can feel as if you are perpetually lost. As if nothing you experience exactly fits any pattern, and the constancy of the new and unknown, the wilderness of uncertainty, has the power to unhinge your mind. I give you this warning myself because I want you each to take it very seriously. *You must self monitor.*"

Ziel had paused here, seeming to stare into each of them until they started fidgeting under the severity of his cerulean eyes.

"You must pay close attention to the strength of your connection to the physical world, because it is entirely possible to get lost in other dimensional planes or confuse your mind to the point of imbalance. It is common to be overcome by fear of the vast and borderless spaces that exist in our practices. No one but you can monitor how you feel, or what you are experiencing, or when you need help." His smile was relaxed as he leaned forward.

"Therefore, your first practice is to ask for help. We rely on each other to anchor, to understand the realms we explore and their effects on our human psyche, to request help and extend it without judgement. For this entire first moon, you are each required to ask for help from someone a minimum of three times every single day. It matters not what you need help with. It matters not what help is given to you, or from whom. You must document each request and submit them weekly to your advisors. The point is learning to self monitor. Familiarize with your own needs and become as comfortable receiving help as receiving food or oxygen. We must value our interdependence to survive and thrive here in the House of Oracles."

Back in her room, Ahna flopped belly down on her neatly-made bedspread, spreading her hands on the comforting patchwork of green and purple fabrics. Mama had made identical ones for her and Aiela, once they'd outgrown their small, childhood bed coverings.

"See?" Mama's jolly voice echoed through her memory. "I combined your favorite colors. They complement each other as beautifully as you two."

Ahna slept on the bottom bunk in a room shared by six, first-year apprentice Oracles. No one else was "home" at the moment and she reveled in the solitude, a rarity in the last two moons.

How quickly she had been absorbed into bustling schedules and swiftly-formed bonds between new apprentices. It was quite an adjustment, unaccustomed as she was to close friendships, outside Aiela—which didn't really count. For the first time in her life she spent more time with people than alone.

Rising, she padded across the brightly patterned carpet to her ornate wardrobe, and pulled a small, eggplant-colored, leather-bound journal off its high shelf. Originally this journal was Aiela's, a gift from Papa at the start of their Ireland trip. But Ahna's pack had been stolen, along with her own journal, so Aiela had let her record the things she'd wanted to capture from the trip. Eventually, it just became more Ahna's than Aiela's.

She hadn't written in it since the day they'd arrived home; the day Ziel and Auntie Sage told them Papa and Mama had died.

Waves of still-fresh sorrow battered Ahna as she curled into one of the room's plush chairs, remembering the day Papa had given them this. The day they'd all said goodbye. None of them realizing it was going to be a much longer parting than they'd planned. Pen in one hand, she opened the journal. Tears blurred her eyes, and she let grief in, like an old friend.

"*I have found my tribe,*" she wrote, sniffling, determined to record the good things before venting her sadness, "*here in the House of Oracles.*

> *There are many like me. I have friends who understand the twists and turns of a sensitive mind, the shame of knowing things I don't want to about people, the wonder of an expanded world that we experience through our 'extra' senses. It's surprised me again and again—this relief of sharing all of it with others who have the same knowing. I realize now how very lucky I am to have had Aiela my whole life, with her own abilities and understanding and sharing of the unseen world. There are some here, who had no one they could tell without being jeered or disbelieved. Papa and Mama and Aiela are my greatest gifts...*"

Ahna paused, letting pictures of the family she wrote about fill her mind, realizing she had been without her sister too much lately, their lives disparate now.

"*I miss them.*" Reaching out with her mind to Aiela, wherever she was, Ahna extended towards her, hoping to connect even just for a moment. But there was no brush of awareness. No connection of answering thought. Ahna returned to the journal with a sigh. *Just have to go find her in person—*

Strange handwriting interrupted her thought. She squinted at it, as if that might help her brain translate why there was handwriting she didn't recognize in her personal journal. It certainly wasn't Aiela's large, bubbly script. It was small and messy and hurried.

She flipped to where it began, five pages back between two pages that were stuck together. Prying them carefully apart, she stared at the drawing of a faerie, taking up an entire page, sketched in light, broken strokes, looking suspiciously like herself, with choppy hair tickling her shoulders, skinny arms and legs sticking out of leaf-shaped clothing.

The leaf faerie perched her left hand on one hip in a saucy wide-legged stance. Her right hand wielded a bouquet as tall as she was. Two real shamrocks and a small blue wildflower were dried and pressed flat, adhered to the page with something sticky.

The bottom of the drawing was where the writing began:

"Golden Ahna, I promised you a birth day gift. It has three parts."

Her heart did a little flip. Could it be? Was it possible this was from him? There was no signature at the end—she checked, to make sure she hadn't missed it.

I give you this poorly done artwork; a reminder that tiny people and their magic exist. You did magic in me. You changed me.

I'll never forget how you stared at my hands like a madwoman that first night on the seacruiser.
Confession—that's not the first time I saw you... I watched you and Aiela say goodbye to your parents on the docks in Armanth and I thought you were the prettiest girl I'd ever seen. I didn't know yet that you would be the strangest, and smartest too.

I give you this blathering note. Could you pretend it's poetry with rhythm, rhyme and layers of meaning? Because that's what I would write to you if I could. Instead, I'm here in the dark of a swaying ship hammock, hurrying to finish and sneak it back into your bag before you wake, in hopes it will surprise you. Maybe bring you a smile when you need it the most.

I give you my truest and best love—which I realize you can't hold or see or smell or taste, but, because of your unique oddities, I know you will be able to feel it. I give you this love for always and always—an appreciation and admiration and respect and gratefulness to have known you.

Another confession; I'm not sure I know what love is. What I feel for you has become my definition though it might be beyond words—still I will try. I care about you so much it hurts. It's like the world trans- formed from shades of grey into a colored wonderland. Like I am strong enough for anything. Like being full or satisfied, balanced, (that's the right word) when I'm with you.

I love your scar—because it united us—and your perfect wrists and the sunlit specks in your eyes. Your body above me in the moonlight is etched eternally in my mind and the pleasure we created together... you trusted me to enter your body—a sacred gift that I cannot match.

Soon now, we will say goodbye. I will grieve losing you for a long long time, Maybe forever. I'm sorry to leave you, I'm sorry to hold so much back from you.

Last confession; You know the best of me, you brought it to the surface —but there's other parts to me that you don't know. I'm afraid for your safety if we try to be together, and mostly, I'm afraid you wouldn't want me anymore if you knew all of me.

So. I will keep this time that we had, this love we created, in my heart and trust that it will outlast the pain of letting you go. I hope you can do the same. —Always

Ahna traced the words as if they were his face, fingers leaving the pages only to impatiently swipe away blurring tears as she read his "gift" over and over, inhaling it into the hollow he'd left inside her. A sob escaped and she hugged the journal, curling into a ball and exor- cising a hurt she hadn't even known she carried.

She'd spent so much time grieving the loss of her parents, and getting used to her busy home with its entirely new way of life. There hadn't been room for processing another loss.

More truthfully, she'd pushed Carver into a corner of her mind. Hid him away until she had the strength to look at what had happened.

His strong-jawed handsomeness flashed into life, hair the color of hematite, grown halfway to his shoulder, the tall breadth of him walking beside her, and his limp when he got tired. Ahna thought about his aggressive strength inside of danger when everyone else was recoiling from the chaos, and his automatic rescue mode to those in harm's way.

He was a Belial. One of three on the Ireland trip. He'd been cold, closed down at first, yet had stepped into her most vulnerable moments. He'd played music for her on his battered old dulcimer with large sensual hands, slowly opening his heart enough to accept her as a friend, and then as a lover.

But he'd refused to talk about his home, or his family, or his plans for the future. Whenever she touched an off-limit subject, he'd go quiet and chilly again.

She'd felt his strong attraction to her, matching her own breathless awareness of him, and taken his resistance to it as a challenge.

Ahna smiled as the tears quieted, whispering into the empty room, "I won Carver. I didn't let you ignore what you felt for me." She rose, feeling both emptier and lighter, touched the journal to her lips, then placed it under her pillow.

"I won. Yet I still lost you."

5

DISCOVERY OF HOPE

9,971 BCE. TEMPLE CITY, BELIAL

"She'd been real and eternal in my arms. Now just a memory—about as solid as smoke. But then so is hope, and hope is magnetic. It calls in things."

CARVER

"Carver!" Mardu's voice thundered ahead into the room where Carver sat, eyes riveted to the leather journal he was reading.

He looked up as his father strode in, long cloak billowing out behind; a recent embellishment Mardu had added, imagining it made him look larger and more commanding.

"Carver!" Mardu bellowed again, this time agitated.

"I'm here." Carver spoke quietly from the corner chair. Rising , he straightened to a considerable height to meet his father's black gaze. They'd always been required to stand when their father entered a room. A forced deference.

"Pack. Quickly." Mardu snapped. "Sarim has fallen ill and cannot be at the mines for High City's first shipment. You'll leave tonight. The Irish ships are due to arrive as early as two days from now and you must inspect the crystals to be shipped, ensure all is in order for the delivery."

Carver nodded. He'd been expecting this since hearing of his half-brother's sudden and violent illness. Rumor said it was an unwelcome gift from the foreign men and women Sarim slept with incessantly.

Mardu usually turned to Carver when plans went awry. Perhaps being the youngest of Mardu's five sons made Carver the most well-rounded, as well as quick thinking, flexible and non-emotional; all attributes Mardu used to remedy the emergencies that invariably came up when running a nation. Especially one that was planning to become an empire very soon.

"It'll be better that you're there anyway," Mardu said. "You made the deal for the ships, and you know more of the Irish than Sarim, though you've not been to the mines... still, you will adapt quickly. Sarim has men there who will show you the whole operation."

"And Meihal's payment for using his ships?" Carver asked, "All that he requires is ready?"

"Sarim was to see to that. I assume he has." Mardu narrowed his eyes, "Meihal asks entirely too much! You should have made a better deal."

Carver remained stonily silent. He'd offer no excuses to this stubborn man. Mardu knew full well it was a miracle that the Irish merchant agreed to work with the Belials at all, delivering shipments of crystals to High City from the Belial mines. The Atlanteans would allow no Belial ships into their ports.

Relations between the two nations sharing this continent were touchy at best, downright explosive at worst. Especially since the Atlanteans learned that Mardu had an army of engineered giants known as the Mutazio.

Official emissaries between the two nations assured each other that all was well, that the Belials meant only to conquer foreign lands and spread out their burgeoning population. They'd long ago outgrown the small portion of Atlantis land, granted after the uprising of Onus Belial.

Atlantean ambassadors wanted desperately to believe this. So they did.

"I want this deal to flow like warm cream. No mistakes, oversights or hiccups. It is more important than I can tell you." Mardu glared at Carver from across the room, always standing at a distance so he didn't have to actually look up to his taller son.

Carver inclined his head. "Yes Dominus, it will be done. I'll visit Sarim now, gather details and be on my way before nightfall."

"Have you found anything helpful—or injurious?" Mardu pointed at the mountain of papers, scrolls, codex books, leather bound leaflets and crystals stacked or spread haphazardly on the floor around Carver's chair. It was an entire collection of documents and information seized from known enemies to Belial, possibly very sensitive secrets— which Mardu wouldn't trust his own spies, assassins and intelligence agents with.

Planning to read them himself, he'd instead started giving them to Carver, who had the mind to decipher codes or catch hidden meanings. Plus, he was the only Belial in Mardu's household to bother learning other languages. Traveling on Mardu's merchant ships had given Carver the curiosity to understand people, and taught him the value of language skills.

"Not yet, just a lot of rambling with no bearing on us. I will keep searching though." Carver lied smoothly, thinking to himself that he'd best throw his father a few unimportant things to appease his suspicions.

"Report to me when you return." Mardu turned and swept from the room as boisterously as he'd arrived, bellowing for Orja as he stomped across slate floors.

Returning to his chair, Carver snatched up the journal he'd been interrupted from. One of three, it had been taken from Ahna's father Drey, after he'd been assassinated in an avalanche while Ahna and Carver were both in Ireland.

The journals had been in Drey's aero.

Mardu believed they must be important if Drey had kept them close, even when traveling.

Carver had read two of them, which were filled with daily mundanities in Drey's life: new plant discoveries, the humorous antics of his various lab assistants, tender thoughts of his mate Taya, and observations, praises or worries of Ahna and Aiela, his twin daughters. Carver soaked in this further knowledge of Ahna, so soothing to his lifelong loneliness. He knew he'd read these over and over.

The third journal was different. It began like the others, detailing Drey's worry of saying goodbye to his daughters too often... was he spending too much time away from them?

Then a few notes about a trip to his Afrikkaan lab, then an abrupt pause. One page over, an account was told, in retrospect, of being taken from his bed and brought to an old stone fortress in England. He told of meeting Nadya, a Banpiro brain scientist being held hostage, and forced to develop a node which could control any person or animal from the pain center of its brain. Nadya had failed to find an organic substance that would protect the tissue from direct contact with the node pulses. Drey had been brought to solve the problem, he assumed, because he was Atlantis' leading expert in plants and the biological materials that could be made from them.

Carver picked up reading where he'd left off.

"The person in charge was referred to as 'the big man'. I was hooded both occasions in his presence but Nadya said his name was Balek. Mardu's eldest son. He struck me savagely, three times during the conversation when we met, even though I was bound and hooded! It created a terror I've not known; having no warning or hint that pain was about to be inflicted on my body. He was a vicious bully, as evidenced by his arrogance and cruelty to both Nadya and myself— though I can hardly compare his treatment of us—I woke almost every night to the sound of screams. Upon inquiry, Nadya admitted Balek was using her for sadistic sexual pleasures. I gathered, from the little she said, this involved a sort of utter dominance by inflicted pain. When she spoke of it, the light in her eyes shut down and she curled into herself in a way that reminded me of many species of delicate leaves that survive hail storms, freezes and tropical monsoons by curling in. I was puzzled why Nadya, who was clearly a predatory Being, submitted to such treatment, and learned that her sister Mahlia, was also being held, to ensure Nadya's cooperation. Nico, the leader of the men under Balek, had fallen in love with

Mahlia. This was the reason he helped us, the only way we escaped. They must have discovered his planned betrayal, for when Nadya and I escaped, we found Mahlia's body, burnt, in the center of a still smoldering mound of coals and Nico's body, still lukewarm, but utterly dead. Nico's throat was slit—after he'd watched her burn I'm sure. (I must write about this clinically. Even now, the roasted meat smell of that air comes back to haunt me. The fastly forged camaraderie I felt with Nico is an ache in my heart. I cannot yet let myself feel it all fully.)

Carver paused, picturing the horrors Drey described. It had Balek's unique seal of evil all over it. This was the cruel tormenter Carver had grown up with; the most dreaded danger of his childhood.

Despite bilious anger building inside, Carver read on.

Drey described in great detail the creatures they experimented on, the guard he killed and the effects all this violence, this taking of life, had on him. A dramatic story emerged of Drey and Nadya's fiery escape, followed by a fourteen-day walk to reach Nadya's people, who helped him return home.

Next came five whole pages devoted to the nodes: how they were built, how they were programmed, what the controllers could do, and the recipe for the all important coating which Drey had found protected the brain tissue from being cooked by multiple uses of the node. Painstakingly, Drey described the exact placement in the brain's pain center so that the tiniest of surges created a pain response in the body. Biologically the node trained the mind and body to respond habitually to any command given, in order to avoid pain. There were labeled drawings, diagrams with dimensions, and a few notes about Nadya's processes.

Later entries had been tacked on, additional memories as they came to Drey. Tiny details, feelings he was processing that he hadn't had time for in the midst of the chaos and high drama.

But Carver caught his breath when he read:

"... however, training is not the single function of these nodes. The nodes were also for killing the animal if needed. A fail-safe to protect

handlers, should the animal threaten their life. Apparently, when you dabble in creating twelve-foot humans, with plenty of gorilla blended in for strength, you get unpredictable, unstable, often dangerous products. Just one of the many reasons, no doubt, that Atlantis, Lemuria, and Mu before us, have absolutely banned (again and again) the cloning of humans. Or even intermixing DNA from multiple species. Every animal that has a node injected can be terminated with the extreme turn of a dial. A diabolical fact I tested when I killed all of our subjects simultaneously. I am ashamed to say I welcomed this killing at the time. Following what seemed like hours of pointless pain, it came as the kindest of mercies—for them and for me."

This was it. Carver felt a thrill go through his body, a shiver of hope.

It came wrapped in risk yes, carried only narrow odds of success, but still... A distinct possibility shone like a rising moon over the obsidian path he was walking. If he could get this information to Atlantis, into the hands of the right people, they could figure out a way to stop the Mutazio army. They'd have what they needed to protect themselves, and therefore, Ahna.

Thoughts of her came fast, dancing together, each one a pang of pleasure edged in loneliness and longing.

Carver rose, packing Drey's journal along with clothing and necessities. He'd best get on with it if he planned to save her.

Pining after her would accomplish less than nothing.

6

AIELA'S SECRET

9,971 BCE. HIGH CITY, ATLANTIS

"If you accept the situation, you will find strength for strategic adaptation."

— LAILAH GIFTY AKITA

AIELA

"*Y*er feet are too close t'gether yer wan. Wide an' low remember?" Kane tapped the back of her head not so softly with a linen-wrapped hand, dancing away again before she could whirl to strike him.

Frustration welled inside of her, threatening to explode out in not-so-dignified ways.

These days were normally filled with meetings and classes, studying and errands—all places she was supposed to appear wise, regal and grounded. *Like a damn puppet being made to perform,* Aiela thought as she took another half-hearted swing at the large wrapped paws weaving back and forth, inviting a hit.

Again the paw swung up to tap the side of her head. "Get yer heart innit wan!" Kane taunted her, dancing away and in again. "When yeh gonna put all that grrrr inna yer hands? Or do yeh like being hit?" The paw swung in and she raised her arm in defense with a roar that pushed energy out with it, blowing his huge hand back like a feather.

Her left fist followed close behind and connected solidly with his shoulder. Kane let the momentum of it take him back, relaxing into the blow even as he turned, howling a laugh.

"Yes yer wan yes! That's it right there. Push back with that force, e'vry time!"

She turned with him, connecting again, this time with his ribcage on the right, her left fist sliding up and whispering by his jaw as he matched her dancing feet, moving with her. Dodging, barely. The energy coming out of her hands moved his long braid as it passed, and he laughed again.

"The *paws* Cailin, get it oot" he whispered and she began to pour out the mounting storm of emotions into his capable hands, screaming as she drove him back, laughing as he let her.

Once the tears came and the onslaught started to slow, he grabbed her tired wrists and pulled her in. A giant bearhug of safety and release.

Aiela rarely allowed herself this; to fall apart completely. No one knew she was here fighting Kane. Not even Ahna. With that thought another wave hit her and she pounded her fists on his shoulders, albeit more gently this time.

He let her. Not speaking, just gently encircling her in massive steel arms, until the tears were spent, and she quieted.

Pressing a soft mound of linen, silently unwound from his hand, into hers he stepped back to let her clean herself up.

"Double use of these things today." She tried to joke, embarrassed at her state.

"Ach, I was raised wi' girls. I know when it's needed." He busied himself unwrapping his other hand, stretching beefy shoulders and arms high and low. "Turner said ye were a feisty one, but I think he doesna' know the half of it." Kane chuckled as he eyed her. "Ye did well today Cailin. I hav'na felt that kind of strength from a girl since wrestling wi' me own sisters back home. An' that was ages ago!"

On Turner's last visit, he'd taken her to visit his distant cousin.

Kane lived and worked at the edges of the last ring of land, before the wall divided the inner city from the outer suburbs, farmlands, and countryside.

She'd been envious of the way the cousins wrestled and rough-housed together. Kane had noticed. He taught the dancing martial arts that were used for sport and exercise here. But back home in Scotland, they were defensive and offensive moves.

When he offered to teach Aiela, Turner heartily agreed but she had laughed at them, brushing the offer away. "I won't have time, nor need for such training."

Yet here she was, weeks later, sneaking away for the third time in so many days to meet Kane for a lesson on her own time and terms.

The first time she showed up, he had asked no questions, only took her to the practice yard and begun training. Quietly intuitive, he sensed in her a strength begging an outlet. A need for something beyond what life was offering her, whatever that was.

She smiled, small but genuine, "Thank you Kane. Guess I needed that." Sinking to the low wooden bench on the side of the practice ring, she grabbed the water jug for a swig. "Why do you call me 'Cailin, and 'yer wan'?

"Did I? It means girl in the auld language. Guess it's habit wi' me girls back home..." his voice faded as a shadow passed over his normally sunny features. He hid it fast but Aiela noticed the dimmed color at his heart.

"I like that you call me 'Cailin'. That here I can just be a girl—a nobody."

He was sitting on the rubber floor now, short stocky legs splayed, stretching forward over them, arms holding ankles. Nodding at the floor he said, "Anytime Cailin. Ye dinna' ha' to be anybody here."

She moved down next to him and began the stretching routine he had taught her, the same one he was doing. For a moment there was comfortable silence.

"It's just—I'm so—frustrated with everything!" Aiela struggled to name the feelings. As much trying to explain her sudden outburst to herself, as to Kane. "My days are filled with too many things—some of it I love, but it's just so *much* and I don't get to be with my sister anymore. It's bad enough adjusting to living apart for the first time ever, but now she's preoccupied with her training, and friends, and house, and I barely get to talk to her anymore..." She ducked her head to hide the tears welling again. Brushed them impatiently away. "I dinna *like* bein' an adult!" Mimicking his Scottish accent, she smiled at him through her sadness.

Kane chuckled a little. "Some days I dinna either lass, an' yet it's a freedom like no other!" He laid back and rolled his legs to one side. "Frustration makes fer a mighty good fighter though! Good way to get it out, eh?"

She grinned unselfconsciously. "Well I did knock Turner down last time he was here. Surprised him—I can tell you that!"

At this Kane roared with laughter. "Good yer wan! Good on ya!" He punched the air as he turned to the other side. "That boy needs taken down from time to time, and yer just the lass ta do it."

Their laughter lifted the mood and she let out a cleansing sigh. "If Ziel saw me, punching you like a wild woman, he might think twice about keeping me in the House of Rulers."

"Or mebbe yer doin' exactly whatcha need eh?" Kane held her eyes for a moment, as he sat up. "We have a saying. It goes, 'Yer a long time deid'."

Aiela stared back. "You're a long time dead? What's that supposed to mean?"

"It means enjoy life lass. Because once yer deid this one's ow'er, and all these experiences yer havin now willna be possible. So yer life is different now. New things are expected of ye. That doesna mean ye let go of the essence of who ye are. That's the verra thing that carries ye thru!" Kane tapped her leg with a gentle fist. "Fightin goes wi' leadin, just as breathin goes wi' sleepin. Ye start dividin' it all up, ye'll lose yerself."

Aiela mulled over his words as they finished stretching. She realized her own assumption; that she had to change completely to shoulder the new position and responsibilities. Here was the source of her frustration and resentment. Kane had given her much to think about.

Thanking him, promising to turn up again soon, Aiela headed out the tall wooden gate, her mind busy with what route she would take to slip back into the palace unnoticed. She didn't see the slight, hooded figure lounging against the outer wall, until a voice froze her as she passed.

"I see you've chosen your teacher." The all-too-familiar voice held dry amusement.

She spun, ready to defend herself. And then the words came through as meaning, confusing her all the more, and she stared into Ziel's eyes leveled at her, hints of a smile crinkling the corners.

"Wha—how did you know—find me?" Surprise colored her face red. Before she could launch a defense, Ziel winked, pulling a ripe pear from within his robes and tossing it to her. She caught it deftly, still confused.

"You've made a good choice in Kane. Tell me, what is it that draws you here day after day?"

She hesitated, embarrassed to tell the truth. As though having frustrations, being homesick, missing her sister and feeling overwhelmed might cause him to think less of her.

Ziel spoke when she didn't. "Did you know I was only thirteen when I arrived to apprentice here in High City?"

She shook her head and he began walking towards the Palace. Aiela fell in beside him.

"I was such a small boy, shy, with no idea how to interact with people—especially men. My sweet mother had loved me intensely, sheltered me. Perhaps too much. I'd lived a very simple childhood in a tiny town and then suddenly here I was in the midst of a world I could barely comprehend. Even the foods seemed foreign. I cried myself to sleep many nights for the first three moons." He stopped to pluck another small burgundy pear, identical to the one Aiela was eating, from trees lining the walkway.

"Some Oracles were kind to me. Some were not." He sighed. "You can imagine which ones made the lasting impression. They teased me about my size, in case I had missed the fact that Atlantean boys were much bigger and stronger than me. They mocked me, calling me High Priestess's boy-pet, bent on proving I had no more ability or power than they did. Their own insecurity and jealousy was taken out on me and I was entirely vulnerable to it. I craved approval. Then I craved respect as I grew into a man, but that too was hard to come by—especially, it seemed, for a man of small stature." He took a bite, dribbling pear juice down his clean-shaven chin.

"What did you do?" Aiela trailed fingertips along a topaz sculpture of running horses as they passed. It was life-size, molded in shades of gold, amber and brown.

Ziel chuckled but it was tinged with something bitter. "I did many things trying to gain approval, most of them foolish. My teachers expected much of me despite my youth and the pace kept me exhausted. Eventually, I learned to listen to my emotions and to take care of myself.

I learned to channel energies that could destroy me, into something creative or skillful. That made all the difference. Still does. Whether it's frustration or fear, or anything else detrimental, I have interests, hobbies, or even chores that benefit from those energies."

He slowed and cocked his head to meet her eyes. "You'll do well to take care of yourself, first and foremost, Aiela. The grief of losing your parents is still fresh. Grief masquerades as anger, seeming to come from other sources. It weights and colors every experience you have until one day, blessedly, it starts to fade. Mastering your emotions is essential but I don't mean denying or resisting them. Mastering means giving them a positive outlet, such as you are with Kane. I'm pleased you're working out your frustrations. When the grief turns to something else, you will find a way to channel that too."

They walked a while before she responded. "Thank you for understanding." How easy it was, to forget that everyone struggles. Hearing Ziel's hardships validated her own, even though their stories were very different. And it hadn't occurred to her that grief might be lurking under all the things she was feeling.

"I've other errands. Pleasant evening to you." He veered abruptly off towards Temple Beautiful.

Aiela took the time to walk the remaining miles to the Palace, instead of catching a trolley. Between Kane and Ziel, she had much to contemplate.

7

CAPTAIN TURNER

9,971 BCE. SOMEWHERE ALONG SOUTH AMERICA'S EAST COAST

"Trust is like a mirror; you can fix it if it's broken, but you can still see the crack in that mother fucker's reflection."

— LADY GAGA

TURNER

"Drop anchors!" The ship Captain hollered in his rollicking Irish tongue. "Launch ah' ferries. Let's see if some'uns in this feckin' godawful place."

Turner grinned as he leaned on the railing, watching deckhands hustle to untie, and launch, two small ferry boats off the hulking wooden ship. Around him, sailors were grumbling and churlish at the lack of buildings onshore.

They'd hoped to find a town teeming with the famed Belial licentiousness, which to these seasoned sailors meant liquor, food, and girls, all flowing in the streets in equal amounts. They'd talked of what they'd find for days during the crossing; a game of topping each other's imaginations, or more accurately, wildest dreams.

Instead they were looking at a generous fringe of sandy beach, bleached colorless under a high-noon sun. Littered with driftwood and other sea trash, the sand led up to what appeared to be a swamp, topped with impassable jungle. It looked an unlikely place for a Belial mining operation and seemed uninhabited, except for hordes of giant bugs which he could see even this far off.

Turner wondered if his father might have made a mistake writing out the coordinates.

"How long you 'sposin we wait and see this is ah' right place?"

The salted rasp came from behind and Turner glanced back at the Captain. Shorter than himself and twice as broad, the Captain was a block of a man, mocha-skinned with heavy, black freckles and a cloud of ghost-white hair that matched his chest-length frizz of a beard.

He was the last of the ancient Captains who'd served Turner's Grandda and Great-Grandda on his father's side. Turner had always been terrified of him with his voice that sounded like rocks being ground together, and his broody stare, accompanied by the least possible number of uttered words.

"I'd say five days—a week tops—Captain." Turner concentrated on keeping the question mark out of his tone. He was meant to replace this man soon and the Captain took Turner's training very serious, always including him in decisions, prodding him to be better, to think more, and work smarter than any other man or woman under him.

"Speak what you're sure of. Work thru questions a'forehand, an' no need of ah' questioning tone." He'd said every time Turner's answers had curled up, or ended in uncertainty.

The Captain nodded, hands clasped behind his back as he stepped up beside Turner. "Twouldn't be ah first mistake your Da made. What orders for ah crew you s'posin?"

His big eyes, wreathed in wrinkles, were much darker brown than his skin. Unblinking, they flicked around the cove, registering every sailor on deck, even the birds swooping to investigate this strange interloper into their world, sticking finally to Turner who was thinking through his reply.

"Anchor the other two ships just outside the cove, visible to anyone looking for us, and keep the lanterns lit all night. Send a crew before nightfall to look for trails or roads. Set some to fish for our supper. I'm fancying a fish-fry on the beach." This last bit Turner added as he noticed the water teeming with a school of fish, curious about the ships. There were probably crabs as well, near to shore.

A heavy hand thumped his back. "Best give ah' orders then *Cap'n Turner. I'm* fancyin' a nap. Wake me when ah' fish fry's hot aye?"

Turner stood upright and turned to face the Captain, mimicking the old man's posture with legs wide and chest stuck out, hands clasped behind him. "Aye Captain."

He could not stop the smile from bursting forth, the thrill of his merchant family's most legendary ship Captain, trusting him to lead in his stead. Their connection went deeper than mere respect. Turner carried this man's blood.

Originally from Greece, the Captain had raised a sizable family there, in between captaining ships for the largest merchant family in Ireland. On a short stopover at the Captain's home, Turner's father Meihal—barely eighteen at the time—had met the Captain's youngest child; his fiery daughter, Diaedra. That once was all it took. A lifelong love affair began that day, and they'd eventually refused to be kept apart, though both their parents tried.

It all caused quite a drama in Meihal's household, but he couldn't care less whether anyone approved or not. Things had stayed rough between the Captain and Meihal, until, with the proving of time, the Captain finally understood. Meihal really did love his daughter as deeply as he professed to. Once the babies started coming, it smoothed away all remaining doubt, or resentment.

"Sleep well Grand-da. I'll pester cook ta splurge on the butter for ya. We'll celebrate this good weather and an early arrival to this 'feckin' godawful place.'"

Grand-da's laughter sounded more like hacking as he walked away, lurching side to side in a stiff, bow-legged gait. He had relieved himself of command until he saw fit to take it back again—a formal passing of the helm that was becoming more and more routine between them.

"Ta me fer orders!" Turner hollered in his best ship Captain's voice.

The men echoed his call; "To Cap'n Turner for orders!" relaying it to those at the furthermost points, and under the decks. They assembled noisily around him as he pointed at two sailors.

"Take a third man with ya, row ta the other ships and relay the plan, soon as I'm finished tellin' ya..."

Carver

Carver swore out loud in the aero, when he spotted the three ships lounging in the bright water far below.

They were early. He'd hoped to have time—at least a day—to orient himself. He needed to talk to those managing the mine, check the entire shipment and prepare for transporting it to the Irish fleet.

Mardu was paranoid of anyone knowing the exact location of the mines, so they'd use river barges to transfer the cargo a good thirty miles downriver.

"What's your problem?" The startled pilot asked.

"The Irish fleet is arrived. There, way to the south." Carver pointed, "Set down close as you can. I need to greet them and give a time to receive the cargo. They're probably wondering if they're even in the right place."

The pilot nodded, squinting into the setting sun as he turned down the coast to get closer to where three big ships tipped and rocked on lazy waves. "I'd've missed them completely. You've some kind of eyes on you."

After three passes, the closest clearing they found, big enough to set down in, was some distance from the beach.

It took nearly an hour of picking their way through the swampy jungle. Little crystals swinging from their belt loops protected against hovering hordes of bugs, emitting a field of frequency that paralyzed insects.

They dodged snakes hanging in lazy curls from low branches, and other legged reptiles that chirped and waddled, sliding in and out of shallow, sun-hot pools of cloudy, stagnant water. Scents of jungle rot and overbearing flowers battled for dominance. Humidity thickened the air and it felt like they'd need gills for a deep breath.

Sweat poured into their eyes as they detoured around the deeper looking swamp streams, and hacked through walls of vines. Carefully, they marked their trail with dead branches, or stacked rock cairns, or carved arrows into tree trunks, so they'd find their way back.

"Sure seems farther than it looked from the air!" Carver remarked.

"Sure would've been a good idea to bring water." His droll pilot returned.

Eventually, the moist green tangle thinned and the ground turned sandy. Stepping out of the noisy, unstirred jungle onto crusty white beach felt like coming out of a too-hot bath. They welcomed the air, sea-fresh, salt-cooled and moving.

Spotting four Irish sailors gathering driftwood into piles, Carver trotted towards them.

"Hello," Carver called in the Irish tongue. "I'm Carver, from Belial, here to meet your ships. Where is your Captain?" The sailors pointed towards their ships anchored far out in deep water.

Eyeing a small-boat Carver inquired, "Can you take me to him?"

The men conversed too rapidly for Carver to follow. When they stopped, the skinny one said, "Sure an' if ya wait, we'll bring the Captain to ya."

Carver nodded. "I will wait."

Thirsty and hot, he and the pilot stood in gentle waves, watching the small-boat row out towards the closest ship. Another small-boat, some distance away, held three men, fishing with pronged spears and cone-shaped baskets. Several more sailors down the beach were casting nets, bare-chested and waist-deep in the water.

"They don't waste time settling in do they? We'd best find some shade to wait in." Carver led the way. "When they bring Meihal's Captain, I'll give instructions to meet us where the river empties in three days. Should give me plenty of time to get things in order."

The figure that stepped from the returned small-boat, and walked over hot sand towards him, seemed familiar. But it had not occurred to Carver that he might know any of Meihal's crew.

He panicked when Turner got close enough to recognize.

"Carver!" Turner shouted and loped the rest of the distance to engulf him in a crushing embrace. "What in the world are ya doin' here?! Da told me, when I go' back from dropping ya in Armanth, that ya were some sort o' messenger fer Mardu. But I didna realize, or think, ya'd be *here*! I thought ta maybe never see ya again! Sure an' I've missed ya!"

He released Carver then, stepping back to clap both hands onto Carver's shoulders, face split in smiles of pure welcome. "I've joost come from High City an' the twins! They'll be so happy ta hear aboot ya!"

"Turner, I—" Carver began.

"He's not a *messenger*." The pilot was defensive and condescending. "Carver is *son* of the great Dominus Mardu and who're you *boy*? We asked to see the Captain!" The pilot's duty was to protect Carver as well as transport him.

Turner dropped his arms and stepped back. Confusion replaced the smile, knotting his brows together.

"GO!" Carver spoke harshly to the pilot. "I've no need of you here. Go and wait for me. I will speak in private to the Captain."

They stood glaring at each other until the chastened pilot muttered under his breath, stalking off to wait in the growing shade of the jungle's edge.

Turner's face was a cloud of doubt when he finally spoke. "Hell of a detail ta leave out mate."

Carver nodded, torn between not wanting to lose this true-hearted friend, the shame of being known, and the fear of Ahna finding out who he really was. If she knew, she could find him. If she found him, he'd either have to reject her outright, or risk Mardu knowing he loved her. If Mardu ever suspected that Carver cared, he'd readily use her against him.

Carver had spent his entire childhood learning how to avoid such obvious controls. He'd sacrificed all connection, built no relationships —just so his father and brothers had no one to threaten, no one to torture him with.

"It is, I know. If you're willing to hear it, I'll explain the best I can." Carver looked straight into Turner's eyes. Eyes full of distrust now, but still Turner nodded.

"Course I want ta hear why. Yer a mate."

Side by side they slowly began wandering up the beach, in the ancient and unconscious motion of turning a difficult conversation companionable, instead of confrontational.

"Can I trust you?" Carver began.

Turner shook his head and huffed breath out. "Yer askin' if ya can trust *me* after I find out yer a *Belial prince* an' have lied aboot it? Seems ya already decided not to, so far." His accent thickened as emotion crept in.

Carver hurried to explain. "I didn't expect to become friends with you. My father is always looking for ways to control me. Anyone I care about is fair game to him. I cannot be close to anyone—it's the only way to keep those around me safe." He paused to let all that sink in before finishing. "Truth is, you're the only friend I've got."

Turner stopped to stare suspiciously at him for a moment. Seeing the raw truth on Carver's face, he simply nodded, and started walking again. "Alright mate. So ya've the devil fer a Da and no one ya can love. I can't say I understand—but I'll try. When ya say 'can I trust you', what exactly are ya asking o' me?"

"Ahna can't know. So neither can Aiela... "

"Ah. Yer only askin' me ta lie ta the person I love most then."

"No! I'm asking you not to mention it to her. Ever. There should be no reason to. My name doesn't need to come up." Silence stood between them for a beat. "How are they?" He couldn't resist the asking, with his heart tugging and yearning for more news of Ahna.

Turner chuckled, squinting sideways at him. "Ya've got it joost as bad as me, don't ya." It wasn't a question. "They're well. Ahna's doin' good as can be expected—oh! Ya probably don' know—how would ya? Their parents died while we were all in Ireland. Aiela and Ahna got back ta High City an' found out. It crushed them a'course—er... *horrible* expression to use, seeing as how the parents died in an avalanche—mostly the girls'r sad all the way through still. An' will be fer awhile. Ya know how much they loved their Mam and Da, just like any o' us would. . ." Turner trailed off as if suddenly realizing Carver's differences.

Carver was trying to decide how not to be dishonest again. But no —there was no way in hell Turner would agree to keep *that* secret from the girls. Carver couldn't admit he knew—that Mardu had boasted about having the twin's parents assassinated. No way.

Instead, he put an appropriately sad surprise on his face, and stopped walking to face Turner. "That's awful! Poor Ahna. I wish I could do something... I cannot risk Mardu finding any connection between us though. It'd put both the girls in danger. I won't do that, even to comfort them."

"Your Da's really that bad? I guess all the stories about him are true then." Turner said, reaching to clap Carver on the back in support.

"Yes, he's really that bad—and then some. I'm ashamed to admit being his offspring. Imagine what that's like and then tell me you wouldn't have lied too, so someone would get to know you without *that* hanging over your head!"

Turner considered. "Guess I might've... I just might've." Then a moment later, "So what are we ta do now?"

Carver smiled for the first time. "Well, we've business to discuss of course. After that, stories to tell on how exactly we both came to be here doing business with each other!"

"Right, right. So business it is firstly, catchin' up secondly. We've a fish-fry planned for supper, yer welcome ta stay fer it. How far away is this Crystal Mine?" Turner's easy smile was back and Carver exhaled in relief at the sight of it.

"The Mines are a ways inland yet. And my aero's set down quite a trek through the jungle. I was headed to the mines to prepare the cargo when I spotted your ships. I do want to talk more, and stay for supper, but that'd put us hacking our way back in the dark... " Carver knew he sounded wistful.

"We've extra hammocks on the ship if ya'd like ta stay ow'er. Yeh could get an early start in the morning?" Turner offered.

"Thank you. I'd enjoy that."

"What do I call ya in front o' the men? Ya have a title?" Turner asked as they made their way back towards the pilot to give him the news about their change of plans.

"Naw, no titles, just Carver. But what's yours? You're heading this for your father I take it, so it'd be 'Captain Turner' then?" Carver said it with a grand inflection and elbowed him, teasing.

"Sure an' my Grandda's the *real* Captain, but I'm meant ta be learning it all."

"Captain Turner it is then!" Carver went off to deal with his pouting pilot, knowing full well he had a lot more explaining to do before Turner would agree to keep his secret.

He stopped dead when the thought occurred.

I could get Drey's journal to them! Turner is the perfect delivery man...

8

SAGE AND ZIEL

9,971 BCE. CHIFFON, ATLANTIS

"When you loved someone and had to let them go, there will always be that small part of yourself that whispers, "What was it that you wanted and why didn't you fight for it?"

— SHANNON L. ALDER

SAGE

*S*age hated that she still desired him so much. Being with him resurrected deep-down yearnings, long ago walled off and glossed over.

Now, that itch that she couldn't reach was back. Maddening and irrational as it was, those feelings swarmed in full force every time she saw him. Or thought of him. Was it love or just wanting what she couldn't have?

Mostly she was weary of missing him. Altogether too much of her life had been wasted on missing him, too much energy spent soothing away the hurt of not being chosen.

Mashing the previous day's food scraps together, Sage wandered outside the cheerful little cottage to feed the hens. "Here you go fat little ladies. Eat up." Taya's chickens pecked and squawked at the winter-barren square of earth that had been Taya's garden. "I'll need to move you lot out of here and plant soon," She told them, "if I want to keep it going for the girls."

Even this brought her mind back to Ziel. He'd loved planting time. Not so much watering, and for sure not the weeding. Harvest was fine, but planting was what made him most happy.

She had so few memories before Ziel entered her life. Three to be exact.

According to the scant information anyone had told her, she'd been born in Belial and probably sold to a group of scientists who were carrying on the legacy of Onus Belial's search for dominion, immortality, and a host of other endeavors.

She had a memory of fixing simple meals beside a severe old woman who taught her the names of fruits, vegetables and grains. Mostly, she remembered wondering where such things came from. The outside world had been nothing but a second-hand story. It was a rare treat when they took her to the upper floor labs where she could glimpse the sky through a window. As far as she knew, the bulk of her childhood was in an underground facility.

The first day she saw the ocean, both wondrous and frightening, was the same day she'd left Belial for good. Or had been taken out of Belial more accurately. Some good soul had rescued her from being only a science experiment, and deposited her in Chiffon; as far away from Belial as you could get on the continent. She was estimated to be about ten years old. After an extended stay in the Healing Temple, Ziel's mother had taken her in.

"Why did you want me?" Sage eventually thought to ask Ziel's intelligent, kind mother.

"Because I understood your illness." Mama had replied, smoothing Sage's bright blonde hair. "Atlantis conducted experiments on Ziel when he was a baby, wanting to test out theories about prolonging human life. I let them because what mother wouldn't want to give her child a longer life? It was mostly reprogramming the mind to slow the cellular aging process, and several courses of drugs to promote absorption of new information at the DNA level. But it made him very ill. He had a difficult time processing regular foods until he was eight or so. I suspect it stunted his growth. I've never stopped feeling guilty for allowing him to be part of that." Mama got tears in her eyes anytime she spoke of this. It was her greatest failure.

"You had the same sort of illness. I recognized it right away when they brought you to the Healing Temple." Mama had been a healer who specialized in herbal medicines. "When they asked who might be able to take you in, I knew it was no accident you'd been dropped off in Chiffon. You were meant for us—me and Ziel, because we understand you like no one else could. You're the daughter I always wanted, you know."

Mama was so full of warmth. She'd made Sage feel like part of a family, taught her what it was to be loved and cared for, and everything she knew about plants and their healing potentials. Ziel's mother was the only mother she ever knew.

Sage and Ziel were shy friends at first.

It quickly became apparent she was growing much slower than other children, just as he was. Long ago Mama had taken him out of regular classes, sending him instead to study with tutors. He appeared to be ten like her, but he was actually eighteen years old. He'd learned and matured mentally at a regular pace, but his body aged very slowly. It was an especially isolating condition because he didn't fit in with the other children—or the young adults.

He'd spent his days helping catch Sage up in learning. She could fix simple meals and knit. Beyond that she'd known nothing of the world or how to live in it. It took four years for them to grow from the appearance of ten to twelve together, playing, learning, and eventually falling in love.

Mama had been beside herself when she found out. "I wanted you to be brother and sister! This is a very bad idea. What if you fall *out* of love? You'll still need to be family…you're *both* my family."

"But we're *not* brother and sister!" Ziel argued in his determined voice that was sometimes squeaky with the beginnings of physical adolescence. Mentally he'd been mature as any adult for awhile. "We've never felt like siblings! You can't understand what it is to be different than the whole rest of the world, and then find someone who is… like me."

Mama's face had cringed with guilt.

"We want to be life mates." Sage had joined in, desperate, both to not hurt Mama, and to win her approval. "I know people won't accept us as officially mated yet, but *you* know we're every bit as grown-up inside as others who mate. I love him." She'd smiled shyly at Ziel. "I always will. Who else could there ever be for me?"

It was only now, thinking back on these memories that she understood how strange it must've been for Mama, having children who weren't children at all.

Ziel had talked of moving around. Sage agreed, maybe they should try living in other Atlantean cities and communities. Maybe even other continents. It'd help them not stick out so much among people who aged regularly. They could build as many different lives as needed.

But then his frequent visions got worse and Mama reported them to the Oracles, fearing Atlantis would be ruined, or disappear like Lemuria had.

When Ziel's psychic abilities came to the attention of the House of Oracles, the Head Oracle, Rowena, tested him and wanted him to come apprentice under her. It was an opportunity Ziel couldn't resist. An opportunity to further his learning far beyond what Chiffon offered. He'd be in a place no one would care that he looked thirteen with the mind of a thirty-year-old.

"I'll come back to you and we'll live anywhere we want. Just not too far from Mama until…"

Sage nodded to stop him from saying it. They'd already talked about the fact that Mama would die while they were still young. Even if she lived to be very old, they'd lose her far too soon. It brought both of them comfort that Sage could stay here and take care of Mama, while Ziel apprenticed in High City.

"Maybe I will figure out what I'm meant to do with my life… " He'd been intrigued with this prospect. "… besides making a family with you. There has to be a reason why we're both going to live to be ancient. We've just got to search until we find that reason."

But he hadn't come back. Not really. He'd visited frequently at first, because he didn't fit in as much as he'd hoped in High City either.

Sage and Mama took in another orphan named Adelay, moving into this little seaside cottage because it was hers, built by her parents.

When Mama died, Ziel spent three weeks at home, helping Sage and Adelay mourn and adjust. Those were hard days. Not just because they were mourning Mama, but because a silent resentment had crept between them. Sage wanted him to come back to her permanently. She wanted it so bad it physically hurt.

He told her there was still too much he needed to learn.

"I've found my destiny." He tried to explain. "I think I'm meant to use my abilities to save Atlantis. Ruler Rowena depends on me for so many things. I just can't leave yet."

The truth was, he liked being special. He liked the endless learning and bustling lifestyle in High City more than he liked living in quiet, picturesque Chiffon. "Come to High City." He begged. "You and me and Adelay can be a family there. There's no reason you have to stay here anymore. We always said we'd live other places. Remember?"

Sage considered it but the thought of living in High City made her shudder. Perhaps it was buried memories from a prolonged childhood in Belial's endless city, and whatever had been done to her there. Perhaps it was simply Chiffon's serene splendor where the forest cradled her spirit and the ocean sang to her soul. Or because this first real home held every bit of love, security or happiness she'd ever known. She couldn't bring herself to leave. Anxiety overwhelmed and almost unhinged her when she imagined living in the city.

In a way, they both broke promises. What made it miserable was the love they still felt, the life together that seemed to hover just out of reach.

He stopped coming home when Rowena passed on and he became Head of the House of Oracles. It just was easier to stop trying to be part of each other's lives when it didn't seem meant to be. They went many decades with no communication whatsoever.

Sage looked around her cottage at the tokens of memories four generations of orphaned girls had left. A legacy to raising them. She'd been so relieved when Taya outlived her mother and grandmother—who'd each died at such young ages. She'd been foolish enough to think the "orphan curse" had been broken.

She absently stroked Taya's multi-colored llamas, while they nibbled daintily at their hemp and oats. Life had brought Ziel to her again. Did he feel their connection as strongly as she did?

Wandering around the cottage filled with spring sunshine, dusting and straightening while Sila, Taya's lavender snake, watched her from the rafters, Sage considered how much time she'd been spending with Ziel. How sweetly he still cared for her, seeming eager for her stories about life in Chiffon.

He still touched her frequently. A palm brushed her shoulder when he gave her cups of tea. Steady fingers supported her elbow, or took her hand while they walked through the rubble of Crystal City. Holding her as she clung to him for what felt like hours last fall, they'd wept bitterly at the loss of Drey and Taya, and wondered how they could help the twins.

Such a flimsy human thing, this infatuation, she scolded herself, vigorously scrubbing the smooth cherrywood table that Taya had made from lightning-twirled cherry trees, after the birth of the girls. How was it still possible at her age?

Admittedly, the infatuation did make her feel young again. She'd made excuses to visit the twins often. Bought new outfits to wear, (never finding appropriate excuses for that) feeling a thrill when his eyes swept her body. When she noticed his gaze linger while twisting her hair up into a messy knot before going to market, she decided then and there to let it grow.

Her last two visits in High City, he'd taken to dropping a kiss on top of her head when she was sitting, or pressing lips to her forehead when they parted.

And now he'd become a craving again.

CHORES DONE FOR TODAY, Sage settled on the old swing out back of the cottage, watching skiffs of clouds turn flamingo pink. A calm ocean, spreading to infinity, reflected the sky's rosy hues until it seemed the entire western horizon flushed with pure joy as the sun slid down.

How many times had she sat here watching sunsets with her girls?

Straight ahead were cliffs that dropped twenty feet to the sea; a constant worry when she had a toddler to keep track of.

Forest trees stood sentry along the north side of the clearing protecting the cottage and gardens from the storms that blew in. At their rooted feet were various stone markers. Cairns, or perhaps a larger stone etched by young hands, marked the spot where beloved animal bones were laid to rest. Only a year ago Ahna had buried her large tawny Yowl who'd been remarkably long-lived for a panther. Not three moons later, Aiela's brindled Charl had passed on too. There'd been plenty of transients, stray hawks, neighborhood cats, even a wolf, but none of them would replace the twin's childhood pets.

Listening to the swing creak, framing far-off crashing of the surf, she sipped cinnamon blackberry tea and reflected on the generations of daughters she'd raised. Orphaned girls, all from the same family line starting with Adelay, had grown up in this cottage, mothered by an orphan who'd outlived them all. Familiar pangs of loss gripped inside her heart. She searched for something else to busy her mind with.

"Like blue wisteria isn't it?"

Sage startled violently at the quiet question from behind. "You're like to cause my heart to stop! What are you doing here?!"

Ziel's smile stretched wide and bright in the fading light. "I missed you." He came to settle beside her, never taking his eyes from her face. Gesturing a careless hand at the fading sky he explained. "I was watching the magnificent colors, trying to figure out how *not* to startle you. I'm sorry I failed." Reaching an arm to wrap and pull her close, he sighed the sigh of purest relaxation, turning pale eyes back towards the horizon. "Does it look more purple or blue?"

Heart beating much too fast—from the unexpectedness of him appearing right out of her thoughts—she settled slowly into the casual comfort of his arm. "Purple. But I—"

"Looks more blue to me." He interrupted. Those eyes the color of clear, sun-warm coves turned back to her. "Can I stay here with you tonight? I'm afraid I forgot to make any arrangements whatsoever. It's the queerest thing. There I was sitting in weekly report hall and couldn't get you out of my mind. I couldn't concentrate on what anyone was saying and they all started getting annoyed with me... so I left." He smiled with delight at his own spontaneity. "I just went to the aero lot, climbed in and came home."

She stared at him, barely able to make out the distinct features of his fine-boned face as twilight melted solid things, bolstering that which can only be felt. *Came home.* "So... you're probably hungry then?" Why was she nervous? Her mind began running in circles, not forming coherent thoughts.

"I am." He paused, his arm tightening around her, ever so slightly drawing her closer. "I've been hungry for close to a century. Sage." He whispered her name. "Could you ever forgive me? Is there any chance for us again? I'm willing to do it your way this time, I can come here when you want or you can come there when you want or maybe I'll just quit—"

This time she interrupted him by pressing her lips to his. Giving up on her skittering mind she simply followed her heart. Kissing him didn't feel the same as she remembered. But then they weren't the same people they had been.

His lips softened and moved under hers. A palm came up to brush her ear, fingers pushing into her hair, pulling her into him. Desire bloomed, but so did fear.

She pulled back. "Last time I loved you it hurt entirely too much."

His fingertips trailed over her cheekbones, along her jaw. "I'm sorry for that. I was too stupid to know the value of your love. I'd like to listen if you're willing to tell me. Maybe together we can heal the wounds I've caused."

"We'll need tea." She rose from the swing and held out her hand.

He took it. "Anything you're offering, I'll be grateful for."

That's what's different, she realized, as they walked inside to wave on lights and set water to heat. *His pride is gone. He's choosing to be vulnerable. He's choosing me.*

TRAINING TIME

9,971 BCE. HIGH CITY, ATLANTIS

"No matter how long you train someone to be brave, you never know if they are or not until something real happens."

— VERONICA ROTH

AHNA

"*I*t feels like forever since we've talked! You look different... " Ahna crossed the midnight blue hall outside Ziel's rooms to embrace her sister, their relief of being together again spreading, like the beach from a slow, outgoing tide.

"*Too* long. I'm not myself." Aiela crushed her smaller sibling, tears springing up.

Then Ziel opened his door and pulled at them, saying, "Inside my dears. Inside." closing the door quickly behind them. "Alright, carry on with your reunion. I'm making tea and when you're ready, we can begin."

The twins turned to each other again and Ahna melted at the sight of Aiela, watery-eyed, reaching for her. "Why didn't you find me? Tell me sooner?" She spoke into Aiela's shoulder, little bubbles of sadness escaped between them, releasing from Aiela's heart center. She felt her sister's shrug, knew she was trying to control her emotion.

Finally Aiela released her, and swiped carelessly at her eyes. "I figured you're as busy as I am. I kept thinking I'd see you at meals, but then I didn't make it to half of them and when I did see you, you were always surrounded with new friends, and I was usually in a hurry anyway. I came to your room several times but you weren't there and I didn't want to wake you or your roommates by coming too late— We have to find times to be together!"

Ahna was nodding. "I know. What if we met for breakfast every morning? Or I could come to your room, spend the night sometimes?"

"Yes. Both." Aiela's response was immediate and full of need. "How about tonight you sleep in my room. We can catch up—I've so much to tell you."

"I'm sorry. I've been uneasy, knew you were off, but I could never seem to find you with my mind." Guilt washed through Ahna for not trying more often, not physically tracking her sister down.

Aiela shook her head, smile blooming with relief, and hugged her again, quick and tight. "It's not your fault, we just didn't know it would be like this." A cough in the the other room brought them back to the moment at hand, and they linked arms just like they used to.

"Better see what Ziel wants."

"Bring your pillow," Aiela added, "I only have the one."

Fully re-connected, they headed around the corner to where Ziel was waiting at his little rosewood table, three tiny empty cups carved from colorful stones awaited, and a butter-colored, soapstone teapot had wisps of steam escaping its spout.

He looked up at them, raising his eyebrows in silent question.

"Sorry we kept you waiting..." Aiela began.

"We've not seen each other much and that's miserable for us." Ahna finished.

Ziel nodded as if he understood perfectly. "I may have a solution, at least for the next few moons. Sit, please, would you enjoy tea? It's toasted rice with green." At their nods, he poured a pale stream. "I wanted to wait longer—let you settle into your apprenticeships—but

I've received more and more information which lends urgency to my need of you."

He paused, leaning forward and pinning them with a piercing gaze, before whispering dramatically, "It is time to begin your training as Keepers of the Crystals.

"The difficulty will be finding time in your schedules and keeping it secret that you come here regularly. That is what we will figure out tonight. Certain deceptions will be necessary. I rely on you to choose what you can drop from your current activities, and still maintain the illusion of being an apprentice. I will, of course, give any relevant permissions you may need."

The twins excitement widened with the smiles on their faces, as they talked through what was being expected of them, what they felt was unnecessary or extraneous in their schedules, when and where they wouldn't be missed.

"We are mostly just *posing* at our apprenticeships, correct?" Aiela asked Ziel at one point.

He raised an eyebrow, "Well, yes, this job I've given you takes precedence, if that's what you're asking. But remember, your facades must be convincing. And every experience has a purpose and a learning to it. You never know when they might come in handy."

It took a solid hour and Ziel ended with a good-sized to-do list of communications with Advisors or Instructors and permission letters to write, but it was finally arranged. The girls would meet here five times a week, some early mornings, some afternoons and evenings.

Ahna and Aiela looked at each other with nothing short of glee. They'd be spending a lot of time together again.

"What sort of training—" They both began.

"—exactly?" Aiela finished the question.

Ziel rose from his low-slung cushion chair with a grunt. "Follow me." He said simply, leading them to a door they hadn't noticed.

It opened into a bedroom, sparsely furnished with a bed and wardrobe, its walls hung with tapestries depicting the four seasons of Atlantis.

Ziel closed the door behind them, turning two locks with a hollow click. "When you go below, make sure you double lock this door. It's a sort of message to me for reasons of tracking you—should anything happen in the maze."

He dug inside his robe, bringing forth two identical keys. They were smaller than the girl's littlest fingers, dainty and complex, hanging on silken cords, one plum-colored, the other jade. "Ahna, you get the green one, and Aiela, yours is the purple. Keep these on your body at all times. This is the most important request I will make of you. They're more than just keys, they're trackers so I can locate you anywhere."

Ziel lifted the winter tapestry away from the wall, running his hand over the smooth, indigo marble, veined with darker lines arcing this way and that as if studiously avoiding pattern. Fitting his own key into a perfectly camouflaged slot, he continued, "The lock sits directly behind the winter sun, turn to the left three turns, then push."

A faint click and he withdrew his key and pushed against the wall. A slab turned in, and they felt cool air whiff gently past their faces, scented with damp earth like the caves they'd visited in Ireland.

"Under the bed are guidelights. Get one for each of us and put fresh spheres in. Who knows how much of their charge your mother used..."

The lanterns were unremarkable. Small polished cedar frames; a hook handle topping a three-sided pyramid which ensconced perfect stone spheres the size and color of grapefruit. The spheres were charged with solar power. The larger the stone, the longer the charge lasted. These were good-sized and could shine continuously for a moon or more on one charge. Waving their guidelights on, they slipped through the secret door.

Ziel led them down a long flight of steps that angled in towards the mountain center. Ever-moist dirt musk scented the air, suffused with an acrid stillness.

They came eventually to a sharply down-sloping tunnel, narrow enough that a broad-shouldered man might get wedged, and short enough that even Ziel and Aiela hunched just a bit to keep their heads from brushing the ceiling.

"This is all a quiet zone." Ziel stopped to whisper back at them, his "s" sounds whistling sharply through his teeth. "From the secret door of the bedroom until we reach the main tunnels, you must take care. No one else knows I've private access and I have no idea where sound might carry in the Palace."

Wormlike tunnels veered off at angles or turned abruptly to either direction and Ziel paused at one, lowering his light to illuminate the dirt better. "These other passages are meant to confuse and distract but can you see how well-worn is the path we walk? Anyone with half a brain can see which way to go. This will be your first task and also your first training; exploring these offshoots, which I call the 'entrance branch', and making all ways look equal. After that, you must become very familiar with the maze in its entirety. It is a defense system. Darkness and claustrophobia, coupled with hundreds of miles to get lost in can be a most effective protection against those who might seek control of the Crystal's power."

He paused to peer at a convergence of three tunnels. Finally choosing to go straight ahead.

"I've maps for you to memorize but it is quite different seeing the maze mapped out in a hologram and actually being in it. Ideally, you'll create landmarks known only to you. You'll memorize how many steps between turns and find ways to navigate even in the dark. I expect you to make all of this your own."

They came to a little transport; a simple horizontal tube with a steering fin on its underside, all of it crafted from bamboo. "The power is here." He turned a dial on the T-shaped bars that controlled it and an engine hummed slightly from inside, lifting it to hover three feet off the ground, barely enough to keep their feet from dragging.

"I've heard about these, but didn't know they still existed." Ahna said, walking round the hover tube, running a hand along its curved side.

"There's quite a few still, stored after Atlantis simplified our transportation. It occurred to me, not long after your mother was here in fact, there was no reason I couldn't use them in the tunnels."

Ziel was referring to a time in recent history, when Atlantis outlawed all hover-type vehicles except aeros. It simply became too complex to manage the high numbers of accidental damages done to structures and people. Controlling the flow of air traffic had taken up too much time and resources. Injuries and death tolls had gotten ridiculously high.

People were outraged about the new laws for quite some time, but eventually came to see the wisdom of sacrificing certain conveniences to simplify transportation. Their vehicles had to connect to the ground via wheels or legs, or be an aero with strict minimum flying heights and rules of travel. Except for sanctioned stops at Poseidon's Palace, aeros were no longer allowed inside the city walls.

"Will it hold all three of us?" Aiela asked doubtfully.

Ziel shrugged. "It'll hold whatever weight you can fit on it but the length might be tight—it's really only built for two."

They straddled it, squishing together, one behind the other and set off with Ziel driving.

Ahna lost count of how many times the tunnels forked, crossed, and split, sometimes one went up and the other down. Twice they stopped and Ziel had them slide disguising doors aside, cleverly stuccoed to match the tunnel wall.

He went slowly, explaining all the way. "There are three levels to the maze, each level is basically a giant spiral that would be fifty to seventy miles long if stretched out. Tunnels that connect the loops are endless and mutable. This will be part of your duties—changing the pathway to the Cathedral at center. We accomplish this by occasionally collapsing some tunnels, barricading openings, using many false walls, and movable staircases. There are quite a lot of tunnels that lead to nowhere. There are 'bottomless' holes, and caches of rock that will fall when an intruder approaches. Terribly dangerous, our little maze."

He steered the hover tube up a staircase that didn't look very moveable.

Three turns later, they came to another flight of steps going down and then two more, down down and into a great unknown yawn of utter dark.

Ahna was gripping the leather handle on the tube tightly and Aiela clutched the other one—both quiet with suspense, more than a little awed at the enormity of what Ziel was showing them.

He climbed off the tube, his guidelight sliding away into inky air and then a grinding sound. The chamber lit up like a high-noon sun on snow.

They gasped, forgetting to wave off their lanterns, sliding off the tube and staring about them.

The cavern was massive, with smooth, white walls and sparkling white marble tile beneath their feet. It was empty except for three towering crystals rising from the center like holy pillars, carved with designs in bas relief with intentional facets sparkling with reflected light.

"How tall are they?" Ahna had gone directly to the blue one and laid both hands on its surface, moving over its glassy smooth, astrological theme. She didn't wait for an answer, distracted by the designs. "This is mapping of more than just our galaxy—there are other universes on here!"

"Yes." Ziel replied, moving towards the girls and watching them closely.

"Your mother used the ancient knowledge of Star people, maps from the Oracles and the Temple of Dreams to depict the three universes we know most about. These Crystals stand just over eighty feet tall."

"*Mama* did all of this?" Aiela was at the platinum one covered with sacred geometry; creation sequenced in shapes. "This one looks taller than the others, probably because of the designs... "

"Every bit was her idea. She spent many many days down here, carving." Ziel's voice echoed proud and tender. "She was here an entire moon, after which she and I brought a team of programmers in to finish the job."

By now both Ahna and Aiela were at the emerald crystal. Its sculptures crowded together with no blank space between; picturing earth life in all its forms from plants to mammals, sea life, reptiles, fruits, birds and clouds, with an oversized human form wrapping its arms around the crystal, as if embracing all that earth offers us.

"How did she do it like this?" Aiela asked, fingers traveling over shapes done in negative space. The designs popped out, almost three-dimensional. "I didn't know she could carve."

"She had clever tools and even better ideas. She borrowed devices and technology from the Temple of Beauty. Your mother was a person with widely varied talents; one of those rarities who seem to master whatever they set their mind and hands to… " He continued reminiscing about his time with Taya and the girls listened closely, drinking in this other perspective on who she had been, as hungry to hear of her as Ziel was to remember her.

It was some time later, after all three had settled onto the icy floor, legs splayed out, backs resting against the Crystals, when Ziel remarked with some surprise, "Neither of you seem affected by the Crystal's energy. It's usually overwhelming or intoxicating, until your body learns to adjust. Do neither of you feel affected?"

The sisters looked at each other and shrugged. Aiela replied for them both.

"Not really. I feel a little spacey."

He gathered himself to rise. "Perhaps it's your age. Although, your mother wasn't' that much older than you when she first came. I will meditate on it. There must be an explanation and it could be useful to know. We should make our way back. I will show you more of the maze's secrets and we can pick up another trolley so you both learn to operate them. That will take some practice too."

Crowding onto the little tube, they set off.

"When we return," Ziel said, "I'll show you where the maze map is and how to access it. I want you to study and memorize it before you start exploring beyond the entrance tunnels. When your training is complete, we will destroy it."

The girls held on tight as they sped through miles of darkness, listening to his words floating back.

"There will be difficult—even dangerous—tests you must pass before I turn you loose in here…" His tone was solemn with warning.

Two days later their new schedules began.

They turned up at Ziel's apartment and he assigned them work, sometimes on the maze, other times on the structure and operating system of the Crystals. Several hours each day they studied and memorized and discussed and quizzed each other on what they were learning.

And each day Ziel sent them in through the little secret door, assigning them tasks like mapping the left side of the "entrance branches" or finding a certain tunnel where he'd hidden something as a reward, or working in the dirt to make all ways look equally travelled.

Ahna discovered she could easily picture where they were in the entrance branch, following the maps in her mind.

Aiela was surprised at her talent for tiny details; remembering a unique indent on this tunnel wall, a narrower space here or patterned dirt layers in the walls there that helped her navigate.

The worst part was an infestation of mice and rats, seeming not the least afraid of getting underfoot, attracted to any light that relieved the pure obsidian black.

TWO WEEKS LATER, satisfied with their practice of learning and exploring the entrance branch, Ziel began their learning of the big maze itself.

They divided it into quadrants, and set about memorizing each section. Through tedious, brain-exhausting work, they persevered, drawing maps again and again from memory to set the quadrants firmly in their own minds.

Actual forays into the maze installed the mapping into their bodies.

Both learned quickly to operate the little tube trolleys, crashing one in a high speed chase that brought Ziel's stern admonitions about taking unnecessary risks. They put on appropriately contrite faces, and commenced their penance of figuring out how to repair the wrecked craft, even as Ahna sensed the satisfaction Ziel was trying to hide. Probably because they could now serve as mechanics for the trolleys—another duty for their expanding job description.

ONE EVENING, Ziel dropped them off in the maze, abandoning them to the chilled, black air. "If you haven't found your way home by tomorrow morning, I'll consider coming to find you." His voice held an amused challenge, as if he thought they might actually get lost, and this might be a lesson to them in the true dangers of the maze.

But they had a few secrets of their own. For instance, he didn't know they'd labeled the quadrants: A for Ahna, E for Aiela, T for Turner and C for Carver. He didn't know they had an intricate system of markings on the tunnel walls, that acted like guideposts to tell them exactly where they were. Or that they now had a fair number of trolleys scattered among hiding places, along with lights, food, water and even blankets.

Ahna had had a vision about surviving in these tunnels. They'd been preparing ever since Ziel let them start exploring the full maze. He didn't know yet that he'd have to remove their emergency stashes, and change all the mutable pieces to make it any sort of challenge.

They knew exactly where they were when he dropped them off. Quadrant C, three loops out from the far side of the Crystals on the middle level.

They ran the five miles to the central cavern, slowing only to feel for the turns.

Lighting up the Crystals in the cathedral, they sat talking about their training, planning more ways to make this maze their own. Trying to think of all variables, they imagined an enemy trying to find their way through with technologies to help.

"We need a way to flood some of the tunnels." Aiela said.

"We need weapons down here too, with our survival stashes." Ahna replied.

"And we've *got* to do something about the rats! They're going to chew up everything."

"What about Sila? She's a good mouser."

Conversation turned to missing Mama and Papa, then memories of Ireland. It was several hours before they took a hover tube back.

Ziel was sipping tea and reading when they arrived. He beamed at them. "How can it be that already you are masters of the maze?!"

As a reward, he gave them the next day completely free. "For the love of every goddess, go to the markets and get some furniture for your room." He said to Aiela. "And both of you need new clothing." He eyed smeared stains on their leggings and poked at clods of earth clinging to their hair. "You stick out like turnips on a platter of cream puffs here. Try to blend in a little more. Wear the latest fashions, visit the Palace beauty people. Get anything you want on my account, I have more credits built up than I'll ever use."

They thanked him with hugs, smirking with victory and teasing him about his doubts in them.

"Next time, we'll wager how long it takes us to return." Aiela said, patting his arm with the compassion of the younger and stronger— who think they're perhaps smarter too.

"Next time you come, I'll have plans drawn up for your contingency of flooding some tunnels, should it ever be needed. It's quite a good idea." Ziel returned with glinting eyes, patting her cheek with the compassion of long-lived wisdom.

Turning to Ahna he continued. "I'm having weapons made for you both already. The delivery should be next week, then you'll start training with them. You're welcome to make any additional requests after you see what I've commissioned. And I've already spoken with Sage. She'll bring Sila for a visit next week, see how she likes the maze."

He glanced at both their questioning faces. "Oh, not to worry, I didn't stay for much of your conversation. Eavesdropping is impolite. I heard just enough to know how to better challenge you. I trust you will propose *all* of your wild ideas to me. They're excellent so far."

Aiela slitted her eyes accusingly. "You really didn't think we could do it! You waited in the cathedral because you were worried about us!" Her tone was indignant.

"Not so. I had business with the Crystals and took the opportunity." Ziel lied smoothly with a bland expression and steady gaze, but he forgot to mask his energy.

Ahna registered it as easily as she dismissed it. Everyone's lies were flavored a tiny bit different, but the energetic feel was like walking along, and running into an invisible wall. The jolt depended on the liar, and how strongly they felt their own deception. People who lie so often they're barely aware of the difference between truth and lie, cause a jolt so imperceptible it's easy to miss. If someone cares terribly much or has any intense emotion attached to the lie, it's very noticeable.

She got up to refill the teapot. "Then why were the lights off when we got there? It's almost as though you were planning to lurk and listen."

Aiela covered a giggle at her sister's impertinence.

Ziel was unfazed. "You were loud as a herd of rhinos, running and shrieking along the tunnels. I heard you coming eons before you arrived. It wouldn't have seemed a test anymore had you found me waiting. I should've followed my instincts and disabled the trolley. Or perhaps the lights!"

"I FEEL LIKE A MOLE." Ahna was lying in bed exhausted, next to her sister. Though victorious and even fun, sprinting in the dark had been grueling.

"You're starting to look like one too, but I didn't want to say anything." Aiela mumbled sleepily, face half-buried in her pillow.

Normally, Ahna might have shoved her out of bed at the insult, but tonight she was too tired for more than a half-hearted kick towards Aiela's leg. "We need more physical training. That run wore me out."

But Aiela was already snoring softly into her pillow. Ahna turned over to fall asleep in the little room at the top of the Palace, feeling for the first time, like she'd earned her new title, Keeper of the Crystals.

THE MAKING OF MARDU

RIVER TOWN IN GREECE

"No you don't know what its like, when nothing feels alright. You don't know what its like to be like me. To be hurt, to feel lost. To be left out in the dark. To be kicked when you're down. To feel like you've been pushed around. To be on the edge of breaking down. And no one there to save you. No you don't know what its like".

— SIMPLE PLAN, WELCOME TO MY LIFE

MARDU

"Stop it! Stop….*please stop…*" Mady sobbed, curling into a ball on his side in the dirt.

Three boys were shrieking ugly words at him, kicking him in the back and head, trying to aim at the tender place between his legs. If he curled into a ball they couldn't get to it. They were much bigger than him, even though Mitera said he was big for seven.

He was bruised and bleeding by the time they grew bored—or tired maybe. Flinging handfuls of rock and dirt at his head, they finally left.

He lay there for awhile, feeling miserable and alone, before dragging himself up. He'd go to the river outside town and wash before going home. He hoped the black bloodstain and dirt would come out of his clothes so Mitera wouldn't be angry at him.

She had just bought him this tunic in the markets. He'd gotten to choose the color he liked best—bright red like the rare apple he was given as a treat. It was the first new thing he'd ever owned.

He began the long walk to the river, watchful to give other boys a wide berth. Continuing upstream until he was alone, he scrubbed his tunic with handfuls of wet sand and then spread it onto the grass bank to dry. Flopping beside it, he watched clouds race overhead, swirling through the bright blue like they could be anything they wanted.

This was the biggest town he'd ever seen. Many many streets to explore, all lined with tan clay buildings, some of them taller than the trees. It was noisy with so many people crowded into the spaces, but Mitera had found a place to live after only one day!

Mady liked their room because it was up the stairs, and had a window to see far into the distance. He liked that he had a real bed to sleep in, not just a pile of torn blankets on the floor. He liked that there was only one man who came to see Mitera. She seemed as happy here as she had with the long-ago man who was not Mady's Pater.

He didn't think about the things he didn't like here. There were only two anyway:

1. The other boys here seemed to hate him. He knew because they always yelled words he wasn't allowed to say, and they hit him when no adults were around. He ran away when he could, but on days like today, they left him a mash of bruises and scabs.
2. The man who came to see Mitera liked to do strange things with Mady sometimes. Mady didn't like it, but Mitera said he must do what the man wanted.

11

THE CRYSTALS CALLED TO HER

9,971 BCE. HIGH CITY, ATLANTIS

"I have come to the edge of the land. I could get pushed over."

— MARGARET ATWOOD, CAT'S EYE.

AHNA

*T*he crystals called to her. Especially the blue one. In her sleep, awake, it didn't matter. Often it was a seduction.

Tonight she'd woken to scene after scene of people: praying, talking, making love, studying, fighting, crying, on and on it scrolled, flinging emotion about till her mind screamed "enough!"

Sitting up in her narrow bed, she threw off the quilt and padded silently to the balcony, careful to open the glass-paned panel quietly so as not to disturb her roommates.

She was a master at silence. This cacophony in her head would drive her mad if she didn't do something about it. Gulping in the cool night air, she leaned slim forearms against the smooth, rounded marble of the rail. *Is this happening to Aiela too?*

Reaching towards the gold thread in her mind, she followed it to where her sister snored gently. Quickly she retreated, not wishing to wake her. It took only seconds for the connection to be made, and she wasn't sure she wanted Aiela to know—if she didn't already.

These foreign thoughts confused her. More and more lately she didn't want El to know things. Why was that?

A push in her mind, subtle but there, alerted her to something else present in the thought. The Crystal's carved image flared in her mind, then abruptly vanished.

An even more disturbing thought came; was it reading her mind? No, surely not. Could it? Her conscious mind wrestled with her deeper knowing. But why? And how? Wide awake now, she reached back to where the push had come from.

What are you seeking? Silence. She began to think she imagined the whole thing.

Then, an image burned across her inner eyes; her twin lying on an altar. It was crude, a rough slab of dull stone, with shadows surrounding her—people perhaps—or something else. But her focus stuck on one searing image; a knife planted deep in Aiela's chest.

Ahna's heart thudded harshly into flight. Panic welled, horror mixed with despair. She'd had visions her whole life, but this felt entirely different. Implanted. Foreign. Devastating.

What? When? Where? Are you telling me the future? Why show me this? Her questions fired rapidly towards the unknown consciousness, more panic than reason, until she stopped herself with a deep breath. Forcing air into her constricted lungs. *Breath in. Breath out. It isn't real. Many visions never happen.*

Willing her mind to empty with her breath, she focused on the stars twinkling overhead, their carefree points of light steady over eons of time and space. When she'd let go of all emotions, she reached again towards the consciousness hovering at the edges, waiting, as if it knew she would come back to it.

There was an infinite sense of patience when she connected. As if it had all of eternity.

Eternity is not time without end—it is what is outside of time. Time-lessness.

Contemplating this distinct thought from the Crystal consciousness, Ahna startled when something fluttered to land on the railing beside her hand. It was a large butterfly, most likely the catopsilia. They migrated to Atlantis from the eastern continent every fall. Huge, some as big as two splayed hands, they were etched in black and colored in with bright orange. Some had variations of reds and yellows.

There was even a festival in their honor with nectar set out to feed them in hordes, while children built butterfly houses of every design imaginable, to house them for as long as they stayed. Scientists believed they were drawn from across the water to the frequencies emitted by Atlantean crystals. Typically, they continued south as the weather cooled, to winter in the islands. How odd to have one out at night.

It fluttered again to land squarely on her hand.

"Well hello pretty." Ahna whispered, still as a statue. "Shouldn't you be sleeping?" A sense of the delicate, short-lived energy of the butterfly touched her just as the Crystal flashed the scene of Aiela lying stabbed on the altar again. "What?" Ahna hissed, exasperated. "I don't understand! You have to be clearer."

Like the caterpillar, the cocoon will give her wings. Be not afraid.

Ahna remained still until the butterfly fluttered off, headed towards the bright night colors of the City.

Feeling her way to her journal, she hid under the quilt with a light orb glowing softly, and wrote it all down. It was her link to sanity, pouring out these experiences from the odd to the impossible.

From the edges of sleep, she reached out. *Thank you.*

The timeless deep answered back. *Remember.*

12

CRYSTAL MINES

9,971 BCE. EAST COAST OF SOUTH AMERICA

"Don't hide your heart but reveal it, So that mine might be revealed, and I might accept what I am capable of."

— -RUMI

CARVER

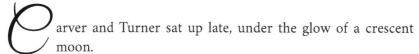arver and Turner sat up late, under the glow of a crescent moon.

As glinting night waves slapped against the ship hull, they lounged on heaps of scratchy rope, discussing all the things there wouldn't be a chance to, once their business transaction got underway.

Turner spoke of how hard it had been to let go his dream of apprenticing in Greece with the uncles he hero-worshipped. "It's been my plan since I realized I needed one ta escape doin' what my Da does an' my Grand-da an' Great-grand-da. I spent a moon every year wi' Mam's family since I was wee. Greece is lovely, hot an' dry. Ya get ta see the sun almost every day! They've buckets o' sweet fruits instead

77

of dirt-tastin' root vegetables and ya wouldna believe the girls there! Every one of 'em bonny and bold.

"But ya see, that's what changed my mind. I can take missin' the sun and fruit an' even no' learning the weapons trade—that was the harder one—but I can't take missing Aiela. She's the bonny, bold girl I want and when I compared the two, Greece or her, well my heart flat refused ta abide the ache o' missing her."

Carver watched the silhouette of his animated, curly-haired friend. It was too dark to make out expressions on Turner's face, but the stout, muscled body spoke its own language. Easy and earnest, energetic and kind. Foreign feelings rushed into some untouched place inside Carver and he reached to clap Turner's thick shoulder. "Wish I had my priorities as straight. I envy your clarity—and your choices."

He felt the weight of Turner's gaze through the velvet night as Turner spoke soft and slow.

"I won't pretend ta understand yer situation mate, but my Da always said 'Yeh've decided what yer choices are long b'fore ya pick one.'"

"Sounds like one of those bitter truths." Carver replied, failing to squelch a yawn.

Sitting up to stretch, he glanced around to make sure no one else had wandered out on deck. Even knowing the Irish sailors had eaten much and drank more, anticipating a full night's sleep rocking at anchor, he couldn't risk them overhearing what he was going to say next.

"I've black things to tell you my friend—and a favor to ask."

Turner only yawned back and waited for him to continue.

"My father commands an army of giants. We call them Mutazio. He plans on using them to conquer the world—and rule it." Carver paused to let this first bit sink in.

"What do ya mean by giants?" Turner asked, quieting his voice to match Carver's. His silhouette wasn't lounging anymore. It leaned forward, facing Carver fully. The ease was gone.

"About five hundred years ago, Onus Belial set out to create the perfect warriors. Wanting them stronger than normal men, he mixed human DNA with that of apes. Our Mutazio are between seven and twelve feet tall, all patterned from the same handful of altered chromosomes. They're purposely bred to be less intelligent so that they're more controllable, but they're very very powerful and have trained their entire lives for one thing; killing."

"Sure an' that's... ominous. How has Belial kept a whole army of giants hidden? When an' where will ya start? Why are ya tellin' me? And why do ya want ta conquer, er rule the whole world? Sounds impossible and exhausting!" Turner's questions held equal amounts of outrage and incredulity.

"Do not confuse *me* with Belial or Mardu!"

Carver softened the sharpness in his tone before continuing. "I'm telling you because I have a plan to stop him, but I need your help."

Turner had insistent questions again, but Carver spoke over him.

"I've a journal from Drey that tell how the Mutazio can be controlled or even killed. If you get it to Ahna and Aiela, they'll take it to Ruler Ziel and Atlantis can move to stop it all. It won't keep Mardu from using the regular Belial soldiers but it'll take away his advantage. No military will be able to stand against the muta army."

Silence stood between them for several beats as Turner struggled to digest these catastrophic words. Finally he whispered, "Who is Drey?"

Carver took a deep breath. He'd already committed. There would be no undoing what he'd just said. "Drey is Ahna and Aiela's father."

He could feel another onslaught of confused questions bubbling up in Turner, and rushed to explain. "My father used him, years ago, to complete the nodes that control the Mutazio. It's a strange story... all in one of the journals they took from his aero. Drey wrote out the science of the nodes and Mardu stole these journals..." *when he had Drey killed.* The truth wanted to rush out but Carver couldn't let himself speak it. Not yet. "...but he doesn't know what they contain. I'm the only one who knows."

When no reply filled the uncomfortable silence, Carver continued. "Look, I realize this is like dropping a boulder on a cake but I can't think of any other way. I've been trying to figure out how to get the information to Atlantis without revealing myself a traitor, and when I saw you walking up to me on that beach I realized I'm being given a chance. A chance to create those choices you talked of earlier." Carver didn't hide the desperation in his voice. "I'm trying to give myself better options here mate."

Turner's head shape bobbed gently in the night. They both breathed in deep, exhaling heavily as if it might lessen the weight settled firmly on their shoulders.

"Alright." Turner finally said. "I will take this journal ta the girls. But how am I supposed ta do that withoot saying where I got it? They *would* understand about ya. I did. An' they'd do the same, I don' know how else—"

"NO!" Carver's word carried force without volume. "You cannot tell them. *Please.* I know Ahna too well. She'd try to contact or come to me and you don't understand the danger if Mardu sees what she means to me. I don't trust myself to hide it. You don't know how vicious he is—how dangerous… " Carver rubbed his tired eyes. How could he make Turner see the gravity?

"If you care about the girls at all, you have to keep my secret. I realize I'm straining our friendship more than it can perhaps survive, but I'm begging you to understand—because Ahna won't. My life, her life, Aiela's or yours are all pawns in his hands. He will use anything and anyone to keep me doing what he wants. It's always been this way. It's why I am who I am."

He stood abruptly and walked to the railing, trying to shake off the despair creeping in. The worry that he'd made a mistake in trusting Turner. Was this Irishman strong enough to share this burden? Wise enough to see the far-reaching implications? Brave enough to move past his own immediate fears?

Currents of warm night feathered by, smelling of mystery and kelp. He felt nauseous and realized it was so late his stomach had emptied and was pinching with hunger; sensations meant to be slept through.

Heavy forearms settled onto the railing beside him, and Carver stiffened, preparing himself for refusal or rejection—or maybe just repulsion.

Turner's tone was matter-of-fact. "Let's ge' one thing straight; I know ya, an' Mardu has'na made ya what ya are. I stand here beside the strongest of men. A man who won't abide evil and is devoted ta stoppin' it. I see a prince who will give up a kingdom, a fortune, huge power and the girl he loves, ta avert evil deeds—even though the deeds be of his own father's hand.

"Make no mistake mate, bein' raised by a right bastard may have made ya strong but it wasna what made ya good. That's yer own doin'. I'll admit, it's a mite baffling how ya could come froom him. Maybe yer soul came ta be guardian angel ta the rest o' us. Who knows? I don' need ta. I'm proud ta be the one yer askin' fer help and I'll do what ya ask. Apologies fer being slow ta understand, slow ta see the truth o' it. Mam says tha's just my head gettin' in the way o' my heart."

Carver felt a shock of relief followed by the fiery pressure of holding back tears. Probably shouldn't have drank so much of the Irish honey wine tonight, it was making him feel. He didn't drink at home ever; couldn't afford to let his walls down.

Grinning into the darkness, he placed an arm across the shoulders of his only friend, affecting an Irish accent. "An' that's when a slow-heided Irishman an' a half-bastard prince became the world's best hope."

They snorted quiet, short laughs together.

Turner straightened. "Best sleep some or we'll no' be worth a damn tomorrow." He led them below decks to the stuffy space slung with hammocks, unpleasantly fragrant with snoring Irishmen.

"Thank you." Carver whispered into the din of sleep sounds as they each settled into the swaying curve of a rough net.

"Best wait an' thank me when it's done mate." Came the quiet reply.

FEAR OF THEFT wasn't the only reason Mardu didn't want the Irish fleet anywhere near his Crystal mine. The mine was located near the northern Mutazio camp.

While foraging and hunting for their food, mutas had discovered the mine just under two years ago. It was mutas that dug and sifted, scrubbed and polished to a sparkle, every cluster and point that Mardu sold.

Carver had visited each of the Mutazio camps at least once, but it didn't matter how many times he'd worked with them, they still disturbed him.

Dense, oversized bones made them look like a prehistoric species. Standing between seven and twelve feet tall, some had little body hair while others sprouted it in the strangest places. Those who grew hair from the scalp seemed to prize it, even if it was only a long thin hank from one patch. Braids swung down the back, or from one side. Many had only short, furry ridges cresting the midline of their skull. Small eyes looked like shiny beads set among shallow, blunt features, and many had extra fingers or toes and double rows of teeth.

Because they ranged in intelligence so greatly, it was hard to gauge how much each one understood. The handlers treated them all like animals, but Carver had seen the expressions on some faces; emotions they didn't know how to hide. He got spooky sensations every time he spoke to them.

Sweat rolled down the middle of his back as he stood in the mid-afternoon sun, watching these huge, nearly naked men load crates packed with crystals onto river barges that were little more than glorified rafts. Built of course, by mutas, the wide, buoyant platforms moved slow, but floated enormous amounts of weight. They loaded each one down within inches of muddy river water flooding its deck.

Unseasonable heat mixed with jungle humidity today. Too far inland for ocean breezes to move the air, the swamp stink was smothering.

"Enough! It's full." Carver shouted to a Belial handler supervising aboard the barge being loaded at the makeshift dock. It rode low in the lazy current. He waved an arm and pointed down river, "Move it out. Make sure all the mutas are off!"

The handler waved in acknowledgement, barking orders at two mutas still on board, then positioned six Belials who would guide the barges thirty drifting miles to the sea. It would likely take the Irish ship crews much longer to transfer the heavy cargo from barges to ships, than the time it took the Mutazio to load.

"Give them a rest and water." Carver said to the handler who was cursing in irritation at his two dozen sweat-slicked giants milling about, drawing clouds of flies while they waited for the next barge to dock.

"They don' need no break. They'll wait till we're done for water!" The handler retorted, slapping away biting black insects. His eyes wouldn't meet Carver's and his tone was pompous. Mean.

Twice Carver's age, he'd probably spent most of his adult life here in the camps. Belials too criminal for society were often sent to work the mutas, used as overseers or trainers. It gave them some importance, along with the authority and violence they craved. But it flourished their criminal nature. Except for a handful of scientists, and the General who ran each camp, most of the Belial workers here were murderers, rapists, or thieves.

Carver's blue-steel knife pressed into the foreman's throat by the time he'd finished rebuffing Carver's order. "Kneel or I take away your ability to stand." Carver made sure his tone was flat and just above a whisper.

The foreman's eyes turned fearful as he slowly bent and knelt at Carver's feet, almost losing his balance in the process.

The Mutazio watched and Carver glanced at them. "Go there" he pointed to the riverbank with his free hand, "drink water and rest in the shade."

They nodded and wandered off with companionable shoves and extensive grunts—words perhaps, that Carver didn't understand. Their master had knelt—the sign of submission to one greater. This made Carver the alpha master.

Shaking his head at what he must do now in this soggy hell, Carver paused, asking out of curiosity, "Why did you challenge me? You know who I am."

The foreman's hands shook, his eyes stayed on the ground. He nodded. "But they's say—"

"Look at me when you speak to me." Carver interrupted.

The foreman raised his gaze obediently. Resigned eyes. *He thinks he's about to die.*

"They's say you're not harsh. That you's more understandin'—

more weak. I's heard you was the runt of the litter." He was muttering, unable to keep from looking away.

"Who's stronger?" Carver asked, "The one who uses his brain or the one who uses his muscles?"

The foreman frowned in confusion. "Muscles. Brain don' make you strong."

Damn. He'd been hoping to appeal to any bit of intelligence this man had.

Carver considered his options. Hot, tired, and thirsty, he was in no mood to fight, but if he didn't at least punish the foreman now, the loss of respect could be dangerous later. Everyone would eventually hear of this, whatever the outcome. Pack mentality was Belial's native dialect. The only language these men understood.

"I don't want to kill you." Carver stepped back a pace and dropped his knife, point down into the soft ground beside him.

"Stand up. Let's see who's stronger." He widened his stance and softened his knees. Imperceptibly building a strong base.

The foreman stood and looked at the planted knife, then rushed in swinging. Carver was taller but the foreman outweighed him by a third. Slow and ponderous, as Carver had known he would be, the man was physically soft from decades of giving orders. It was why they needed the control nodes. No way could these lazy, criminal handlers win against their bred-to-fight mutas.

Carver dodged loose fists coming at him in slow arcs, backing up towards the nearest tree.

Breathing hard in the punishing heat, the foreman threw his weight forward, fist leading, thinking his target was trapped.

Carver stepped aside, allowing the fist to connect with the tree.

The foreman howled with rage at the pain but kept swinging. Encouraged that Carver wasn't hitting back, he lunged again.

It was exactly the force Carver needed. Angling his body slightly and throwing his weight forward, he drove his knee into the charging man's groin, left fist sinking deep in the high belly.

The man dropped like a chunk of molten iron.

Leaving the foreman to his huffing moans, Carver retrieved his knife and water jug, chugging without pause before going down to the river. The lounging Mutazio watched him wade out upstream to refill it, then dunk under the lukewarm eddy. Sweat rinsed away, heartbeat returned to steady, he dripped on the bank while the last barge was tied up.

"Load it." Carver spoke to the Mutazio and nodded towards the barge. They rolled to their feet and trudged off to wagons, stacked with remaining crates.

Soaked and refreshed, he watched them work, a little awed at their physiques. Tremendous broad backs, thighs and calves bulged with muscle under darkly bronzed skin. Their smashed looking faces, with pronounced brow bones and tiny ears must be courtesy of the ape DNA.

He walked back to where the foreman still nursed himself on the ground. Moved at least to the shade of a tree, he still moaned in pain, breathing shallow. Squatting beside him, Carver held out the water jug.

The foreman took it and gulped. Then promptly turned and retched it all up.

"Take small sips and hold it in your mouth long as you can." Carver advised. Growing up youngest in a house of boys had taught him all too well how to inflict precise pain—and survive its aftermath.

"Kindness is not weakness." He watched the man take small sips. "And the mind gives a truer strength than muscles."

The foreman nodded in understanding before Carver went back to the river.

Almost done here.

13

MIND CONTROL TRAINING

9,971 BCE. HIGH CITY, ATLANTIS

"In almost every act of our lives, whether in the sphere of politics or business, in our social conduct or our ethical thinking, we are dominated by the relatively small number of persons [...] who understand the mental processes and social patterns of the masses. It is they who pull the wires that control the mind."

— EDWARD BERNAYS. 1928. PROPAGANDA

AIELA

"*A*iela, see that young man over there?" Ziel tipped his head towards a boy just younger than Aiela herself.

Across the park, sitting on still-green trimmed grass under a maple tree ablaze in purple-reds, the boy laughed along with a girl whose hair matched the leaves above them. Styled recently, with equal amounts of face paint and gaudy clothing, they were awkward and shy together, but clearly lost in their own romantic world.

Aiela nodded. "Yes."

"Use your mind and influence him to kiss her. I'm timing how long it takes you." Ziel began watching his little pocket crystal that acted as clock, compass, thermometer and light.

Aiela frowned. This was supposed to be their day off, and she was still eating as though she hadn't for days, scarfing down chewy millet rolls dipped in a fiery spiced, sweet plum sauce. With a full mouth she replied, "Mind control's illegal! You probably helped make it so—aha!" She held up one sticky finger. "This is a test!" She slitted her eyes at him.

Ziel exhaled his impatience. "I *was* involved in those particular laws. Although controlling someone's mind was considered impolite and unloving for ages in our society, we needed a way to stop those who practiced it with malevolent intent—that's why I pushed for laws against it. And no, this is not a test. Stealing is illegal too, but yet we study its nature to understand what actually makes a thief. You need to understand mind control for when it's used against you."

Dark plumy stains around Aiela's mouth disappeared with a swipe of her tongue as she sat straighter on the branch sculpture, woven into chairs and table in one continuous, still-growing piece. "Fine." She muttered, tossing her braids behind her.

Concentrating hard on the boy, she began thinking "kiss her, kiss her, kiss her" staring so hard she wouldn't have been at all surprised if he'd started steaming. "C'mon!" She yelled in her head. "Kiss her now. Do it! You must do what I say—kiss her, kiss her, kiss her!" Frustration rose as the boy took out a book and appeared to start reading to the girl.

"El." Ahna whispered close to her ear. "Go into meditation mind. Even your breath. Close your eyes and go deeper… deeper—now, picture the boy kissing the girl. Picture it in great detail, maybe as a huge image encompassing them. Or maybe lots of that same image surrounding them. Now—plant that picture in both their minds."

Aiela was following her sister's instructions. Getting into meditation mind came easy. Years of daily practice had trained her psyche well, and her breath followed automatically.

"Well done!" Ziel's voice sounded. His hand landed on her shoulder and she blinked open to find him smiling.

The boy and girl's faces were inches apart. The girl traced his brow, then planted another kiss on his mouth.

"With practice, you'll do it in far less than eight minutes, though I've seen it take a week of daily, hour-long practice to effect an action from strangers."

"Ahna," he tipped his chin down and gave her a hard stare, "you interfered."

Ahna glared back at him. "You can't expect her to know what to do! She's had no training in this yet. You might've given her some bit of direction first."

"Your sister is fine without your instruction." Ziel reached to touch Ahna's elbow while he spoke, but she pulled away from it.

"I know what you're doing. You're *programming* me."

"Oh?" Ziel's cerulean eyes twinkled, as if he was holding back laughter. "And what am I programming you for?"

"Not to *interfere* with Aiela's training. Ridiculous! Of course I'm going to interfere, we use each other's powers and abilities almost as easily as our own. It's hard for us to even separate them."

"Really." Ziel leaned closer. "Tell me more about that. What do you mean you use each other's—"

"We don't know how we do it. And anyway it doesn't matter, it just is." Aiela interrupted, from her place between them. "You're going to teach us these mind... games, I'm guessing?"

"I am." Ziel answered, nonchalant. "Our maze won't defend the Crystals long if someone takes you over. So, your mind control training has officially begun. Next lesson; Ahna, cause that little girl to catch the ball."

Ahna's forest green eyes scanned the park. A girl of six or so was playing catch with her father, grasping at the soft, melon-sized ball with both hands, clapping them together on empty air every time.

Ahna closed her eyes and breathed deep, in once, out once, face blank as a mask. The little girl caught the ball against her belly, giggling and falling in the grass as her father celebrated with her.

"Huh." Ziel grunted. "Children are too easy, let's find something—" he was watching the constant stream of people pass by the park, to and from the market where they'd gotten their midday meal, "—better. There. Let's have that man trip over his own feet."

Ahna's head swiveled to follow a young man walking hand in hand with a lady who looked older than him. He seemed starstruck, carrying a delicate glass sculpture in his other hand. Probably a gift from the market for his lover. "No. It would embarrass him, probably break his trinket, maybe even seriously hurt him."

Ziel turned to Aiela. "Your sister is making excuses. Giving someone an extra little push to do something they desire to anyway is simple, as is anything with children—the younger the easier. Most difficult is getting an adult to do something they *don't* want to, especially when it goes against their moral code or involves threat of physical pain. The mind and body's natural defenses must be overridden. Although Ahna has practiced the techniques of influencing people since she was small, she's spent only a short time learning intentional methods."

Aiela looked at her twin. "What's he talking about?"

"Which part?" Ahna stalled.

Aiela turned back to Ziel. "She hasn't been controlling people our whole life. I was there! I would know."

"I will explain how it works. You may see what you saw differently." Ziel settled back into his branch seat. "Your brain must enter alpha wave to connect psychically to another. Theta works better but we'll just speak of alpha today. People notice your sister's remarkable calm, yes?"

Aiela nodded.

"Her calming influence stands out to others, so much so that they speak of it and are themselves calmed by it, and this has happened your whole life. Am I correct?"

Again, Aiela nodded.

"Ahna spends much of the time in alpha or theta waves. It's why she is often psychically tuned in. Without realizing it, she projects her own state of being, a balanced, peaceful energy, in such a way that those around her are influenced, you could even say, controlled by it. It's somewhat of a defense mechanism, causing others to act in such a way that makes her comfortable."

"But that's not *always* true, plenty of people act in plenty of not-calm ways around her too." Aiela said defensively.

"Yes. Because she hadn't learned the skills of intentional mind control. You, my dear, do it too."

"I do not! Never have I caused anyone to be calmer or more balanced, if anything it's much the opposite!" Aiela's face flamed with indignance. She was still trying to adjust to the fact that Ziel, a Ruler, was training them in a highly illegal practice.

Ziel chuckled. His long silver hair glinted in the sunlight as a lilt crept into his voice, "Charming Aiela. The leader, the instigator, the one whom anyone will follow into all sorts of mischief, mayhem and mystery—am I correct?"

Ahna couldn't help but laugh too. "He knows altogether too much about us."

Aiela's face was still defensive but harbored a tiny smile. "Alright. I see where you're going with this. But I disagree that it's anywhere near mind control, because if it is, then most people are practicing it most of the time without conscious intention."

Ziel inclined his head to her. "Well said. It may ease you to know that I don't approve of controlling another for any purpose or intention. But I will train you to do it and defend against it, because the dangers are very real. We've an enemy who shares no such morality."

His eyes were pools of kindness as he held each of the girl's gaze in turn. "If you are to safeguard the most lethal weapon this world holds —which safeguards the most advanced society, the largest collection of history and knowledge and therefore unlimited power—you must be equipped appropriately. I'm glad you object to what you know to be wrong. I'm heartened when you question me and uphold your own boundaries."

A smile curved his lips as he looked at Ahna. "You told me 'no'. I cannot even recall the last time anyone said no to a direct order from me. But your reasoning proves you both are trustworthy, of learning and practicing something so powerful it's been outlawed. Now that you understand my reasoning, may we continue?"

Two heads—one light, one dark—bobbed in agreement.

"You said Ahna's been learning intentional methods." Aiela turned to her sister. "Is that true? You didn't tell me..."

Ahna nodded. "Because of Jaydee's attempt to get into my mind in Ireland. Remember?"

"Yes but—" Aiela began.

Ahna continued over her. "I haven't forgotten it—I didn't know what to do. What if I hadn't known it was happening? What if I'm sleeping or unconscious? Can someone penetrate my mind and get information, or cause me to act in ways I don't want to? I felt it was important—learning defense at least—so yes, I've been researching and studying some on my own. The real question is," She leveled a stare at Ziel, "how did you know?"

"Because access to any subject outside of our laws is monitored. I imagine you've noticed, there's not a lot of information on it in our archives. Just the basics."

"I did notice. I've read everything there is and watched all the talks you did when you convinced the Rulers to outlaw practices of psychic influence."

"Excellent." Ziel nodded in approval. You can catch your sister up on all that you learned. I'll give you both access to this subject in the Restricted Archives so that you can study further and fully. Atrocious experiments, truly horrific things have been done to people and animals in the name of science. I expect it will be shocking to you. Therefore, we will have many conversations as you learn and digest these things. I will give you exercises so that your knowledge becomes practice, and there will be tests."

Aiela looked at Ahna, saying lightly. "Anything else I don't know about that you've been learning?"

Before Ahna could reply, Ziel interjected. "You know well that Ahna is not the only one to choose new pathways of knowledge. I am due for afternoon meetings. Enjoy the rest of your free day." Extracting his wiry body from the comfortable woven branch seat, he hurried off towards Poseidon's Palace, whistling.

The girls remained silent until he was out of sight.

"Wanta shop?" Ahna asked, bouncing off her branch bench. "We could find some stuff for your room. Let's spend more of his credits than he expects. It'll serve him right for trying to play us against each other!"

Aiela laughed, rocking to her feet. "Agreed. We'll shop our little hearts out! And after that, the spa. I haven't had any bodywork since I got here! Have you seen Jai lately?"

They started towards the nearby market which teemed with people enjoying the mild, late-autumn day.

Hundreds of shoplets stood in rows, with vendors selling everything from clothing and technological devices, to food and furnishings. This was the largest of High City's dozen markets, some of which were seasonal or temporary for specialty merchants traveling through, or festivals. Other markets specialized in one category like jewelry and clothing, or foods, but this one held a little of everything, and often, the newest or best of the goods that flowed into Atlantis were offered here at the Palace Market first.

"I'm sure that's just another of his subtle tests." Ahna said as they walked over thick grass the color of light emeralds.

"What, mentioning things we didn't know the other is doing?" Aiela said.

"It's natural for us to have separate interests, and not have to tell each other everything. There hasn't been time! But even if there was, I expect we both need private areas and I trust your reasons for privacy. I don't need to know all that you do and learn."

"Which is why I absolutely adore you." Aiela replied merrily. "I was just a little shocked that you're studying something considered illegal. It's refreshingly *bad* of you." She paused as they reached the edge of the market. "I've been fighting."

Ahna laughed outright, then realized she was serious. "What sort of fighting?!"

Aiela told her of Kane, the Scottish instructor who seemed to understand girls and stress and the art of physical combat, in equal proportion. How Turner had introduced them and she'd been compelled to turn up in Kane's arena day after day, to work out the pressures of her day to day roles, in a life she felt alone in for the first time ever. "Ziel knew. He was waiting outside the gate one day, just after I started."

"What did he say?" Ahna's fingers skimmed the wood grain of a gleaming maple table top.

"That's too big for my space don't you think?" Aiela rested her fingers on the wood. "He approved. Said we'd both have to train in combat anyway. He was glad I took the initiative of self-care, and found an outlet for my frustrations from being plunged into the deep middle of this new life. He told me a story of when he came to apprentice at thirteen, and how hard it was to adjust and keep up with the expectations and pace here. He thinks I'm working out anger from Papa and Mama dying."

Ahna's eyes softened as she focused her full attention to Aiela, no longer interested in the small set of bamboo nesting tables. "Is that true?"

Aiela nodded. "Probably. I *am* angry they're gone, that we had no choice in the matter, that we are now in a huge city, surrounded by strangers and working so hard in things they will never know about. I miss their unconditional love, their encouragement, their guidance. It's not fair that everyone else our age still has parents and we don't!" She was crushing a large, embroidered pillow to her chest as though it might plug her feelings, keep them from getting too overwhelming.

"We'll take the pillow, and those bamboo tables." Ahna spoke softly to the lady vendor, handing over the little crystal cylinder Ziel had given them that tracked his credits.

The lady nodded, and hurried silently to complete the transaction, while Ahna asked more questions about Aiela's fighting experiences.

"I'm good at it! Even Kane is surprised how naturally it comes."

"Of course you are... name one thing you're *not* good at." Ahna muttered dryly. " 'Built for physical things' Papa used to say." Her mouth curved up. "I can't wait to see you fight."

They got so much stuff, they had to set up a delivery to Aiela's room. Evening had darkened the sky to new denim by the time they wandered back up the mountain towards the Palace, marveling at how life can change so drastically in a few moons.

Still full from sampling foods at market, they decided to forego supper and visit the Palace spa for hair treatments and massages. Grateful to be together, overwhelmed at all the luxury available, they reveled in this day of rest. It felt like a well-earned reward.

14

MIND CONTROL TRAINING LL

"While initial attention should be toward degradation of human performance through thermal loading and electromagnetic field effects, subsequent work should address the possibilities of directing and interrogating mental functioning, using externally applied fields."

— THE AMERICAN AIR FORCE 1982 FINAL REPORT ON
BIOTECHNOLOGY RESEARCH REQUIREMENTS FOR
AERONAUTICAL SYSTEMS THROUGH THE YEAR 2000

AIELA

"Tell me what you learned about mind control this week." Ziel angled his body to hear better in the moving, open-air trolley.

Aiela's answer came fast. "Culture is the biggest subtle influence of all. Our beliefs and parameters of living, even our thinking patterns, are programmed from birth, by expectations to conform to the societal norm. No wonder different cultures fight so much. We're literally programmed for different worlds!"

"We're literally *reduced* to a program you mean. By the time our parents, teachers and," Ahna shot a look at Ziel, "leaders get done with us. Not to mention that great animal instinct—herd mentality."

Ziel smiled. "Well the good news is, your mind is like any muscle, push it in new ways and its expansion is rapid." He was dressed in the loose pants and tunic of a country Atlantean. It was rare to see him out and about without his customary robes.

Taking an overdue day away from Ruler or House of Oracles duties, he had requested that Ahna drive the three of them out of High City to Old Forest; a thousand-acre grove of ancient, soaring trees, many of which had been turned into homes over the centuries.

The oldest tree-homes were passed down through many and more family generations, their unique living spaces grown and cultivated within the host's massive trunk and branches. Craftsmen, trained in the art of living sculpture, worked in Old Forest generation after generation, twining the massive growth into living rooms.

"Go south here." Ziel directed Ahna, who had struggled to navigate out of the busy city on this, her first time driving a trolley.

She lurched to a stop instead. They sat in silence at the intersection of five, leaf-strewn roads, cobbled and curving in broad strokes among the enormous trees. Like Old Forest's homes, its meandering roadways were laid out to accommodate forest growth more than human inhabitants. Casting a frustrated look at her sister, Ahna admitted "I've lost all sense of direction in here. Which way's south?"

"Left." Aiela prompted, searching out the sun's position to check her innate compass sense. The canopy overhead was dense. Even deep into autumn, with the trees shedding spent growth, not much sunlight reached the spongy ground.

It was early morning. Ahna turned the trolley towards rays slanting in from the east, a newborn yellow that would only light the treetops once the sun climbed higher. Absent of people, the ancient forest felt like elegant chaos, yet not at all still or empty.

Far far above, goldfinch flashed in the lower branches like escaped drops of sunlight. Hummingbirds trilled as they whizzed to and fro. Echoing rat-a-tat-tats of woodpeckers came in bursts, and in the pauses, the soft mhoop mhoop of motmots floated down. Aiela's favorite was the cuckoo, calling out its dependable rhythm as it flitted between branches.

"Is it time yet to tell us what we're doing out here?" She asked Ziel.

He watched the forest passing, a little smile of enjoyment softening his features. "Soon enough... we're almost there. And," he was careful to add, "we will be working today."

She and Ahna both squealed in delight when they stopped at the end of a long lane. "Is this yours?"

"It's so well hidden. I wouldn't even know it was here!"

Ziel's smile was proud. "It's small and I've neglected it, but yes. It was a gift, a hideaway I rarely come to. I'd hoped to retire here, but that day has not come any closer than my daydreams." He sighed with relief, the sound of letting burdens disappear for awhile. "You two are my only family. It'll be yours when I'm gone, so get on with it. Go explore!"

Ahna and Aiela shared a look, then went to hug Ziel.

"We'd rather you show us." Aiela looped her arm through his.

"And tell us its story." Ahna took his other side.

This host tree was slimmer, and regally tall, towering above its neighbors. But for shallow toe-steps carved into the tree trunk, no signs gave away the cozy rooms cradled high inside its branches.

Breathing fast from the climb, standing in the main space, which served as lounge and kitchen both, Aiela felt the dim as a hush. "Definitely older than Charis' tree." They'd first visited their mother's cousin in her bright, airy, Old Forest home years ago. "So natural—as much a part of the tree as a squirrel's nest." Dropped leaves were ankle deep, heaped up to knee height in the corners.

"I *feel* part squirrel after that climb!" Ahna had skinned the heel of her hand on the rough tree bark, slipping on the upper parts of the stairs.

Ziel moved about, replacing solar cells in the light sconces, then waving them on. A gentle glow made it seem as if sunlight had found a way in. He stopped to consider. "I haven't yet named this... 'Squirrel's Nest' it is!" He pointed to tattered holes in the hemp-thatch layered over branch rafters to form a roof. "We share it with the little vagrants anyway. I'll wager my bed stuffing has been filched to nothing. It's up here." He pushed through small, twiggy new growth, crackly with leaves, and climbed between two branches, thick as the pillars in Poseidon's Palace. Narrow steps led up and beyond.

Following him, they entered a bedroom as big as the main space. Its mattress was large but dipped in big, threadbare, deflated patches. Trails of foam and fabric confirmed it. The squirrels had indeed robbed a majority of the mattress to line their own beds. He frowned when his light came on, further illuminating the mess. "I've neglected my hidey hole entirely too long."

"But it *could* be cozy." Ahna enthused. "If you get someone to fix the structural things, El and me could do the rest. You know, blankets, dishes, soap…"

Ziel touched Ahna's cheek. "You two making this your own is exactly what I hoped for. If we can make it habitable, I'd like to train you here at times. The Forest is a great teacher you know."

They swept away a dozen season's worth of leaves that disintegrated at a touch. Dried out twigs, fallen branches and dust layered every surface. Birds had summered here, leaving bobbins of feathers in nests surrounded with seed shells, and copious amounts of shit crusted to the long-ago sanded and oiled wood floor. Autumn's sweet farewell scented the air a warm, rust-colored musk.

The kitchen corner was such a mess Ziel only shook his head at it saying, "I will find and contract a restoration expert. Someone who will know the relevant technicians and woodworkers and finishers. Once it's habitable again, you may commence with the decorating."

Glad for the thermoses of tea beside clay jugs of stew and small fresh loaves of rustic bread, they settled into chairs that were now a little cleaner, with cushions deflated by furry and feathered forest inhabitants. Sipping a roasted black tea blend, Ahna and Aiela waited for Ziel to begin.

"Awareness through knowledge, is the number one defense against mind control. I will tell you all that I know, and my understanding of what is still being practiced today, mainly by the Belials. With your reading, and watching experiments from Atlantis' darker history, I should hope we can cover every eventuality." Shifting to get comfortable, he continued.

"Mind control could be summed up as the attempt to turn human beings into machines, or programming a brain in such a way that the person reacts to specific stimuli predictably—in the desired way. Of course you fully understand the various brain wave spectrums and what can be accomplished in each frequency?"

The girls nodded. Starting in primary school, Atlanteans were well versed in this basic knowledge and how it affects everything from meditation to healing.

"The earliest scientists knew less than you when they began archaic experiments on minds. They searched for what was possible to alter—or create—in a person, with various external stimuli. Worst extremes included splitting personalities and creating multiple entities or egos within a person, known as 'alters'. The controller—usually the creator—holds complete control of each alter created, often without the host person's knowledge. Their conscious mind can only be with the surfaced—or acting—personality. Specific memories remain also with the acting personality.

"It is rather like watching different characters act their parts in a play, each character unaware of what the other characters do, or even that there *are* other characters. The stage would represent the conscious mind, and the audience would be the person's unconscious mind, which stores everything that comes across the stage, but is inaccessible to the host's consciousness without very specific therapies. You're understanding so far?"

"Yes, we've found some of these experiments, usually done on children because they're most susceptible to splitting. It was... difficult to read about. I haven't been able to stomach watching the holograms all the way through yet." Ahna's face was stone.

"Why do we even keep records of such atrocities?" Aiela felt anger rise at such things being done to innocents.

"So that it's not repeated. Remember, repulsion is a reverse magnetism, and is forcing one to *not* look at something. One often has to get past that to discover the truth. Humanity is wired to explore. To push and expand outward into every experience possible. Those of scientific mindsets want to know what might result from certain experiments. What we already have answers to, should preclude the need to repeat the experiment. At least that's our hope."

They sat for a silent moment digesting this lesson, and then Aiela shook her head. "It's still terrible. I don't like this part of our training."

"Neither do I." Ziel's face softened. "There's a great lot humans have done that I don't like. Yet, we who stand in love, must hold knowledge of the despicable too. Else who will stand against it?"

"All of mind control is despicable!" Ahna spoke with outrage. "I read in the third epoch, our armies were trained by breaking down the personality or individuality of the soldiers. It was barbaric—utter control of the soldiers, from talking, to food, to bodily functions. They used intense humiliation, sleep deprivation, excessive repetition of routine activities, social isolation, constant undermining of the person's confidence in themselves, or their own judgement."

Her tone became accusatory, as if those who did this were on trial. "They removed self-confidence, and replaced it with confidence only in the military establishment and its superiors. Indoctrination by rewards and punishment, and dependance for their basic survival, along with injections of drugs to break the stronger or more resilient personalities..." Ahna's tirade faded, as she said sadly, "It must have reduced them to less than animals."

Ziel nodded, mirroring her tone. "It was all very... purposeful. Corrupt leaders don't want anyone questioning their motives. They want armies who fight without morals and follow orders without hesitation. Even then, Atlantis knew that a thousand individuals acting within each one's natural strengths, are more powerful than ten thousand programmed soldiers. Thankfully, our current epoch reflects that learning, acquired at great cost."

Pausing to take a long drink of the cooling tea, he stared absently out the window at two squirrels chasing each other, before adding a soft afterthought. "But armies are so rarely used for noble purpose."

The girls shifted in their chairs, not glancing at each other while coming to silent agreement.

"We're wondering too... " Aiela broached the subject. They'd been waiting for an opportune time to ask. "... about psychotronic weapons, and sound eye technology. Does Atlantis still use any of it today?"

Ahna leaned forward, focused intently on Ziel's energy field. Would he tell them the truth? Did he even know there was proof in the Restricted Archives that it was in fact, still being used via the crystal grid?

He hesitated, drumming fingertips on the chair armrests, as his eyes shifted sharply to Ahna, then Aiela. "Yes in a way—the later evolutions of that technology anyway, which is really what you're asking. I see you already suspected. Do you want to ask your questions first or shall I explain why?"

"Explain why." Ahna's tone was hard, edged in betrayal.

Aiela felt a mixture of shock, and, surprising to her, interest.

"I won't attempt to justify it." Ziel began, "I will explain what we have and why it's utilized. Decide for yourselves if it's right, wrong, both or neither. My own opinions haven't made much difference over the years—but I have them, if you're interested. You understand how our 'sound eye' technology works?"

The girls shook their heads.

"The 'sound eye' uses an originator programmed within a stone or crystal. An originator duplicates the energy fields created between humans when we make eye contact, or speak to each other, touch or even think about each other. It operates solely inside these energy fields, established through the connection of conscious awareness. In essence, once eye contact is made between a person and the originator, an energy field is created. Those caught within the field are held in trance. They can be controlled in ways limited only by the imagination."

Aiela sat back in her chair, musing, "And the imaginations of 'controllers' go quite dark. No wonder they banned this. And we still use this for…?"

"For our weapons. The originator itself controls those caught in its spell. We use sound and magnetism. But light, and scrambling of the body's nervous or electric systems were explored, then determined less effective. A true 'sound eye' can be used on crowds. With some of our weapons, several *hundreds of people* can be magnetized to the originator—or repelled by the force field of opposing magnetics."

A loud rustling of wings came from just overhead and then bird-song, trilling and sweet, belying the dark story being told.

Ziel continued. "As you know, sound can create or kill, with all sorts of effects in between. With a 'sound eye', the connection is not only invisible, it's undetectable, with no effect on those who haven't established a connection. All of the effects are contained within the energy field established through the initial eye contact. This same technology can be used with touch except it's often more difficult to initiate touch than eye contact. Thoughts, of course, create energy fields too, but they're too subtle and interwoven. Impossible to isolate or control." Ziel paused and looked at Ahna as he said this.

"I'm hungry. My brain needs food to follow this." Aiela spoke into his pause.

Ahna nodded and rose from her chair. "You talk, we'll eat."

They grinned when Ziel frowned. "That hardly sounds fair. Save me some."

Dividing the food into thirds, the girls curled back into their seats with stew and hunks of bread, ready to hear Ziel out, still unsettled by the admission he'd made; the idea that their trusted government might be using a form of outlawed technology on the general population.

"We use the 'sound eye' technology in weapons for the Knights and in military defense systems. Also to guard valuables, such as the Restricted Archives. Even the gates of Atlantis are armed with origi-nators. They can render unconscious—or kill—those coming against us. The problem with using such weapons, is distinguishing between those we want affected by it and those we don't. Also, the energy field created by just one glance is rather short-lived and short-distance, and if a person knows to not make eye contact, the technology becomes useless. I have thought it might help guard the Crystals. We can discuss that later though."

"The simpler, so called 'psychotronic weapons' you speak of, are in use today, though infrequently. I promise you, the Crystal grid already produces harmonic frequencies. The only thing we do is enhance peace in areas, or persons whose frequency is fallen out of harmony. I know, I know," He held up a hand as if to ward off the girl's mutinous expressions, "any artificial control crosses the line.

"The Rulers argue that our little 'enhancements' have created the longest lasting peace and abundance of any age yet." He paused again, no doubt expecting questions, or more likely, arguments.

But the girls continued spooning up their stew, so he did the same, savoring the meaty warmth for a moment, before continuing.

"Belial, on the other hand, uses this technology freely to subdue its population, reducing the general intelligence level. Which renders the public even more controllable. Do you understand how psychotronic technologies work?"

Ahna and Aiela shook their heads mumbling "very little" and "not really" through full mouths.

"It's all a matter of energy vibration, or frequency, that manipulates the emotions via the nervous system. Typically, the devices use directed energy beams or broadband radio frequency. Obviously, the broadband weapons can produce mass effects, while the directed energy beams are very specific. Range is limited with both.

"Then there are acoustic psychotronics that transmit messages outside the human range of hearing. Literally planting thoughts or ideas in the mind. Entire ranges of frequency undetectable to the human ear, can hide behind music. Visual messages can masquerade behind any mechanical image, such as holograms, without anyone's senses picking them up. But the human brain absorbs the messages and the body responds accordingly.

"In Belial, Mardu has scientists dedicated to monitoring the people, and using these weapons as needed to prevent—or fix—noncompliance. Psychotronic weapons work best on sick bodies and weak minds—which is why Belial provides poor health care for their people, and promotes over-processed and unhealthy foods; much of which is purposely tainted, along with the water supply." He sighed heavily, then forged on with his grim accounting. " Alcohol and drug use is encouraged. Addiction is rampant."

Aiela's stomach soured. "Why would they want a nation of weak or sick people? How does that benefit them?"

"When people are healthy, free, and content, they instinctively know love from unlove. Or scientifically speaking, high frequency from low. They create their environment accordingly, which means electing leaders that serve higher purposes such as beauty and wisdom and peace."

"Which describes what we do." Ahna said.

Ziel nodded, standing to stretch and pace slowly back and forth across the small kitchen space.

"Yes. You must understand, control over others is a type of power that negative people crave. The power a leader has, is either offered by. or stolen from, his people. This power is finite. Imagine each one of us had our own little pile of sand labelled 'personal power', which we either keep, or portion out to others, such as a leader, parents, mate, or teachers."

He stopped in front of the girls. "You understand?" He made a fist with his right hand, and put it atop the back of his straight left hand, "If the leader is all powerful, it leaves the people powerless." Then he switched his hands, opening the left fist so his fingers pointed to the sky, "Conversely, if the leader has *no* power, chaos reigns because the people have all the power, which could pull in a thousand different directions." Bringing his fingertips to touch in a loose pyramid, he said, "The trick is balancing the two polarities so as not to get lost in either direction." Ziel sat again, heavily.

"To answer your question Aiela, this controlling power, this 'sand', is the most addictive thing that exists on earth. And let me tell you, people rarely give away *all* their power, willingly. So then, it must be taken from them, to support the leaders addiction. This defines The Sons of Belial."

"So if I were to go to Belial, would their psychotronics affect me?" Ahna asked.

"Yes, but to what extent I don't know. You're healthy, with a powerful will and strong mind—which is its own defense system. Awareness and understanding of the technology is the best immunization. Ironically, the only total protection is to program your own mind against any outside influences that would go against your core nature, your beliefs and your body.

You won't be surprised when I tell you we have spies in Belial. Many are short-term, and rotate in and out, others long-term. They spend much of their adult lives there. All must be programmed before going, in order to combat the psychotronic weapons being used. Because they must emulate the population behavior, these spies can tell you how powerful this type of control is."

"I wonder if we need to be programmed then?" Aiela knew Atlantis had developed better methods before they gave it up altogether.

Ziel nodded. "If you are to be immune to mind control, that is exactly what I believe we must do. But first, finish your studies. Learn and practice the exercises I give you. Your programming must be completely voluntary, and I want you to understand fully what you are agreeing to. I'll expect you to help write your own program."

This lesson complete, Ziel ate while Aiela and Ahna explored the tree, discovering higher spaces that could be made into rooms.

The peace of nature, deep and primal, thrummed through them as they climbed down, and wandered this corner of the forest. When they returned, Ziel led them through mind exercises; splitting focus to work through problems, interact with a person, and plan their next actions, simultaneously.

SUNLIGHT REACHED in from the other side of Old Forest, by the time Ahna drove them out, dropping Aiela off to train with Kane.

He'd advanced her to weapons—but not the razor-sharp Atlantean thin swords, and certainly not the laser guns or sound wands. Mainly just any object that might naturally be at hand. Rocks. Water and cloth. Pottery or glass.

"It's a fine stick ye've brought, yer wan." Kane circled her, eyeing the stout branch she'd found in Old Forest. "Ye surely canna mean ta use it 'gainst me?!"

Grinning, Aiela crouched in a fighting stance. "Sure do. Unless you can take it away from me... "

15

THE SHAPING OF MARDU

FORTY-SOME YEARS AGO. RIVER TOWN IN GREECE

"I was diamond on the outside, and I would not break.
Inside, though, I was already broken."

— SHAUN DAVID HUTCHINSON, WE ARE THE ANTS

MARDU

"Go ahead and tell. Next time I'll cut out your slimy eyeball and keep it with my treasures." Mady sneered the words, pricking his knifepoint under the boy's left eye just hard enough to well a tiny bead of red.

The boy was already whimpering because of the blood dripping from his nose. It had been such a small cut. The left side of his nostril was so thin Mady hadn't even felt the knife slice through it, but the boy screamed so loud he'd had to clamp a hand over the blood-slick mouth and threaten him further. When Mady had removed his hand, disgusted at the sticky mixture of red snot, the boy sobbed and blubbered, "I will tell Pater what you've done."

Mady mimicked the boy in a mocking tone. Then turned harsh. "I think, instead of telling your Pater about this, you should steal something from him. Something I will like. If you do this, maybe I won't hurt you anymore." Mady was eleven now. Younger than this boy, but bigger. He'd had lots of what Mitera called "growth spurts". He'd gotten to pick out many more tunics, quickly outgrowing each one.

The boys that used to taunt and hurt him were all afraid of him now. This made Mady laugh. He'd found out what his limitless supply of hot anger was good for. Making people afraid. When people were afraid, they'd do whatever you wanted them to.

He'd found out he was smart too. Smarter than all the other boys, which is why he had a whole roomful of nice things. He could make the boys give him their own things and then lie about it to their parents. He could make them steal things for him.

He lowered his knife from the bleeding boy and stepped back. "Tomorrow you'll bring me something nice so we can be friends again, won't you." The boy nodded frantically, and Mady let him run off towards the river.

The red was drying into black stains on his pretty little blade, and he stooped to wipe it on the grass, thinking about what he could do next to pass the time. Even though he had the upstairs room all to himself now, he spent as little time there as possible. Mitera had moved downstairs with the man she wanted to be Mady's Pater. But Mady would never call the man that. Not ever.

Mitera hadn't been feeling well lately and it worried Mady, but he refused to think too much about it. This was their forever home and Mitera was happier here. It wasn't so bad now that Mady was getting big and strong. Mitera's man didn't come to Mady's room as much lately either. Mady knew it was because he was getting so big. The man seemed disgusted that Mady's body was growing dark hair in lots of places.

The man had left today, traveling to far away seaports to fill his wagons with things he would bring back and sell in the market. This happened several times a year. When he returned, Mady would have to help unload and pack it all neatly in the sheds. He also had to help in the marketplace lately because Mitera wasn't well enough. Thinking of Mitera's recent weakness made him feel sad.

Mady decided to take Mitera some flowers. It would make both of them happy.

He wandered to the meadows outside of town, and set about picking wildflowers that grew in abundance. Only the yellow and blue ones, he decided, because they looked nice together and didn't smell bad. He was hot and thirsty by the time he had a big enough bunch, an entire armful!

"They're so pretty! Look at all of them!" Mitera clapped her hands together when he held out the flowers. So many he could barely wrap both hands around the stems. She rose to help him stuff them into a clay pot, and pour a little water in so they didn't die so soon.

He noticed that she moved slower today, even though she wasn't old.

"Mitera, are you sick?" He couldn't bear the answer, but not knowing was even harder.

"Only a little Mady. Just a little... but your Pater will bring medicine for me and then I will be fine." She reached up to brush his thick black hair away from his eyes. He was bigger than she was now. He'd never before realized how little she was.

He dodged away from her hand muttering "That one's *not* my Pater!"

Mitera dropped her hand and stood smiling at him with pride. When she smiled, she didn't look much older than the big sisters of the other boys. This he realized with a bit of shock. And she was much prettier, with her large eyes like a rabbit that slanted up at the corners, and her long black hair like a stream down her back.

"How many years are you?" He blurted it out as he ladled up a drink of water.

"Twenty and five this year... I think. Why do you ask?" She reached again to caress him and again he dodged away. He didn't want to be touched.

"I don't know." He shrugged at her question and gulped the water.

"Sit with me. I will tell you some things." Moving slow and careful, she curled back onto the couch bed. Staring at the bouquet of flowers, though her eyes saw something else entirely, she answered the questions he hadn't asked.

"I was not much past childhood when I birthed you. No one taught me how to prevent babies, and I'd had to start working—because my Pater died you see, before he could marry me off. We were poor and had moved around so much there were no friends or family to take me in. Pater found work where he could—usually for a harvest, or fishing season. He was a kind man, but with one good hand he could only do so much."

She stopped, and Mady hoped she might resume the story. Instead she gestured at the cupboard. "There are apples and bread still if you are hungry." Her eyes were wet before they drifted shut. "I need to rest a moment."

He was always hungry these days. Taking his snack outside to enjoy this fine, cool day, he thought about going down to the river to fish. Maybe he'd get lucky and catch something for their supper. On a whim, he returned inside and invited Mitera to come too. "I can help you walk and carry a blanket for you" Mady coaxed when she looked doubtful.

She nodded and even though it took a long time to get there and even longer coming back, it was nice not to be alone.

He even caught two small fish to roast when they got home.

16

WINTER SOLSTICE AND FIRST DAY

9,971-9,970 BCE. HIGH CITY, ATLANTIS

Lord of the Dance

I danced in the morning when the world was begun
I danced in the moon and the stars and the sun;
I was called from the darkness by the song of the earth
I joined in the singing and she gave me birth.

Dance then, wherever you may be!
I am the Lord of the Dance said he,
And I'll lead you on wherever you may be,
I will lead you all in the Dance said he!

I sleep in the kernel and I dance in the rain,
I dance in the wind through the waving grain,
And when you cut me down I care nothing for the pain—
In Spring I'll be Lord of the Dance again!

I see the maidens laughing as they dance in the sun,
I count the fruits of the harvest one by one;

I know the storm is coming but the grain is all stored,
So I sing of the dance of the lady and the lord.

We dance ever slower as the leaves fall and spin
And the sound of the Horn is the wailing of the wind;
The Earth is wrapped in stillness and we move in a trance,
but we hold on fast to our faith in the Dance.

The sun is in the south and the days lengthen fast,
And soon we'll sing for the winter that is past.
Now we light the candles and rejoice as they burn,
and Dance the dance of the sun's return.

They cut me down but I leap up high!
I am life that will never, never die.
I'll live in you and you'll live in me --
I am Lord of the Dance said he!

The moon in her phases and the tides of the sea,
the movement of the Earth, and the seasons that will be
Are rhythm for the dancing and a promise through the years—
The Dance goes on through joy and tears.

AIELA

Poseidon's Palace was festooned throughout with lighted silk buntings, anchored and punctuated by bouquets of stark white poinsettia flowers larger than a man's head, creamy winter roses, and delicate snowdrops. Every fountain pool floated lotus blossoms, and the old fireways, thin reservoirs lining each room, hall and banister—once lighting the Palace before solar technology—were replenished, ready to fulfill their yearly duty.

All of the decor ranged from ivory to white, except where it sprouted silver holly berries. This sacred fruit of winter was touched only by women and used to transform barrenness into fertility.

Musky layers of rose and teakwood scents filled the Palace hallways. Closer to the kitchens, the air turned spicy with nutmeg and ginger, then sweet with orange and vanilla.

Tonight was Winter Solstice and tomorrow, the First Day of a brand new year cycle.

Aiela felt groggy when her sister tapped faintly on the door. The morning still held full-dark. She was careful not to wake Turner, slipping from their bed, wrapping her brushed-velvet cape around her. A shocking shade of turquoise, Mama had designed it. Intricate embroidery made it fancy, the generous hood made it practical, and now it served as her meditation robe whenever she went to a communal space.

Ahna'a pale hair was still sleep-tousled, excitement lighting her hazel-green eyes.

In hushed reverence, they whispered to each other of plans for the morning, as they hurried through the long, curving hallways of the Palace, making their way down to the first-level meditation room. Only a quarter full, it would host less meditators than usual because so many had gone to their family homes.

This first half of Winter Solstice Day was a traditional observance of old year's end. Quiet celebrations united the extended families across the continent. Gratitude was given for blessings, abundance, and lessons the passing cycle had brought. Meditations were focused on how time had served or changed each person. Light meals were shared, and tea rituals drunk to health enjoyed and work accomplished. It was a time of whispers and softness as all of Atlantis bowed to the sacred endings of cycles.

Sitting cross-legged on grain-filled cushions, the customary hour seemed to stretch twice as long. Though Aiela had come to depend on meditation, it still wasn't easy.

Afterwards, they visited the empty dining hall for a bit of fruit to tide them over until their planned tea ritual. Though most apprentices were with their families this morning, she and Ahna had already addressed this sadness head on, planning out exactly what they wanted to do and who they wanted to do it with.

"When is Jai coming?" Aiela asked, crunching pomegranate arils big as almonds, the juice turning her fingertips and lips a bright magenta.

Ahna shrugged. "Sometime after the sun rises. He's always hungry —so probably sooner than later. He was glad for our invite, with his family too far away to go to. Are you bathing now or this afternoon?"

Breathing in the invigorating malty scents of roasted mate before sipping at it, Aiela raised an eyebrow. "We'd be better off napping this afternoon don't you think? It's going to be the *wildest* night of fun we've ever had!"

Ahna nodded, stuffing the last grapefruit wedge in her mouth and grabbed an apple from the large basket of fruits. "We better get going then."

Aiela pulled a green banana from the giant bunch and followed her sister back into the hallways.

Without discussion, they both returned to their rooms, selected clothing, then met in the communal women's bathing area near Ahna's room. Fresh and dressed, they hurried to a kitchen to prepare food and tea things.

Sunrise had passed in a wake of washed-out colors by the time their guests arrived.

"You remember Jai from Ireland?" Aiela said to Turner.

"I do! Sure an' it's good ta see ya again Jai." Turner pulled the tall, willowy man into a bear hug, and Jai smiled wickedly over Turner's shoulder, winking at Ahna.

Ahna grinned, shaking her head as Jai replied in his unique purr. "And you, lovely Irishman, it's always a pleasure to see *you*! It's said you're practically a citizen of Atlantis nowadays."

He found Turner very attractive—especially the accent—and hadn't been shy about telling Ahna, when they first met in Ireland on the student trip. Mocha-skinned, with overly large, bright eyes, a sassy tongue and endless energy, Jai was prettier than most men.

"It's lucky I am, gettin' ta stay here wi' my love." Turner's attention flicked to Aiela for an instant before returning to Jai who was removing a long, bright-coral outer tunic trimmed in tiny pearls.

"Yer bundled. Chilly ootside is't?"

Jai nodded. "The breeze had a bite for this thin-skinned, southern-bred boy. It'll warm if the clouds burn off. I'm starving, what delicious fare are we breaking our fast with?"

"You southern boys eat anything and everything so what does it matter?" Ahna countered, embracing her friend in greeting.

"Anticipation! It's half the fun."

They were in the smallest of the palace kitchens. Creamy marble slabs veined with pink served as counters, with strips of copper warmers down the center. Gleaming maple shelves offered pottery dishware stacked in matching sets of every color and shape a potter could dream up. Three sizes of cook-boxes for various types of food niched in the walls.

Aiela finished packing baskets of food alongside tea accoutrements. Her heart held an odd mixture of excitement and aching nostalgia. For the first time, she'd miss the traditions Papa and Mama had knit into every Winter Solstice and First Day she'd ever known. But there was pleasure too, at the freedom of creating her own.

"To Ziel's then?" She asked Ahna. "If it's chilly, the Observatory won't be so perfect after all... ocean view or not."

"Yes—"

"*Ruler* Ziel's?" Jai's eyes went round. "We're going to Ruler Ziel's?"

"Yes, but he's gone so you won't get to fawn over him. Can you carry this one?" Ahna handed a basket to Jai as Turner lifted the heavy one. Aiela held a bowl heaped with prepared fruits, and Ahna hefted the remaining warming crock.

Traipsing the considerable distance of winding hallways, the four of them chattered, eager about their plans for the day and night.

Settling into Ziel's familiar rooms, they heated water for the tea to brew. Jai told funny stories about his daily work as a massuesse. Turner described mystical parts of his voyages. It comforted Aiela's undercurrent of sadness, this friendly banter, even though she and Ahna didn't mention their own current activities.

She still hadn't found the right time to tell Turner about her training. Ziel had left it up to her. She did *want* to discuss it all with Turner. His wisdom and common sense would be an aid, a ballast in navigating such highs and lows, excitements and atrocities which had become her daily learning. Already, she'd come to depend on his support, and already it felt like too many secrets were piling up between them.

Turner had arrived only yesterday with his fleet of ships full of crystals; which High City would distribute across the country. "Sure an' it's a strange errand, ferryin' goods between the Belials and Atlanteans." Uncharacteristically, he'd been choosing his words with care, and she sensed there was more to the story than what he said—but he must have good reason. Maybe she was imagining his secrecy because of her own.

Such a relief it was to spend this holi day with him. Between their all-consuming romance and High City's sumptuous and glittering observance, it distracted her from the constant ache of missing her parents.

Turner had elaborated about Ireland's Solstice celebrations. She knew how much it meant that he was here to enjoy this time with her, and not his own family.

Aiela watched his face light now, as she unlidded the warming crock full of savory roast lamb and root vegetables to honor his Irish fare.

He inhaled with an "mmmmm", reached for her hand, and squeezed. "I told ya naugh' ta bother wi' my traditions. Plain an' simple compared ta yers—but many thanks ta ya both!" He beamed at Ahna too. "Sure an' I feel right at home! My parents will be delighted ta know ya helped celebrate in the auld way."

Jai whooped his elation at the bounty, folding his hands in mock prayer. "Thank you great goddess for providing this gorgeous, hearty Irishman to us so we have an excuse to eat something substantial!" He grinned widely at Turner. "Usually, we're stuck with winter fruit and light cakes. Nary a shred of meat in sight and I spend all day and night hungry as a heron." He held up a hunk of soda bread he'd pulled from a basket, "I like your food better." Setting the bread on his plate, they all inhaled the earthy aroma, as Ahna began pouring tea.

"Time to say the words so we can eat while it's hot." Aiela declared. "Ahna, as the eldest woman among us, this honor goes to you."

All four pressed their hands together, thumbs nestled at the heart as Ahna spoke the ancient thanksgiving and blessings.

"Goddess Earth and Father Sky,
thanks be for food and warmth of fire.
On this last day of greatest dark
we gather, love, and eat to mark
an end, a death. The cycle done.
Begin anew with next day's sun.

We bless our families and friends.
We bless our food and drink.
We bless this merry day and night,
with song and dance in fading light,
each heart filled by love and plenty,
compassion grace and joys many.

Vows make we now by hands we link."

Mama had always spoken these words before—should be speaking them today—but at least Mama's presence was with them. Aiela had felt it as she was reaching to clasp Ahna's hand when her voice wavered.

Jai took Turner and Ahna's hands and they were indeed a circle linked, completing the vow. After a tender moment, Ahna released the hands she held to spoon heaping amounts onto each plate. "Let's eat!"

And so the celebration began.

Midday passed on this shortest day of the year and with it the mood turned from quiet to jubilant.

Following their meal, the four wandered outside where, as Jai predicted, intermittent sunshine had replaced winter's chill with festivity.

Excitement mounted in rapid conversations between those hurrying to and fro from the canals, unloading exotic wines and water, and docking every manner of floating vessel along red-lined canal walls. Food smells filled the air as bonfire building crowded the streets.

Walking through the Palace Square and park, they watched dance companies and acting troupes prepare for the first performances of the day.

They joined in unloading trolley trailers heaped with wood scraps, broken or outdated furniture, Old Forest deadfall, even sawdust logs. Working beside strangers and acquaintances, they stacked fuel up into bonfire heaps, higher than Aiela's head.

Two hours of hard labor later, Aiela asked Turner. "Ahna and I want to nap before dressing for tonight. What did you have in mind for the afternoon?"

"I'd like ta see yer performances. We don't have such things an' I can brag aboot it all back home." Turner brushed away hair strands stuck to her cheek.

Jai's face lit. "I'll take you! Most of my friends act or dance and I've promised to see them *all* onstage—which'll be tricky. If you want abundance of performance, stick with me. I'll show you the variety of your life!"

Turner thumped him on the back. "Thanks mate! Ya get ta be *my* guide this time. We will see you two beauties in a couple hours then." Kissing Aiela lightly, he was off.

DUSK BROUGHT the entire city roaring to life as musicians turned out in droves, filling every venue, playing odes to the coming night. Once darkness fell, it would escalate to rousing and rowdy heights.

"How do I look?" Ahna asked, twirling so her long, lace train spread out around her.

Aiela paused, eye-paint brush held aloft, to take in her sister.

Ahna wore silk tights of deepest brown, threaded with golden sparkles and clinging to every slender curve. Draping low on her hips, burnished-gold lace flowed out behind her. Her midriff was bare and her sleeveless top matched the bottom with barely enough material to mold and cover her breasts. More lace trailed down her back from dainty shoulders. Her hair was curled and piled high, ringlets spilling beside her face and down her nape. Encircling her head, a diadem dangled a teardrop of amber, and her armbands, earrings, and necklace all matched the burnished gold lace. Eyes and lips were outlined in broad brown strokes, cheek hollows brushed with gold dust. She floated like a seductive song.

"Like a princess of the night. Carved in forbidden chocolate then gilded." Aiela answered.

Ahna laughed. "So eloquent! It was your brilliant idea. Mama would love it. You want me to finish your face paint?"

Aiela nodded, handing over the brush.

Her own outfit was similar but in cool silvers. Its base was deep pewter with sparkles of every color, as if diamond powder reflecting the light. Burnished-silver lace and jewelry accentuated her muscles and curves. Her long black hair was in the usual tiny braids, each one threaded with a shimmering silver strand, and piled up artistically, adding inches to her height. Her top was mostly straps, showing more of her breasts than it hid, but theirs wouldn't be the most provocative outfits tonight.

Feminine sexuality was honored—especially celebrated—during Winter Solstice, with women dressing to display their beautiful bodies. Some would wear little more than painted-on flowers, feathers, or elaborate body jewelry.

She barely recognized herself in the mirror when Ahna finished with her face. She'd grown lean these past moons, her muscles sharply defined from the workouts with Kane, her skin pale from too much time spent underground. The silvery blue tattoos she'd been collecting seemed to glow.

Ahna stepped back to stare at her, finally answering the unasked question. "You look half goddess and half warrior." A shiver rolled through Ahna, so intense Aiela felt it too.

"What?" She held her sister's gaze.

Ahna's eyes held foreboding, then she blinked, forcing it away. "Just—seeing all your potential. Let's not talk of it though. Tonight we can be whoever we want. Let's dance like life is only a stage."

"Dance like life is only a stage." Aiela echoed back, as Turner and Jai came through the door, arms slung around each other, laughing and handsome. They stopped short at the sight before them.

"Holy bleeding gods!" Turner breathed, stepping closer, reaching towards Aiela. His hands stopped in mid air. "Can I touch? Ya look... splendid, like starlight on a waterfall."

"Everyone's a poet tonight!" Ahna laughed, reaching up to brush a palm against Jai's cheek. "You're lovely tonight too—mmm, you smell already of bonfire... and wine. Let's go. I'm ready for music!"

This longest night of the year was celebrated in as much of its entirety as each person could withstand. Bonfires would blaze from sundown to midnight, and every park, street or open space would be a mass of dancing, singing humanity.

Foods were roasted en masse, but not consumed, in preparation for First Day Feasts, filling the air with tantalizing scents thick enough to taste. Traditionally a night of fasting, wine flowed freely. Sensuality was celebrated in many a bedroom, dark niche, or private balcony, instigated by the irresistible feminine, in honor of the goddess that rules night with her inward focus and romantic, erotic play.

Most wore black or darkest hues of color to honor nighttime, the hibernation of winter, and the death that must precede rebirth. Tomorrow would dawn, and High City's clothing would reflect its first light of a new year cycle, but tonight, the shadow was celebrated. Night became an Elysium.

Aiela and Turner got separated from Ahna and Jai somewhere between their third music stage and fourth bonfire.

Dancing made her thirsty. Finding a cart with water led to finding new and interesting wine to drink as well. By then, Aiela was chilled so they'd head towards another bonfire. Warming up, she'd begin writhing to some enticing beat and follow its sound to yet another stage, Turner booming laughter and egging her on with his delicious, rough sailor hands. And so the night went.

"Which canal are we close to?" Aiela slurred only a little. A throbbing warmth coursed through her as she danced with Turner below a stage full of hang drums, flutes and dulcimers. This piece featured a front line of skin drums keeping a slow heavy rhythm. They were locked together and her body was fully aroused, aided no doubt by wine and Turner's hard maleness pressing against her, his hands roaming and kneading.

"Middle one. Mabbe eastern... " Turner lifted his face from the warm valley between her neck and shoulder to glance around. "Mmmm, ay've no idea where we are." His accent rolled and dipped more than usual.

Aiela giggled at him, pulling away, catching his hand to lead him out of the knot of gyrating bodies. "Had a bit too much wine have we?"

"O' course not! It's joost my full attention 'as been on you, ya fine beautiful, moonlit goddess... gondess... god-dess." He pulled her hard to him, his thumbs wandering upwards to brush the underside of her breasts, his mouth covering hers in a devouring sort of way.

She matched his passion for a moment, then pushed apart. "Not here my love. It's not proper. Let's see, I think we're on the second land ring still... "

"I *need* ya in th' woorst sort 'o way mo ghealach." His growl intensified the warmth, his words grown thicker still, like the night.

"I know, me too. Come on, I'll find us a boat. You look for drinking water while I figure out which way to go. *Water...*" she elbowed his ribs for emphasis, "not wine or we'll be hurting in the morning."

He dipped his head to suck at the top of her breast, puffed grandly above her pewter top.

She smacked his springy curls and danced away, though she dearly wanted his searing lips around her nipple.

Pulling him behind her, she threaded through throngs of people, navigating by the dim outline of the Palace in the distance behind them. What a marvel, this intoxicating mixture of chilled winter air, smoky wine perfumes, music, and the laughter of thousands of people as they pirouetted under silent stars. Her body begged sexual satiation, and her heart threatened to burst with love for this man at her side.

Stopping for lemon water, Aiela finally brought them to the east canal. She led the way across a high, arching bridge to where stairs angled down the sheer canal wall ending in a small dock lined with anchored boats. There wasn't enough moonlight yet to make out the orichalcum lining the canal walls, but come morning, they would glow red, sparking like hot coal embers in the rising sun.

Turner was close behind, his hands on both of her hips, often straying to other parts.

"That one. It's small with a little privacy." She pointed with her water jug and pulled him around a group of people, boisterous and fumbling in the dark as they boarded a craft.

"How kin *you* see evera'thin an' *I* canna keep from stumblin'?" He nuzzled her ear.

"Moon goddesses can see in the dark silly, it's night that makes us shine—surprised you didn't know that. Careful now, do you see where to step down?"

The boat rocked as his weight settled into it.

She handed the water jug down to him. "I'll untie, can you hold us steady until I'm in?"

Aiela laughed when his outline indignantly replied, "Ship captains kin hold anythin' steady shilly—s'prished ya didn' know *that*."

They started the whispery little engine, and she steered down river, dodging a few other vessels that had set out early too.

Turner held her from behind, his legs wide around her hips, warmth practically steaming off of him. His hands roamed lazily between breasts, belly and hips, one stroking down between her legs, making her stiffen, gasp and moan.

People lined the bridges arching overhead and tossed down flowers or songs as they passed. Once under the great gleaming wall, the busy canal widened, with less congestion, quieter and darker.

Prolonging their need of each other, she turned to tease him in a sweet agony of caresses and kisses. With the anchor still dropping, she pushed clothing aside and straddled him, sinking onto him with a long sigh of pleasure, holding him still until he threatened to dump her overboard.

Oblivious to the chill, they moved together, the frenzy of sexual need replacing inhibition until they collapsed, gasping, on woven hemp benches in the wildly rocking boat. Heart to heart, letting everything calm, she reveled in this pure beauty, this bouquet of sensations her body experienced.

"Shoulda worn something warmer. I'm f-freezing!" She pressed tighter into Turner's warmth and he sighed with satisfaction.

"Ah. Is that why yer tryin' ta climb inside o' me." He ran his hands over her. "Yer cold as a fish joost hauled up froom the deep! Let's see if there's anythin' aboard."

Rooting under both benches they found hemp tarps, rain cloaks and a blanket.

"A bit stiff and smellin' o' hemp oil but better'n nothin'. C'mere, I'll warm ya. We hearty Irishmen kin cross glaciers withoot chillin'. Yer Atlantis 'winter' is the *tropics* ta us."

Bundled in the boat's bottom, floating under fire-fragrant breezes with distant city-wide drums pulsing, Aiela lamented. "We're missing the midnight Phoenix Festival... I suppose we can watch it on holo-gram tomorrow." She didn't really feel like fighting their way through crowds again.

"Let's stay right here—where we kin make loove again." Turner coaxed. "Tell me aboot it instead." His warm, calloused palms made circles on her back. "What ezz-actly is yer 'legend o' the phoenix'?"

"A sort of magical remembrance that's sung and danced on every stage at midnight. The costumes are elaborate with fiery effects so intense, somebody always gets burnt." She paused as the stories flooded in. "Papa insisted phoenix birds exist still and are actually of the dragon species. He saw one once in another land. Their feathers are incredibly colorful he said, brighter than any sunrise. They're big as a man and live over a thousand years. When they feel their end coming, they build a pyre-nest of cedar twigs, lining it with fragrant spices, frankincense resin, and myrrh oil. When the bird chooses to die, it simply ignites the pyre.

In our performances, after the old Phoenix melts away into ashes, we dot ash marks on each other's forehead to symbolize death. An old year gone, and with it, the person we each have been. Right at midnight, all the bonfires are quenched, making giant clouds of steam (somebody usually gets steam burns during that too) and plunging the whole world into darkness—well, as much darkness as we can muster when our buildings glow with solar paint!"

"Sounds verra mystical." Turner lay beside her, quiet for so long she thought perhaps he'd fallen asleep. She startled when he spoke again. "Tell me of this holi day when ya were wee. How did ya cele-brate it then?"

"Well," Aiela inhaled deeply, smiling into the night as memories danced in her mind's eye. "Papa and Mama let us stay up late for the music and performances and village bonfires; which weren't as big as the ones here, but they seemed enormous to me then. Then they'd bundle us up in Papa's little fishing boat and he would tell us the Legend of the Phoenix until we fell asleep under the stars—kind of like now.

"Mama always made white rose honey taffy for First Day, and we couldn't wait to have the first piece. They'd bribe us with it to eat our eggs. Oh! but first, Auntie Sage kept a special red saffron tea blend that she mixed with foamed nut milk for hot lattes. She'd wake us with them, and we'd sit in our beds sipping and guessing what gifts we'd get. Gifts were what we looked forward to most of course. And watching The Rebirth hologram from Poseidon's Palace.

"After that, Teacher Mia and her mate joined us; that was our Fourthday teacher who taught music and meditation. And Zan," Aiela giggled, "I dubbed him my 'still life tutor'—trying to ruffle him. It never worked and neither did any of a hundred antics I pulled. I struggled in meditation and he tried to help me. You'll find this hard to believe but I couldn't sit still long enough—or focus."

Turner snorted. "I find it harder ta believe that ya overcame it!"

She pinched him but kept talking. "Those teachers, and of course Auntie Sage, shared First Day Feast at our house, after which we would get all dressed up and go into the village to watch the perfor-mances. Our gowns were always the prettiest of course, because Mama made them." Trailing off, she cuddled Turner to her, letting nostalgia wash over her. "Bittersweet memories my love" she sighed, feeling sleep overtake her.

"We'll make new ones." He assured her.

"Mm. We already have." She planted a kiss on his curls.

Ahna

In the earliest hours of morning, parties migrated to the water; a final bow to the feminine in her element, a cleansing away of the ashes—of the last remnants of death.

Younger children and the elderly dragged their spent bodies into bed, while High City's canal rivers became clogged with boats, rocking gently as the occupants tried to stay awake. Music still floated upon the air but quieter now, more introspective and soothing, a soundtrack for the ancient starlight winking above. These few hours of deep night represented earth's womb as it nurtures, growing and shaping new life. Most, eventually fall asleep—if only for the pleasure of awakening to a brand new year.

Ahna slid through throngs of drifting people, relaxed into a wine-haze that softened and muffled everything around her.

Jai's lover, a solid, studious looking man, somewhat older, led them. Jai held his lover's hand and Ahna's. Linked to her and forming the end of their chain was a friend of Jai's lover... or was it a brother? A cousin? She couldn't remember—couldn't even see him in the dark.

He'd danced the Phoenix onstage wearing an elaborate beaked headdress, huge feathered wings, and little else to cover a gracefully muscled body that danced as if born to it. As the blindingly gorgeous Phoenix, he'd fed on berries and nuts, soared and floated on the airwaves, drank dew, hunted, and mated, before ceremoniously building his funeral pyre. Dramatically, to crescendos of music, he chose the time of his death.

Ahna had moved closer to the stage, mesmerized by his red bronzed skin, oiled to glistening. He moved like no dancer she'd seen before.

Finally stepping into death, dignified head held high, he met his end in a blaze of flames and fireworks. That beaked head had finally drooped, then disappeared in the last explosion that had everyone cheering and backing away from its bursting heatwave.

She'd wanted to weep at the loss of him.

But Jai and his lover had whisked her away, sharing a bottle of blackberry wine behind the stage while they waited to gather their Phoenix.

Now, as they wound through the throng, she imagined they looked like a serpent curling its way among a sea of grass people.

Much earlier she'd danced for hours by firelight, sometimes partnering with someone, mostly just moving with the crowds and letting Jai keep track of her.

One boy she remembered—probably her own age—had short, light hair and gentle wide-set eyes that reminded her of a friendly dog. She'd felt the first stir of arousal since Carver when they'd danced with his chest brushing hers. He'd stayed for awhile, offered her mint water and steered her to sit when she tired.

She'd left him to get a closer look at the Phoenix.

Perhaps it was the wine, or the festival energy, that heightened sexuality. Maybe the exotic strangeness of utter freedom. Or just loneliness. She didn't care—refused to think about the person she wanted most right now. He wasn't here and this phoenix-dancer was.

His hand felt silky and strong in hers. It didn't make her heart pound as if trying to climb from her chest to get to him, or her brain forget to tell her lungs to breathe.

Black-hearted gods! Even with mind-numbing amounts of wine, her heart insisted on thinking of Carver.

"Did we bring more of the night wine?" She asked Jai, swaying against him when he slowed to look back at her. His thin, elegant fingers steadied her.

"We're almost there darling." His voice reminded her of the complex, darkly fruited wine she'd drank entirely too much of already. "There'll be some aboard—perhaps watered for you. You're much too small to consume such vast quantities. Here we go, three steps down, turn, three more." Jai's soft voice guided her and she floated on it, settling into deep cushions that surrounded and sucked her down into warmth.

The boat's outline was large and luxurious and she lay there, staring up at a sky filled with stars like little sparks of eternity. The calm seemed sudden.

The swish of water as they moved through it began to clear the swirling, smothering energies pressing in from the crowds of people all night. She realized it was partly why she'd drank too much. It dulled her senses, made her able to bear the overstimulation of being in the combined energy of so many people.

A goblet hovered over her and she roused slightly to accept it, murmuring thanks and gulping. It was water but it tasted good. "Where'd Jai go?" She asked the form settling beside her, drinking from his own goblet.

The form shrugged. "It's a big boat with a goodly number of rooms." His voice was medium-toned and husky, as if dried out from the performance. He smelled of cedar-smoke and myrrhed jojoba oil.

Without thinking, she sat up and kissed him, parting his lips, searching his hot mouth boldly as though to figure out who this Phoenix was.

His initial surprise gave her advantage until he returned her kisses, his free hand reaching to touch her, molding the parts he could not see.

She broke away to drain her glass and he did the same while she maneuvered on top of him. When he dropped his empty goblet into the cushions, she took his hands, tracing them slowly down her body like an introduction. Pushing beneath the cloak he'd donned off-stage, she felt, rather than saw, that he still wore only the small loin covering he'd danced in. The light, dry oil sent her palms gliding over his red skin and she pulled off her own clothing, wanting to feel her whole body glide like this. Her seduction was swift and sure. She knew exactly what she wanted and he responded fully to every invitation given.

Once inside of her, he moved in measured beats that heightened her arousal. Remembering his lovely strength as he seemed to fly, she focused on this pleasure, pushing away any thought that tried to distract her.

Using his hands and mouth to paint her body, he brought her to climax and she melted on top of him, letting the waves subside, slow as a spent storm.

Shifting from his warmth into the cushions beside him, she felt him rise, then return to settle blankets over them both.

Reclining, he watched the stars in silence, offering her sips from his water jug.

"You're a skilled lover." She whispered, from the edges of sleep.

"Dancers are." His voice sounded drowsy now, instead of husky.

"We study body movement, specialize in providing pleasure." He went on, probably saying more wondrous things—but she couldn't keep herself awake any longer to hear it.

SHE WOKE to Jai sitting beside her, folding her strewn clothing into precise little squares. The sun was just peeking over the horizon and its rays stabbed rudely inside her cranium. She groaned and squeezed her eyes shut, but smiled in Jai's general direction when he began massaging her temples.

"There there my pretty canary," He clucked. "Let's stop those nasty after-wine pains. I told you not to drink so much, didn't I?" Long fingers pressed and held points on her achy skull. "I deduce from your nakedness, and the distinct scent of sex on your blankets, you were attempting to assuage the loneliness. You still miss Carv—"

Ahna jammed a hand onto his mouth, partially missing it, her eyes still squeezed shut. "No. Stop. I just spent a night forgetting there is anyone to miss. I danced and sang and had sex—because I *can*. Because there is no one else." She let her hand drop from Jai's face, rolling to bury her face in the cushions.

"Fine," he spoke gently, "but it's only a temporary bandage. Talking about it might make it better."

"Where's my Phoenix?" She said stubbornly, sighing as he resumed massaging her, pressure melting away inside her head.

"Flown home I imagine. He wasn't here when I came up."

Ahna sat up with effort. Gathering the blanket to cover her breasts, she chanced slitting her eyes open. "Thank you sweet friend. You're a magician! It doesn't hurt as much!"

Jai pulled her tangled head to his chest, in a fond hug. "Happy First Day darling. This magician had a magnificent Winter Solstice and it seems you did too with your charming Phoenix. Let's get you dressed and home so your sister won't worry."

"My Phoenix…" Ahna said dreamily, pulling on garments as Jai handed them to her. "I don't even know his name."

· · ·

TURNER

If Winter Solstice was a celebration of feminine energies, First Day was its masculine counterpart; a formal day of feasting and performances. Everyone dressed in their finest, presenting gifts to each other, sharing meals and making toasts. The brightest whites or palest shades of color would be worn to honor the returning light, marking the turning point where days grew longer instead of shorter. Traditionally, clothing was brand new, and acquaintances made on this day would be especially blessed. More couples had commitment ceremonies performed on this day than any other, believing it enhanced their union.

Poseidon's Palace welcomed the City with a traditional Gala of all things new and fresh and bright. "The Rebirth of the Phoenix", a cherished play enacted at sunrise on First Day, was going on in the packed Palace square. Attended mostly by children and the elderly, it would be replayed in holograms all throughout the day for revelers who slept through the performance. Afterward, the children would receive a gift inside the palace, and break their long night's fast with fire-roasted dishes in a morning banquet. Special music and dancing would follow to honor the youngest members of society.

Turner was waiting for the opportune time. He'd wrapped the little leather-bound journal in canvas and tied it with string, lettering 'To Ahna and Aiela' on its stiff paper tag. At least there was no need to disguise his handwriting. He could barely write Atlantean, though he spoke it well enough.

After considering for some time whether to have it delivered before he left or after, he decided definitely after, and added a delivery date to the tag. What if he couldn't feign ignorance well enough? What if Ahna sensed he was lying, simply by omission? No. Better that they opened their father's journal, and absorbed the shock of all it contained while he was an ocean away. By the time he returned, they'd have given it to Ziel, who would know exactly what was needed.

Now, all he needed was a few moments alone to deposit it in the delivery booth outside the Palace gate.

127

Waking at dawn, bleary with too few hours of sleep, he and Aiela had taken a trolley home from the east canal gate.

Now, they managed to crowd into the Palace square just before an enormous ash pile onstage began moving. Music soared dramatically, and child dancers costumed as birds of every sort, flapped, sang and bowed, rejoicing as new life wriggled into being.

An ashy shape arose, and all went still, save high, clear, expectant notes from a single flute, as the shape shook itself free of the ashy coat, revealing a newborn Phoenix. Gusts of simulated wind blew the last flakes of ash from its vibrant purple, red and gold feathers.

It blinked and looked about, stumbling out of its ash mound, toddling curiously from bird to bird, awkwardly tipping over, much to the delight of the children filling the square.

"Listen to them laugh." Aiela said in his ear. "Is there anything merrier than children laughing?" He squeezed her hand, wondering suddenly if she wanted to make their own babies someday. Best wait until later to ask.

"Come on." Aiela tugged his hand. "It's almost over, and we're on gift duty."

Breakfast tables were lined up, covered in pale lemon silk, and hovering low to the ground. Hundreds of long, white floor cushions streamed along either side and the air smelled of citrus and yeast bread. Stacked neatly in the corners were cheery white and yellow-wrapped packages. "What's inside all o' them?" Turner asked, stretching up but failing to reach the tip top of a pile.

"Moving picture books, spinning tops, bouncy balls, long-tailed phoenix kites—the usual things we all played with." She'd helped wrap them, had told him earlier how the House of Rulers worked together for a week to accomplish this gift undertaking.

"Not all of us." Turner muttered. He hadn't any idea what most of these things were. "How will we know who gets what?"

Aiela pointed at the other corners filled with gifts. "That one's for age five to seven, the far corner is seven to ten, next one's ten to thirteen and this one's under five."

Turner frowned at her. "We're supposed ta know how auld they are?"

Aiela nodded. "Most of them know exactly where to go. If you're not sure, just ask." She handed him two bananas and set a plate stacked with bite-sized, orange-flecked cakes on the windowsill beside them. "You might want to eat now. I imagine we'll work without stopping. The little ones sometimes need help unwrapping. Then there's all the trash to bag... "

He sighed. That opportune moment slid further away.

As it happened, the gifts went quickly because the children stampeded them. Massing in ear-splitting decibels of chatter, the littlest ones, dressed in puffs and bows and lace, bounced up and down, shrieking until they got one, some running off to find a seat at the tables, others plopping down where they stood, to open new treasures.

Turner was exhausted by the time it was over. His knees ached from kneeling on marble when little hands tugged at him, begging him to help untie ribbons or read their new storybook.

"What's next?" He asked Aiela, as they sat in the din watching a sea of children play, sometimes remembering to cram a bite of sweet bread into sticky little mouths.

"I think we're done." She glanced at their corner, now filled with bags of wrapping and ribbons. "Next, they'll play music and bring out garlands in the square for the little ones to dance with. But *we* might sneak away—have a nap before feast time." She yawned, rubbing at her eyes.

"You go ahead. I need ta bathe." He could finally drop off the parcel tucked securely inside his dawn-blue tunic, with plenty of time left to clean himself up.

"Happy First Day!" Ahna and Jai appeared, looking fresh in their new whites. Hugs were exchanged and they surveyed the wriggling mass of children. Not bothering with conversation in the din, Aiela pointed and they all followed her into the hall, walking a ways before the people and the noise thinned.

"I figured you'd sleep 'til noon." Aiela said to her sister.

"Good. Then you weren't worried about me. We stayed on a boat. Got back an hour ago or so."

"I see." Aiela was looking at Ahna in that spooky way they had, exchanging information not meant for anyone else. "Well, I'm hoping to fall asleep. Turner's going to bathe. Save us seats at the feast?"

"Along the north wall." Ahna confirmed. "I'm due in the kitchens to help prepare, and Jai is leading the dancing with the children."

Turner exhaled the breath he'd been holding. Everyone was going to be occupied. This was, after all, the opportune time.

THE FIRST DAY Feast began at high noon.

Revelers dragged their bodies from beds and boats, to wash and dress in fine new clothing. Convening at Temples, gathering halls, homes across the city, or at the Palace, everyone contributed food. Afterward, gifts were exchanged. By early afternoon, performances filled the City venues: formal plays—often newly written by the young—and concertos newly composed.

As dusk fell, Turner and Aiela picked half-heartedly at leftovers set out from the Palace feasts. "It's quite the party." Turner yawned. "Ya know, I used ta think Atlanteans indulgent and spoilt."

"Really? I suppose we are... what do you think now?"

He shrugged, searching for the words to explain. "It seems abundance is somethin' chosen. I canna fault yer people fer creating somethin' so happy. I see now. It's verra intentional."

First Day came quietly to a close as people travelled home. Turner helped Aiela put food away and wipe tables. Falling early into bed, sleep came quickly after two days full of celebration.

17

MARDU UNMADE

RIVER TOWN IN GREECE

"Man is a spirit but his body is resonant to the world of beasts. To deny this relationship creates an imbalance which results in all sorts of ills upon the world."

— PETER MOON, MONTAUK REVISITED

MARDU

"*I* will not leave you here Mitera. You cannot make me!"

Mady stormed around the room, picking up his mother's things and slamming them down again as she tried to reason with him. Her voice was weak, and she stopped to take a breath every few words, but he did not care. She wanted to send him away and this was terrifying. He'd never been away from her. He didn't know how to make friends, and he couldn't trust anybody.

The fear was trying to paralyze him, so he stomped it out and let anger come instead. Anger always helped him get his way.

"Mady please... please stop... come sit here beside me... there's so many things... I need to tell you..."

"NO! I don't want to hear ANYTHING! I won't listen!" He screeched in his changing voice, then stormed from the room, running outside, pounding up the stairs to his room.

Breaking things helped him feel in control so he broke everything he touched, ripping and shredding the blanket until it looked like rags littering his bed, throwing gourds and clay cups against the wall, beating the bed posts with staffs he'd collected and carved, before snapping them over his knee. Kneeling on his dried grass mattress, he stabbed it again and again with his prettiest knife. Even the spear he prized, stolen from a boy's Pater, he bent and bowed until it finally gave way, cracking in his bare hands. He raged until there was nothing left to break and then he hit the rough wall until his fists were mangled enough to leave blood smears.

For thirteen, he was very strong.

He woke to vicious stabs inside his head. Everything felt sticky and clogged. His eyes, his mouth, even his nostrils were stale, gummed up. Groaning as the pain of light entered his slitted eyelids, he dragged himself upwards and immediately started retching.

Words he didn't understand were crooned in a female voice, and a shape appeared in his blurry vision. Hands held his shoulders, cool when they cupped the back of his neck. A gilded bowl hovered under his chin.

Nothing came out and the nausea subsided along with the blurriness.

The women were magnificently beautiful. One small, with a quiet smile that reminded him of his mother, the other older and much taller, with hair the color of living fire coals.

They said the same words over and over, looking into his eyes, holding water in a clear cup and guiding his lips to it. The water tasted so clean. He didn't seem able to move his own body like usual, and when he did, it was slow and achy. Finally he blurted out "I don't know what you say", startled at the raw sound that came out of him.

A flurry of new words came at him from both women.

"Where am I? Where is my mother?"

The women looked at each other, speaking back and forth rapidly. The small one left, and the old one with the bright hair smiled kindly, smoothing his hair back and urging him to sip more water. Arranging cushions behind him, she pushed to settle him back, then started sponging his face with a wet cloth that smelled of flowers.

His mind didn't seem to be working any better than his body, and he couldn't make sense of the things he saw around him. Perhaps it was all a dream.

WHEN HE WOKE AGAIN, it was dark and he felt better.

No one was in the little room, but soft light came from a glowing sphere the size of a lemon, perched in an ornate holder on the wall.

Stars hung, in the night outside a window, and he heard sounds, maybe voices, in the distance. Spying the clear cup of water on a table by his bed, he drained it, feeling it flow into his empty belly as strength.

Scooting to the edge of the low bed, he put bare feet onto the polished wood floor, frowning at its glossy feel. Where was this place? It was like nothing he'd seen or heard of. The room was a peculiar shape, all odd angles, even the roof.

Standing, Mady swayed a bit but the door was just a few steps away. It had no rope handle like the ones at home, nothing except intricate carvings. Tentatively, he pushed and it swung open easily into a larger, plushly furnished room.

The two women lounged in strange chairs, each holding clear cups of something dark. Doors stood open at intervals around the large room, and Mady saw people inside those rooms, doing things he didn't understand. What riveted his attention was a moving picture—a wide beam of light shining upwards from the floor with people dancing and singing in it. He could barely make out the sound of their voices from this far away, so he moved slowly towards the darkened room, fascinated by what he was seeing.

He tripped over something, almost falling, making enough noise to draw the two women's attention. They rushed to him, speaking more of their strange words, clutching his elbows, supporting his back. When they noticed him staring at the moving picture, they laughed gently, making gestures that seemed an invitation, helping him walk to the room.

Soft cloth seats held a man with a small child cuddled against him. They looked at him with smiles and the women took him to the seat next to them.

People in the moving picture were beautifully dressed. He could hear them, even though they were only made of light and he could see the wall of this room behind them. What magic was this? It was enthralling, and he didn't notice the women had left, until one of them returned with a small platter of food. Grapes he recognized, but not the small white discs that were chewy, soft, and tasted faintly of herbs. He was ravenous and hoped they'd bring him more. But he ate it all so quickly, he felt sick again.

They brought him bitter green tea in a mug. At least it was pleasantly warm.

Eventually, the other woman returned with a man who squatted down beside Mady saying "Greetings".

"You speak my words?" Mady asked eagerly.

"Little." The man pronounced it strangely but held his finger and thumb close together to ensure Mady understood.

"Where am I? Where is my mother?"

Everyone else in the room was focused on Mady and the man's conversation.

"Mother?" The man shrugged and spread his hands. He didn't know. Pointing at the floor, "Atlantis. You home Atlantis."

Mady shook his head. "This is not my home! I want my mother, where is she?" He was close to tears. When the man shrugged, this time with a sad and helpless look in his eyes, Mady felt a sob bubble up. He buried his face in his hands to hide his shameful tears from these people. Whoever they were.

The women tugged Mady to his feet, helping him back to his room. He cried into his hands as they lowered him gently onto the bed.

"Look." Said the man in Mady's tongue. He held a strange tablet and writing stick. He drew a picture of a ship on waves. Then mimed drinking something. "You. Drugged. Left here." He hesitated, then tried several words. Mady shook his head, swiping at tears. He didn't understand.

The man tried again. "You blood Atlantean. You Atlantean. Atlantis is you home."

"NO!" Mady shook his head. "This is not my home! I want to go home, I want my mother, she's sick and she needs me…" It dawned on him then. She'd been trying to send him away, babbling about his Pater being Atlantean—which he'd ignored, too outraged that she wanted him to leave.

He had fought with her, ran away, fell asleep in the wreckage of the bed he'd destroyed. It was the last thing he remembered. Surely this wasn't her doing. She wouldn't drug him and abandon him in a foreign land with nothing. Besides, she was too sick. Too weak.

It was her man! He did this. He'd dumped Mady somewhere far far away across the sea so he couldn't return to his mother. If this really was Atlantis, he must be far from home—but that wouldn't stop him. He'd find a way back. He would!

ANOTHER DAY PASSED before Mady was strong enough to go outside. What he saw out his window in daylight, was even stranger than the oddities and glories inside.

The food here was good, and the people smiled at him and talked a lot, always gently touching him, sometimes bring him little gifts. He shied away from their outstretched hands, unsure what they might want from him—especially the men.

The man who spoke Mady's language came to visit again. They exchanged names. The names he spoke, gesturing to the ones who lived in this house, were so strange Mady couldn't remember them. He didn't bother trying to pronounce them, just stared, trying to decide what threats were here. Everywhere had danger. It unnerved him further that he couldn't figure out what the danger was in this surreal place.

When they took him outside, he stared around in wonder. It was a town unlike any he'd imagined, much less seen. The buildings were all the same, half-dome shape, with the same number of angles and planes. All a uniform sandy color.

It was much later, long after he learned the layout of the city, that he finally had words for it.

Honeycomb City had one of the most striking Atlantean architectural styles. Each home had six sides, all of them grouped together with linking walls, like cells in a honeycomb. In the middle of each cluster of six houses was a garden. The small cluster formed a cell in a larger cluster, cells within cells, aggregating until they formed a city with hundreds of houses. All the linked walls made this design incredibly strong. Built close to a fault line, the inhabitants became experts in earthquake resistant building.

Central gardens in each cluster were a popular feature, giving children a contained place to play, or adults private spaces to socialize and enjoy. Groups of friends, like artists, scientists or counselors often chose to live around a shared garden. The only disadvantage to this design was that some of the rooms had very strange shapes.

Because all the houses looked the same, Mady often got lost.

Eventually, it was pointed out by his kind hosts, how all the front doors were painted in bold colors—red, blue, yellow, green, orange, violet, and he learned the code of their color spectrum. These colors followed each other clockwise in spectrum order, and everyone knew where these colors fit in the overall map of the city. The doors of the outermost cells were the strongest hues, paling as you moved into the middle of the sector. So at a glance, you also knew how near the center of the city you were.

MADY WORKED HARD to master the Atlantean language with one goal in mind; going home. He mimicked the people around him, learned to smile, be gracious, act charming.

They lavished praise on him, and love—though he didn't trust it. Eventually things always went wrong. Eventually, someone would try to take advantage of him or hurt him.

The family he lived with, explained how they had found him as if it were the greatest story ever told: A riverboat carrying merchant goods had stopped in Honeycomb City to offload cargo. One of the crates seemed heavier than the others, and when the dockhands heard coughs and moans coming from it, they opened it right away. Mady was curled inside with a ragged blanket and a jug of water, very ill from whatever he'd been drugged with.

"You might have died!" They would exclaim in horror. Their Pater —whom they called Father—had been working at the docks that day, and took him home. Both his mate and her mother were healers. Plus, they had an extra room in their home—which they took as a sign; they were meant to find and take care of Mady.

They even commemorated the day they'd found him each year, since he didn't know when his birth day was.

18

ZIEL'S SPIES

HIGH CITY, ATLANTIS

" Hence the use of spies, of whom there are five classes: Local spies; inward spies; converted spies; doomed spies; surviving spies".

— SUN TZU, ART OF WAR

ZIEL

*B*elial spies are not hard to come by.

What is hard to come by, is accurate information of any sort from them. The Belial leaders, which is to say the military, is so secretive, it's difficult to find out what they like for breakfast. Or if they've moved their bowels today. They spread elaborate stories constantly—a somewhat brilliant strategy, as what filters to me becomes impossible to sort out as truth or lie.

Most of the information my Belial spies give me—demanding payment for it of course—is absolute whale shit. Fortunately, there are a few Atlanteans who sacrifice themselves for the greater good by living as Belials—though it pains them—waiting for any hint of attack against us.

The particular man who came to me today, I haven't heard from in over a decade. Not once.

From a balcony of Poseidon's Palace, I watched the city being cleaned of First Day's aftermath. Fire rubble was hauled away. Streets were scrubbed clean of the spilled wine, and buildings of smoke stain. Though tired, I felt happier than I'd been in a long while, after my two-day sabbatical away for the holi day.

I spent it with my secret lover. It isn't strictly forbidden anymore for one in my position. Remaining unmarried is more habit, from centuries past when we believed Oracle's powers were strongest with few distractions pulling at their focus. I'd asked Sage (trying not to beg) to join me in my hideaway tree home in Old Forest.

She did—bringing Taya's snake, Sila, for the girls, who hope the reptile will help thin the maze's overabundance of vermin.

Our rendezvous was long overdue, tender, spectacular and fulfilling. My soul wants that woman at a level I don't understand.

I stood reflecting on it for quite some time, feeling elation and regret both. Regret at the years I'd passed without trying to explain, or asking forgiveness for the hurt I'd caused. Elation, of knowing my magnificent Sage is every bit as dazzled by our renewed romance as I am.

I jolted back to my present balcony scene when Maya found me, knowing my habits and quiet spaces well.

"Pardon the intrusion Ruler. A man is here insisting to see you immediately. I thought it best you hear him." Maya's noble face was lined from sharing my burdens, her graceful body aging faster than it might have, had she chosen a simpler occupation. She knew I trusted her instincts implicitly.

I nodded, turning to follow her.

He waited in my office, hooded and somber. A tall, thin figure, that made me think of poets and young saplings that die prematurely but don't fall for decades.

"I cannot tarry." He opened the conversation. "My aero leaves within the hour. Mardu plans to invade Greece at Spring Equinox. The troops will start moving into place at the waning quarter-moon." He rushed his words as if to prevent interruption before he finished.

"They expect it will take three weeks, moving the Mutazio and launching the ships. You have two moons to prepare."

I was stunned to silence longer than I should have been. We'd avoided war for so long, few of us alive had experienced it.

"Ah—alright. Should we warn Greece?"

"I don't know. Some there have been bought. I wouldn't know who to trust. That is your concern, not mine." He waited, still hooded.

I wished I knew what he wanted me to say. "Well done. I will take this to the Rulers immediately. How can I communicate with you?"

He shook his head. "You can't. I'm monitored always. If I can, I'll arrange a go-between."

"What else can you tell me?" My mind was going in circles trying to imagine what questions the Rulers would ask. What questions I should be asking.

"They claim the Mutazio are undefeatable." His voice held despair. "We should never have let Belial get this far. Now they have an army of giants. Understand, our only hope is bringing ten times their number against them. Even Atlantis and Greece combined do not number that many."

It would be futile at this point, to argue the reasons we haven't stopped the Belial mutations and experimenting. (In short, it would violate our Law of One by limiting the free will of individuals when we had no authority over them. It's a fine line—controlling some so they don't control others.)

Maya placed a hand on the spy's arm. "Have faith my friend. Because you have risked greatly, because you have sacrificed these years of life, we now have time to prepare."

The spy bowed to her. "I've been too long inside, watching a government become ever more powerful. I've lost hope they can be stopped—unless we violate our own morals."

"Then perhaps it is time you come home." She said softly.

He nodded, considering. "I will try to learn more first. I must go." He stepped away from her touch, glancing at me. The long face grew darker. "If Atlantis aids Greece, war will be waged on this continent. Either way, we stand to lose too many lives. Peace be with you." He bowed.

"And with you. Is there anything that you require?"

But he was already stepping out the doorway and didn't pause or turn to answer.

SEVEN OF US were seated around the polished, zebrano table laid with food. No one was eating. It had taken a little over four hours to assemble everyone—some having just returned from their holi day destinations.

"We must warn Greece!"

"Yes, but we are allies. They will ask that we come to their aid."

"If we aid them against Belial, war will be fought on our own continent as well, risking the lives of every Atlantean! The very well-being of our country!"

"If we don't aid them, we lose an ally and empower Belial all at once."

"What if we're next? Grecian armies combined with Mardu's could overcome us."

The conversation swirled around me in rapidly firing voices. These women I ruled with, were used to considering things in their depth and entirety before making a decision. I feared we hadn't the time for it, but for now, I kept quiet as they went round the table.

"Perhaps we should negotiate, find out what Mardu wants and see if we can settle with him peaceably. We've been able to so far... "

"But then we reveal our knowledge of their plans. They'll just change them and what little edge we have will be lost."

"Not if we can successfully treat with him. Maybe what he wants is simpler than we think."

"Doubtful. If he's going after Greece, what he wants is bigger than anything we can give."

"That's an assumption."

"We know the Belials operate as a military nation and they're in desperate need of expansion. We know their philosophy is opposite our own, and we know they've been building power as fast as they can for decades. Centuries."

"What about the weapons?" I interjected. Six sets of eyes turned to me. We all knew what I meant. Our weapons were relics from when Atlantis warred far and wide, conquering any society that threatened us—or might one day—establishing our supremacy. Now, we cared only that other countries left us alone to thrive. I'd often wondered, how much our long-lasting peace had to do with the reputation we'd made, before we became practicing "Children of the Law of One".

"Do they still work?" I pressed.

Eirene, the Head of the House of Foreign Relations nodded and spoke up. She'd stayed peculiarly quiet thus far. "Oh yes. We maintain and study them still, in the event we must defend our borders. The problem", she said slowly, articulating clearly, "is they are *mass* weapons, designed for use against an approaching army. We can't pick and choose the targets. All in their range will be... affected."

"You're saying we'd be using them against Greece as well as Belial?"

"If they're both on the battlefield, yes. Also there could be civilian casualties. If we ally with Greece in time, and if the setting is favorable, we may be able to position them against only Belials armies. Of course we have no idea if they'll be effective on the Mutazio and there is the matter of powering them on Grecian soil. They're designed to work within our power grid."

The volley of opinions started round the table once more.

"Unacceptable. We can't harm innocents—even for the purpose of defending ourselves. It goes against every code we have."

"Yes, but it would resolve the war on foreign soil. At least Atlanteans would be safe."

"Then we might as well use the weapons against the Belials *before* they go to Greece! Avoid harming *our ally!*"

"That's oppression. Right back to before our predecessors made the decision to grant the Sons of Belial freedom to live and rule how they want."

"Yes and that decision had caveats. We can defend ourselves. There are consequences if they harm us in any way."

"The treaty does not speak to our situation."

"But if they harm our ally, is that not the same thing as harming us? Should that not bear the same consequence?"

"Why then, wouldn't we prevent such loss of lives, move against them before they attack Greece?"

All eyes turned to me. I was the expert on future happenings.

I sighed long and deep before answering. "Because the taking of a life for a deed one hasn't committed yet, violates the law of free will. We can't know for certain an event will take place. There are too many variables."

I didn't even like my own answer.

Talk went in circles for hours. There was no clean, perfect, or safe answer and we all knew it. It was decided to reconvene tomorrow morning. We would each spend this evening in meditation, and study of our Law of One. How does one find balance between allowing free will—without letting powerful ones oppress the weaker?

19

FINAL PREPARATIONS

9, 971 BCE. TEMPLE CITY, BELIAL

"Let your plans be dark and impenetrable as night, and when you move,
fall like a thunderbolt."

— SUN TZU, THE ART OF WAR

MARDU

*T*he obelisk General's tower rose fifty-some stories. Jutting against a bright winter sky, it dominated the crowd of columned buildings ringing it.

Surrounding those were structures of every shape and size, modeled after real temples across Atlantis, perpetually mocking the spirituality Atlanteans held fast to. All of the crowded buildings, levels and parapets were linked by spidery layers of walkways forming Temple City, the capital of Belial.

For all its shining regal length, the General's tower was abuzz like a shaken wasp hive this morning, when Mardu arrived.

Soldiers were everywhere, clumped in loud-talking knots, slouching in pairs against walls, or striding to unknown destinations on endless errands for their commanders. Excitement gusted as high in the center atrium, as the winds whipping loudly against buildings outside, bending weedy bushes, redirecting abandoned clothing and discarded trash into maelstroms of rot.

Just inside, Mardu paused, watching the mill of bodies go slowly still as they realized he was in their midst. Surrounded by his personal guardsmen, he stepped up on the edge of a water fountain, and waited until a relative quiet cloaked the space, then spread his arms wide. "Greetings warriors of Belial! What a pleasure to see your industriousness! What good it does me to feel your excitement. You know the time is drawing near when Belial will earn the right to lead our world and—"

Applause, stomping, and shouts thundered over his words as the men showed their appreciation and fervor. It died away and Mardu, teeth glimmering stark white in a ferocious smile across his smoky bronze face, shouted "Until then, carry on and remember, victory belongs to those with the greatest power!"

He jumped down to the black marble floor and strode towards the elevator that would take him many stories below, to the chambers where his Generals were waiting.

The men pushed in as close as his guardsmen would allow, lining his path, cheering him, chanting "Dominus Mardu" until he disappeared from their view.

Still smiling broadly, spirits high from the devotion he inspired, he stepped into the war room where his dozen top Generals all rose from their seats around a long polished table, clamping their right fists to their heart in salute to their leader.

He took his time savoring this moment, eyes roaming the room with its wall-sized battle scenes painted so realistically they pumped adrenaline. Slim side tables showcased displays of weaponry as if they were national treasures, and sword-shaped sconces lit the room in sharp points of light, their hilts glittering with jewels set in ornate metal workings.

Every General wore black uniforms made of very thin and supple leather. Slim pants carried a wide stripe of black satin down the outer legs, topped by stiffer tunics that fell just below the crotch, accented with rows of orichalcum buttons, and more wide satin stripes that spread from the neck base across the shoulder top, down the arm and from the armpit down to the hem. Lesser officers would also wear black, but with dark grey stripes and the soldiers wore uniforms of gunmetal grey.

"Like a thunderstorm with the power to reshape our landscape." Mardu often described his army when he inspected their drills and training regimes.

"It is time." Mardu spoke softly, almost tremulous on this cusp of all that he had worked towards his entire, violent life. His voice rose with gladness. "Take your seats men, let us first celebrate!

"A toast, in honor of all that we have become, and the triumphs soon to come. Look around you, and take note! This is the eve of a new beginning. This is the tipping point my friends, a time of balancing the scales, of branding a new freedom on the world, and claiming more of it for ourselves! Let us drink to what we leave behind, but most of all, to the glories that lie ahead!" Mardu raised his chalice, a beautiful topaz-colored glass embraced by a finely wrought orichalcum lion standing on its hind legs to form the stem.

A dozen generals raised equally beautiful glasses, echoing back, "To the glories that lie ahead!"

Gesturing to maps covering one wall, Mardu took his seat. "Report in. I want to hear each of your plans from beginning to end, including adjustments for weather and other unforeseen delays." He swung his gaze to the man on his left. "Begin."

It sounded flawless. Even easy. But Mardu knew better than to believe everything would go according to theoretical plans. Even now, Atlantis or Greece could be learning of Belial's plan to attack. Some traitorous weakling could betray them at any moment. Paranoia edged up, convincing and solid.

"How long until you can have the Mutazio in place?" Mardu asked General Rogan, sitting as always, on his right.

"From now? Fifteen days, give or take."

Mardu calculated mentally.

"Then we attack in fifteen days." He announced it calmly and immediately a storm of voices began. Astonishment. Questions. Dissent.

Mardu stood, staring down his Generals until silence reigned. "The element of surprise is our only defense against spies and oracles. We are ready. You are ready. I've just heard it."

20

DREY'S JOURNALS

9,970 BCE HIGH CITY, ATLANTIS

"If everyone helps to hold up the sky, then one person does not become tired."

— ASKHARI JOHNSON HODARI, LIFELINES: THE BLACK
BOOK OF PROVERBS

AHNA

*I*t was bedtime before the sisters came together to open their mysterious package, delivered to Aiela's door this morning. Sitting cross-legged in her bed, Aiela untied the string.

"What is it?" Ahna crouched to peer at the little leather book in Aiela's hands.

"Somebody's old journal looks like..." Aiela flipped through the pages. "It's only a little over half-full. Why would someone send us an old journal?"

Ahna shrugged. "Start reading." She flopped onto Aiela's mattress, stretching out on her stomach as Aiela propped her back against the wall and began to read.

*"It is half dark, yet morning paints the horizons once again. Does
Terra ever tire of it I wonder? Creating such spectacular and unique
art that few see? It reminds me of the temporary nature of all things—
both the great and the miserable. We were never meant to cling. Not
to experiences, or beliefs, or beauty even. I must learn to accept and
experience and release.*

*The sky glows now, like the center of a ripe melon. Just enough thin
clouds to provide a palette for new sunbeams.*
*This morning I say goodbye once again to my precious ones. I'm off to
the Afrikkaan lab to study with Rik and Carla. I'm sure they have
gathered many new specimens by now and it's been at least four
moons since I've visited... "*

Aiela trailed off, glancing at Ahna who'd sat up, eyes stretched
wide.

"Keep going." She whispered.

*"... since I've visited our desert facility, which I miss. It's quieter
because my Atlantean colleagues don't care for the stark barrenness of
it. I think its beauty is unique. There are few desertous places in the
world and we're lucky to have one accessible to study.*
*The girls will be up soon—which will awaken my Love. I'd best get
breakfast going for all of us."*

"Papa!" They breathed in unison.

"Is it really him?" Ahna reached to touch the leather book, scooting
to sit beside Aiela so she could see his writing for herself.

"But why wouldn't it be at home with the others?"

"And who would have sent it to us?"

They hadn't thought to read any of his journals yet. A whole trunk
of them waited in their abandoned childhood home. How did this one
get here?

"Maybe Auntie Sage thought it would somehow be good. Healing."

"Maybe." Ahna said doubtfully. "Read more. The answer must be
in it."

"Today I named a new flower. Or rather, Carla did. She discovered it and had a name picked out already..."

Aiela's voice softened in reverence, savoring each word as she continued.

Tears blurring her vision, Ahna rose to make tea, listening intently, seeing her father's kind eyes the same green color as hers, his honey-blonde head bent over the book as he wrote. Missing him ached intensely as his words opened a doorway to his soul. Such a gift. Like hearing him speak again, and yet it hurt—almost too much.

Aiela stopped reading, her sudden silence stretching. "Hm, strange. He skipped a page and now the writing is different. Sloppier. Listen to this;

'I was taken. A Belial man named Nico came with six others in the night, dragging me from bed. They had an aero and we put down in England—far south I believe—at a ruined stone castle. There I met Nadya, a Banpiro, which species creation I'd heard of but had no idea still existed. She was astonishing in beauty and intelligence, though she was being abused. Her sister also was being held to gain Nadya's cooperation, but I never laid eyes on her. Mahlia was the sister's name and they killed her the night we escaped. They burnt her, alive, to a charred shell and forced Nico to watch because he loved her and was helping us escape. I weep still at these atrocities, as though there aren't enough tears to cleanse such horror from my body.

I'm telling this badly... I will compose myself and start again.

The person in charge was referred to as 'the big man'. I was hooded both occasions I was in his presence but Nadya said his name is Balek and he is Mardu's eldest son."

Aiela left off to look at Ahna in amazement. "When was this? Did you ever hear him speak of this?"

Ahna shook her head as Aiela thumbed back through pages, searching for a date. "This would have been when we were about seven! Did Mama ever say anything? Or Auntie Sage?"

"No. You want me to read for a bit?"

Tea forgotten, they continued on, stopping often to exclaim or discuss the things Papa had written. Coming to the final pages, explaining what the nodes were, the sisters read of how they were constructed and how they worked. When only blank pages remained, they sat looking at each other in confusion.

"We should take this to Ziel." Aiela stood, stretching.

"Now?" It was late. Everyone would be asleep.

"No, I'm too tired to explain it properly tonight. But first thing in the morning."

"I wonder what he'll make of it."

Changing into nightclothes and falling into Aiela's bed, they talked late into the night, trying to process it.

"Why did Papa never talk about such an important and terrible thing?"

"What about the Blood Code? Wouldn't that have applied to everything Balek did?"

"They say every family has secrets but I would have sworn ours didn't! Maybe Mama and Auntie Sage didn't know."

"Somebody knew. And now they've sent it to us."

"IT TELLS ABOUT WHAT?!" Ziel didn't bother to hide his astonishment.

"Papa was taken to England by Balek, Mardu's horrible son, and forced to work on some brain nodes Belial needed to control animals. Papa thought they might also be used to control their Mutazio." Aiela repeated what Ahna had already said.

"How did you come by this?" Ziel clutched a steaming cup, still wearing his long, linen nightshirt. The twins had knocked at his door before meditation, or breakfast, or even dressing.

Aiela shrugged. "It was delivered yesterday morning to my room. Wrapped in canvas, tied with string and a paper tag that said 'To Ahna and Aiela'. We'd like to know the same thing, who sent it?"

"And why?" Ahna added. "All his journals are at home so we thought maybe Auntie Sage...?"

Ziel was shaking his head. "If Sage knew about this she would have come in person. She'd never do such a thing without being here to support you. No, it was someone else." He closed the door belatedly and pointed at his table. "Sit. I've dire news to tell you and then you'll understand the ramifications of *this* arriving at such a precise juncture."

Ziel talked while he heated more water and brewed a fresh pot of tea, telling of the news his spy had delivered, the circuitous deliberations between the Rulers. "We're to meet again early this morning, though I can't imagine we'll make much progress."

"We've just two moons to prepare for war then?" Ahna asked, voice deliberate, calm.

"Or try to treat with them, or dream up options unknown." Ziel set out two cups for them and poured, before settling into his customary cushion chair at the table.

"Will Belial overcome Greece if we don't aid them?" Aiela was thinking of Turner and his beloved Grecian uncles. Perhaps at least they could be warned, could flee or prepare somehow.

"Yes. I believe they would. I have too little intelligence on the Mutazio—mostly because we can't find them. The Oracles have visions of giants—mutations of primates and men—yet somehow Belial manages to keep them hidden. It's said they're unbeatable in battle."

"If Papa's right and the nodes are used to control them, maybe our scientists can help. Give us a way to interfere or take them over."

Ziel flipped open the little book and started reading, ignoring the girls as they discussed all he had told them and foraged in his cabinet, pulling out fruit and baked cheese crackers to break their fast.

"Why wouldn't he have come to me?! Surely Taya would've told me... " Ziel murmured to himself, scanning the writing rapidly until he came to the last few pages about the nodes.

Reading carefully now, he finally looked up, hope lighting his peculiar blue eyes and blooming into a smile. "This is it. This is option unknown! I must dress and tell the Rulers. Meet me here tonight, I'll have supper brought up."

21

INVASION

9,971 BCE. NORTHERN BORDER OF GREECE

"Bullying builds character like nuclear waste creates superheroes."

— ZACK W. VAN

ROGAN

*G*eneral Rogan waited, back propped against a twist in a stunted tree trunk. Watching the grey morning light, his annoyance grew as the horizon brightened, with no sign of the last batch of cargo. If they weren't here very soon, they better stay put until dark fell again.

Next he paced to staunch his irritation, while eggs boiled in water. Perhaps breaking his fast would help.

Full morning had dawned in bands of thin, vivid gold when the loud drone of engines sounded overhead and three large transporters came into sight. *I should beat the stupid outta that boy and be done with it!* He raged inside, always careful to contain it.

Touching down, the aero doors slid open and Mutazio filed off to stand in crooked lines, awaiting orders. Wide-eyed, the giant men looked slightly bedraggled, no doubt from long travel and encountering a startlingly vast world beyond the familiarity of their primitive camps.

Balek stepped off last and bellowed at the nearest muta for food and blankets. As if the just-arrived muta would know where to find these things. *Fool.*

They were ten miles outside the border of Greece in a region thick with bushy dwarf trees and shallow, snaking rivers. Winter felt frigid to these tropical born and bred Belials, but the rivers and streams weren't frozen, General Rogan had reasoned, so it couldn't be that cold. Mardu had entrusted this first phase of the invasion to his eldest son, and Balek was all puffed up with the pride of his importance. The assigned duty was simple; oversee transporting the Mutazio army from sea cruisers to three points along the border and await the signal to attack. It was expected to take three full nights.

Glancing around at the terrain in daylight, Balek strutted to where General Rogan stood breathing deeply to control his anger. "I'm satisfied we shall be undetected here. Perhaps we'll creep closer after I've got the lay of the land." His eyes were still puffy with sleep. The foremen and handlers had no doubt done all the work, while Balek dozed in the aero. Even now, those same foremen and handlers were directing this Mutazio company in setting up camp, while Balek played pretend.

Pompous little rat. General Rogan didn't bother to hide his scowl—or to answer—before turning away to attend to his eggs.

MOST OF GREECE's armies were naval.

No other nation had the technology to aero an entire army in, and the vast swathes of empty land would starve out a land march, so Grecian border defenses were light. Historically, their attackers came from its seaside.

Greece had always been at peace with Atlantis. Themselves descendants of first and second epoch Atlanteans, they had no fear of the technology that Atlantis used. They would certainly not be expecting an army, possessing Atlantis' advanced capabilities, to sneak up on them from behind.

Once the entire Grecian fighting force was engaged with the land battle, Mardu and his naval generals would lead the Belial soldiers in an attack from the sea.

Mardu himself would treat with the Grecian rulers. Soon as they realized they were surrounded by these giant, animalistic men, hopelessly outnumbered, they'd do anything he asked. His intent was to conquer Greece, with its army wholly intact. The highly trained military was what he wanted—to ensure eventual victory over Atlantis. Knowing Greece would come to Atlantis' aid if called, Mardu would turn them to his side first, tipping the odds solidly in his favor. One more army at his disposal.

BALEK WAS SCREECHING about something else as General Rogan stalked off to have a word with the pilots. It wasn't worth his life to lose control and wring the boy's neck.

"64649! Yes *you* ugly wretch—I'm talking to you! Get a fire going. I don't eat raw meat like you animals. Bring it to me cooked and it better be clean. Hurry up! And somebody bring me a girl. I'm fucking sick of having to smell you ugly oafs all night! Is everyone here stupid? Deaf?" Balek was screaming, but staying a distance away from the huge Mutazio so he didn't have to crane his neck to look up at them.

The muta he addressed, broke branches off stunted trees and nodded vigorously at Balek's demands. "Yes. I build fire. Cook meat. Clean meat. Bring girl." He was eager to please this master. This master was unusually cruel and took offense at any perceived slight disobedience.

"Rogan!" Balek continued shouting, full of his own power now that the General was a safe distance away, "Get this camp in order! I want these mutas fed and resting. They are to be kept in top form until we march."

Mardu's number one General merely ignored Balek. Always trying to prove his power, playing at the errands Mardu sent him on.

General Rogan suspected the errands were simply a way to get rid of his obnoxious eldest. Come to think of it, this coming battle might just be the perfect opportunity to permanently rid them all of the dangerously stupid boy.

General Rogan was perhaps the only Belial who wasn't afraid of Balek—probably why he got stuck with him. It had become increasingly annoying as Balek became an increasingly reckless man.

"Not so loud Balek!" General Rogan turned back to stop the bellowing before it riled up the whole camp. "They've set you a place to sleep just over there. Food will be brought to you soon, then you should sleep. Refresh for tonight." General Rogan may be the only friend to this boy's father, may be the most trusted of Mardu's Generals, but that didn't exactly make him superior to the offspring of Mardu according to Sons of Belial laws. He had to tread carefully, play along with Balek's pretend command, while still maintaining control.

This was the exhausting part; letting Balek play the part of commander, but not letting his frequent bouts of stupidity throw them all off course.

When Mardu had first sent Balek to the Mutazio camps for training, the teenage boy took out his considerable boredom and rages by maiming or killing mutas, honing vicious skills on those who were prevented from fighting back.

General Rogan had threatened going to Mardu with the problem of his army being wasted. Balek had backed down from that particular sport for the time being, but managed to find someone he could bully and kill regularly, often the girls he demanded brought to him.

General Rogan may not have been the most honorable man himself, but he was disgusted by Balek—a spoilt coward who took advantage of his position rather than earning it.

Mardu

"Run that ship down. We cannot risk it warning the Grecians." Mardu pointed at a shape far off to port, heading towards Greece.

He'd equipped their warships for just such an occasion, knowing they'd likely be spotted in the narrower channels before reaching Grecian shores.

Four Belial soldiers hustled to board an aero.

Mardu watched the small, triangular craft lift off the sea-sprayed deck and shoot across the water to hover over the unlucky vessel for a few moments. A beam of light, with a girth larger than three bundled men, flashed where the ship had been.

The resounding boom traveled belatedly across the water. Mardu knew the remaining pieces of the disintegrated vessel would be smaller than the size of his fist. Sea creatures would feed on chunks of its crew and with no wreckage ever found, their families would forever hope they lived still—stranded maybe, or lost.

"Tonight you will aero to General Rogan's base and see if all is ready." Mardu spoke to General Pompeii, youngest of his military leaders, grecian-born like himself. "You know this terrain better than anyone. It's been four nights since Balek started transporting the Mutazio. They should be in position by now. Have them start the march at tomorrow's sundown as planned. We'll hold here until they send someone to confirm the entire Grecian army is engaged."

General Pompeii bowed. "Yes Dominus Mardu. I'll leave at full dark. Let's hope for a clouded sky."

Mardu continued as if the General hadn't spoken. "I expect it will take several days, once the fighting starts, for the leaders to launch everything they've got to stop the land invasion. Several more for their troops to actually get there. If they decide to send their navy the long way around, to flank the Mutazio, we'll see them from here. Destroy them. Though I hope that doesn't happen. I prefer their navy intact to help take Atlantis." None of this was new information to the young General. Mardu was talking from boredom. They still had a few day's wait ahead of them.

The aero landed back on deck, sending a flurry of water droplets to mist him. "What sort of vessel was it?" He asked the pilot climbing out of the control seat.

"Fishing boat I believe, Dominus. Rather big one, probably a whaler."

Mardu nodded, satisfied. "Good. Not a battleship then. Well done."

The pilot bowed low. "Thank you Dominus. Do you require anything else?"

"No." Mardu waved him off, turning towards his quarters for dry clothing.

Carver

"Thank you Orja. This smells heavenly." Carver smiled at their gently aging servant as she set before him a plate of steamed vegetables and fish.

It was very late and he was working in his father's library, sitting behind the monstrous desk crafted from a slab of thin, black pyrite balanced across a dragon skull dipped in illumine. "Why aren't you sleeping?" He thought to ask, stuffing buttered green beans into his mouth. He was famished, and exhausted.

Orja frowned at him. "More importantly, why are not you? Great strength you will need to run this country until your father returns. Full of vipers and thieves, who will take advantage of you." She clicked her tongue. "I hope you doubled your guard."

Carver nodded, unable to speak around a mouthful of moist whitefish before swallowing. "I'm not helpless Orja. You still see me as a boy, but believe it or not, I'm a man with many skills. I'm cunning, well-liked *and* dangerously handsome." He could see how worried she was, wanted to make her smile.

She just stared at him, fatigue creasing her still beautiful face and dulling her eyes.

He sighed long and deep. "The entire City Council wants to meet with me in the morning. Food distribution is demanding new warehouses and additional personnel. Some gang has grown quite large and is menacing the poorest sections—our judges claim that every time they capture one, three more take their place—and we have no soldiers to send. There's a hiccup in Conrectus production, because some of the creators were reassigned to replace soldiers in other positions, and the High Priest of the Temple of Mind Power is practically threatening me if I don't solve it for him.

"Everyone wants Belial to keep running at full speed on less than half the manpower. Mardu hasn't been gone a week and they're already dumping things on me they wouldn't dare even mention in his presence."

Shaking his head, Carver bent to eat more before it got cold.

Orja came to stand beside him, laying a small brown hand on his shoulder. Something she never would have done if his father or brothers were in the room.

"What will you do?" She asked simply.

"I'm devising a plan to give the Council. If I go in with orders, I won't have to listen to them debate and argue what should be done—or what they each want or expect from me. I will penalize the worst of them for dereliction of duty. Threaten to replace them. You know, bluster and blow and scare everyone."

Orja patted his shoulder. "Good boy. You're thinking like your father."

"Yes." Carver replied, hating to admit it out loud. "I'll have to if I want to keep order. Please gods, may this time be short."

He already loathed this job with a passion—which surprised him even more than the shock of Mardu announcing Carver would rule Belial in his stead during the Greece invasion. It was the last task he'd been expecting and his brothers were all livid—until they remembered they wanted to go to war more than stay behind and babysit a country of addicts and thieves. Then it was all sarcastic jibes and mocking "the baby dominus" until they finally boarded the warships and aeros.

"I can write." Orja picked up his pen. "Dictate while you eat and I'll finish the documents."

"No Orja. I'm almost done and I'll need you bright and fresh in the morning to see to things here. As you said, we're vulnerable right now —despite doubling the guard. I need you to be my eyes and ears, fixing my food and drink personally and all that."

She squeezed his shoulder, replacing the pen. "Alright. You'll ring for me if you change your mind?"

Carver smiled. "I will not. Sleep deep—because it certainly won't be long."

He bent to writing again.

In truth, the plans for his morning meetings were already

complete. What he worked on now was contingencies. So many things could happen. The invasion and takeover of Greece could take weeks or moons longer than Mardu expected. Someone might attempt to oust Carver and take over Belial—several of the gangs were suspected of uniting, forming an overlarge force. Atlantis might go to Greece's aid and defeat Belial. What then?

He'd been unable to sleep last night, thinking up a hundred different scenarios. What might he have set in motion by sending Drey's journal to Atlantis? Not knowing was a torture. These days could be the end of his lifelong imprisonment. What if he was free to find Ahna soon?

His heart grasped at this thought. Then hardened back into a lump of dread at the next one. What if Atlantis did go to Greece's aid, thereby going to war with Belial. And what if Mardu won? It was possible, even likely with the Mutazio.

Which is why he must finish this contingency and start executing on it tomorrow. Just knowing he had a way to get to Ahna—could move her and Aiela out of High City and to safety before Mardu occupied it—might relieve his mind enough for sleep to come.

Orders for strategically placed aeros filled with weapons, food and survival gear would go out tomorrow. Orders to others for the aeros to be moved would follow. Layers of orders to low-level personnel, those too ignorant to think much about anything other than following orders, would all be signed and sealed by Dominus Mardu. Sent, fulfilled, forgotten.

Until Carver needed an escape.

22

KEY TO AN ARMY

"Appear weak when you are strong, and strong when you are weak."

— SUN TZU, THE ART OF WAR

ZIEL

"Ｗhat do you mean you've scientists working on it this minute? We have not yet discussed this!" Ruler Kenna sounded tired, not to mention, cross.

"It's very doubtful the Belials are still using this technology in their Mutazio. Didn't you say the incident happened years ago?" Ruler Eirene was as steady and pragmatic as ever, even at this early hour.

"You got us out of bed for this?" Another grouchy voice chimed in.

"Where is this journal? I wish to examine it for myself."

Without a word, I passed around copies. I'd known they would ask. Paper rustled in the hands of overly tired Rulers. I'd only given them the pages detailing the brain-nodes. The rest of it felt too private. Eventually, they'd demand the whole story and that would ignite a whole different discussion involving blood laws being broken

—or not, depending how you looked at it. Technically, the Belials hadn't taken any Atlantean lives. But they had forced Drey to do things against his will, abused him and allegedly planned to kill him.

I was certain now that Drey and Taya had been assassinated. The timing—right before Belial used their muta army to invade Greece—was too convenient. This also convinced me Belial still used Drey's technology.

But all of that would be dealt with later. Right now, I felt like a boy who'd deliberately rolled in dirt, hid the evidence, ate all the cookies, and now faced his mother. Only, in this scenario, there were six mothers.

I spoke into the silence as they sat reading the copies of Drey's journal pages. "I strongly believe this is the solution to our problem. Perhaps the only one that will protect our ally *and* keep us from going to war with Belial."

One by one, the other Rulers finished reading and looked at me, listening.

"I sit here with the wisest women I've ever known, and I have the utmost respect for each of you. We've known each other for decades and we've weathered enormous difficulties together. I'm asking you each to trust me on this. At the very least, consider my reasoning." I searched their eyes, reading their energies and body language.

They nodded. Mirroring back respect and even a little hope—which I was about to ruin.

"We are, quite literally, out of time. Belial's army shipped out yesterday. I only heard of it this morning—moments before I messaged each of you. More likely than not, their Mutazio army is also being positioned. I propose we ready our troops—some to go, some to stay at our borders. But before we decide that, let me tell you my hope for the nodes." I held up a hand, as if to physically stop the words hovering on each set of lips, barely contained under rounded eyes that would be panicky if they didn't belong to such seasoned Rulers.

They stayed silent.

"You all know Drey was like family to me. Drey struck a deal with Mardu. He bargained his silence, concealing this incident and information from Atlantis authorities, in return for the life and safety of himself and his family. Though I cannot prove it, I suspect Mardu had Drey killed, believing this information would never come to us. Now that it has, *we must use it*. Drey most likely ended up giving his life for it. Yes, the possibility exists that Belial developed some other technology to control the muta army. That is a chance we must take.

"I believe our first plan of attack should be to annihilate their giants, using controllers our scientists are creating right now based on Drey's information."

Papers shuffled as the Rulers let their minds catch up.

"How might it be accomplished?" Ruler Eirene was the first to speak up.

"We could send in an aero by night. Destroy every muta on the battlefield with a flip of the switch, without even landing. Greece would outnumber Belial's remaining soldiers. If that doesn't work, then we send in our troops to aid our ally and we prepare to defend our home. But if it does work, Belial won't even know it was Atlantis. I will ensure that. Perhaps they'll think it was an accident from their own controllers."

Moments of silence stretched after my impassioned plea, until one of the Rulers called for tea and food. Platters were brought and set before us, and the apprentices sent away before discussion began again.

"I cannot think of any reason this should not be our first plan of defense." Ruler Kenna admitted.

"I agree—with every backup we can conceive of, should it fail." Another Ruler chimed in.

Nods and murmurs of assent travelled around our circle of seven. Finally, everyone looked to Ruler Eirene, Head of the House of Foreign Relations; Leader of Atlantis' Armies.

She nodded thoughtfully. "I agree also to Ziel's plan being implemented immediately." Her hawk-like eyes fastened onto me. "You have the people and aeros and anything else you require to carry this out, once the scientists complete your controller?"

"Yes." I had vague ideas of who to use. Everyone at the table knew this mission had to be untraceable, which meant it belonged to my ghostly, and technically illegal, network of spies, not Atlantis' proper military channels.

Her deep, steady eyes travelled around the table. "Then I would like to position our weapons heavily along the Belial border and at the shores where High City's rivers meet the sea. The major Sound Eye I will position to protect High City from aero invasion. The minor sound eye I'd place in Ziel's care." She turned to look at me again. "Since you protect the Crystals, it may prove useful should anyone slip our defenses and get to you. I imagine the Crystals can easily be weaponized and I imagine you're prepared for this eventuality."

All eyes landed on me, waiting for the answer. "Yes and... yes. I'm prepared." How many of my secrets were really secret from this quiet, formidable woman? It wasn't the first time she'd startled me by asking pointed questions. It wouldn't come as a surprise to find she was psychic. Or somehow listened in on everything that was said by anyone who held power.

Discussion came slower this time—reminders, more than objections.

"Positioning weapons at Belial's border breaks our treaty."

"Not if we have reason to believe they will attack us."

"If you start moving troops, word will spread quickly. Belial will be alerted as quickly as our own public."

Ruler Eirene nodded, acknowledging the truth of these statements, waiting for any other concerns before responding. "We will call it a training exercise. It's been quite some time since we've conducted a massive initiative involving all branches of our force. This way, we can prepare for war, and cover it from everyone but my Generals. By dawn we will launch."

Watching until each of us nodded assent, she made a note, then continued. "Movement of the weapons I can keep quiet. We'll get them as close to the border as possible without alerting Belial's border towns. Weapon placement will begin as soon as the soldiers are moving, to distract attention. The Sound Eyes—I'll have in place by noon."

23

VISITING BELIAL

"If there is pain, nurse it, and if there is a flame, don't snuff it out, don't be brutal with it. Withdrawal can be a terrible thing when it keeps us awake at night, and watching others forget us sooner than we'd want to be forgotten is no better.

— ANDRÉ ACIMAN

AHNA

"I'm to deliver this to the Belial border. Leaving now." Ahna gestured vaguely to her pack—in truth, containing two changes of clothing and some food—then handed the letter she'd forged, to an attendant at the aero lot atop High City's wall. The letter bore Ruler Ziel's signature, topping his personal seal branded onto the page.

"You're licensed? Or you need a pilot?" The woman yawned—likely had been on duty all night.

"A pilot." Ahna turned to check the eastern horizon, still a soft, well-worn indigo. She hoped to be away before it lightened.

165

The woman spoke into a communique. "Immediate departure. Belial border."

"I'll need that letter." Ahna wasn't about to leave behind evidence of her bad deeds. She knew full well this was foolish, irresponsible, dangerous—and if her string of well-placed lies were discovered before she returned, would cost her the trust and wrath of those she loved.

She'd starting planning right after Ziel told them Belial's army was enroute to invade Greece. And that scientists were close to recreating the brain nodes and controllers based on Papa's journal notes. A deeply hidden hope that Carver might eventually come to her, had died a little more.

His country was going to war. Maybe, eventually, with hers. She had to try to find him. How hard could it be? Belial was geographically a small area. Surely she could find someone who knew him. Or Drommen or Lister. Impending war might even convince him to come back with her.

Ziel would stay preoccupied with the urgency of stopping the invasion, moving their own defenses into place, and arguing with the other Rulers whether to attack Belial if all else failed.

Aiela was focused all the day long on her apprentice role; supporting Ruler Kenna by researching pertinent history that might assist in their decisions. Plus, Turner was back for an extended stay, occupying her nights.

No one would miss her for a few days. Especially after she'd invented an Oracle apprentice assignment involving solitude, and told them she'd be at Squirrel's Nest in Old Forest to complete it.

"Ready to go Miss?" A stout young woman, not much older than Ahna, stepped into the light and beckoned with a cupped hand. "You're early enough to avoid the morning rush and the weather's fine over the mountains so we'll take a direct route. Get you there and back before supper."

"Actually I'm staying for a few days. It's an opportunity to um— offer Oracle services to those in the border towns, since I'm going all the way there." When had she become such a prolific liar?

They reached a small, bright orange aero. "You ever been? The pilot asked, climbing into her seat.

"No. This is the farthest south I've seen." Ahna settled in while the pilot took them up and away from High City's colorful nightglow.

"The border's pretty dreary. Once the mountains end, it's mostly just dust or Belial's great ugly heap of buildings all the way to the coast." The pilot stretched and yawned, never taking her eyes from the radar as they shot through a morning sky still too dark to see. "We're over 20,000 feet in altitude" she explained, as if Ahna had asked. "The birds are probably just starting to stir, but still, hitting a flock of migrating geese, or the odd early-preying giant eagle, would do deadly damage at this speed."

"Belial's really that bad?" Ahna hadn't been able to find out much before she left. Atlantis didn't bother to keep many records of their neighbor who shared the same continent.

"It's not pretty." The pilot muttered. "Or nice. I've had to land there twice and wouldn't ever again if I could avoid it."

Ahna smiled. "Well then maybe I can bring some cheer—to the border town at least. Reading dreams and advising in life dharma tends to motivate people, especially when they're stuck in a rut. Gives them new ideas, new direction, new hope." The pilot looked doubtful and shrugged.

"If you say so."

IT WAS SIMPLER to cross the border into Belial than she'd dared to hope. Dressed in black tunic and pants four sizes too big, wearing no face paint, with hair unstyled, she looked like any other teenage boy here.

Nestled against the south side of Atlantis' expansive central mountain range, the terrain flattened abruptly into dusty plains with sharp grass and even sharper rocks. It didn't seem the Belials cared for the landscape at all. Clearly no one shaped or improved it. It was near as desolate and ugly as the horrible island they'd visited in Ireland where the Chief sacrificed the babies of his wives to keep them obedient.

Lack of soldiers on the Belial side was prominent, and this border town was small enough that people might know each other. She wouldn't tarry long enough to register in anyone's memory.

The sun was high and hotter than home, even behind sketchy clouds, when Ahna found a place baking small egg pies filled with mushrooms, leeks and spinach. Next was to bribe a pilot to take her to Temple City.

Scouting the available pilots from afar, she finished eating before approaching the youngest, skinniest one. He looked hot and bored ,awaiting customers beside a shabby aero.

"I've cheese, meat and fresh fruit if you drop me in city center. Actual gold if you help me acquire accommodation there for a few nights."

She'd gone to the far side of High City a day ago, to cash in all of her credit for the pure, white-gold bits Belial used for trade. Dispersing it between her shoes, pockets, and pack, she hoped any would-be robbers wouldn't get it all. It was said, Belials coveted quality food as much as anything, but she'd believe it when she saw it. Atlantis provided plenty of food to Belial, according to scant information she'd found.

The boy nodded, eyes following her movements as she took out a small, woven-hemp bag.

Something about him reminded her of the desperate boy in Ireland who had stolen her pack, accidentally cutting her face in the process. Marked by the long puckered gash from high cheekbone to chin, she'd spent the first part of the trip healing and the rest trying to hide what felt a hideous ruin. But Carver hadn't even seemed to notice it—except to ask if she was in pain. He'd made her feel beautiful when all she could see was damage.

Fresh-roasted quail scent filled the air and the boy reached for the parcel. "I'm yours long's you needin'." His voice cracked on the 'needin', and she wondered how risky it was to hire such a young pilot.

Once they were airborne, Ahna introduced herself. "I'm Erin and I claim neither Atlantis nor Belial as home. I plan to see the world before settling anywhere."

The boy's eyes flicked to her chest as if trying to determine her gender.

Glad she'd worn a tight undershirt and loose clothes, she continued, "In Ireland, I made three friends from Temple City. I'd like to find them." She described Carver, Drommen and Lister, hoping to get lucky and find somewhere to start looking. But the boy just shrugged and shook his head.

"Never heard of 'em, but city center is the place to ask 'round. Ever'body goes to market there 'cuz they got the best of what comes." He paused to dodge another aero coming straight at them, almost unseating Ahna.

Clutching the sides of her torn seat with both hands, she tried not to watch the goings-on outside the narrow windows. Belial air traffic was notorious for frequent crashes. She'd placed an energetic pyramid of white light around them for protection but that might only do so much in this recklessness.

"An' the arenas—you gotta see the arenas! Best killin' show is at central arena. Might even find your friends. Ever'body goes to watch there 'cuz they get the fiercest fighters."

She noticed his light brown, dirty looking hair had been combed, his clothing was simple but fairly clean, much like his energy felt. "What's your name?"

"Timen. Ever'body calls me Tim. How much gold you got? I could help you find 'em. Long as I bring home food, goods or gold, ain't nobody care how long I stay away."

Ahna squelched a gasp as the aero dove through a tangle of walkways that connected structures. Ramps and bridges went every which way in the monstrous pile of buildings. They all looked to have been added for convenience as the need arose, following no discernable pattern or plan.

Landing hard on a wide strip that spanned between two tall buildings, the boy grinned at her as if everything was completely normal.

"Is... is this it? This is city center?" Ahna felt dizzy with the bustle even before she got out. Aeros whizzed by to land, disgorge passengers, and take off again.

"I'm not sure where to start..." Suddenly this felt like an incredibly bad idea. There was as much height to this city as there was breadth. High City had tall buildings, but they were stunted in comparison to what she saw here. Layers and layers of city towered above and below. She'd somehow imagined it all smaller and simpler.

"C'mon. I kin show you 'round." Tim held out his hand so Ahna put three small gold bits into it. By the way his eyes lit up, she knew it had been too much.

Taking what was left of the quail meat—which he'd savored steadily in huge bites since they'd departed a quarter hour ago—he carefully locked each aero door before leading her to the edge of the strip. In High City, the aeros didn't even have locks.

A too-loud gasp escaped when she saw the vertical, mechanical rungs meant to transport them from this bridge to the ground—far far below. Affixing her pack onto her back to free both hands, she took a deep breath, watching how Tim stepped easily onto a ladder rung and hung onto another one.

"Hurry up. It on'y slows for a count of twenty." He called.

She'd barely closed both fists around the rung at chest height before they dropped so fast, her stomach seemed to float up behind her heart.

Abruptly, the moving ladder slowed again and they stepped off. She felt shaky all over but there was no time to think about it as Tim darted through a throng moving in every direction around them.

Stumbling a few times, she learned fast how to dodge a hundred different transport devices that hovered, rolled or flew. It was a flowing river, all moving to some unfathomable rhythm, faster in the center of the streets, slower close to either side. The streets felt more like tunnels, with building additions and walkways crisscrossing overhead.

City center was the original part of Temple City, Ahna knew from her reading. Built like miniature temples, every building they passed was grossly ornate, gilded with man-made jewels and metals. Pyramids looked crowded here, crammed rudely against each other—not like home where they flowed out into lawns and gardens. Towering rectangles leaned forward, as if propping up their faces on over-carved columns. A cluster of tall cylinders were topped with gleaming half spheres. A giant plinth foundation was formed into balconies and stairways supporting a stepped building that seemed to reach into the heavens.

She'd grown used to the ever-changing fashions, coiffed styles, and pampered body care of High City. In contrast, Belials looked cheap, dirty, and patched together. They made up for it in gaudy colors and crude ornaments that must pass for jewelry here, hanging off every body part.

Between the noise, the sea of transports and the visual overstimulation, claustrophobia began to close in. Before it turned to panic, she grasped her pilot-turned-guide's arm to shout, "Can we go somewhere quiet?"

"But we're almos' to the market."

She shook her head. "Let's find me a room first. Then a map—for after you leave."

He veered abruptly to the left and pointed at a grouping of spires in the distance. "Cathedral's the place to sleep. If you're rich, you kin git a real big room, if you wanna work for your stay there's the underground beds, and then there's ever'thing in between. 'S close to the arena too! If you're lucky you kin even watch fights from a window. They do two shows ever' day—three on rest days!"

It felt like miles, battling their way to a tall cathedral that was pure white and glittered in the sunlight. Intricate layers of architecture might have been gorgeous if it weren't for the overabundance that surrounded it. Instead it just competed, without dignity, in a city of chaos.

A man with jowls so fat they fell close to his collarbone, greeted them. "Welcome to Cathedral! A place that has it all—for a price." He rapidly flicked a bright orange tongue in and out between lips dyed the same shocking color. "Two young lads... very sweet..." he reached a fat hand towards Ahna's cheek but she scowled and dodged away. "Oh! And feisty too! We've plenty of patrons who'll like you!"

"He's wantin' a room and he'll pay with *gold*." Tim cut off the man's leer, while backing up a step.

"Oh? Already given somebody good fun then. How much gold do you have sweet laddie?"

"None of your business." Ahna scowled again and squared her shoulders. "Just show me to a comfortable room. Something small—and above ground." She glared into the fat man's droopy, bloodshot eyes. "I will tell you what the room is worth once I see it."

"No need to be snotty." The man gestured to a small elevator. Even that small movement sent a wave of terrible body odor. Were they short of water—or soap—in Belial, as well as food?

"We'll go the steps." Tim said quickly. "Which level?"

The man pouted like a toddler who'd lost his sucker. "Thirteenth."

"You'll wanta stay far away from *him*." Tim coached cheerfully as they climbed an endless staircase. "Let's tell him you're the son of a merchant, or maybe a councilor—if he thinks you're important he maybe won't try to rob or rape you."

"Maybe?" Ahna forgot to hide her shock.

He stopped to face her. "How much you know 'bout Temple City? Nevermind. Jus' don't trust nobody. Keep your weapons handy an'... " He rolled his eyes at Ahna's expression. "You came *here* alone an' with *no weapon?*"

"I—I didn't realize..." Maybe she should just go back now. This was getting worse and worse.

"C'mon." He started climbing again. "At least you don't look too rich or too poor an' at least you ain't a girl—you *are* a boy ain't you?" He stared suspiciously at her.

Ahna hesitated, unsure whether to trust him with the truth. "Of course I'm a *boy!* Are *you* a boy?" It wasn't hard to sound extra defensiveness. "I can't help it that I'm not very big."

"Me neither." He said simply. "We'll get your room an' worry 'bout a weapon after. Maybe I should jus' stay with you... " This last part was muttered under his breath as though she might be the biggest idiot he'd come across in awhile.

"Would you?" Ahna smiled brightly at him. "I'd pay you as much as I have. We could say we're brothers or something and you could help me look for my friends and—" They reached the thirteenth level where the sloppy-jowled man waited impatiently.

"Hurry up!" He lumbered down a dirty hallway lined with doors. "How many nights you wantin'?"

"Just two." Ahna replied. Figuring she'd add another night if needed. Hopefully, she'd find Carver long before then.

The fat man leered, his revolting orange tongue flicking, making them squeeze past him through the door into a small room. It had a window, and the bed was big enough for two. "One gold bit a night for this one." He said, holding out a plump hand.

"I am the son of Councilor Drommen from the south and I will pay *one* gold bit for *both* nights." Ahna retorted. "*If* they've been peaceful and no one has molested me!" She narrowed her eyes at him until he turned and left, slamming the door behind him.

"You're learnin' fast!" Tim said admiringly. He was already at the window. "Hey lookit' you kin see the arenas from here! I'm stayin'! Since you don't know nothin' 'bout city center an' all. You need me!"

Ahna slid the heavy bar in place across the door and dumped her pack on the bed. The room was cleaner than the hallway but the carpet had ominous stains. "Clearly I do need you. I need to wash too. And then you can show me where to get a weapon and food."

"Then the arenas?" Tim asked eagerly, scratching at his groin.

"Sure." Ahna tried not to sound so wary. "Then the arenas."

It seemed the only blank space in all of Belial. Air devoid of towers, spires, or walkways, loomed like a giant sphere above Ahna and Tim as they waited to enter an elevator.

Dropping in the closely packed box deep into the earth, Ahna felt anxiety's clench grow tighter and tighter.

The markets had been bad enough. So many people and heavy energy, all permeated with oily food scents and raucous voices. Fresh food cost a lot here but she wasn't about to try any of the garishly colored concoctions offered for less. They smelled nauseating and looked more like toys or decorations than food.

She had bought a triple-edged blade as long as her forearm, and so sharp its sheath was made of a hard-as-stone plastic instead of leather.

It was only as big around as her middle finger and strapped quite neatly to her ribcage under the oversized tunic. On Tim's recommendation, she also bought a hard, fingerless glove with little razors that popped up from the knuckles and a stone roll that was grasped in the palm. Only soldiers could own advanced weapons but the general population had endlessly creative and lethal armaments. Probably the skill to use them too, Ahna thought.

"So many people still, with all the soldiers gone..." She commented. How could they fit more bodies into this mess?

Tim shrugged, scratching his left armpit. "This ain't a lot of people. 'Bout a third is gone right now. It's nice. Here's where you buy our seats."

Ahna shook her head. "We're not here to sit. We're here to ask about my friends, remember?"

"Aww, but we'll get tired. Don't you wanta see the fights none?"

"No. I don't want to see fights." She didn't even know who would be fighting or for what.

"Kin we at least get a mask? I'da brought mine but I did'n know we'd be comin' to the *arena*."

Ahna followed his attention. A cart selling animal masks and parts was right beside them. You could buy ears, trunks, claws, beaks, tails and entire animal heads or faces to wear. They looked alarmingly real.

"No! We're not buying anything!"

He pouted, pointing down a tunnel. "That way."

She felt like an ant, skittering along with a stream of others through winding, dark tunnels. Evening was coming on, but still, the light at the end felt welcoming.

Emerging onto a balcony, she saw the whole of the arena. "How many fit in here?" It was breathtaking, if ominous. An enormous cylinder sunk in the earth, with rows of seats, twenty deep at least, that lined the cylinder's walls.

"'Bout a hunnerd and fi'ty thousand seats. But with the hologram, eight times that many kin watch. We have three other arenas but they're littler. This is where ever'body comes to watch fightin'."

Just below, the arena itself was a circle of green so charming it relieved her anxiety a measure. Looking up, the cylinder towered high, ending in another perfect circle of blue sky. Seeing the second moon glowing, she realized the clouds were clearing. It had been cloudy since they'd left Cathedral. Manufactured clouds to ease the heat.

Tim had explained it all to her earlier in the markets. Here on the southern coast, the sun combined with city power stations and massive numbers of bodies, turning everything sticky hot, even in the middle of winter. Belial weather generators created clouds to block sunlight, but sometimes they became a cap that held the city heat in, so the weather scientists created wind, but then it would blow the clouds away. It was almost impossible to balance, but they tried.

"You better start askin'." Tim advised. "It'll get too noisy once the fights start."

Glancing around at the nearly full seats of this level, Ahna took a deep breath and walked along the front aisle. "I'm looking for my friends named Carver, Drommen and Lister. They're about twenty years. Does anyone know them?" She called as loud as she could, watching faces turn to look at her.

Some shook their heads. Other's just stared with glassy eyes. Many, she couldn't see behind their assortment of animal parts. Someone wore the long neck and head of a giraffe with eye holes cut around the throat area. Scorpion tails were popular as were giant paws with sharpened claws curving from the ends.

She paused to make sure no one was going to respond before moving to the next section, calling out again and again. Often someone would say something rude. "None of your business, less you pay for it." Or, "Wouldn't say if I did!" Or, "Sure, I know 'em. Come sit on my lap sweet boy and I'll say where." These were accompanied by a leer, or rude tongue movements with some garish color of tongue, or even a groping hand.

One fat man opened his shiny silk robes to show off a penis so enlarged, it could've belonged to an auroch in Ireland. Even more shocking, it's tip and the sagging testicles were dyed the same bright blue as his tongue and lips. She'd forgotten about the rumors that most Belials enlarged their sexual organs as a matter of fashion. Apparently, they dyed them as well. Trying not to show disgust—or stare in fascination—she forced her eyes down and hurried in the opposite direction.

Half of the spectators chewed on long, thin strips. The other half smoked things in all manner and shape of pipes, or rolled tubes. The air filled with scents both sweet and acidic.

"I feel like I'm floating." Ahna heard herself giggle as she walked. "Why're their eyes so big?"

"It's the drugs." Tim handed her a grubby rag. "Here, tie this over your mouth an' nose so you don't breath it all in. Your eyes are big too. Ain't you had drugs before?"

Ahna shook her head. "I don't know what you mean." Suddenly she realized she hadn't been asking people about her "friends" anymore. They'd just been floating along, listening to the crowd murmurs get louder as the stadium filled and people got rowdy with inebriation.

"Wafers, powders, chews an' smokes? Makes you feel good and forget all your troubles." Tim picked his nose and contemplated the mass. "You can just be and nothin' matters anymore. Ever'body's addicted to somethin' here."

"I'm looking for Carver, Drommen and Lister. You know them?" Ahna felt bolder now that she'd remembered her mission. She walked right up to groups of people, interrupting their bored chatter. The responses changed.

"Lemme think....heh that feels harder than it should... I don't *think* I do. Think... hahaha tha's a weird word."

"I know three Listers. One's just a baby, one is his father, and the other's his Oldfather. Which one you want?"

"Carver... that sounds sorta familiar. Where have I heard that name?"

Suddenly, spectators began stomping their feet. The wave of movement ran around the cylinder, up and down, until the whole stadium was shaking and deafening.

"It's startin'." Tim shouted in her ear. "We might as well go topside. Nobody'll hear you or care now." He sprinted back into the nearest tunnel, hurrying, only to wait impatiently for the elevator.

Ahna's head began to clear after the long, brisk jog. "Why are we in such a hurry?"

"So we kin at leas' watch the holo. C'mon!" He dragged her into the elevator, empty save for two girls, scantily dressed and wearing more face paint than she'd ever seen. They looked about her own age. One had a shaved head and a see-through shirt showing off nipples as large as her palms. They were yellow, bright as sunflowers.

Seeing Ahna and Tim looking, the girl flipped up her short skirt for a glimpse of a glaring yellow vulva. At least twice the normal size, it was positioned more on the front than between the legs and reached halfway to her belly button. "You boys want suh feel-good?" The voice was both husky and child-like.

Repulsed and averting her eyes, Ahna decided she might as well ask. "I'm looking for some friends. Carver, Drommen and Lister. They're about twenty years and went to Ireland with me. You know anyone of those names?"

The girls turned away, shaking their heads but Ahna persisted. "Carver is tall, with black hair—"

"NO. Don' know no Carver!" One spat.

She was lying. Ahna felt the familiar invisible jolt. Maybe if she paid them for the information. But she was already worried about running out of gold bits now that she knew how much decent food and lodging cost here.

I could influence them. Just a teeny bit. It seemed like the easiest thing in the world. "You *do* know one of the names. Tell me who."

"Yeah, I know a Carver. Dark an' good with a blade?" This from the yellow vulva girl.

Ahna nodded. A surge of excitement shrilled her voice. "Yes! Yes, where is he? I need to find him—it's important."

The girls whispered to each other loud enough for Ahna to hear. "He jus' a boy. If he ain't Carver's friend, the gang'll take care of it. If he is, we doin' Carver a favor." Their black-ringed eyes travelled up and down Ahna's small, baggy form.

"He with the un'erground gang. Call themsel'es Talons."

Ahna looked at Tim. "You know where to find them?"

Tim looked suspicious, but he nodded.

"Thank you so m—" But the girls had stopped the elevator and were already out the door. "Finally! We got something. Let's hurry. Maybe we can find him tonight."

"You believe *them*? They're jus' pleasure girls! Prob'ly lied to shut you up. S'prised they even talked to you at all. We ain't goin' to find no gang at night. That's asking for killin'! Better to go in the mornin'."

"What are pleasure girls?"

Tim looked incredulous. "Don't you know nothin'?! They do whatever anybody wants. Sex and stuff."

Topside, they stood looking down at the circle arena. "Opening ceremonies are real pretty ever' time I been here." Tim said, and Ahna wondered if he'd ever seen something that was actually beautiful.

The arena circle was no longer green. Now it was a picture of a mediocre sunset. "Wasn't that grass there before?" Ahna asked.

"A'course! Only the best for our central arena. Grass is rare here—you prob'ly don' know that. The arena grass grows thicker and greener than even Dominus Mardu's gardens. It's all the blood they say. Fed and watered by the blood of a thousan' creatures."

Pictures of conrectus started appearing where the sunset had been. Each one stayed for a few seconds and the crowd either cheered or hissed. But these were not the simple, cow-like conrectus that helped to work their farms and orchards in Atlantis. These were creatures she never knew existed. A snake with a human head and arms that ended in crab-like pincers filled the air with wild cheering. A giant sloth with a scorpion's tail drew bored hisses. What looked like a shaved gorilla with huge, female breasts and a mouth full of fangs got mixed reactions.

"How are they doing the pictures?" From this height Ahna couldn't make out how the images morphed from one to another.

"Arena rats. Childrens that work here, keepin' the Things fed, and dead hauled out and new fighters ready. The rats sell stuff an' clean the arena after fights. They have colored cards that together make a picture. 'Bout five hunnerd of 'em down there, holdin' up cards in order. See, they only do the fighter pictures for a grand match. That means the winners of lotsa fights get to fight each other. It happens once a moon so you're lucky to get to watch it! I told you we shoulda got seats!"

A dark blue rhinoceros head on a thick, elongated neck, topping a sea lion body drew hisses, but now cheers and pounding boomed up at a snarling wolf head on a bird with huge wings.

"They'll close the holo soon. C'mon. Let's go back to our room so's we kin watch."

Ahna's belly was churning and she felt nauseous. She needed to get whatever she'd inhaled out of her system.

Grinding sounded as they walked towards the tall spires of the Cathedral and she looked back to see two crystal half circles coming together over the arena pit. "What's that?"

"The holo. I tol' you, it projects ever'thing from the arena up so ever'body kin watch the fights. The fighters are a hunnerd feet tall in the holo so you get to see more. But it ain't as fun as what happens in the arena." His face went back to a pout.

Ahna was relieved to see no leering, jowly man guarding the Cathedral's entrance when they returned. "He's probly at the arena." Tim explained. "Lucky for us."

She lay down on the too-soft bed which smelt of raw potato and sweat, holding her palms over her roiling stomach to send healing energy.

Tim hung out their opened window, laughing and cheering at what he called the "showcasing". Apparently, each of the main fighters was paired with a "throwaway Thing" to show off their killing abilities. A sort of warm-up before they faced each other.

The holo image was indeed huge and she caught a glimpse of the naked gorilla with breasts, picking up a creature that had an oversized ram head with big curling horns, on the body of a kangaroo. The gorilla gripped a horn and the thick, long tail, suspending the terrified creature overhead for a moment while the crowd's frenzy grew, before bending it backwards to break its spine. Sinking oversized fangs into the ram face, the gorilla bit off the tender white snout and spit it towards the stands. Blood dripped and ran everywhere but it wasn't done. It ripped the fine, long tail off and swung it around, flinging blood in great arcs, charging towards the stands where people rushed and trampled each other in their frenzy to get away. But then it fell abruptly, clutching its ears, mouth wide in a soundless scream.

Ahna gasped, horrified and shocked. "What happened? How did they stop it from attacking the people?"

Tim poked his head back in from the window, a grin spread wide on his face. "Did you see that? That Thing's strong! The arena's lined with sound lasers. They kin stop or kill any of the monsters. Still, I wouldn' sit on the lower levels. I hearda some they couldn' stop."

The nausea increased and she rolled over so she wouldn't see the horrors going on outside. How could they all watch this? And every day—multiple times a day even?"

She turned her thoughts back to finding Carver. When she'd heard that Belial was going to attack Greece, she'd felt such an urgency. Like this might be the last chance before visits became impossible between their countries. Or before war broke out. He might even be gone with the soldiers. The thought hadn't occurred to her until Tim said at least a third of Belial was gone.

But she was already here and she was going to look for him every moment she could. And now they at least had a place to start.

She sat up to pull the little eggplant-colored journal from her pack. It opened automatically to the pages he'd written to her. So often she'd read his words, immersing herself in memories: the feel of his lips on hers, the yearning in his ice blue eyes, his perfect hands strumming the dulcimer, coaxing notes from it as haunting and gentle as rain.

After they parted, she'd hoped her love would fade. Convinced herself that it would, as every bit of energy got sucked up grieving her parent's death—and then invested in her secret training.

Becoming Ziel's Keeper of the Crystals was the perfect distraction, but it had only distracted her mind. Her heart stubbornly held onto Carver. Her love hadn't diminished at all. If anything, it had increased, becoming a longing that ached all day and burned all night.

Exhausted from her long, strange day, she dozed in dots and dashes, head on her pack, weapons still strapped to her body, unsure whether to trust even Tim.

Soon as the killing games were finished, he flopped into bed beside her and started snoring.

Turning in the dark room, meaning to watch him in case he did anything suspicious, her eyes followed the gigantic hologram still beaming into the sky outside. The image was a battlefield of fallen bodies and animal parts. Several creatures still writhed or tried to drag themselves over blood-slick grass. Uniformed children and teenagers appeared, cautiously approached each body, and fired a laser gun at the heart. A thin beam flashed and then the body would go limp.

AHNA WOKE FEELING GRITTY, achy and exhausted. Hurrying across the hall to the bathhouse to pee, she stripped and stood under lukewarm water for a long time. Finally, she could let tears come. The guilt at her lies, the ugliness and despair of this place, frustration at how hard this was turning out to be, all demanded to be felt, before they could be washed away.

Finding Carver would redeem it all. Wouldn't it? Just to talk to him, look into his face, feel that connection again. All this would be worth it.

"Why was you in the *girl's* bathhouse?" Tim was waiting outside their room, arms crossed, when she returned.

"Was I? Stupid of me. I didn't know—good thing there weren't any other girls in there! Let's get going. We can eat on our way to wherever the Talons are."

Tim frowned. "The gangs'r dangerous. They stay underground. I *hate* the un'erground. I kin show you where to go but I ain't goin'."

There was no way she'd make it without him—especially if the underground was worse than what she'd seen so far.

"What if I give you everything I have, including my weapons when I leave? Will you go then?"

"Depen's how much you got. Why you wanta find these friends so bad anyways?" He followed Ahna back into their room and she dropped the heavy bar into place across the hardwood door.

Should she trust him? It seemed like too much effort to make up a believable lie. The longer she spent with him, the more childish he seemed. This was all a grand adventure to him, not to mention, very profitable.

"My name is Ahna, not Erin. I'm a girl—"

"I knew it! I knew you was a girl. You *act* like a girl!"

"Yes, well I'm sorry I lied to you. I'm looking for someone I love very much and this might be the last chance I have to find him. I have to try. Have you ever loved someone like that?"

Tim stared at her a moment, his eyes turning puppy-like. "I think so. She lived in Bordertown awhile. I taught 'er how to fly my aero an' we had the most fun jus' talkin' and she kissed me once." He was gazing out the window now, his mind somewhere else.

"What happened?" Ahna asked softly, feeling his longing.

"She said I weren't rich enough an' they moved back here." He shrugged. "That was after I told her I loved her. So I'm gonna get rich enough and go find her."

"I'm sorry. I hope you get to be with her again." She touched his bony shoulder, just starting its metamorphosis into a man's body. "Since you understand, will you help me?"

Tim's brown eyes turned wise. "Maybe... does he love you back? 'Cuz if he don't, the gang might do anythin' they want to us."

Ahna smiled. "Oh he loves me back alright." She sobered. "But perhaps you should tell me about the gangs and the underground. What are they? What do they do? Why are they underground?"

" 'Cuz ever'body up here ignores ever'body down there. We pretend it don't exist. An' the ones who live down there—ain't nobody want 'em. Some Things escape before they're sold to the arenas an' that's where they go too. It's like the garbage dump for ever'thing Belial don't want."

"If it's such a problem, why doesn't Belial just destroy it all?"

" 'Cuz all the drugs come from down there."

"Ah, I see." She began to make sense of it. "And up here, every-body's addicted to something."

"Yep."

The thought of Carver living in such a hell, or manufacturing poisonous things, wrenched at her. She pushed it away, along with the doubts that flew in from all sides. Surely he wouldn't participate in something so dark. But if he didn't, that meant she would not find him down there, and this was the only lead she had.

AN ENTRANCE to the underground forked from the hollow roots of Cathedral.

This information cost the last of Ahna's berries and mangos to an old, bent woman with furtive eyes who cleaned rooms in Cathedral. She confirmed Tim's suspicions that they wouldn't have to go far to find a way in.

"Bring all your weapons an' leave your pack." He instructed, before they left their room.

"No. What if it's stolen?"

He shrugged. "If we hide it good, prob'ly be fine. If you take it—stolen for sure."

Ahna loaded grain bars and the rest of her gold bits into the pockets of her clothing, tucking her crystal communique underneath her left breast. If things went too awry, it would be her link to home.

The elevator only went a few levels below ground where doors still lined plastered halls. Stairways got increasingly narrow and steep the lower they went, each level seeming dimmer than the one before.

Finally, they reached a basement where the walls were no longer plastered to cover raw stone and mortar. Instead of halls, tunnels led between rooms with low ceilings. Bunks niched in the walls, stacked so close together it made Ahna claustrophobic just to think of sleeping so enclosed. She was thankful to find them empty, save for heavy spirits and dank thought forms abandoned in the black boxes and corners.

Tim stopped by a light sphere, rapidly losing its glow. He squinted at the maplines crudely drawn on his inner forearm from the old woman's instructions. "This way I think….'spose to be another tunnel somewheres aroun' here… "

It had been boarded off. Repeatedly, judging by the broken boards that littered both sides. Ahna stumbled as they picked their way through.

"Shoulda' brought a light." Tim muttered, squeezing through spaces in the boards.

Ahna's baggy clothes snagged on splintered board ends like harsh fingers grabbing. Her eyes had adjusted to seeing in the shadows, but on the other side of the grasping boards no light shone ahead.

"This's a terribler and terribler idea." Tim heaved a sigh and went back to wrench the dimming light sphere from its sconce. The sconce looked like a wire cage and he yanked to pull the whole thing off the wall. It didn't budge. He worked at the cage for several moments and Ahna was just crawling back through to help him when he bent wires far enough apart to pull the sphere out. Holding it on one palm, he led the way into a black unknown.

A stench soon hit them. Sewage mostly, leaving a taste of rot on the back of their tongues. "Ugh!" Tim pulled his shirt up to cover his mouth and nose.

Ahna did the same. It helped very little.

Sounds filtered to them. Things being struck against each other. Shouts. Motors revving, then dying down again. Ahna wrapped her free hand around the knife handle, wishing suddenly for a vision of what lay ahead. Usually they came, distracting and unasked for, and she ignored them. Now, she would welcome even a hint of the immediate future.

She took it as a good sign though. Oracle training had taught her a bit more about visions. They had to do with diversions in energy streams. Each lifetime is a stream in time and space, with thousands of possible diversions like little currents that join and leave it. When a diversion is strong enough in relation to the stream, it registers on the screen of those with the frequency of precognition. Even though many events Ahna saw seemed mundane or tiny, they represented a major energetic change in the lifestream. Because it is human nature to give more attention to negative energies—in attempt to avoid them—there is simply more energy build-up around events that cause negative reactions, such as death, disaster or violence. Therefore, the visions often portrayed harmful scenes.

She smacked into Tim's skinny back when he stopped short. The sounds had broadened into a jumble of noise.

"There's light ahead." His voice held fear.

She slipped by him to keep going. It was true. Enough light shown now to see the crumbling earth clods they walked on, the uneven tunnel ceiling and walls that seemed to contract or expand abruptly and at will.

They both stopped when they saw a circle of dimly lit space just ahead.

"Turn off the sphere and leave it here in case we come back this way." Ahna said, creeping towards the edge. Her breath caught as she glimpsed the height and breadth of the underground.

She'd been expecting labyrinthian tunnels and mole rooms. Something similar to the the Crystal's maze perhaps. What she saw was an enormous space, many levels high, with walkways and ladders and entrances to even more areas. Massive square pillars made of metal and stone, lined up symmetrically, supporting the underground structure. Equipment and machines filled much of the ground just below them and people were operating them, working on them, repairing walkways or ladders across the way. She couldn't see very well. There was some light source, but its effect was rather like a very bright moonlit night. She saw headlamps winking from workers and realized their shapes and sizes seemed odd.

"Lot more Things down here than I thought." Tim murmured, nervous beside her.

"Those are all conrectus?" Once her brain knew what to interpret, she could indeed make out nonhuman shapes.

"Not all, just more'n I thought. We goin' down or what? Prob'ly should jus' go back... "

She knelt in the gloom to peer at a rickety ladder that stretched from the tunnel opening to a ground about twenty feet below. What she could see of it was missing more rungs than it had. Turning around to swing one foot down, she felt for a toehold. "Hold onto my hand. The first rung is too far..."

Tim knelt and let his shirt drop from his face. "Ugh! Stinks bad!"

She held his hands with both of hers. He was smaller and skinnier than her but a better anchor than nothing.

Tentatively, her other leg dropped, searching over the edge. She scooched down an inch at a time. Something caught her right toe and she brought her feet together on the rung, lowering her weight, hanging onto Tim until she found a lower one and clutched onto the first.

Tim slid, feet scrabbling, between the gap.

Ahna was not quite halfway down, attention diverted, dirt peppering from above when the rung broke beneath his feet. He slid into her with a thin squeak.

Clenching tight with one hand, she tried to catch him with the other. Tried to swing out of the way so he had a place to land. Missing on both counts. He was falling too fast and their strength was too little.

He ended on the ground below in a heap and she scurried down the rest of the way.

"My leg…" he stopped to breathe in sharply, exhaling a whimper, "… hurts! Mus' be broke." He sat hunched forward, upper body rocking, hands around his right knee.

Then a headlamp was shining in their eyes.

"Who. you." The tone sounded like a cow's moo, though each word was enunciated very precisely. The face of a musk ox bent close to peer at them. It walked on cloven hooves and had long hair covering its body, but it had arms, hands and speech.

"We… we're from up there… looking for someone. They said he'd be here… I-I just need to find him… we came from Cathedral and now Tim fell. His leg might be broken, we need help, can you help us?" She heard herself babbling. Struggled to stop.

The ox blinked at them, expressionless. "Come." It straightened.

"Can you walk?" Ahna tugged at Tim, helping him stand. He cringed and she could see tears from the pain of it.

"Come." The ox repeated. It seemed to tower above them. Its size and expressionlessness suddenly terrifying.

"Yes, we're trying! He's in too much pain, I don't know if he can walk."

"Come." This time louder. It gathered both their arms in one huge, leathery hand and turned, dragging them along.

Tim cried out.

"Stop! You're hurting him!" Ahna wrenched this way and that, trying to get free, but the Thing kept going, dragging them along like rag dolls. Tim screamed when he tried to hobble, and choked, losing his footing entirely. She thought maybe he'd lost consciousness the way he went limp.

"I said STOP!" She kicked at its bony legs and punched the bit of backside she could reach. It hurt her fist. "You must carry him! Stop!"

It did. Blinking back at them, not letting go of Ahna's arm, it picked Tim up by his shirt and slung him over its beefy, sloping shoulder. Then set off again.

Tim whimpered, but it had to be better than being drug.

They passed close to an enormous machine with a thousand moving parts. The grinding and squeaking was deafening. Other Things worked around it, putting substances in one part, removing what looked like broken glass from another. Many of them looked human except for stray animal parts. One man was covered in scales. Another had a long reptilian tail. Several had heads that resembled an eagle or a snake. A hundred questions formed and she wished there was someone to ask. What had all these been made for and how did they end up down here and what were they doing?

Her hand was going numb from the ox' grip pulling her. She tried to notice everything, especially the way they were going. A concrete ceiling was not far overhead, now that they'd crossed the huge expanse where the machine was.

They went up ramps and walkways and stairs, slick and wet and stinky. She felt almost glad for the iron grip that kept her upright.

Tim was wide awake now. She could see his face when they passed near rooms where brighter light shone out. There were piles of what appeared to be garbage everywhere and the stench was overwhelming. She used her free hand to pull her shirt back over her nose and mouth.

Mostly, the structures were concrete, and all of it looked wet. Slime ran down some of the walls and her sandaled feet squished through puddles.

Up, up and up they went until they were on the topmost level that looked over the expanse. The ox pounded on a shabby door made of thin metal, then pushed inside.

Ahna blinked. Perhaps forty people were scattered in here. Some of them were eating, many merely lounged, inhaling from tubes or bulbous pipes. The air was smoky but this acidic smell was a whole lot better than the sewer stink. Tattered couches and cushions lined much of the wall space and she saw a girl in the corner using a cooking box.

The ox just stood there, waiting for someone to acknowledge them. Several glanced their way, but kept doing whatever they had been.

Ahna grew impatient. "I'm looking for Carver." She called out. Does anyone know where he is?"

An old woman came over then. Her face, harshly wrinkled, loomed over a thin body that looked strong. Like a slow wave, others in the room stopped their conversations, eating and smoking. Several came to stand behind the woman.

"What's that you say? Who're you *boy* and whatchoo want wit' Carver?"

The ox hadn't relaxed its grip at all. Tim was wriggling, trying to see, even though his head hung down the creature's long-haired back.

"I'm Erin—just a traveler. Come to find my friends. Carver, Drommen and Lister are their names. I was told Carver might be here."

"Jus' a traveler. Huh. Wha's wrong with that one?"

"He fell on our way down. His leg may be broken. We'll need a healing temple."

"Huh." She chewed on something, baggy eyes roamed over Ahna taking in every detail.

The others wore mismatched clothing. All of them had knives of every size and shape, many had electric weapons or barbed clubs. They all bore scars too. There were missing ears, mangled noses, empty eye sockets. Hostility steamed from them and Ahna's skin prickled as danger seemed to come alive like a beast waking from hibernation.

"Wake him." The woman snapped at a man whose upper lip was

twisted into his nostrils. She stepped forward and grabbed Ahna's biceps. Running hard hands quickly down her arms, then around her waist, squeezing up to her armpits.

"Huh." The woman reached under Ahna's tunic and wrenched out the blades in a blur of motion, before continuing down from her hips.

The long, triple-edged blade came out next and the old lady almost smiled. "Huh. Very pretty that. Not as pretty as you though *boy.*" Her hand slapped hard between Ahna's legs and squeezed.

Ahna yiped like a pup, trying to step away but the ox still had her wrist in its deadening grip.

The old woman pushed close to Ahna's face, still pressing her sex. Close enough for Ahna to see the coldness beneath all the baggy layers of skin. She blew towards Ahna's mouth and it smelled like sour milk, laced with chemicals.

"You come armed and lyin', huh. Tell me true, who are you and what's your mission?"

"I-I-I'm a girl, yes, but it was safer to not be. The rest I said is true and the weapons are n-normal here are they not?" She stuttered to show submission and fear, her mind and senses working overtime. What was the best course here? What if it wasn't her Carver?" She pushed thoughts into the woman's mind. *Girl is safe. Treat her well.*

The woman raised her hand from Ahna's crotch and slapped her. Hard. "Stop it." Her chest heaved with sudden fury and she slapped Ahna again. "So you're mind player too. Huh!" She looked at the ox. "Put 'em in a slave cell. A empty one. Let her speak to no one else."

But the crowd behind the old woman had parted as a tall man with dark brown skin strode towards her. Three more men came with him and they all looked like warriors compared to this rabble. Dressed in thin leather armor, they wore weapons—probably laser or sound. Ahna wasn't familiar with what Belials weapons looked like.

"You wake and summon me down here... for what?" The man seemed quiet in an ominous way. Large, black freckles dotted the sides of his face and he might have been handsome but for symbols branded under each eye, glowing pale and deep in twisted flesh. One was a snake circling back on itself to swallow its own tail, the other a snake with a second head where its tail should be.

"She seeks you." The old woman said simply, stepping aside so that the space between Ahna and this stranger was free.

He eyed her up and down, his black eyes either bored or confused.

"You-you're…" she gulped as fear nauseated her stomach. Her last brittle strand of hope snapped. "Is your name Carver?" It came out a breathy squeak.

He frowned at her. "Who are you?" Then he stepped closer and his voice dropped to a growl. "Who sent you?"

She desperately fought back tears. "You're not the Carver I was looking for. I'm sorry, I've made a mistake. I'll go home and never bother you again."

He ran his eyes over her but turned to the woman, who nodded at him curtly.

"I'll take care of it. Thought to check her story first. Jus' in case."

"I'm entertaining tonight. Bring her with the other pleasure girls." He turned to go, paying her no more attention.

"She a mind player." The old woman called after him.

He glanced back. "Some product should take care of that. Might be we'll find out something interesting."

The crowd of rabble closed a circle around her, and the old woman grinned. Three teeth were missing, the rest were various shades of gray.

"Welcome to the Talons. No more mind games for you birdie—jus' body games with your little boy body, huh… oh don't look so frightened. It's all the drugs you want here. You come to enjoy it." She felt for Ahna's nipple and pinched. "Lucky—bein' a girl and pretty. Else you be making powder an' glass like the res'."

Shoving her towards the ox, she ordered, "Take 'em to a cell. Fetch the healer for that'un. He young enough to give us years of work."

"You unnerstand—we're slaves now." Tim muttered despairingly, soon as the ox shut the gate to their cell. "Nobody knows where we are. Nobody ever will neither. I *tol'* you we shouldn' come! Once you disappear down here…" His voice trailed off into tears.

"Shhh. It's going to be alright Tim." Ahna moved to his side in the dark. It wasn't pitch black, but she couldn't really see either. She felt for his shoulders and put her arms around them. He was shaking from pain and fear. She felt it like a barbed, suffocating blanket. Pulling his head to her shoulder, she held him, rubbing soothing circles on his back until the tiny sobs stopped. Whispering in his ear, Ahna spoke hope.

"I've my communique still. I can contact my sister and they'll come for us."

THE NEVERENDING NIGHT

"My task is set before me, girl. My mission clear and true. There'll be black knights and dragons, girl. But I will always come for you..."

— EMME ROLLINS

AIELA

*A*iela's comm vibrated against her leg. It would have to wait. She turned her attention back to the small council, to Ruler Kenna's long diatribe of concerns about Belial's attack on Greece.

It vibrated again. And again. And again. Exasperated, she reached to shut it off.

Help! Need you!

A picture formed; Ahna with a chain around her wrist, sitting in a bleak cell that she couldn't see. But that wasn't true. Ahna was at Squirrel's Nest in Old Forest studying some abstract Oracle thing.

Help. Need you!

Was this some kind of trick? Part of their training? Maybe Ziel had figured out a way to access their mind-to-mind communications.

The comm vibrated again and Aiela pushed back from the council table so hard it displaced the table with a resounding screech. "Relieve bladder." She mumbled to no one in particular, interrupting Ruler Kenna, who had stopped speaking to frown at her.

"It can't wait?"

The others were trying to right the table, its clawed, silver feet shrieking against marble tiles as too many tried to straighten it at once.

Aiela shook her head on her way out the door, already holding the comm to her jaw.

"Ahna? What's wrong?"

"El! I'm in trouble... city... underground..." Broken whispers. She could make out few words. "What? I can't hear you."

At the other end, Ahna hissed loudly "Tim, go... gate... watch for lights."

"Who is Tim? Who are you with and where—?"

"Listen!" She pushed her energy out like a raised voice, speaking quickly.

"I'm in the underground beneath Temple City. The Talons have taken me and Tim as slaves—they make drugs—I need you to come get us. Do not come alone. Bring weapons and plenty of fresh food: meat, vegetables, fruit. And gold bits. It's bad here..." And then in answer to the unvoiced question. "I didn't find Carver."

Aiela sighed, hearing tears edge her sister's voice.

"I just... had to try. One last time... you know? Before all hell breaks loose."

"Are you safe until we get there? It'll be hours." She didn't actually know how long it took to the border, much less to Temple City.

"I don't know. Probably. Just come as soon as you can. Please don't tell Ziel?"

Aiela snorted. "How am I supposed to do that? Bring protectors and weapons, use an aero, get money but without Ziel's help? It'll all go much faster if—"

"Please? I can't bear his disappointment. I lied to everybody, forged his seal. Please, can you just try to figure it out without him knowing?"

193

"The Talons you said? In the underground?"

"Yes. We're in some sort of cell. It's too dark to see anything and we came in underneath Cathedral but I wouldn't recommend that way if you can find another. The Belial soldiers are all gone but it's still rough here. Worse than we know. Poor and ugly and cruel. They'll do anything for money... or food." Ahna paused, no doubt registering the anger Aiela was feeling.

How could she go and do something so reckless and stupid? On the verge of a possible war—the first one in their lifetime. Didn't she understand this was what they'd been training for? How important they were in protecting Atlantis? Aiela tried to block her own thoughts.

"I'm sorry El. I know how bad an idea this was and I hate to put you at risk for—"

"We can talk about it when I get you." The anger clenched as she digested her twin's complicity and the danger she was in. "Just make sure you don't lose your comm. I'm coming." She snapped off the audio and flew to her room, her mind racing ahead. She'd have to get an aero and money. Turner could be in charge of weapons but she needed to find him first...

"She left when?" Turner gripped the sides of his seat.

Aiela hadn't earned a license yet, had only flown a handful of times before. It showed in their lurching, wavering take off. "I told you—I don't know! I haven't seen her since Firstday morning. It could've been that night—or anytime since." She tried to temper her words. Tried not to sound so annoyed at every question Turner was asking. If he'd just shut up for two minutes and let her concentrate on getting them in the air and away from High City...

She'd practically stolen this aero from the lot. Flashed a forged letter and stolen license (if Ahna could do it, so could she) and demanded a black one, on Turner's advice.

"How many gold bits did ya get?"

"I don't know! A lot. My entire account and some from Ziel's—which I technically stole. Can we *not talk* now?" They'd hit a band of gusting winds and she struggled to keep them level. Plus, the sun was getting low, blinding her.

Instead of silence, his voice changed, like when they were in Ireland and he was calming the teachers after the bloody Islander's attack.

"It'll be fine Love. Yer doing so well an' I can hardly b'lieve it—look at ya—you can fly!" He chuckled low and easy. "I can sail and you can fly. Between the two o' us, there's nothin' we canna manage. Sure an' it makes me admire ya more, watching ya take us inta the air…" It was magical how he could soothe her. He talked slowly about nothing that mattered, building up her confidence, reassuring and solid.

Finally, they were above the turbulence, high enough to set their course and let autopilot take over. She turned to him then, and quietly wrapped her arms around his solid shoulders. "Thank you. I'm sorry. It's not you I'm angry at, it's my sister. I can't believe she did this! She's supposed to be the smart, logical one. I don't even know how to react. I've never been so angry at her and—"

"Yer scairt for her. Anger's just the armor. A way ta be… em, brave about it."

She considered this.

"Can I ask some questions now withoot ya snappin' at me?" His eyes held amusement, but also concern. She nodded.

"Why did she go *there*… was it Carver?"

"Yes. There wasn't time to find out more, she just said she hadn't found him… and she was sad about it."

Turner stayed quiet then, gazing out the window. She couldn't see his face.

Studying the instrument panels for awhile, she eventually glanced back at the bags he'd lugged aboard. "You had no problem getting the weapons?"

"They were righ' where ya said. Grabbed everythin' I could carry, tho' I've no idea how ta use them." His words came short, ringed in frustration. No—more like deep in thought.

She tried to let him be but her thoughts went in circles, all that she didn't know making her more and more anxious. "How are we going to get her back Turner? We don't have a plan and I don't know enough about Belial. I don't even know where to start or who to ask—"

"I do." Turner looked at her then, angling his body to fully face her, his expression deadly serious. "There's somethin' I want ta tell ya. Somethin' aboot Carver that ya don't know—because he asked me ta keep his secrets... " He stopped, gauging her reaction.

Aiela kept quiet, careful of what showed on her face.

"I promised him that I wouldna tell ya but now it seems important that ya know." He inhaled, then exhaled sharply. "It doesn't seem the right thin' ta break a promise..."

She realized he was arguing with himself.

"... yet we may have need o' Carver ta get Ahna oot and... I know where ta find him."

Her eyebrows rose before she could stop them. "Where?"

"The thing is, ya canna tell Ahna. If she knows—"

"She'll go to him. Yes, clearly! But I don't see the harm—"

"I'll need yer trust. There's more harm than ya know. Before I tell ya, could ya jus' promise me ya won't let on ta Ahna? Can ya even do that wi' all yer mind sharin' going on?"

Defensiveness reared. "You want me to make a vow based on *your* judgement about *my* sister? How about you trust *my* judgement!? I would never risk Ahna. I have the right to determine what might harm her. No I won't make that vow! Keep your damn secrets from me if—"

He laid a gentle hand on her leg, leaning closer. His eyes were steady and clear. His absolute calm was like water to her fire. His touch cut off her tirade. "Carver is the son of Mardu."

Turbulence whipped up inside, greater than any they'd just flown through. "Dominus Mardu? Belial's *leader?*"

Turner nodded. "Yes. But Carver holds no love fer him. Says his father would use anybody he cares fer as, em... leverage. Carver's as good as a prisoner ta his own family. They *canna* learn about Ahna... and you."

"So... if Ahna were to know... to go there—"

Turner was nodding, watching her mind catch up. "Carver would either reject her outright—try ta convince his people he cares noothin' fer her—"

"Or Mardu would use her... to keep Carver in line." Aiela finished. She'd heard plenty of brutal tales about Mardu. Especially in High City where the folly and abominations of Belial were whispered like evil ghost tales in the night.

Aiela took a deep and heavy breath. Truth sank in. "We can't tell her. Ever. She obviously doesn't care about the dangers." She wondered if she was even capable of keeping such a secret from her twin. The one who'd shared emotions, thoughts, every nuance of experience since the day they'd been born.

An insistent hum began from the instrument panels. "We're coming up on the border. We have to set down here. Our aeros are programmed not to cross into Belial."

"So, you wanna pay me *five* gold bits to use my aero for less'n a day?" A gnarled hand spread its five fingers wide to make sure they were both talking about the same number. "An' I don' even hafta pilot for you?" The beady-eyed woman seemed suspicious. Or disbelieving that such good fortune could be happening.

Night came early during the winter moons, and there were only a handful of pilots willing to ferry people from the bordertown to Temple City, instead of sitting down to suppers and going early to beds. Fewer people watching in the night served Aiela's purposes perfectly.

She nodded. "Yes, I *like* to pilot, see and it's just a quick errand." She fervently hoped it was going to be quick. "I know you're not supposed to, so I'm willing to pay extra, just to say I've flown in *Belial*." Leaning closer, she smiled conspiratorially. "You know, bragging rights and all."

The beady eyes didn't blink. "Whatsa errand?"

She thought fast. Decided to make it juicy and shameful. "See, my sister likes drugs. This isn't the first time we've had to come fetch her. This time she's with the Talons and I don't know if she'll even come back with us. She's older—doesn't ever listen to me. But I have to try. My parents are willing to spend everything to get her back and keep our family, our neighbors and village from knowing about it."

She put on a shamed expression. "It's very... *looked down upon* for us in Atlantis you know. She will lose her apprentice if they find out, may even be *punished...*" her tone took on desperation. "I'm sorry I didn't tell you the whole truth before. Look, maybe it'd be better for you to pilot us—"

The woman was shaking her head, backing away before her night and day of highly-paid leisure was snatched back. "You go on. I always felt sorry for you's with the rules and the high-handed morals. Seems to me a person should do what they want."

Aiela was already holding the gold bits out. "Thank you for understanding. Really. You don't know how much you're helping us. My... brother—he's getting our bags—will be so thankful too." She dropped them one by one into the woman's palm, with five little tinks. "I'll bring it back soon as we've found her. Shouldn't be more than a day."

The woman nodded, poking at the warmed golden clots in her hand, a smug smile hovering. "Make sure you keep it locked. Thieves all over Temple City." She walked away, then turned back. "Hey. Girlie. Happens I gotta old sister too. She a boss with the Talons. You go to the God's Temple an' ask for Drinara an' you tell her Rhena let you use her aero to fetch your sister back. You'll need to pay her better'n you did me even. But she'll help you. For me—an' for gold."

"Thank you Rhena. I owe you a kindness."

The woman snorted. "You done bought a day's worth of aero for the price of a *moon*. The kindness is free."

Soon as the woman disappeared inside her stone and plaster cottage, Turner appeared by the aero. He carried both bags, small, but heavy with weapons and a considerable amount of gold bits, along with all the meat and winter fruits Aiela could haul from the kitchens without raising suspicion. She opened the door, helped him clip in the bags.

"This is much older than ours." Climbing into the pilot chair, she studied the levers and knobs as he clipped himself into a seat. "I'll have to figure out how it works." Pushing a few wrong buttons and flipping switches to see what happened, they finally rose, wavering, into black air. "The pilot woman told me where to go and who to ask for." Aiela recounted her conversation with Rhena.

"What *would* they do if Ahna—or any Atlantean—were addicted ta drugs?" Turner asked, full of curiosity.

She shrugged. "Probably just put her in the Aades of Sacrifice. Addictions come from physical, emotional or mental imbalances. They just need healing."

"Why are we bringin' food? They don't have enough here?" Already the ground ahead was lighting up brighter and brighter. The map indicated they would pass over Midtown and three others too, but the spaces between towns had filled and all of Belial was now one huge, unending city.

"Ruler Kenna says we send plenty to feed the Belials, but the rich ones take all the best and waste too much. The 'problem of uneven distribution' we call it. They have levels to their society, and the lower levels—slaves and such—live mostly off the waste of the upper. Kenna says they make a powder from the throwaway food, the garbage. The powder can be reconstituted and at least keeps lower citizens from starving—most of them." Aiela couldn't quite imagine it. It was all just stories to her.

"I think we're here." Turner interrupted her thoughts, staring below at Temple City, lit up bright as day. Smog hung in layers on top of the city, but the city lights turned it into a colorful haze.

They were way too high and it was a good thing. Aeros whizzed back and forth in the vast colorful cloud, dodging each other at dizzying speeds, diving to land or shooting back up in vertical take-offs from bridges or platforms strung between towers, pyramid peaks and spires. Ramps and walkways wove a web connecting everything and her heart dropped.

How was she ever going to land them in this mess? Her skills were new, her courage fraying, and this aero was on the backside of ancient.

"Hold on." She spoke shortly. "With any luck, we won't die trying to rescue my lovesick sister from this insane place." She'd already begun their dive.

"Sure an' I've been wondering something... " Turner was watching her. Seemed unconcerned with the fact they were falling, pointed straight down. They narrowly missed two building tops, grazing a walkway which threw them into the path of other aeros—which careened expertly away from her clumsy spin. "Would ya've done the same fer me?"

She knew what he was asking. Would you have abandoned reason and rules like Ahna did, would you have lied and stolen, would you have risked your own safety, to come find me?

She leveled them out at the last minute but they still landed rough. Hard enough to bounce twice, making her bite her tongue.

Tasting blood, she gave Turner a triumphant grin. "I'd chase you around the whole world if I had to. Only I wouldn't have waited so long. C'mon, I'll show you how to use our laser wands and sound guns, then onwards! To this 'Gods Temple'... wherever that is."

He took her face and kissed her desperately. As though it was the first time—or maybe the last. "Yer a right bonny hero and I'm glad ta not be deid from landin', and truthfully? Ya scare me."

She climbed into the back of the aero, unbuckled the heavy bags, and laid out five weapons. An unremarkable, grey hard plastic covered metal and crystal mechanics inside. "These are illegal in Belial unless you're military or judges—so we'll need to conceal them."

She opened the aero door, letting in air so moist it felt like the wet sauna in the bathhouses, except this air stank of garbage and burnt chemicals and sour bodies. She wrinkled her nose. "I wish there was a place where you could practice using these." It hadn't ever occurred to her that he might need some of the same training she and Ahna were getting. "When we get back, I'm going to teach you everything I know. You should learn to handle an aero, practice with our weapons, learn defenses against them, study the layout of our country... "

But Turner wasn't listening. He'd climbed out to watch a few people race towards the moving ladder that dropped off the landing bridge. People ran as though *from* something. "I think we should mabbe be gettin' down."

Aiela had barely registering they were the only ones left up here, when a blast of air knocked her backwards. Moist wind slammed against her so hard it pinned her to the aero wall inside. The weapons skittered across the floor and she worried the aero itself might lift up and blow away.

"Turner!" She couldn't see him. "Turner!" The winds stole her scream before it even reached the aero door. He was out there in this. Air was pulsing now, gusts heaving one upon the other.

She pushed away from the wall, using the seats to pull herself towards the open door. It was hard to look up with the wind pushing into her eyes. Then she saw his fingers wrap around the door's edge and he slid slowly into view. Just the edge of him at first, then he carefully wrapped his body around and inside.

Once she'd closed the door they sat staring across at each other. Turner spoke first. "No natural storm blows like this."

She shook her head. "It has to be their weather generators. But how they can do this— *why* they would do this, I've no idea."

"I wonder how long it might go on?"

IT DIDN'T LAST LONG. Enough time to eat a bit, slow her heart rate from the fearsome landing, and calm her energy for whatever lay ahead.

They were halfway down the moving ladder, tunic pockets saggy with gold bits, food and weapons in packs on their backs, before she noticed the air didn't stink anymore. It smelled of food cooking and underneath that, the sea.

At the bottom of the moving ladder, at least a dozen people were brawling. Shouts, taunts and curses were deafening as she prepared to step off the rung.

Turner had gone first so he shoved against the punching, slicing tangle to make space for her. He tried to yank her quickly out of the way, but not before an elbow caught her in the chest.

"Ouch!" Automatically her arms went up to guard just like Kane had taught her and Turner blocked a wayward hand holding a stunted blade that might have grazed his ear. Together they finally broke free of the fight.

Even at this late hour, hordes of people filled the streets.

She and Turner held tightly to each other, gaping at gaudy buildings that soared out of sight overhead. People moving about them swayed and stumbled into each other, and occasionally, a wall.

An old man sang at the top of his lungs, waving his arms, and gazing up as if serenading the starless gloom overhead. Couples kissed and groped each other or yelled and slapped each other. Knots of teenagers, some of them still children, shared bottles and pipes. Most of them had brightly dyed lips and liked to flick matching tongues. A few people carried bags, hurrying as if to get out of the madness soon as possible.

"Where is the God's Temple?" Aiela asked a large lanky woman, wearing red lace and lounging on the steps of a giant foundation supporting a stepped pyramid.

The woman shrugged, eyeing Turner up and down. "I'd take you's there... for a taste of that 'un." Her voice sounded like a man speaking in falsetto. "An' I give you a taste of this." Parting the red lace, she revealed an oversized horror that looked to be a vulva with a penis coming out where the clitoris should be. It was stark white and positioned higher on the front of the body than normal.

Turner backed away pulling Aiela with him. "We'll be askin' someone else."

"What in the world o' insanity was *that*?! He hissed, as they moved with the tide again. Aiela shrugged, as shocked as he was.

In the middle, the concrete street was still smooth, and various shapes and sizes of trolleys, most of them hovering like the tunnel trolleys, whizzed by. They had to duck to avoid a small aero. On both sides where foot traffic never stopped, the concrete was cracked and crumbled. Holes hadn't been filled and more than once, both of them stumbled and tripped.

Turner grabbed the arm of a passing woman. "I'll give ya five oranges an' a roast quail if ya take us ta the God's Temple." Her face was long and thin with dark hair pulled back tight, making her look pointy and mean.

She studied both of them, then nodded. "I'll have the meat now, the fruit when we're there." She wasn't slurring like the other voices around them. Turner rummaged in Aiela's pack and handed a white, waxcloth-wrapped package to the woman.

She sniffed it and pointed to the direction they'd come from. "This way and hurry up. I been working since dawn and I'm tired."

Cutting through a passage so narrow their shoulders almost touched the walls, they came into another busy street. It wasn't far until the lady stopped in front of a glowing, three-sided pyramid.

All the other pyramids Aiela had seen were four-sided and much smaller than this one. It was lit from within, in shades of red, with gold glowing at the base and up from the tip. Wide steps formed its base, their cracks and pits sprouting seedy weeds grown tall as Aiela, so that it looked like a splotchy field. Trash tangled in the weeds.

"It's a ruin, but there ya go." The woman sounded exhausted.

Aiela slipped two gold bits into the bag of oranges before handing it over. "Many blessings on you. We thank you for your help."

The woman snorted. "No such thing as blessings here. We work, we live, we die." And she faded into the passing flow.

Aiela tried to smile at Turner, but it came out halfhearted and thin. "Onward?"

"Onward." Turner took her hand and together they picked their way through the trashy weeds up, up and up. There seemed to be no door in the pyramid face.

"This way, maybe." Seeing a flow of energy, Aiela led them to an angle joining the faces. Sure enough, the walls didn't quite meet, leaving a space wide enough to enter. They stepped inside to red-toned light, somehow darker than even the night outside. "It's playing tricks on my eyes." She said, wondering if Turner's eyes were having trouble adjusting.

They walked along a passageway that ran inside the pyramid wall as if another pyramid was nested inside the outer one. Currents of air coming from an angle above washed against her face. Rank smells and blurry sounds rode the currents. Human sounds, occasional raised voices, clunks and rustles of noises she couldn't identify, rose and fell like waves.

When they had traversed an entire side of the pyramid, another false wall hid another entrance to another passageway.

Three times they went inward. Three times they walked a passage the length of one pyramid wall. And each time the noise and smell and red-hued light grew more intense. The last hidden entrance opened into a courtyard. The pyramid was shells within shells, but its heart sprawled vast and lifeless. The structure's point, high above, interrupted a starless sky.

"This must've been beautiful once." Aiela still held Turner's hand, pulling him toward the center where a triangle of steps went down. Around them were deteriorated fountains with defaced sculptures, the water gone still and stagnant.

"Look at the trees." Turner was almost whispering and she noticed the sounds had faded, replaced with currents of air that swirled in invisible patterns inside the pyramid. Skeletons of trees still reached out with bare branches and she noticed the dusty patches of earth around them were in shapes. "Probably grass grew in these, little lawns to sit on. All the terraces might have held flowers once."

"What gods ya figure, was this temple for?" Turner asked.

Aiela stopped to study what she could see of the courtyard. "I think... earth, air, water and probably fire. The statues look to be metal, wood and stone. It might have been to Gaia and her many children—the gods of earth."

They both startled when a male voice spoke. "Gods what serve us now! What you've come for? What manner of pleasures you seek?"

Figures stood at the cusp of the descending stairway. It was too dim to see more than their forms, but the fact that there were close to a dozen of them, spread in a line, appeared threatening.

Aiela squeezed Turner's hand when he started to step forward. *Let me handle this my lover.* "We come on an errand to Drinera. Her sister sent us."

"What errand?" The voice was less friendly.

"It was asked I speak only to her. I've—"

"Take off your packs." The voice interrupted. "Search them." Forms came at them.

"Gun." She breathed. But Turner already had one in his hand, its tiny laser locked on a target. The two men were almost upon them when their bodies crumpled with a squeak and a grunt to the earth.

With a clear line of sight to the rest of them, Aiela sprayed the line, toppling forms from one end to the other. Some of them tumbled backwards down the stairs.

She and Turner ran to another side of the stairs and started down. "How long will they be out?" Turner asked.

"Should be a couple hours at least but no guarantees. Hurry!"

The steps didn't go down very far. They ended in a concrete vault lit with enough spheres to guide them. Tunnels and rooms opened off this central area, with people coming and going. No one paid them any mind, but Aiela didn't want to waste time going in the wrong direction.

She stopped a man with small goat horns protruding above his ears. "We're to find Drinera."

He didn't seem suspicious of them at all.

"Foller the north tunnel, keep going up. She be somewheres at the top. Jus' ask around."

Aiela made her voice impatient, careful to dumb down her wordage. "How'm I spose' to know which is north?"

Goat man scowled. ""An they say *I've* got no brain! This'uns south. Figure it out."

The north tunnel was wide and sloped sharply down. Slimy wet with standing puddles, and mostly deserted, its stench grew the further along they went. Smaller shafts angled away before it ended in a balcony. Before them yawned a space so big Aiela could barely see the bottom. What she could see was shapes of machines, and distorted colors of energy surrounding forms scurrying around like little ants. The noise told her more than the sight. Everything got amplified in here.

Huge pillars supported layers of balconies below the one they stood on, and Turner leaned far out to look up. "Only two levels above us." They searched until they found the stairs.

At the top, a half naked woman with blue-black skin splotched with white, and the ears, whiskers and mouth of a cat was starting down. "We're to find Drinera. Where'd she be?" Aiela asked, hoping to cover for Turner's shocked expression.

The cat woman stroked around one white breast as if petting

herself. Another white patch on her belly disappeared below the waistband of a short skirt. "Six doors to the left but she sleeping." Her voice was a soft purr and a thick black tail flicked into view, curling and bobbing as she continued down the steps.

"What in the name o' everything holy was *that?!*" Turner hissed.

"Shhh. Cat's have excellent hearing. I'll explain later."

Reaching the top of the last staircase she felt suddenly nervous. "When we find Drinera, I will ask for Ahna and offer payment. If she refuses or causes any problems, we threaten her. March her at gunpoint to get Ahna if we have to."

Turner nodded, squeezing her hand.

Counting doors, they tried the sixth but it was locked. Aiela knocked sharply and loudly, then waited a beat. "Drinera" she called through the door, pounding again with the flat of her fist. "Rhena sent us."

The door opened. The lady behind it looked older than Ziel, but was fully clothed in leather tunic and patched leggings. "Who this Rhena, huh?" She spat suspiciously, eyeing them both up and down.

"Your *sister* Rhena. I'm here to buy my sister back and Rhena said you'd help me... she even let me use her aero." They stood there, staring at each other. Drinera seemed unsure and Aiela got the feeling she was never unsure.

Drinera peered up and down the deserted passage. "Huh! Come in then. What you payin'?"

She closed and locked the door behind them and entered another door into a small sparse bedchamber. Lighting three candles, thickly misshapen with wax drips, Drinera muttered to herself. "Shows up ina night askin' to buy a sister... huh! tellin' of *my* sister... probly jus' a dream..."

"It's not a dream. But if it is, you'll wake with something to show for it." Aiela was pulling out parcels and bags of goods they'd brought. "This is roast lamb, this is fresh quail, this is six pomegranate, a dozen figs, and two bunches of grapes. Oh, and I've gold bits of course. Five. This is more than enough for one slave girl." She inserted the assurance into Drinera's mind.

"Ah, so you's a mind player too. An now I know which un's your sister. Twenty gold bits for her."

"Ten." Aiela had the twenty but she could see the old woman liked to bargain.

"Huh." Drinera clucked with recrimination and shook her finger. "Sure, she a sister but you won' pay top price? What's this of Rhena? How you know her?"

"I flew her aero here and paid her many times over for it. She said you would help me. Sisters helping sisters."

Drinera rasped a laugh, reaching up to touch Turner's cheek. "An' who this curvy thick cock? He keep you warm at night huh? He talk?"

"Yes and no." Aiela spoke to keep him quiet, pushing Drinera's hand away. "Ten gold bits if you bring her before I get impatient. Another ten when you deliver us safe topside."

"Huh! You kill my temple guards then?" Drinera didn't sound like she cared one way or the other. "That cost you more. In fact, you and muscle pet here can jus' stay and work it off…"

Aiela rolled her eyes. "Your *thugs* are only stunned. They'll wake good as new. And who's the mind player here? If you know of your guards, you know we've weapons. This can go only two ways. You get many times the price of my sister or you get nothing and we take her anyway."

Drinera stared at them long and unblinking before she spoke. "How much you give for the other one. You give all you got? Weapons too? He your sister's friend and he leg hurt. He little and skinny, not much use…"

Aiela exhaled impatiently. "Just get them up here… or take us to them. You're wasting my time old woman! Your sister trusted me, why won't you?"

"I'm *not* my sister." Drinera paused and her stare grew harder. "Just as you not your sister. I can see. Huh." She shuffled out both doors and to the railing. "Ox! She bellowed down into the void. The single word echoed and bounced back and forth before getting lost in the din from below.

Shuffling back into her room, she bent to examine the bags and parcels of food laid out on her bed. "Smells good anyways." She leered at Turner, tongue moving slowly around wrinkly lips. "You feed me grapes while we wait?"

"Get your own damn grapes." Aiela snapped.

Drinera let go high snickers that sounded like "huh huh huh" and set about opening the bags. They watched her rummage through the foods, noisily chewing.

A shape filled the open doorway. Huge and hairy, it looked like an auroch with extra long hair, except it walked upright and had arms with hands.

"Ox." Drinera said in a merry tone. "Bring me the sandy girl you found, huh and the boy with the broke leg. They leaving us already..."

Ox turned and lumbered off as silently as he'd come.

Drinera continued to eat, chewing each bite loud and overlong.

Turner squatted, back against the wall, to rest, and Aiela did too. Her feet hurt from hours of walking and standing. Her head hurt from gods only knew what. The air was probably poisonous down here.

"I'll maybe see Rhena again when I return her aero. Is there anything you want me to tell her?" Aiela spoke grudgingly to this mean little woman who liked to play head games. Still, if she got Ahna back safely, she'd happily deliver any message.

Drinera chewed like a cow on its cud. "Tell that bitch to come visit. I never see her. Huh! Almost seem she don' like my home."

"Maybe you should go see her. This place is... dreary. And it stinks. I wouldn't come see you here either."

"Huh huh huh" Her high snickers sounded again. "You viperous as me."

It was only perhaps ten minutes, but felt like hours, before Ox returned, shoving a small form into the room.

"Ahna!" Aiela stood but didn't go to her. Didn't examine or hug her like she yearned to. "You alright? Did they harm you?"

Ahna shook her head. Shivering and barefoot, she wore a silky, pink shift that barely covered from breasts to thigh. White face paint caked her skin, raccoon-like circles darkened her eyes, with little dribbles and runs from sweat or maybe tears striping through the white. Traces of garish pink still outlined her lips, making them appear fuller. She looked exhausted. *Just get us out of here.* "Let's go home. That's Timen, we're taking him too."

A skinny boy was slung over Ox' shoulder. He groaned whenever Ox moved.

"Huh, she all safe. See? The boy too. He hurt hisself, weren't us. So here's your sweet sister huh and now you give me everything." Drinera demanded.

Ox hadn't let go of Ahna's arm.

"Ten gold bits." Aiela tossed a bag onto the bed. "The rest once we're topside." Waves of outrage at these horrible people, warred with concern for Ahna.

"Ox", the old woman didn't even hesitate. "Take 'em up through the west sewer. Bring me their packs an' everything on 'em. Don't give the girl over til you got it all."

Ox turned and lumbered out the door, dragging Ahna with him.

"Wait. That's it? You're not coming? Not sending a… a… human? Can that… Ox even talk?" It was all happening too fast and Aiela couldn't tell if they were being tricked.

"Aiela!" She heard Ahna's panicky call fading.

Turner yanked at her hand to follow Ox.

"You tell that bitch to come visit. Huh-huh-huh." Drinera's snickers followed them out the door.

They passed few others on the long way out. It must've been twenty flights of steps down to the bottom, where machines were deafening and partly-human workers moved lazily, shoveling or pouring substances in, taking bins of something out.

Nobody bothered trying to talk. Concentration on where the next step was in the dim, along with weariness, and the noise multiplying in endless echoes, colluded to keep them trudging without words.

The west sewer was a square shaft, sharply pitched, with at least a foot depth of running waste. It smelled so bad, Aiela thought she might vomit. Ahna did, though not much came up, and Ox didn't slow its pace or take any notice.

Aiela's sandals slipped and slid so badly, Turner took her by the elbow and propelled her so they could keep up. She refused to think about the lukewarm clots and slime that slid over her feet or the sludge that sucked at her sandals, or the fact that Ahna's bare feet were probably getting cut up on the broken glass and smashed stone goods. Nothing she could do about any of it right now.

When it got so steep and slick even Turner was sliding backwards some, they finally reached a vertical shaft with a broken ladder affixed to one wall. Ox began to swing Tim down but Turner intervened. "Give him to me. I'll carry him."

Aiela handed both of their packs to Ox and only then did he release Ahna.

"Ox, if y-y-you w-want to leave h-h-here, you can c-come to Atlantis. They'd b-be good to y-you." Ahna spoke kindly to the conrectus, though her teeth chattered badly.

It nodded its wide head in understanding. "Go. Up." Its voice sounded like a cow's moo and it gestured at the ladder with hairy hands before turning and trudging back the way they'd come."

"How's your feet, can you climb?"

Ahna nodded. "I'm j-just c-cold in this s-stupid thing." She fingered the silky pink shift. "Turner and T-Tim sh-should go up f-f-first." She was rubbing her arms briskly and bouncing up and down, trying to warm up.

"Careful!" Turner called back once he'd started up the splintery rungs. "Ladder's slimy as th' rest o' this nasty place."

Aiela was already taking off her calf-length leggings. "Here, put these on. They're wet at the bottom but they'll warm you some."

"Your t-tunic's not l-long enough…"

"I don't care. I've got undergarments—plus it's dark. You're freezing. I should've thought to bring you clothes."

"I sh-should've thought to not c-come here!" Ahna pulled the leggings on, and Aiela followed her up the slippery rungs, cringing at the foulness that squished between her fingers and caked under her nails.

"Tim's aero is s-still here, he might be able to f-fly us back."

"I brought an aero. How bad is he hurt?"

"Broken leg I think. Can you ch-check him? *You* piloted here?!"

"Yes but a healing temple would be better. And a bathhouse and clothes…"

"Tim will know where to g-go. You still have any gold? Everything c-costs here. Probably even a healing temple… " She was already shivering less and sounding stronger as the underground chill gave way to humid heat above ground.

"A little." Aiela replied. "Maybe five bits."

"Ho there! NO!" Turner yelled at someone fixing to pour a bucket of something down the shaft. The form backed away and ran off, no doubt startled.

Topside, they saw it was a well of sorts that served as a dumping place for garbage.

"Tim," Ahna put the back of her hand against his forehead, "how you feeling?"

"Hurtin'. Hungry. Wantin' to go home." His voice was faint.

"I know. We'll help you. Where's the healing temple and is there a bathhouse and clothing we can buy?"

Tim was riding on Turner's back, clinging to him with his unbroken leg and both arms. The injured leg, Turner held carefully against his side. Tim looked around, studying the buildings that crowded together. "I think… go that way and then I'll see where we're at. He pointed behind them.

They got strange looks and everyone gave them wide berth, wrinkling or even covering noses at their stench.

Once again on a main street, Aiela paid for a ride to the healing temple. An older man and his mate seemed eager for the gold, but complained about their passengers' disgusting odor the whole way.

The Healing Temple turned out to be a shabby suite of rooms at the Temple of Mind Power. Packed with people from Belial's middle-of-the-night madness, there was everything from knife wounds to drug overdoses being treated by a grouchy staff who didn't seem to care all that much for the people they healed. A gold bit got Tim into a healing chamber ahead of everyone else. A tiny shower space and stained robes were placed at their disposal. Belials gave you anything if you had money. Aiela wondered what might have happened if they didn't.

She sat on the floor of an empty hallway beside Turner, waiting for Ahna to get done bathing so she could go next. Tired to her bones, she laid her head on his shoulder, and closed her eyes briefly. "I can barely look at my feet without gagging." They were covered with shit and rotted things and other people's hair.

"Sure an' ya need good stout Irish boots next time." He lifted one foot to show his off, though they were no cleaner than her feet. "I'd be the man ta see aboot that and I'd only charge ya twenty gold bits."

She let go a mad giggle, the hysterics of exhaustion and relief taking hold. They weren't out yet but it seemed the worst was over. She had Ahna back. They'd soon be on their way home.

She startled when her Comm vibrated. "Can't be good news. It's the middle of the night!"

She dug it out of a pocket. "Who's this?"

"Where are you?"

Bugging her eyes to Turner. *Oh no! Not good!* "I-I-I'm not at the Palace." She stammered. "What's wrong?"

Ziel's voice was clipped. "I've just received the controllers. It's time to make a plan—to use them. I need your help with it."

He's speaking in code in case anybody else is listening. The Belial attack must be underway.

"Ahna's not in her room either and she's not answering her Comm... " He paused to let her answer.

Because she's bathing off Belial sewage. "She's with me. It's a long story—"

"No time for long stories." Ziel cut her off. "Maya just showed me where you are."

He's tracking our Comms.

"Are you safe?" He couldn't hide worry in the question.

"Yes. Turner's with us too."

"Good. I'm going to give you coordinates—the shortest distance between us. I'll meet you. How soon can you leave?"

Aiela rubbed her eyes, then cringed at what she may have rubbed in them. "We can leave in half an hour."

He gave her a set of numbers, and finished with, "I'm glad Turner is with you."

The door beside them opened and Ahna smiled as steam swirled out around her. "That was the absolute best shower—what?" She saw Aiela's face, no doubt registering the emotions too.

"It seems this is the neverending night! Ziel just contacted me. We're to meet him along the Belial border. He's got Papa's node controllers and needs our help. Belial must be attacking already or he wouldn't be in such a hurry."

"He's wantin' *us* ta use them?" Turner's eyes were wide.

Aiela shrugged. "I don't know what he wants us to do but we'd better hurry up. I'm not leaving until I wash this shit off! Can you get Timen ready to go?" She asked Ahna.

Ahna was already headed away, mopping at dripping hair with a small cloth. "We'll be here by the time you're done."

THE KILLING GROUND

"I said it was a brutal thing."

"No, it was a human thing. You should not insult the brutes by such a misuse of that word; they have not deserved it."

— MARK TWAIN, THE MYSTERIOUS STRANGER

ROGAN

*G*eneral Rogan had trained half his life for this moment.

Blood thundered in his ears to the rhythm of the muta march. Even barefoot, the ground trembled under them, a fast-growing drumbeat that pounded towards the still-assembling Grecian army, camped just over the next ridge.

It was full dark, but starlight guided them between smatters of dwarf trees and shrubs. Rough rocks studded their path to the killing ground, causing a grunt here and there when a leathery-soled muta foot found a particularly sharp edge. Otherwise, the night was muffled and expectant. Shadows of shallow ravines snaked their way across the innocent landscape. A rising crescent moon climbed over the horizon at their prey's back, outlining targets perfectly.

At first, General Rogan had led the wedge formation of eight to twelve-foot-tall bodies. But their long strides and bloodlust had them flowing around him and far ahead, like a fast river current, rushing towards their promised kills.

Though it had snowed lightly during the evening, he'd had the trainers run a few fight rings. Nothing drove Mutazio into a frenzy quite like fight rings. Starting with four mutas, they fought until only one still stood. He hadn't let them kill each other, even told them to draw as little blood as possible. Still, those gathered a hundred deep around the rings had stomped and screamed for the fighters. Fists pumped the air—with plenty landing on each other until half the spectators were blooded. The animal shouts of a hundred thousand Mutazio warriors had been so deafening, there was no way the Grecian army hadn't heard it. Only two miles separated the camps.

He'd considered it their battlecry.

Sprinting now, he panted up the naked, rock bluffs he'd chosen for his vantage point. The Greeks had positioned behind it, probably imagining it would provide some level of protection from this massive army that came against them. Perhaps they hoped the giants they'd face would wait to meet them on a level field, or at least be winded and weakened by the time they descended from the long, unbroken line of bluffs and cliffs.

General Rogan had come himself, yesterday morning, to spy on the assembling camp. There looked to be maybe ten thousand soldiers, building fire rings and setting up crude tented shelters to keep off the cold winter rains that wavered occasionally into snowfall.

Grecian soldiers wore armor tunics. Made from layers of woven linen glued together with a substance made from the skin of rabbits, they were dyed the color of red apples and trimmed with gilded leather. Short sleeved and falling just below the crotch, they permitted the soldiers to move freely. Knee-high boots and leggings made from the same materials covered legs and feet. Gold painted helms protected their neck and head. Metal and leather gauntlets guarded forearms.

Rogan knew these armor tunics were deceiving. Appearing no tougher than good thick leather, they could stop arrows and even most blades with the strength of a man behind it. Muta strength however, was something else altogether.

More Greek soldiers arrived in a continuous line that trailed to the horizon. Ox drawn carts dripped water from their wooden tanks, and food wagons lined up in neat rows. This land force was but a fraction of the Grecian strength. Their Navy would have word by now, would be scrambling to get here as fast as they could.

The muta Rogan followed, wasn't even breathing hard as he topped the ridge. Black hair streamed behind the sub-human giant, like a ribbon of ink pouring from the meridian of his blunt, oversized skull.

It was here General Rogan stopped for his own safety. Waves of animalistic roars rolled like thunder, shaking Grecian soldiers out of slumber and into nightmare, as Mutazio attacked the frontmost fringes of the camp below. Snarls, grunts and screams marked their progression.

It had been a race. He'd told the Mutazio there wasn't enough men here yet for each to have a kill. So they'd competed for it.

Holding a laser weapon in one hand, a panel of node controllers in the other, Rogan looked upon the beginning of the slaughter. Once the Mutazio bloodlust was up, they would kill anything that moved.

Machete knives flashed every now and again, reflecting faint moonlight. Pale tents collapsed into tangles of bodies and dust and death cries. Both sides of the camp were encompassed, and more muta shapes, taller than the trees, were running to attack from the back, even as the front and side waves worked their way inward.

Battle clamor shuddered and lurched, one moment a din of screams, the next an echoing pause as if choreographed. Furious fits of dull clangs heralded the triumphant howls or guttural grunts of the mutas who bothered with blades.

Their orders had been simple. Box them in. Kill them all.

This was to be the sacrifice. These doomed first arrivals would be torn limb from limb and left for their brothers-in-arms to find. Rogan hoped the horror, the totality of it, would win the war and cost no more Grecian casualties.

He and Mardu had bigger plans for the brothers of these soldiers being butchered below. They were to help Belial conquer the world.

It was too dark for General Rogan to see the gory details playing out below. The tail-end of his ranks passed by, rushing down the ridge like an orderly avalanche, piling into battle. Memories of training filled in what happened next.

For the last two decades, Judges and Generals had sent a continuous supply of throwaways to the camps: Belials too criminal for even their own society, slaves who turned out to be worthless, enemies of Mardu. The camp commanders could do with these men and women as they pleased. Mostly, they became training fodder for the Mutazio.

It was too dangerous to let Mutazio use advanced weaponry, so they fought with blades. Machetes were preferred; one for each hand. Huge two-handed swords were popular as well. Daggers tucked into the muta's belts as backup would likely be forgotten. More often than not, they simply used their hands. Training exercises always ended with humans dismembered, beheaded, torn apart. Body parts strewed the training arenas, seeping blood and drawing maddening amounts of flies, until gathered and buried, or burned.

Even up on the bluffs, the battle grew loud as Rogan watched the entire camp razed.

Small shadows broke out frequently, racing back towards home, trying desperately to escape the killing frenzy. None did. The farthest anybody made it was a few hundred yards before a muta caught him.

They crumpled, they toppled, they folded, caught in a tidal wave of death.

At the ridge's base he saw a muta snatch a soldier by the neck, the man's legs still running in the air. The muta tossed the man, one-handed to another muta nearby, who caught him with two hands by the crotch and the head. Raising the man high the muta broke his back over a knee, as one might break sticks for kindling. *Well at least they're sharing and working together.* There were moments when General Rogan noted his own lost humanity.

Occasionally, pale wisps of cloth waved frantically back and forth from some part of the camp. The Mutazio had not been taught what that meant.

Somewhere along this same ridge, Balek and the other trainers sat holding weapons and controllers for self-protection, just like him. And like him, they wouldn't risk wading into the muta melee to honor a flag of surrender.

THE MUTAZIO WERE RESTING easy around the edges of their carnage, by the time night lightened into dawn. It had taken less than an hour for the camp to be overcome, but the killing had continued methodically. Thoroughly. Then slowly, the Mutazio had settled, losing interest or simply tiring. Retreating to an empty patch of ground, they sat against trees and rocks or even stretched out to sleep.

Freezing cold as he listened to the deep silence, Rogan waited until light seeped across the killing ground, until he could see the frost of his own breath. A horn no larger than his palm roused the Mutazio. They formed up near the base of the ridge and awaited his instructions.

"All companies except Stone will return to your camps. Clean yourselves, eat, and rest. Stone, you will spread across this field and ensure no man still breathes. When you finish, take the Greek weapons and food wagons back to your camp. Dismissed."

He walked to the edge of what looked a sea of body parts brined in blood. He watched Mutazio of the Stone company check pulses, gathering spears, bows, arrow quivers, and blades of all sorts as they went. Sometimes a pulse would be found and the muta might chop off the head, or simply stomp a heel into the face, crunching it underfoot like a ripe melon.

It was too cold for flies, but overhead the sky began to fill with dark wings and the raucous shrieks of crows, vultures, kites and ospreys. This sharp blood scent would need warmer weather to give way to the stench of rotting flesh. Likely their Grecian brothers would arrive, surrender, and bury them before the stink of death ever putrefied.

26

THE NEVERENDING DAY

"Always protect those who live justly. For the wheel of power turns in dependence on the wheel of justice... "

— TESAKUṆA JĀTAKA FROM THE JĀTAKA (JA.V.109)

AHNA

*H*unger pangs stabbed at Ahna's belly but that took a backseat to the conversation with her sister. "Well what exactly *did* you tell him?"

"Nothing! Just that I wasn't at the Palace. That you and Turner were with me." Aiela was fiddling with knobs and levers, readying the aero for takeoff. At least there weren't as many aeros whizzing in and out of Temple City at this hour of the night—or morning.

"He didn't ask where we *were*? Or what we're doing? Something's very wrong."

Aiela didn't answer, looking out the windows in every direction and then studying her screens, waiting for an incoming aero to land next to them.

Ahna settled back into the seat just behind her sister. Turner had the other pilot seat. Glad to be clean and warm again, guilt joined her hunger pangs. None of this was Aiela's fault yet here she was peppering her with questions, making everything harder. All because of her fears of what Ziel might do once he discovered her folly.

She desperately wanted to sleep a bit. But that wouldn't be fair either. Aiela was every bit as tired, but she still had to get them out of this madness. It felt so good to be warm though...

She woke with a start, realizing they were no longer moving.

Aiela was curled into the opposite passenger bench, and Turner lay on his back, snoring lightly on the floor between them. She shut her eyes and dropped back into restless slumber.

"WE'RE HERE... sleeping in the aero... be right there." Aiela sat up, speaking to her Comm, braids tumbling like a sleepy Medusa.

Ziel. She said without speaking aloud, as Ahna pushed herself upright. Sunlight streamed in the windows and Aiela moved down to wake Turner.

Rousing quickly, they opened the door to what awaited them. Aiela had set them down on the Atlantean side of the border, but only barely. The pale concrete wall that marked it was just yards away and pine trees grew so thick, it seemed a miracle they had landed safely at all. Foothills rose sharply around them and Aiela pointed at one to their left. "He's on top." She yawned, which set them all to yawning.

"It's good ta have ya back little sister." Turner wrapped an arm around Ahna's shoulders and squeezed as they set off through tall grass. "Ya think Timen will be alright do ya?"

Ahna smiled at him and nodded. "I think he'll be better than alright. We gave him five gold bits remember? That's more than he'll have in one hand again. I'm sure he made it home just fine. He's used to piloting in that mess."

"Technically, *Ziel* gave him five gold bits..." Aiela amended.

Ahna stopped walking. "Listen, before we get to Ziel, I just... I want you to know how sorry I am—" She was close to tears and trying hard to mask them.

"I know exactly how sorry you are." Aiela interrupted. She looked at Turner. "Ahna's very sorry and grateful we got her out. What you don't know about is the few hundred times she saved my wild, irresponsible, crazy ass from getting a whooping—or worse. If Mama had known all the things I got up to... "

Ahna laughed a little then. *"That's* true! I got good at misleading Mama... I'd say you were just out doctoring animals or practicing your meditation. But this is a little different..."

"Not really." Aiela started climbing again, weariness evident in the slope of her muscular shoulders. A figure appeared on the hill's lush, rounded crest, and headed towards them. "I knew your crazy would come out eventually. And now I consider us even."

"You're piloting a Belial aero?" Ziel's bushy silver eyebrows pushed up, creasing his forehead deeper than usual. He was wearing black pants and tunic which made his hair look almost white. Ahna had only seen him wear cream and white, outside his deep blue Ruler robes.

"We didn't steal it if that's what you think. We paid to borrow it." Aiela wasn't giving anything away. *He'll have to ask the right questions if he wants the whole story.*

Ahna fought a smile at their shared thought. Just like when they were twelve.

"Belial aero's can go off continent without showing up on their radar." Ziel mused, smoothed one eyebrow with a forefinger over and over; sure indication he was thinking some deep thought.

They were back down the hill, standing around said aero. It looked shabby in the morning light, flat black paint chipped in places, peeling in others. Dents stole any former sleekness. It was small, with seating for six including the pilot, and no cargo hold to speak of.

"How long can you use it?" He asked, still worrying the eyebrow.

Aiela shrugged. "Long as we need to, probably. What are you thinking?"

Ziel looked them each in the eye before answering slowly. "I had planned to send a pair of my spies with the controllers... spies who are currently on our eastern coast. They'd need to modify an aero to keep it off any radars or tracking logs. I hoped you would take the controllers and meet them with instructions but..."

"But we might as well take the controllers to Greece and do it ourselves." Aiela finished into his pause.

Ahna finally understood Ziel's distracted pondering. "Using a *Belial* aero solves the problem of proof. It'll be hard for anyone to say it wasn't a Belial who did it."

Ziel looked uncomfortable. "Your parents would be terribly unhappy that I'm even thinking it. Sage will likely never speak to me again if I send you into this danger. But yes, it would save considerable time. Mardu began the attack last night. It would take you half a day to get to our coast and find my men. All night for my spies to prepare an aero—make it untraceable. They wouldn't go until dark, so that'd be two nights from now."

"Sure an' that's too *late!*" Turner burst out. "Mardu will've slaughtered the Grecian army by then—or they will've surrendered. My *family's* in danger! We could be there by sundown tonight."

"I *am* a pretty good pilot now... sort of trial by fire... " Aiela added, in support of Turner.

"It's our best choice all around." Ahna decided. "Show us how the controllers work. With three of us, El can pilot while Turner and I do... whatever it is we need to."

"How will you find the Mutazio? They could be spread over miles." Ziel had already opened his pack on the floor of the aero and started to unload it.

"We'll use the aero's radar and heat signals to search them out." Aiela sounded so confident. "And I'd want to take the scanner from your aero. This one's too old to be reliable. How close do the controllers have to be?"

Ziel laid out three long, white tubes, no bigger than Ahna's forearm, lining them up carefully on the aero floor. "The controller's signal should work within three miles. Maybe more—"

"And if they don' work at all?" Turner voiced what they were all thinking.

"You'll have a backup plan. Sort of." He pulled a large, grey metal box out next. "We call this the minor sound eye."

Opening the polished steel lid, he removed a felt-wrapped object as big as three hands laid side by side. "Put those on and take turns looking at it. Turn around if you must, but do not look on it except through the eye shields." He pointed to two eye masks in the box.

Ahna reached for one. A simple half-circle band of corn-colored plastic had ends that rested on her ears. The eyeholes were crystal and slightly rosy, turning the day brighter.

Aiela and Turner already had their backs turned and Ziel had the other eyeshield on when he unwrapped the dense black felt.

The crystal was milky with veins of blue, green and yellow warping through it. Shaped like a flattened diamond, it was only a bit thicker than her palm. One long point attached to a staff top. Thick hammered copper, also attached to the staff top, formed a frame in the same diamond shape around the crystal, but not touching it. "This screws into the rest of the staff." Ziel gestured to three more lengths of rod disassembled in the box.

A vision flashed. *She was underground. There were stone steps she didn't recognize and a stone pedestal table, similar to the table she'd seen Aiela die on. Men surrounded her, held her eyelids open, forcing her to see and she was fighting them, rolling her eyeballs to look anywhere but straight ahead. They simply brought the crystal on the long staff up so close it filled her vision. Magnetized her to its milky white colors. And she lost control of her own will...*

"Let the others see it and I'll explain what it is and how you'll use it." Ziel was saying.

Ahna's breath came too fast and her hands shook when she removed the eye mask, handing it to Aiela.

What's wrong?

Tell you later.

"Eye contact with this stone creates an energy field." Ziel began, returning the metal box to the weapons bag. "Once you are held within that energy field, you no longer have control over yourself in any way. You will do what you're told, think what you're told, and feel what you're told. Your own will ceases to be in control, and the will of others can be imposed on you any way they choose."

He paused to stare sternly at the three of them. "Should the controllers fail, the minor sound eye can be used to overtake a Belial Commander, or as many Mutazio as set eyes on it. I trust you'll be creative and wise if you must use it. Its power is so cellularly disturbing, the mind may not fully recover without healing."

"H-how many of these do we have?" Ahna swallowed, still trying to recover from the vision. She'd tell Ziel of it, but now wasn't the time. It felt more a memory—from another life perhaps.

"This is the only portable one left—the rest were destroyed to avoid misuse. We've larger ones for protecting our city gates, and of course, the Major Sound Eye utilizes this technology on a much grander scale. I meant to bring more eye masks, but failed to in my rush to meet you. There's only the two."

"And if we look on it unprotected?" Turner inquired.

"The effects wear off in approximately three to six hours. But the feeling of it, you will never forget." His tone was enough of a warning.

Aiela asked. "If we're too late, if we can't find them, or something else goes wrong—"

"Then you get back home." Ziel interrupted. "Contact me on the Comm soon as you're in range. Either way, I'll be waiting to hear."

"And what'll happen then?"

He sighed. "Then we decide whether to launch a thousand aeros and ships to Greece—or not. The Rulers still aren't agreed. But the three of you only need to worry about getting back home. Not in this aero of course. You'll need to destroy it, or leave it in Belial somewhere and find another way…"

"We can just return it." Aiela assured him. "The woman who owns it thinks we're in Temple City. She won't connect us with being in Greece, or a fallen muta army. Plus, I've got a pocketful of gold bits off your account. We'll get home just fine."

Ziel smiled then, as he usually did at her impertinence. "If this

works, I'll gladly give you every gold bit I've ever had and then some."
He sobered suddenly, shooting a long, narrow-eyed look at each of
them. "The day *will* come—when this is over—you will tell me exactly
what you've been up to the last twenty-four hours!"

He talked them through everything the engineers had shown him
on the controllers. There were even paper diagrams with instructions.
"Burn these when you're done."

"The controllers too?"

He thought a moment. "Yes. The controllers too. Better you're not
found with any evidence." Pulling three light guns from the bottom of
the pack, he looked at the girls. "You'll show Turner how to use
these, yes?"

Ahna nodded, managing a smile. "I was hoping that was food." Her
stomach gave off a loud rumble.

Preparing to leave, Ziel laid an aged hand against Ahna's cheek
first, then Aiela's. "When you return, we must complete your training.
It appears we've less time than I anticipated." His tone become oddly
formal. "I trust you understand the importance of this task to the
safety of your country and will make wise decisions?"

They both nodded, faces reflecting the gravity, affection and
sadness in his cerulean eyes.

Wrapping her arms around this man who trusted them with so
much, Ahna remembered the last family goodby they'd said before
leaving for Ireland. It seemed years ago, though it had only been seven
moons.

They'd returned from Ireland to find only Ziel waiting. He'd been
the one to greet them, the one to help Auntie Sage hold their world
together as they learned of their parent's deaths.

"I'll make sure they come home safe ta ya." Turner promised,
bowing formally to Ziel as an Atlantean might.

"I know you will, and I thank you." Ziel replied quietly.

THEY FLEW to a small harbor town on Atlantis' south-eastern coast.
Ahna wondered if Ziel's spies were here, or in another of the many

little villages that clung to the sea. They'd landed well away from the clean, quaint townsite, not wanting anyone to question the Belial aero.

Walking a mile to a well-provisioned market, they procured warm tunics and soft, leather leggings to replace the ugly Belial robes they wore.

"We'll need food and jugs of water too." Ahna said.

"Look, stuffed figs!" Aiela gathered some, cramming an entire half in her mouth while Ahna picked out bars of seeds, nuts and dried fruits.

Well provisioned for the night, carrying portions of hot seafood pies and roasted root vegetables to satisfy them now, the three settled at a sculpted stone table, overlooking the sea.

"Why were you wearing that pink silk and so much face paint?" Aiela asked. They'd talked of their mission so much, nothing had been said of Ahna's follies.

"I was to be a pleasure girl." At Aiela's blank look, she explained. "There are girls and boys who do whatever brings pleasure to their patrons. All manner of sexuality, or massage or singing—I'm not sure what all they do actually. They just said I was to look pretty—their idea of pretty is lots of face paint—and do whatever was asked of me." She stopped to wolf down more supper turning her face to the clean salty breeze lifting her hair.

"What—did you have to do anything... ?" Aiela looked horrified. Turner had stopped eating to listen.

"No." Ahna had felt such relief at the lonely, elderly man who'd picked her out of the lineup. She'd been the only sober pleasure girl, the rest already "sailin'", a term used to describe how the drugs set them free in one way or another. "An old man just wanted to dance with me. I listened to him talk about his dead mate for awhile and then I massaged his hands and feet. He just needed touch. Poor lonely old man. He fell asleep and I thought I could maybe escape but there was Ox, waiting right outside the room we were in. It dragged me right back to the cell."

"I'd heard o' Belial's Things before, but seein' them was right shocking." Turner said.

Ahna nodded. "There's more in Belial than I thought. They're treated awful! Slaves and cruel amusements… do you think the Rulers know?"

"Of course they do." Aiela replied. "But short of taking authority over the Belials, what can they do about it?"

A STORM HOVERED over the sea between Atlantis and Greece. The little aero bounced violently on turbulent air waves, and lightning arced on all sides.

Aiela's jaw was tense as she worked to get them above it. "Gods! Does this feel like the never-ending day? Last night went on and on, today seems to have no end point either. It's like we've found some place where days and nights elongate right into hell."

"Last night was my fault. I never should have gone. Today—we volunteered for." Ahna massaged Aiela's tense shoulders. "Your skills are what's never ending. My sister, the fighter, pilot, and preventer of wars! It's going to be alright. We can do this."

Turner's nose was pressed against the window. "Would ya look at the lightnin' from up here! Vera much prettier when yer no' fightin' rough seas in a wooden ship, gettin' soaked… tryin' ta guess which course would avoid the worst o' it." The storm mass flashed fiercely beneath them. Filtered by clouds, shards of luminosity flickered back and forth, like colossal fireflies winging across the night.

"Let's hope this isn't over top of the muta army." Aiela still worried. "Lightning makes the radar a little wacky." She tapped the screen. "I can't tell what's below us."

Ahna got busy setting all the node controllers, turning the dials as high as they'd go. All that remained was to power them up, set the correct frequency, and push the right buttons—once they'd located Mutazio.

She thought of Ox, and the spirit she sensed in it, a spirit that was innocent. It was the same as any animal, only with more awareness, and perhaps more thought patterns. What sort of spirit was inside the Mutazio? Were they more animal, more human, or something else?

"Do you think it'll hurt them? You know, when they die?" She hated the thought of any creature being helpless and suffering. Likely, they didn't deserve this death flying towards them. "It's Dominus Mardu, and the other leaders of Belial who deserve to have something explode in their brains! Do you think the Mutazio have souls, same as us? Is there anything incarnating them, or are they more animal, without individual consciousness?" This question had long been debated in Atlantis and the lack of answers, the problem of inter-mixing species that might or might not be incarnated by advanced awareness, had led to outlawing it altogether.

Aiela didn't answer. Ahna could feel how much she hated what they were doing too. Aiela was a healer. She charmed people, made them laugh and gave them grand adventures. Most of all, she took away their suffering, whether human or animal. How much worse must this be for her?

"Whether the muta're 'real people' or no', it's like ya said when the islanders attacked. We'll save many lives fer the price o' a few." Turner spoke of their time in his country when violent outcasts had stopped their wagon train and tried to take what they wanted. "I know what ya mean though. It's likely no' the muta's fault—yet they're the ones who'll die."

During the Ireland attack, he had argued that he could reason with the islanders, buy them off.

But Ahna had a vision of the carnage they would wreak. They would kill every Irish driver and Atlantean male. They would take the wagons, supplies and all the Atlantean girls for their own.

Aiela had killed a man that day. So had Turner and Carver and Kinny...

"I know it sounds right—but it still doesn't *feel* right." Ahna was grateful he understood at least.

Aiela finally spoke. "We're only killing the *tools*—to stop them killing innocents. We're doing nothing to the source. It doesn't even sound right." Her voice was bitter and hopeless.

All three of them were overtired. The relief of a couple hours sleep early this morning had worn off. They'd rested before leaving the safety of Atlantis' eastern coast, but couldn't sleep. Too many unknowns lay ahead. Likely as not, night would be gone before there'd be another opportunity.

"We should be over Greece now." Aiela pointed to the landmass shown in yellow on the radar. Water showed as green. They'd been flying over yellow for awhile with Aiela carefully marking the miles. "I'm taking us lower. Help me watch for warm bodies." Any source of heat showed up red on the radar.

Little red masses blipped here and there as they descended. Most likely fires warming homes scattered across the countryside. A small grouping marked a town and they flew a wide berth, not wanting to be seen. Clouds were intermittent, the wild storm moving off behind them.

"Moon's pretty bright. Ya think anyone could see us?" Turner asked.

"Only if they're looking, and if we fly between them and the moon. Once we fi—" She drew in breath as the entire top of the radar screen lit in red dots. Moving red dots.

"Found 'em" Ahna murmured, moving to peer out the windows.

Red began to take over the screen as they got closer. Aiela veered to the left. "Let's see how spread out they are. If we can find the edges, we can make a full pass with the controllers. Make sure we get them all."

"Why do I feel like an exterminator?" Ahna muttered, studying the ground. "It's too dark, I can't make out anything."

The radar screen was mostly a mass of red now. "Looks like they're pretty bunched up. Does that mean they're fighting? Or marching?"

Turner shrugged. "Either way. They're aboot ta die."

27

THE QUIETUS

"... and in a single day and night of misfortune all your warlike men in a body sank into the earth..."

— PLATO, TIMAEUS/CRITIAS

GENERAL ROGAN

*G*reece had not surrendered. Not after seeing their bloody, dismembered land soldiers. Not after the Iron company, all of them ten to twelve-footers, stood at a distance pounding their chests and waving machetes. Not even after meeting with Rogan wherein he gave the Grecian leaders Mardu's overly generous terms.

Disappointing.

But if they wanted to be stubborn, there was nothing he could do except go forth, cutting them down until they changed their minds.

Mardu would not be happy about this.

It felt a repeat of their first attack, only now they marched on the entire Grecian force. Impressive really, that it took only a few days for so many to cross the country. This was the Greek Navy. Their land

230

troops were just a fraction of the power Greece could muster. The land troops, slaughtered two nights ago by the muta, had always been enough to protect the border. Most attacks came from the sea, due to Greece being a series of islands, peninsulas and fjords. Only one border was on land.

Again, the ground trembled with bare giant feet, this time marching, deliberate and orderly, into battle. This time, they must go further and this time the Greeks had assembled, preparing for war on an open plain where they could not be hemmed in, could see their enemy approach.

So this time General Rogan had brought an aero.

The Mutazio companies were named Oak, Iron, Stone, Ice, Storm, Sun, Fire, River, Wind. The nine Belial commanders used hovercraft to give orders from behind their companies.

Balek raced his madly back and forth even though Rogan had asked him to stay close by. Allegedly so General Rogan himself could keep Mardu's son safe, but really to keep the boy from giving stupid orders and creating chaos. To make sure, he'd disabled the speaker crystal Balek carried.

This attack was as organized and precise as the first one was a free-for-all. Like calling a dance, General Rogan could give a cue and the companies responded in a carefully choreographed formation.

Earlier today, Rogan sent two of his commanders to spy. They'd returned white-faced—and not from the winter chill they were unaccustomed to.

"They've thrice our numbers and more!" One had panted, even though he hadn't been running. "At the very *least* General Rogan, we are outnumbered two to one."

"It appears they've swelled their ranks with every countryman able to fight." The other commander added. "There are twice as many men out of uniform as there are soldiers."

General Rogan had merely smiled; a rare occurrence that frightened those who knew him well. "All the better. The muta will enjoy a challenge. I didn't come all this way, after a lifetime of preparation, to accept a surrender without earning it."

The commanders had found their courage then. Begun bragging of the victory they would have, wagering how long it would take the muta to cut through only three men apiece.

It did worry General Rogan a bit. Mardu didn't want a butchered Grecian army, he was counting on a formidable force bowing to, and then joining, his own.

A waning crescent moon popped out between clouds that moved across it to drape their march in frequent shadow. Where before, they could make out the land contours and vegetative forms by starlight, this night kept its secrets well, as though playing a game of hide and seek. It made little difference to the Mutazio.

General Rogan followed at a distance, making abbreviated hops in the aero, setting down at the army's broad back as they loped steadily along. Something glowed on the horizon and he lifted off, flew towards it to investigate.

A crescent of fire burned between the advancing Mutazio and the Grecians. Swooping low, he estimated the wall of flames at perhaps fifteen foot wide in a curving line that reached for at least a mile. Behind it, rows of archers and men brandishing spears formed up. They were ready.

He thought he saw another aero high above, from the corner of his eye, but when he turned, it was gone. Probably Mardu being too impatient to await General Rogan's message that the Grecians surrendered. Or, just a figment of his imagination.

Hovering a safe distance from the sickle of fire, he watched the front ranks of Mutazio reach it. They didn't hesitate, nor did they speed up. Simply kept their jogging pace and moved through it as though it wasn't there.

He lifted off to monitor the battle starting behind those dramatic flames. Mutazio were grabbing the bristling spears, yanking to pull men into range of their blades. Arrows flew so thick it looked a horde of locust swarming in one direction. Some of the Mutazio fell, or slowed at least, to yank shafts out of themselves. Most kept going, immune to a few sticks protruding from their flesh.

He'd ordered them to go slowly. To maim, but not kill, disarm and disable, but preserve. With a single word, he could set them to butchering if needs be. This restraint he showed was a sort of peace offering. He would only hold it for so long.

The muta's unrelenting advance pushed the Greeks a fair distance behind the flame wall, which waned, stomped to death by muta feet in spots.

Then suddenly, those Mutazio nearest to the archers rushed in, hacking and slaying in destructive frenzy. Frowning, General Rogan set the aero down, already shouting orders before leaping out. That's when he saw Balek.

The ignorant tyrant had taken someone's speaker-crystal and was screaming commands to the Mutazio, racing back and forth on his hovercraft, goading and spurring them into a craze.

Sticky red sprayed those soldiers trying to fight against giant men almost twice their size. Mutas used decapitated bodies like a scythe, swinging them back and forth, clearing anything standing out of their blood-spattered way.

The Greeks fell back, turning to run, stumbling over each other in a panic before these great monsters who tore them limb from limb.

Cursing, General Rogan spun as Balek came whizzing by on his left, and aimed his sound gun.

Balek fell, unconscious, from the craft, which crashed, cartwheeling across the ground.

General Rogan barked orders to the nearest commanders. "Go! Restrain the Mutazio. They're slaughtering them!"

Stalking to Balek's crumpled body, he dragged it back to dump beside his aero. He'd tie the fool up and gag him if he had to. Hopefully, the fall had broken something. Something that would be terribly painful for a good long time. Again it entered his mind to simply rid them all of Balek, permanently.

But then he saw Mutazio begin to fall.

The tail end ranks passed by, flowing around him and the aero. One by one they collapsed, slumping to the ground, melting, buckling, sinking and toppling, as though a great ghostly mowing machine swept over.

His disbelief was so great, he stood gaping to see if they'd get back up. His mind couldn't make sense of what was happening.

A commander raced towards him on hovercraft, almost crashing into him. Shouting incoherencies. Something about nodes.

Then it clicked.

"Where are the controllers? The controllers! Where are they?!" The commander was screaming over and over.

General Rogan leapt into the aero and lifted off, desperate to see how many were falling.

It was like following a wave of invisible death. It spread and spread and spread, rippling out across the pond of bloody battle below.

The mass controllers were right here—and some in the transport aeros, though each commander carried a small one for emergencies, but those wouldn't have this capability.

Then he remembered seeing the other aero—if it hadn't been his imagination. Could somebody have taken one with the controllers and used them? But who?

He rose above the clouds, intending to find anything else in the sky.

He might have missed it, had it not flown between him and the moon at just the right moment. It was small, a quick black shape like the bats you see only in periphery. Definitely not one of his much larger carriers. Nor one of Mardu's weaponized triangle crafts.

Rage surged as he aimed, speeding west in pursuit, away from the arrested battle. Readying his aero's laser he determined to shoot it down. It had to be the culprit. Perhaps he could stop it before the entire muta army fell.

There it was! He aimed and fired. Missed.

Again and again he fired, but the little black bat dove and bucked, dodging right and left, up and sideways and under.

When it disappeared beneath him, he worried that it would be on his tail now—but it was too small to be armed well. He flew a wide circle, scanning for it.

Suddenly it rose. Too close and coming straight at him.

He could see figures inside the window when two flashes of light beamed out, the first shattering his front window, the second striking his neck. Crystal shards from his windows stung where they embedded in his flesh as more shots hit his carrier. The little aero circled around him, continually shooting until his engine stopped.

His mind still worked but his hands wouldn't and the wet wind whipped inside, in mad rushes of dizzying onslaught. Spinning, limbs flinging out as if boneless, the last thoughts he had while his aero plummeted, were of the Mutazio. Decades of work, now lying wasted. All those magnificent, muscled bodies would only rot—or maybe the Greeks would burn them...

Such a pathetic reaping of great power.

Frustration at his failure melted slowly, giving way to relief. He welcomed his end.

The *Quietus.*

28

THE DAY AFTER

"In the path to self-realization and mastery there are many ways, many paths and many choices. Neither is better than the other. It is simply that each choice brings with it consequences."

— MARY MAGDALEN

AIELA

No one spoke. The aero's steady hum suspended the adrenaline rushing through their systems. Or maybe countered it.

Aiela registered only the constant pressure of her twin's hand. Ahna knelt behind her and Turner, one hand clutching each shoulder. She was connecting them, channeling strength from herself and Turner into Aiela, holding her up as she brought them safely down to earth.

The aero scraped a dwarf tree, which leaned away and broke as the craft settled, gently crushing it.

Aiela groped at her door latch and fell out onto bare ground. It felt like a bottle of panic had been shaken and shaken and shaken inside of her and if it exploded it might take her with it. She didn't know how to release the pressure and she couldn't breathe. She couldn't breathe... *Breath out. You must first push all breath out before you can draw in what you need.* Zan's accented sing-song played in her head. Her "still-life tutor" from so long ago... she wished he was here now. *Breathe out to breathe in. Breathe out..."*

She was on her knees, forcing air from her lungs, and the effort made her retch. But then she could inhale. Forced it out. Inhaled.

She could feel the thin gold strand linking her and Ahna. It seemed her only tie to sanity. She sucked breath in, forced it out. Hard raindrops landed on her head and they awakened her. She clenched her fists so tight, fingernails bit palms, forcing out another breath—this one carrying sound. Something between a scream and a howl lurched off into the night. She rose to follow it.

Tripping twice, then gaining speed, she ran and ran and ran. Like she used to outrun the panic of her dreams, she ran out this panic. This nightmare that was no dream.

Drops turned to downpour and lightning flashed soundlessly in the distance. Bushes snagged at her and rocks stubbed her toes, bloodied her shins, and turned her ankles but she outran them too.

She ran until she couldn't anymore and then she dropped once more to her knees and let out the rest of the sound. The rest of the bottle of panic, covering a deep new horror, poured from her mouth, her lungs, her soul. Screams turned to howls until howls turned to sobs and then there was nothing except the cleansing rain sheets falling on her bowed head, soaking into her spent body.

Tipping her face skyward, she let it wash away the desecration, the mania, the unthinkable. Inhaling her lungs full to bursting, she let it all slowly release.

Icy mud trickled over her scraped, bruised feet and she felt grateful for it. Patted it lovingly with her palms.

She had killed thousands.

She tapped on her meridians as she searched out the core of the panic. *I snuffed out a hundred thousand lives tonight.* The energy of it was like a tidal wave, engulfing her with no way out. The panic of drowning loomed, but she tapped until it disintegrated into the storm's sudden mad dance around her.

Grief crushed her chest like a pillar of stone but still she tapped. Forced breath out. Dragged breath in. Tapped. Faced the pain. No more running from the carnage she'd caused.

"Breathing is cause and effect." Zan intoned every day. *"For each action there is reaction. What enters must exit. Every action returns in some form. You may hold your breath or you may refuse the breath, but these too are actions with a reaction. All of life offers cause and effect. Breathing is our reminder—and source. Without breath, you cannot cause—nor experience the effect."*

Pounding rain softened to drizzle and peace finally started seeping at her roughened edges. It was freezing cold and her limbs were numb.

She reached for the gold thread, rose to follow it back. Thoughts of Turner and Ahna hurried her. What were they experiencing? How would they mitigate the effects?

Energetically, taking so many lives created a vacuum. It felt like a tidal wave containing every emotion those beings were experiencing as they ended. She only hoped the lives they'd saved would balance it in the end.

"Ahna!" She called, turning in circles trying to see in the dripping dark. Both of the aero doors gaped open but no one was inside.

A shape sat up several yards off.

"I'm here." Her voice sounded drained. The body dragged itself up from the ground and came to Aiela, wrapping sodden arms around her. Mud caked Ahna's entire back.

"We're a terrible mess." Ahna shivered.

"Mama'd be so mad."

"She certainly wouldn't let us in the house."

"She'd make us walk all the way home."

"From here!" Their tears made way to include raw chuckles.

"She wouldn't care that we had to swim a few hundred miles."

The weight of the moment lifted some, and they pulled back to examine each other in dim light cast from inside the aero. Ahna's blonde hair dripped blobs of mud. This seemed funny to Aiela. "You look like your head is melting."

"You look like you scrapped with a jungle and lost."

"Where's Turner?"

Ahna shrugged. "Last I saw, he was growling, kicking trees and yanking shrubs out of the ground. He threw rocks for awhile until there weren't any left." She pointed to a large dent in the aero tail. "Big one slipped out of his hand, went the wrong direction... are you worried about him?"

"Naw." Aiela turned to search the aero for a jug of water. "He needs to fall apart same as us. Exhume the awful of what we did."

They sat and shivered side by side, legs swinging out of the passenger door, gulping water and sharing the last stuffed fig in silence.

Ahna laid back, and curled into a shivering ball.

Aiela shook from being soaked and cold, worry seeping in before Turner's compact form finally appeared.

Disrupting mist that swirled, replacing the rain, he stood in front of her and took the water jug she held out. Usually thick and bouncy, his curls were a soggy mop. His round face was set in a mask.

"Lover, you must tap before we go home." was all she said.

THE SUN WAS high when Rhena started to inspect her aero but Aiela jiggled gold bits in an outstretched palm. "I'm sorry I kept it longer than I'd planned. This should cover it."

The sound of gold tink-tink-tinking together earned the old woman's full attention.

Behind them, Turner had unloaded the weapons bag and was walking away.

"I took her to see the fights." Ahna interjected quickly in explanation. "We don't have such things at home you know. But then it got late and we decided to stay an extra night." She shrugged. "Temple City has too many... distractions."

239

"Drinera wants you to come visit." Aiela had almost forgotten about the evil old woman. So much had happened since then.

Rhena perked up and made a scratchy sound that may have been a laugh, or only clearing her throat. "She want me to come to that nasty ol' dreary place? I don' think so!"

Aiela smiled. "That's exactly what *I* told her! It is dreary. She should come see *you*." Relief surged. They were almost home. She reached out to hug the hard woman. "Rhena, I can't thank you enough for all your help. You and your rotten sister helped me get mine back and I'm grateful. If you ever come to High City, look me up."

Rhena remained a stick, as if dazed by the hug and warm words, piled on top of more gold. Before the stiff, old woman had stirred herself to respond, Aiela and Ahna were walking away, headed towards the gate. Turner was waiting for them somewhere, with the bag of weapons.

They had stopped at the same harbor town they'd left from, to clean themselves up, wipe mud out of the aero, try to hammer its dent out, burn the controllers, and eat. The brief respite had returned sanity, but not two nights of lost sleep.

The twins slowed when they saw the gate. It was manned. All Belial's soldiers were still in Greece—or perhaps en route home, *if* the battle was lost with the fall of the Mutazio. These men were dressed plainly, but armed.

Atlantis didn't bother staffing the gateways between their land and Belial's because they welcomed any Belial who wanted to visit or even change citizenship. They did however, keep soldiers near the borders to ensure peace.

Belial manned their gates, paranoid in checking the origins and purposes of those passing from one side to the other. Rumor said if they caught Belials trying to defect, they were punished with heavy fines, or any other way the soldiers saw fit, even death in some cases.

"Didn't you say nobody was watching the gates when you came through?"

"They weren't. But it was night." Aiela veered off towards a sparse market just down the street. "Maybe if we wait till after dark. Watch for Turner, he must be here somewhere."

"But we said we'd meet on the other side. At the aero pickup…"

"That was when we thought walking across the border would be easy."

"Don't you think Turner will still stick to the plan?"

"He's not going to get across with that bag. They'll take it—and probably him—because of it."

"He'll find a way. Maybe climb the wall farther down, or wait till night, or cause a diversion. I think we should trust him. We can't cross with him. All three of us together plus the bag could be even harder."

Aiela stopped her headlong charge towards the market. "Alright." She looked at Ahna, realized worry was muddling her thinking. "You're right. I just don't like leaving him behind."

"He might already be waiting for us over there."

They circled around, heading again for the gate. "So what's our story going to be?"

Aiela grinned, a little mischief creeping up to ease the worry. "They're men and we're pretty. Flirt a little, tease 'em with a kiss, tell 'em we needed some Belial fun…" She shrugged. "Simple."

Ahna grinned back and led the way.

Before they reached it, the gatemen suddenly rushed inside their shabby guard hut. A commotion of shouting covered Aiela and Ahna as they hurried under the cracked arches.

On the other side, they searched the Atlantean aero lot, hoping to find Turner lounging and teasing them about being so slow.

But he wasn't there.

"Transport to High City please." Aiela mumbled to the lot attendant. "But we're waiting for one more. He should be here any moment." *Please, please let him be here any moment.*

"We're terrible spies." She sighed, as they slumped down on waiting couches. "Why didn't I just drop him on the Atlantis side to begin with?"

"The worst." Ahna agreed, staring tiredly out windows at the occasional person passing back and forth under the gate arches. "We can't even keep track of three people."

"We wiped out an army of giants. That's something." Aiela whispered, scooching further into the comfortable cushions.

Silence lulled them both into drowsing until a hand shook her shoulder. "Best be going *now*." Turner took their hands pulling them up, glancing behind him. Outside the windows, three stormy-faced Belial men paced under their gate arch, scowling and staring in their direction. "They're none too happy wi' me. I'm surprised they didna chase me in here. Rather no' push my luck."

All three were on their feet when Aiela realized he wasn't holding anything. She looked around frantically. "Where's the bag Turner? Where's the *weapons?*"

His face said it all. "I'm sorry. They took it when they caught me tryin' ta toss it o'er the wall. I couldna find where they put it. I knocked one oot an' escaped when the others went ta contact their commanders. They were makin' plans ta take me ta Temple City... couldna let that happen. I looked fer it long as I could. They almost got me again."

"You're bleeding." Aiela examined his hands. Both knuckles had cuts and scrapes across them. One eye was already puffy. Red smudged that temple and Aiela suspected the red would turn darker colors soon.

Ahna scrubbed her eyes. "I can't think of anything we can do about it El." Her voice was quiet. "It's not like we can march over there and demand it back. We have no way to threaten them. If Ziel wants to get it back, let him figure it out. Let's go home."

Aiela stared into Turner's tired eyes. Hating this sudden tension between them.

He looked away, pulling his hands out of hers. "Sorry I failed ya."

They traipsed to the waiting aero in silence.

29

MARDU'S GRIEF

"There are times when the mind is dealt such a blow it hides itself in insanity."

— PATRICK ROTHFUSS, THE NAME OF THE WIND

MARDU

*H*e killed the messenger.

Slowly and softly, Mardu watched his own hands ease towards the man's neck.

The messenger backed away.

"Come." Mardu's voice sounded forced and hollow to his own ears. "Stand right here." He stabbed his finger at the deck in front of him. "Right. Here."

He waited until the messenger stepped back to the exact spot where he'd stood when he'd uttered those deafening words. "Say it again." Mardu knew his own mouth was moving and his tongue was forming words but the voice sounded so strange he wondered where it had been hiding inside him and why it was coming out now. "Say it just like you did before."

"The M-Mutazio are all d-dead Dominus." The man cringed. His voice was hoarse and his eyes dark with terror. "Someone must have accessed the nodes. They all just... dropped... and the main battle barely begun." He rushed through the last six words.

Mardu reached up again as though his hands were underwater, slow, like he didn't want to cause waves.

Wrapping them around the man's throat, positioning them carefully, he squeezed. *They've gotten just a little plump.* He studied his own hands. *Much too pale.* Black hair grew thick along the little finger side. *Like the spine of a book. My hands could tell entire stories.*

The man gurgled and hacked.

Mardu squeezed tighter. *He carries to me an unwanted truth. I shall kill this truth. Make it not so.*

The messenger pried at Mardu's recently plump hands, beat at the bones along the top of his arms, pushed and grabbed, kicked and even buckled his legs perhaps thinking Mardu couldn't hold his weight.

Mardu simply held the messenger closer. Intensely, intimately close. *Almost like a lover. All lovers are liars. All lovers deserve to be punished.*

The dying man's squashed face was red and darkening. He wriggled in violent spurts now. It reminded Mardu of the worms he fished with as a child. They too had wriggled on the hook, some of them as plum-colored as the man's face.

"Dominus, it—it wasn't this man's fault... " One of the commanders protested feebly. They stood in a semicircle. Only six of the original nine. And none of his Generals.

"It was *someone's* fault." Mardu said softly. Pushing the last of his strength into his hands, he crushed the man's throat. "You are so certain it wasn't this man..." he released the limp, plum-faced body and stomped to the one who'd protested. Thrust his face nose to nose with the quaking, wide-eyed commander. "... you must know who it IS! So tell me, was it YOU? WHO DID THIS?"

"No! I-I-I do not know Dominus. I swear on my life, I don't kn—"

"Where is General Rogan? WHERE ARE MY GENERALS?" He'd moved to thunder into the next face.

Another commander stepped out. "General Rogan is dead Dominus. He went up in an aero. I watched him get shot down. But Balek is alive. We found your son. He's with the others, t-taking the carriers home."

Rogan is dead? Must not think of that now.

It was too much.

It was all too much and he thought he might implode with what he was feeling.

Pacing back and forth, his breath coming too fast he snapped. "Tell me. Tell me all of it." *Have to keep moving. Find out who did this to me. Who did it. Who did it. Who did it. Who.*

"We'd barely begun the attack. The entire Grecian force was there. So many. They outnumbered us... "

Five steps to the right. Five steps back. One two three four five. Turn. One two three four five. Turn.

"... wall of fire but it didn't even faze them. Then they fell. They just... went down. And then General Rogan lifted off and was shooting at something and it shot back and his aero crashed. We returned to our camps on the hover trolleys—to the aeros. The humans were all that was left. We got out of there before the Greeks could find us. We just left. There was nothing else we could do."

One two three... "What was in the sky? Did anyone see it?" *Turn. One two three. Turn.*

"No Dominus. None of us did."

"They're returned to Temple City in the carriers—except for General Rogan—the other commanders and all the trainers and handlers that were with us. They sent us in the only aero small enough to land on a ship, to report to you. Dominus, what would you have us do now?

HIs boots echoed hollow on the ship deck.

... two three. Turn. One two three. Turn. Could take the Greek capital, while their navy is still inland. Take their leaders hostage. Force them to turn over their country. But it wouldn't last long. Their numbers are too great. Without the Mutazio they will overpower us.

He didn't answer. Didn't even look at the commanders again. He just walked over to his aero. The one that had shot every ship to splinters that had passed by since they'd anchored, waiting for word that the Grecian military had surrendered to the massive muta army.

Waiting, he'd dreamed over and over how he would fly into the city and claim his victory. He'd treat with the rulers and plan their newly formed alliance. It was to be a brotherhood of countries. The beginning of his world empire.

"Pilot!" He muttered softly, climbing into the aero. Someone went running to fetch the pilot.

A mistake to sit still. He rocked forward and back. *Rogan is dead, dead, dead. My only friend, gone, gone, gone.*

The tears tried to come but only got as far as his temples, making them throb and ache, burning the backs of his eyeballs. He remembered his sweet mother. *Rogan is gone.*

He wanted to cry. He wanted to roar. He wanted to do whatever it took to stop this terrible terrible pain.

The pilot climbed in. "Dominus. To which ship?"

"Up. Go up. Go up up up... " He watched the commanders mill with soldiers below as they rose. Some of them craned faces up at them with dumb expressions. Faces that looked as numb and blank as he felt.

The Mutazio are gone. Those commanders didn't protect my army.

He reached over and flipped the switch that charged the laser.

The pilot looked around. "I see no ships that aren't ours... what are you—?"

"Go higher. No, move back over the ship. Go back. Directly over them."

The pilot's expression turned incredulous. "Dominus, your commanders... our soldiers... you can't—"

"My muta are dead. Someone must pay."

Mardu reached towards the red blinking light. Poked it with his middle finger, without hesitation. A high-pitched ripping sounded and the flash of light was blinding as the ship below exploded.

Did it explode or did it melt? He wasn't sure. It happened so fast.

Now there was nothing but a frothing hole in the water and the air filled with debris, some of it peppering harmlessly against the aero. A million little bits rained down into the water hole.

He felt the tiniest thimble of sanity return.

"Take me to General Pompeii." He couldn't remember which ship that would be.

3 0

HOME

"Home isn't always where you're from, it's where you find light when all grows dark."

— PIERCE BROWN, GOLDEN SON

AIELA

*A*iela had accomplished her mission—both of them in fact. It should have been a joyful homecoming, but exhaustion and grief had stolen her joy and Turner wouldn't let go of losing the bag of weapons.

He buried himself in the seat, facing away, surly and silent. Didn't respond even after she apologized a third time for blaming him.

"It could've happened to any one of us. I'm just glad you got away." She insisted.

But he shrugged her off, not meeting her eyes.

Poseidon's Palace glowed as majestically as ever, spiraling away as the aero turned and settled lightly onto a landing pad ornamented

248

with weathered copper. Even this small bit, as sumptuous as the rest of the Palace, now seemed surreal and dirtied by the horror of the last few days.

Ziel waited alone, midnight blue robes and long silver hair lifting and swirling in the considerable gusts at this altitude.

Holy Mountain rose sharply above them, disappearing in grey-white clouds crouched protectively over its summit. The four of them stood watching as the aero lifted off and angled away towards the gleaming white wall where it would recharge.

The rush of water filled their ears, competing with a restless wind. Two gushing springs had been created by Poseidon, flowing from high on this mountain. One cold and sweet to water the plains, irrigating crops hundreds of miles away via the canals. The other hot and mineralized. These steaming waters circulated through the Palace bathhouses. The rest was piped to Healing Temples across High City, serving its inhabitants and visitors.

Ziel beckoned them close and they huddled around him to catch his words.

"Judging by your cryptic message on the Comm, it is done?" He pushed his voice towards them through nature's noise.

All three nodded. He waited for someone to speak.

"The controllers worked. They fell—the Mutazio. We couldn't see them much of course, even with the moon, but the radar showed they stopped moving…" Aiela's jumbled speech trailed off and Ahna took up story fragments.

"A Belial aero came up for us—only one. We shot the pilot. It was a close thing with its big weapons and much longer range. Aiela's maneuvering saved us. Can we go inside now? I'm freezing."

Ziel nodded. "I'll make tea."

They followed him down steps carved seamlessly into white marble walls, and wound along seemingly endless hallways to his rooms.

Slumped around Ziel's rosewood table, hands wrapped around soapstone mugs of winter milk, deep golden with tumeric and ginger, they told him everything.

Aiela admitted how scared she'd been, piloting their aero through the storm and dodging the Belial aero's guns over the battlefield.

Ahna confessed her impetuous, covert trip to find Carver, describing with horror the fighting pits with conrectus they called Things. She ended by praising the courage of Aiela and Turner's rescue.

Glum-faced, Turner announced his brief capture by the Belial border guards and their seizure of the weapons bag. "I'm sorry I could no' find it again." He made no excuses.

Aiela wanted to protest his self-flagellating tone. Remind him how very tired they all were, how they'd been surprised to even find guards manning the border. Instead she slid a hand into Turner's and held on firmly.

Ziel's fingers steepled in front of him, elbows resting on the polished, rosewood table. "I am immensely proud of each of you." His tone held professional respect but his eyes were pools of compassion as he studied each of them. "I see how troubled you are—as you should be. It is no small thing to take a life, even lives manufactured from the darker side of humanity. Ahna, as foolish as your act was, I am glad it caused you to experience Belial culture, to taste what our world can become, if we, as a society, abandon the Law of One."

He laid a hand on Turner's shoulder. "You are forgiven. I want no more berating of yourself—it only serves to cripple. Our minor sound eye is significant but you did right to abandon it and save yourself. I gladly accept that loss over the loss of you.

"Aiela," he beamed approval at her, "you have demonstrated much wisdom in your actions. Now..." he reached to touch each of them in turn, "... I want you to rest. Sleep as much as you can. Soak in hot water and visit the Temple of Healing when you wake. I have much to discuss with the Rulers so I shall expect you each to take excellent care of yourselves. Come for supper tomorrow. Yes?"

"Yes." They replied.

Gathering his Comm, donning his diadem, he left them to their orders.

Ahna gulped the rest of her spiced milk, padding across thick carpets to root around Ziel's cabinet for something to eat.

Aiela rolled her head, neck popping and cracking to release some of the tension built up from days of intense pressure.

Turner finally looked at her, eyes heavy but relieved. "He's no' angry wi' me?"

"Anger only multiplies one problem into many. He's disappointed in losing the sound eye, but anger won't bring it back." Aiela watched him process this.

"He's right aboot one thing. I've been self-flogging an' bein' awful ta ya in the process. I'm sorry."

Aiela leaned in to brush his lips with hers. "Apology accepted. You hungry?" She went to join Ahna's foraging.

"There's only a little fruit and two grain bars here." Ahna complained.

"What did you expect?"

"Fresh caught shark, preferably smoked and juicy. Fire-roasted vegetables. Warm crusty bread." Ahna gave a small laugh, realizing it was the first one in what felt like weeks. "Wishful thinking..." They helped themselves to the little that Ziel had, carrying it back to his table, eating in silence.

"Meet me in the spa? Maybe a hot soak will help me sleep. I'm so tired—but can't seem to settle my mind." Aiela spoke softly to her sister then kissed Turner's curls. "This one needs to be tucked in." His forehead was sunk onto forearms folded on the table.

Ahna nodded, crunching a green winter apple. "I still don't feel clean after Temple City. Maybe that'll help."

THEY HAD complete privacy in the Ruler's luxurious spa. Normally, Aiela wouldn't think of soaking here, but she knew the Rulers would be hours and hours discussing whatever Ziel chose to tell them.

Besides, it would be worth a reprimand to be able to speak freely while they soaked—unlike the public hot pools.

Bouquets of fresh jasmine and winter peonies from the south, competed to scent the air. Statues of opal dolphins spouted scalding hot water from their mouths and a waterfall tumbled down sheets of crystal formations to mix cool water with hot. The shallow, pink quartz pool was shaped like a rose, each scalloped petal just right to cradle a body. It could have seated ten and though its beautiful room was spacious and filled with light from an entire wall of windows, the steam was so thick you couldn't see more than an arm's length away.

"Do you get the feeling there's important things Ziel isn't telling us?" Only Ahna's face floated above water.

"Yes. Always. We've trusted him to tell us what we need to know." Aiela paused, swirling her hands back and forth across the surface. "Do you think we trust him too much?"

Ahna's shrug rippled the water. "I just wonder... why us? You wouldn't believe the level of talent in the House of Oracles. I'm not anywhere near as gifted as many of them. You're a great healer and leader, but I'm sure there's better equipped people than both of us. He *recruited* us—remember how strongly he suggested these Houses to us way back when we were sixteen? Even then it seemed he knew us better than we know ourselves. It all points to something bigger than what he's told us so far. Don't you think?"

"I think it's odd he sent *us* to kill the Mutazio army. Any other non-military Atlantean who kills would spend moons, years even, in the Aades of Sacrifice yet he barely blinks an eye at all we've done."

Contemplating, soothed by the music of falling water, Aiela's naked body finally began to relax. She felt her systems ease into peace one by one, slowly convinced she was no longer in danger.

"The crystals have been telling me things." Ahna blurted.

Aiela lifted her head from its petal rest and stared at her sister's closed eyes, not understanding. "Tell me. I've suspected you've been shielding me from something." *Just as I must now shield you from who Carver really is.*

This thought wasn't welcome.

"Thoughts. Visions. Ideas... It's like they're calling out to me. Like they want me to *do* something about the things they know. It's almost like they're a person but without emotion. Which seems cold or uncaring. They can see and hear things because of the grid, and they detect patterns of danger which they pass to me. I figure Mama programmed these abilities into them, but I don't know what other things she might have programmed. We need to spend some time with them. Find out what all they're capable of."

"Maybe we should go down in the morning. Meditate with them. Get some answers."

Ahna nodded. "Good idea. It's felt like too much for me handle alone. But you've had a lot to do for Ruler Kenna... "

"You don't have to take care of me anymore you know." Aiela smiled to soften her tone. "Maybe it's better that we start telling each other everything again. Look at the trouble we get in when we don't!" As she said it, her heart gave a tiny twist of guilt.

"You mean, look at the trouble I get in." Ahna was still floating with her eyes closed.

"I didn't realize you missed him that much. I'd hoped maybe your love for him had faded some... " She watched her sister's delicate eyelids quiver, long honey-colored lashes dancing just above high cheekbones.

Tears began to leak from the corners. Small, rose-tipped breasts broke the surface when Ahna inhaled deeply, sinking under again at the bottom of the long exhale.

"Me too." Her voice was dense with emotion. "I know it's ridiculous to still miss him, to still think about him and want him. I've tried ignoring it, replacing him, distracting myself. I even had another Oracle apprentice program me under trance to not be infatuated with him. It's like there's a connection that I can't disconnect from or turn off no matter what I try. So the only thing left was to try to find him.

"I had a dream about him—about us together when we were older. I thought it was a sign. Now I think it was probably just a dream... "

Maybe if she knows who Carver is, she could get over him.

Or it might add more pain if she thinks he lied.

And then she'd know exactly where to find him—which could have disastrous results. Aiela's thoughts went round and round as she patted the water's surface with her palms, sending miniature waves to collide with the edges of Ahna's face and the far scallops of the pool. It felt so odd to keep anything important from her twin. She wished they could just talk about it. Talk through it. But she clearly could no longer predict what Ahna might do—the risks she might take.

"I do understand why you went. If it had been Turner, I'd have done the same thing."

Ahna's eyes blinked open then. Like glistening pools of seafoam, they slid to look at Aiela. "But you wouldn't have waited so long." They shared a knowing smile.

MARDU'S RAGE

"Men in rage strike those that wish them best."

— WILLIAM SHAKESPEARE, OTHELLO

MARDU

𝓜ount Vulcan was rumbling when Mardu woke. Half dark with late winter morning, the still air outside his windows suspended thin white smoke. It happened every few moons.

One of the lesser mountain peaks, Vulcan squatted on the Belial side of the towering, jagged, central mountain ranges layered between Temple City and High City. Vulcan made up for its lack of height by venting often; great clouds of hot steam, smoke and sometimes even ash that engulfed Temple City.

Probably one of the reasons Atlantis ceded this portion of the continent to Onus Belial so long ago. Mardu spat morning mucous into the toilet before pissing. *They probably still laugh at his stupidity every time that mountain goes off.*

Just perfect. Everything else had gone against him. Now he'd have to contend with this too. Belial's hordes of mindless, desperate, addicts would riot again, stealing food with frenzied panic, stock-piling drugs, killing anyone who got in their way. Fear made them controllable—but chaotic and stupid too.

Mardu never worried about perishing from earth's upheavals. It was the violence of men that kept him up at night. Betraying, lying, greedy, corruptions of men was what he feared.

Orja appeared with fresh-squeezed juice. He sipped it in the bath. Maybe soaking would dispel at least part of his troubles. In his spacious suite, Orja would be laying out clothing, along with fresh armor.

"Put spirits in this." He called, setting the molded glass of spiced pomegranate juice on the sunken tub's red jasper edge. Orja bustled in with a bottle, adding clear liquid with its comforting sharp odor.

Two glasses later, he welcomed the numb that finally offered respite from his losses.

CARVER WAS WAITING in his library with Ramon and Norse. Sarim was at the crystal mines preparing the next shipment to High City. They stood, as he'd always required them to, when he entered the room.

"Where's Balek?" Mardu settled behind his dragon skull desk and pushed away the plate of fried roots and steaming slabs of bacon a servant set beside him.

"Haven't seen him since yesterday, late morning." Carver replied.

"Find him." Mardu snapped. "He's two days late in reporting to me. Ramon, take two of my guard and visit the Generals. Escort each to a different cell on lower level 24. Give no explanation and no comforts. I'll take it from there. Norse gather two units and deal with this." He waved a careless hand at the choked air outside the window.

It didn't occur to him to be grateful he had sons to trust with these tasks. Instead, his mind was on the Generals. Fury as hot as the steam spewing from the mountaintop crater miles and miles away, pushed through the numb and he welcomed it.

He'd find the culprit. No matter how much pain, no matter how long, no matter what it cost him, he would find who had destroyed his Mutazio and stolen this chance of ruling Atlantis.

General Hercule would be first. He'd always been jealous of Rogan's position as Mardu's right hand. It'd be no surprise that he eliminated the competition. And then there was the business of having to kill Hercule's idiot son. Likely Hercule had harboured resentment all this time, just waiting for a chance to get even, plotting and planning for the best—the most damaging way to retaliate. *I played right into his plan, leaving him behind instead of assigning him to the invasion. I know better. Enemies should always be kept close at my side.*

Yes, he'd start the interrogations with bitter old Hercule, then root out anyone who'd backed him or known about his scheming.

But first, let them all stew in the cells for awhile. Let the fear build. Let them be hungry and thirsty and shivering and very very afraid by the time he went to them. Getting things set up for interrogation would take some time anyway. Maybe he'd take the wife or a child or mother on the visits. Someone to make the arrogant, scheming Generals more truthful.

"Carver." All three boys were on their way out the door.

Carver turned back at the barked summons. He was dressed in the simple black tunic and leggings he favored, but with an armored vest now. Tall boots reached almost to his knees.

"Balek can wait. Probably passed out in some whore's bed. Tell me everything that you did from the time I left until now." Mardu pulled the plate of food back, realizing with some surprise that he actually took comfort from this boy's company at times. "So I can clean up the messes you made—fix your mistakes."

He took a bite, scowling that the ham had gone lukewarm. "Start with who took advantage of my absence. I'll reward those who did us well and repay those who didn't... "

"Ah Hercule my wretched friend. You are still lying to me—"

"I would never lie to you Dominus. I have not... I w-will not. What is it I have done to be treated this way?" The man wasn't much older than Mardu himself but too many excesses had drained his health. He'd been in a perpetual state of grieving since his son died so violently, right before his eyes.

Grief irritated Mardu.

Standing behind the large center post, Mardu contemplated whether Hercule might indeed be innocent.

Outside the floor to ceiling windows, sunshine warmed the air, still clouded from Vulcan's spits and sputters. The annoying little peak had continued to vent longer this time. No matter how much they used the weather machines, Vulcan stubbornly made more clouds from its tons of steam, spewing a steady stream of smoke and ash into the atmosphere. The scientists had come to him yesterday with dire warnings and grave predictions saying they should all prepare to evacuate.

He'd told them to stop being scared little rabbits hopping about like the sky was falling. "Go figure out how to make it stop. If man can't triumph over nature, what good are we?"

Hercule was craning to look over his shoulder, where Mardu stood with his wandering mind.

Naked and shivering, flesh sagged from Hercule's pale arms, stretched behind him to where his wrists were chained on the backside of the post. Bruises and whip marks from scalp to heels added interest to his otherwise dull, misshapen body and blood clotted on his upper lip, crusting jaggedly down across mashed lips to blacken the stubby remnants of his beard. He'd been standing here a night and a day, since being brought up from the tiny underground cells. Beaten regularly at two hour intervals he'd been asked the same question over and over. "Who killed the Mutazio? Who killed the Mutazio? Who killed the Mutazio?"

He'd had nothing to eat in three days and very little to drink. He stank of feces and urine, but even more of fear.

Not one of the Generals Mardu interrogated had offered anything helpful. Three had died. One from internal injuries, one from electrical shocks and the third from a heart attack or something similar, while being burned with chemicals on strategic body parts. Several had admitted to killing the Mutazio just to stop the pain.

But once hooked up to a mind machine, all their admissions of guilt turned out to be lies.

Hercule's voice cracked now and he hung his head in defeat. "I will say anything you want to hear Dominus. If you want me to confess to something, I will do it. *Gladly.*"

Ignoring the despairing plea, Mardu went to the door and summoned a guard. "Bring me a healer and someone to clean him up. Food and drink too. Be quick."

The guard nodded and hurried off.

Turning back to Hercule, Mardu arranged his face into compassion. "I am sorry for all this. I had to be sure. You understand of course, when an unknown enemy works from within, robs me of my most valuable assets, I cannot spare anyone until that enemy is found."

Hercule sagged against the cold, sleek post, tears of relief dripped down his cheeks. He tried to hide them, keeping his head bowed. "I will not rest until we find our enemy." His voice was thick with emotion.

"Unchain him. Bathe him and give him food. Clean up this mess." Mardu snapped as the healer appeared, accompanied by two servant women, as if it were their fault Hercule was found in this condition.

Stepping out of the scene of torture—Hercule's own luxurious apartment—Mardu waited for his best chemist to arrive. Hercule would be fed and bathed, no doubt believing he could go back to his padded lifestyle of privilege. Hope was a very strong motivator. Chaining and interrogating him is his own home was a cruel hope, dangling like a carrot just out of reach.

The chemist, a very tall and very thin man, arrived.

"You brought the improved truth serum you keep promising?" The chemist reminded Mardu of a hawk with barely a pause between shoulders and jaw, a large beaked nose and hair that stuck up in odd colored tufts.

Hawk man nodded, opened a satchel full of liquid vials, needles, masks, gloves and other accoutrements of his trade for Mardu's inspection.

"Hercule is in his bath. You'll administer the serum now. How long until it takes effect?"

Hawk man stared with dead unblinking eyes. "Seconds."

Mardu nodded. Beckoned one of his guards over. "Come with us."

Hercule was reclined in his huge tub, filled with steaming mineral water. Eyes closed, he clutched a glass of juice with both hands and took sips every little bit.

The healer was placing crystals around him and one of the servant women was dabbing carefully at his injuries.

"Get out." Mardu ordered.

Hercule's head jerked up and his eyes grew desperate with a new terror when he saw the men with Mardu. "N-n-no. Please please please, no more…" He began to sob.

Hawk man ignored the hysterics and knelt beside the tub to inject his murky brown liquid.

Hercule scuttled and splashed away, out of reach.

A guard stepped into the tub and grabbed the old man by his dyed black hair. Dragging him back in a wave of water that sloshed out onto the floor, the guard slammed the whimpering head against marble. A knee held it until Hawk man had emptied the needle into the fleshy neck.

Hercules eyes widened, bloodshot white showing all the way around his irises. He made little squeaky noises and cowered back as far as the tub would allow. His gaze began to jerk this way and that around the room as if it were some new atrocity full of demons and monsters.

"Is he ready?" Mardu asked.

"Yes. I believe he is." Hawk man replied.

"You hate me for killing your son don't you?" Mardu began.

Hercule stared up at him with those stretched wide eyes. He gave a very slow and exaggerated nod.

"I dooooo. I haaate you Marduuuuuuu." His mangled lips twisted into an exaggerated smile that split the clotted cuts open, trickling fresh blood. He didn't seem to feel it. "Heh heh, I made a rhymmm—."

"You were jealous of General Rogan because he was my friend, weren't you?"

Again the slow bob of the head that took his chin almost to his chest and then his forehead to the ceiling, ornate with carved moulding framing paintings of an orgy.

"Yesssss. I wishshsh you would like meeeeee."

Mardu's voice softened as though in understanding. "And so you had to kill Rogan didn't you?"

Hercules face turned slowly all the way over to his left shoulder and then all the way to the right. "Nooo. We need Rogannnnnn."

Mardu's eyes narrowed at Hawk man. "You said this would work!"

"It is." Hawk man's dead gaze was unperturbed. "The other serums had subjects agreeing with the questioner whether it's the truth or not —simply taking the path of least resistance. He's telling the truth over agreeing with you. He has no capacity to tell lies anymore. It takes creativity, imagination, to make up a lie and those areas of his brain are shut down presently."

"Shut dowwwwwn..." Hercule agreed with another exaggerated nod.

"Why did you kill the Mutazio?" Mardu barked.

The shoulder to shoulder head shake grew slower still. "I did not killllllll themmm." He seemed distracted by the way his mouth and tongue worked to form very distinct syllables.

"Who killed them?"

Bushy eyebrows rose comically high. "I don't knowwwww."

"What's the most terrible thing you did?"

The eyebrows fell a millimeter at a time, pushed down down down as Hercule squinched up his entire face. "Let you kill my sonnnnn." Tears leaked out of both eyes.

Mardu turned away in disgust and muttered to his guard on the way out the door. "Drown him. I'm done here."

"New Generals. Faithful ones." Mardu addressed his men gathered in the lavish room at the top of the General's building.

They stood at attention, faces carefully blank.

"You have heard the rumors about my former Generals. I assure you, those disloyal to our cause have been rooted out. There were many kinds of traitors yet we still do not know who ruined us in Greece. I charge you now; find those responsible for the destruction of the Mutazio. No one will rest until you bring me this enemy. Tell your soldiers; 'the man that discovers who did this, can name their reward'." He pointed to a map of Belial. "Each of you will take a sector. Seize every aero, check their logs, interrogate their pilots."

Many aeros had trackers with automatic logs so that workers couldn't cheat their bosses. Many also didn't, so owners could do what they wanted.

"Question every person you remotely suspect. Find out who was doing what, when, and why. Somebody somewhere knows something." He made eye contact with each of the twelve and received a nod and a bow from each.

Cast a wide enough net, Mardu figured, *give enough incentive and maybe he'd get lucky.*

"Yes Dominus."

"It will be done."

"We will not rest until we bring you something."

He smiled as the new Generals stumbled over themselves, assuring him of their undying allegiance. *Time to make nice. Bind these ones to him.* "We've had too many cruel and grim days. Tomorrow begins your investigations. Tonight you will rest. Each of you and a guest may come to dinner at my house."

Grins, raised eyebrows and nods shone back at this announcement. The last time he'd entertained at his home was to celebrate the birth of Norse. Carver hadn't warranted even an announcement—being birthed from a foreign whore.

Mardu studied their faces. Some of the smiles seemed forced. *Not a one of them I can truly trust.*

"Dominus, if I may ask a question?" From his right, General Pompeii bowed low, the only General that escaped the interrogations simply because he'd been with Mardu that night.

Mardu gave a curt nod.

"What of Atlantis? Could they not have conspired against us, perhaps used spies to discover our use of muta nodes and secretly come to the aid of Greece? They are, after all, allies."

"Improbable—but possible yes. My spies are combing High City for clues as we speak. Between the Atlantean's sacred Law of One and the blood laws that stand between our nations, it's doubtful they would violate either, just to save Greece."

Satisfied, General Pompeii bowed again. "We will not fail you in this task Dominus."

"It was one of the small border transports. Owned by an old woman named Rhena who isn't talking." General Pompeii accompanied Mardu to the bordertown where the aero and woman were being held.

"She'll talk. Does the log show when it was in Greece?"

Pompeii smiled, showing large white teeth, waiting a beat for effect, which only irritated Mardu. "It's the one Dominus. It has to be. Of course the internal log doesn't give dates, just a string of coordinates for everywhere it goes, but it was recent. The Greece coordinates are the only time it's been outside of Belial."

Mardu was pleased. *Finally something.* "And what does this woman have against her own country that she would do such a thing?"

Pompeii shrugged. "She won't speak. Won't even acknowledge us. She knows you are coming. She's a hard old bitch and doesn't seem to care about anything we promise or threaten her with."

Mardu rolled his shoulders and reached for his flask. A challenge would be welcome. It'd been too long since anyone had defied him outright or tried to outsmart him. *The most boring thing about ruling; everybody just rolls over.*

"Rhena." Mardu bent to push his face close to hers as he said her name low and soft, almost warmly. She looked at him with absolutely no expression on her disgustingly old face. A thrill shot through him. He could push the bounds of pain with this one. She'd probably hold up longer than most.

He studied the brown eyes with bags under them and wrinkles folding away towards gray streaked hair. Delicate skin sagged under her jaw and flowed in lines and creases down her neck. Horrible. Her whole body probably looked like this. He'd know shortly.

"Why did you kill my Mutazio?"

Her chin came up and those eyes shone with sudden defiance as if she could read his thoughts. "I didn' do a thin' to your Mutazio, Dominus Mardu. But it sure nice for you to come see me personally. I waited for *you*." Her voice was calm with a hint of jeering.

It angered him, but he stored that away for later. "Who did it then? Your aero was there. Why was it in Greece?"

She shrugged. "Some man pay me to use it. Big un—look like you in fact. He Belial but I don' know him. Never seen him a'fore or since. He pay me plenty gold, he take the aero for two days, he bring it back. I don' ask questions when some'un pay me gold."

Mardu leaned close to whisper in her ear. She smelt of ancient fried things. "I'm going to hurt you until I'm sure you're telling the truth. Then I'm going to hurt you until you help us find this man. After that, I'm going to hurt you just because it'll bring me pleasure."

He pulled back to give her a wide leering smile. "Right now, my men are finding who you love, who your family and friends are so they can help too. See, some people don't care about their own pain, but they sure care about those they love."

He located the nipple on her left breast. It felt more like an empty skin pouch than a breast but he could feel the enlarged tip through her tunic. Rolling it, he noted how she pulled away the slightest bit. Almost a subconscious movement. He pinched savagely then and her jaw clenched.

As if to overrule the uncontrollable responses of her body, she thrust her breast against his hand. "You wanta play Dominus? Untie me." She leered at him, licking a dry, thin lower lip. "I'll give you more'n you ever had a'fore." She spread her knees apart as wide as her foot chains would allow.

He straightened and slapped her face with all his strength. It knocked her and the chair over.

She only laughed at him. A high pitched titter that made him want to snap her ugly old neck.

"I don love nobody an' nobody love me. I'm jus' old with nothin' to lose." She rested her head against bare concrete that had been painted, looking sideways up at him as if she hadn't a care in the world.

A sharp knock sounded on the door to her home.

"Dominus Mardu there's an important message for you." His guard's voice called from the other side.

"Know this; I'm going to kill you—but not before I grow tired of hurting you. That could take... years." He turned to go.

"Aww, leavin' so soon! Pity. I told the truth y'know. You can thank me tonight. Ever'one says the Dominus like it rough but I'm bettin' the Dominus don' like it rough as ol' Rhena do..." Her taunting faded away as he stepped into cold sunshine and slammed the door behind him.

"What?" Mardu snapped at his guard. He hated being summoned.

"General Pompeii found border guards who know something. He's still questioning them but wanted you to know without delay."

"Show me where." Mardu noted the abandoned streets as they walked the short distance towards a gate house that squatted beside the arch separating Atlantis and Belial. Plain and poor compared to Temple City, like the other three border towns, there should still be people selling at the market, townspeople going about their business, children running here and there. "Where are all the people?" He inquired, as if his guard would know.

"There are all sorts of rumors flying about why we're here. I'd guess they're hiding." The guard replied.

"People are stupid." Mardu grunted.

Three wide-eyed men inside the gatehouse stood when Mardu ducked inside the door. General Pompeii bowed and they followed his example.

"These men have a very interesting story Dominus." Pompeii turned back to the men. "Start with the bag of weapons." He seemed very excited.

Mardu wondered what he would ask for as reward.

"It's right here. We fetched it to show you's." The fattest one began. He gestured to where a plain black bag lay open on a metal table.

Mardu walked over to examine the items in it. There were light guns, sound rays, and laser knives. "These are Atlantean!" It surprised him. One item he didn't recognize; a metal box with some sort of lock on it.

The fat man continued as if it wasn't that important they had seized a bag of Atlantean weapons. "We stopped a man 'bout seven days ago, tryin' to leave Belial into Atlantis. Young 'un, with queer curly hair an' talk funny. Queerish accent, an' he—"

"What accent?"

"Er, uh, well, I don' know—"

"Well talk like he did. Maybe one of us will know." Mardu said impatiently.

The fat man looked at his companions. "I don' think I can mimic it right. Gaby, you do it. You kin do voices good."

A stocky man with short dirty hair cleared his throat. "Sure an' its nothin', ya know, I was on'y here ta partake in the famous debauchery ya offer." He spoke with a heavy brogue.

"Irish?" Mardu looked at Pompeii. "Sounds like Irish."

Pompeii nodded. "It certainly does." He looked at the three men. "You're very sure that's what he sounded like?"

All three of them nodded vigorously.

The fat one said eagerly. "Exactly like it. I tole you Gaby does voices good."

"Sit down." Mardu ordered the three men. Taking the chair across from them he settled in. "Describe this Irish man. Leave nothing out."

"He was just shorter than me. Very curly hair that was, ah, light brown or maybe a little reddish. Eyes… Gaby, you see what color his eyes was?"

Gaby shook his shaggy head.

"Er, we don' know 'bout his eyes but he was muscled real good. Thick shoulders an' arms. That's how he got away see, me an' Gaby left to get orders, figurin' you's would want this queer man with fancy weapons brought to Temple City, an' while we was gone that shit let him get away."

The "shit" was the third man with hunched shoulders and a ragged, almost emaciated look to him. He hadn't said a word so far and with everyone's attention turned on him, he only hunched lower.

The fat man recounted every word spoken between them as close as he could remember, with occasional questions to Gaby to fill in blanks.

Mardu asked every question he could think of, glad to finally have somebody cooperate. The sun had set and the early darkness of winter chilled the room by the time he rose and stretched. His stomach rumbled. *Time to go home.*

Gathering the weapons and mysterious box back into the bag himself, he smiled at the men. "You've done well. Very well. You shall be rewarded for it. Pompeii, thirty bits of gold for each of them."

The men clamored to each other with excitement. Even "the shit" stood straighter and managed a grateful smile.

Standing at the door, bag in hand Mardu addressed the men a last time. "If you think of anything else or learn of anything, you will come to me immediately?"

All three nodded vigorously, bobbing bows and heads at the same time. *Idiots.*

"A'course we will! Thank you Dominus, thank you. We're honored to serve you. Honored!" The fat man blabbered as Dominus walked away into the night, his guards falling in around him.

"Bring the old bitch. I'll want to interrogate her where I have all my... tools. She knows something that she's not saying. I can feel it."

A guard veered away to Rhena's stone and plaster hovel where she was tied hand and foot to her only chair.

Mardu was settled into his aero, warming his belly from a flask when the guard returned. Alone.

"She's dead." He stood a safe distance outside the aero's side door.

Mardu choked on his brandy, had to cough before he could reply. "Dead?! How?"

Shrugging, the guard shook his head. "Don't know exactly but it looks like she managed to get to that big crystal receiver she had and fall on it. It's embedded in her throat. She's still tied to the chair.

Bloody mess in there. She's definitely dead and it can't have been an accident—"

"Nobody else went inside?" Mardu confirmed. He'd left three of his personal guard outside the tiny house. Those three were arriving back at the aero now.

All three shook their heads. "No Dominus. No one even approached. Didn't see another person within twenty yards the whole time."

"You see her do it? Hear it?"

"Huh-uh."

"No."

"Not even a peep."

"Find anything else there?" He knew these three would have been going through all her possessions for clues to what she knew or why her aero had been in Greece.

Again they shook their heads, climbing into the aero one by one. "Nothing. She did have more gold than usual. Besides that, just clothing, food and woman baubles."

Mardu sat thinking for a few moments. *She definitely knew something. Was willing to die to keep it from me.*

"Bring the body." He spoke to two of the guards. "We'll give it to the Temple of Mind Power." They had endless uses for cadavers—what, Mardu did not want to know.

CREATING GATEKEEPER

"I warn you, the trip will not be easy. Once you choose to walk in the light, your path will lead you places you do not want to go."

— DAVE WOLVERTON, THE COURTSHIP OF PRINCESS
LEIA

ZIEL

I would have to take the girls into another dimension to do it and there was only one person in all the world whom I trusted to help.

She would be like a fury from hell when I asked her—but by now I was resolute. This had to be done, no matter how distasteful.

I'd communed with my Higher Self, my Angels and Guardians, a longtime Pleiadian friend, and the Oversouls of both girls, in building the process I would use. Each and every time I'd asked the same question; "Must this be done?"

It was more of a plea. *Give me another way.*

But each time the answer was the same. "Their human minds will break under what is coming. You must create in them a gatekeeper. A system of protection."

When Ahna ran off to Belial and witnessed their atrocities, enduring abuses on her person, I suddenly had hope. After Aiela and she killed the entire muta army and seemed to weather the barrage of psychosis that followed, I believed they might be strong enough to withstand anything. I almost abandoned the plan to create alters in them. Even after Ahna confided in me how they both lost themselves for a time afterwards, I still hoped.

Bright with the belief I had dodged the proverbial bullet, I again visited with the girl's Oversouls. "Surely these tests have changed them. Strengthened them." I said.

"No. There is not time for them to heal fully. What you call 'tests', created trauma in their brains and bodies. Trauma that will reactivate, multiply, when additional trauma is introduced. It is more important than before, that they have a gatekeeper."

"Then heal the trauma! Or give me a way to!" I insisted, stung by the implication that I had made a mistake in assigning them to the killings.

"It is not to be. These experiences and lessons were chosen. You know this." Came the ever-calm reply.

"THEY'VE ALREADY AGREED to it my love." I pleaded, quavering as any man might when trying to reason with a dragon. "They won't remember any of it. We'll take them into another dimension so they won't even miss time—or we can do it during the night and they'll just think they were sleeping. I can program them so they will have no memories of it. No idea they were even split. And you *know* there's a way to do it without pain—"

Sage attacked me. I'd expected no less.

First she came at me, clawing and hitting, screaming I was evil incarnate.

I let her. The entire idea deserved to be punished. When there was blood on my face and I was wincing, probably cowering away from her bruising fists, she physically backed off but continued to batter me psychically. I'd forgotten how truly formidable she was.

She broke me in places, before her rage was exhausted.

"You cannot." She slumped in the corner chair now with tears streaming down her face. We were both drained and I was crying too. "What must I do to change your mind?" Her whisper was dejected.

"I've tried a thousand ways to change my *own* mind." I pled. "But it always comes back to this;" I waited until she met my eyes, until she was listening fully instead of being defensive.

"The day *will* come when Ahna and Aiela are subjected to mind control. Whether by the Belials or travelers from another time. Even our own Atlanteans might plot to control the Crystals. The girls *will* succumb unless we take precautions now. And if they succumb, if we don't do this thing, everything I've done, everything you've done, everything *they're* doing will be a gigantic waste. They're keepers of the most powerful weapons this world has ever known."

I came then to kneel at her feet. Taking her clenched hands in mine, I opened fully to her, wanting her to see into every part of me, to see I had no hidden agenda. I gave her total access and had she chosen, she perhaps could have changed my mind for me right then. It was only within such complete vulnerability that she might finally come to trust me on this. It seemed an age before she responded.

"Did... was... you did this to Taya?"

I nodded. "Yes. With her permission. It was actually her idea."

Sage's face crumpled into another sob. "She never told me."

I pulled her down into my arms, and this time she let me. We clung together on the new plush carpets of Squirrel's Nest. I concentrated on the bright, comforting colors and the feel of her surrendering finally. "We used drugs, deep trance and the bliss vibration. She was programmed to retain no memory of it, so we never spoke of it after it was done."

I couldn't bear the fact that I was triggering such pain in this woman I'd loved across many ages of time.

She'd been split. Back when the only method known was extreme physical pain and unbearable fear. They had traumatized her mind so badly, the terrorized parts split off to protect the rest of the person.

Complete utter barbarism it was, practiced by immoral scientists. Creating alters allowed them to experiment on a human being without driving them wholly insane or making them comatose. I'd found Sage's case in the restricted files—stolen from Belial laboratories long ago. I knew much about her origins, her programming, her greatest wounds.

It took my breath away to understand what she'd endured. Her father was one of the scientists and her mother, another experiment who birthed Sage at the age of thirteen and died soon after. But I'm not sure if she suspects or not. She seems to have no conscious memories of her parents.

Sitting up abruptly, easing out of my embrace, she wiped tears off of full, high cheekbones, then rose and filled the warming pot with water.

I suppressed a groan as I stood, soreness already setting in. Meaning to visit the bathing closet and clean myself up, I stayed instead, to wash mugs for the tea Sage was making.

Taking my hand she pointed to the bamboo table lit with the glow of the evening light. "Sit so I can clean up this mess I made."

"The mess *we* made." I fitted my lips to hers tenderly for a moment.

"I'm sorry." She said, and I knew we were both thinking of all the times we've said those words to each other. Why is it that those we injure most grievously, are those we love most intensely?

"I'm sorry too."

We drank gallons of tea while we planned. Sage was passionate and brilliant once committed to something. Getting past her defenses was like facing a dragon, but the rewards of having her on my side was more than worth the damage she could inflict.

An ornate bottle of summerberry wine accompanied us outside later. We shared in silence, walking pathways beneath the boughs of towering giants. Forest shadows grew black as we contemplated the task we'd undertake tomorrow. Passing the bottle of burning sweetness back and forth, we took long pulls, needing the warmth—and courage—it created in our bellies. Birds and small animals skittered, rustled and flitted about, preparing for rest. Their plaintive songs echoed our moods.

Shivering in the full dark of early winter night, we finally climbed back up to rooms made cozy by the sisters who'd reunited us. The ones whose personalities we plotted now to split, thereby creating an alter, a persona whose sole task would be locking anyone out who tried to access their minds.

"Are you hungry?" I asked Sage, fingering strands of her hair. It had been golden blonde in her youth, now streaked with equal amounts of white, creating colors that reminded me of white daisies with pale yellow centers. Or freshly churned butter. Still luxuriously thick, she'd let it grow to her waist. "I remember you chopping it all off in the summer."

"The better to swing from vines and climb trees and swim in our pond." She turned to put her hands on my face. Finally, at our advanced ages, we were the same height. In our youth she'd always been taller than me.

"Yes indeed I'm hungry..." She set to kissing me and, as though I was still twelve, I became entirely and eagerly moldable to her will.

"Give Ahna another milligram." I said, watching her digital numbers fall.

Sage nodded, dosage already prepared to place under Ahna's tongue. "Her metabolism is fast. She'll require more, more often."

The drug would keep them in deep trance. The machines they lay in were administering just enough current to suspend them in a physical state of bliss. The only time humans naturally reached this frequency was during extreme sexual pleasure, or when accessing Source during meditation.

Checking every holographic readout to ensure their brains were ready, I began giving the commands. Isolating a portion of the personality, I named the parts simply, Gatekeeper. The list of its duties that Sage and I had comprised was lengthy—we'd tried to think of every eventuality.

I'd refreshed my knowledge of all the mind control methods and experiments from the records, when unscrupulous scientists had explored the far edges of the human mind's capability. Everyone's limits are different but we all have them.

The Gatekeeper personality would activate and take over, at any attempt to access knowledge of the maze or Crystals, from someone they didn't trust. Once activated, it would shut out anything they knew related to the maze or Crystals. It would turn off their physical and emotional senses, so no form of torture could be useful against them while Gatekeeper was activated. It would in essence, be like trying to access an iron block.

Gatekeeper would recognize and guard against attempts of remote viewing, and also prevent any other alters or splits being created in the girls. It loved no one, experienced no emotions, was ruthless and dangerous to those coming against the girls, and would be put to death rather than allow access to their knowledge. The girls would not remember anything that Gatekeeper experienced, just as Gatekeeper would not remember anything outside of its own experiences. Such is the nature of alters. Each is its own fully developed, distinct personality.

I'd needed Sage to bear witness so we could enter the dimension where this equipment was kept, relics from nearly five hundred years earlier in this epoch. These machines were supposed to have been destroyed, but I'd discovered they had been hidden instead. Hidden in a place that could not be found unless you knew exactly where to look —and how. Alternate dimensions require a creator and a witness before they physically manifest.

Sage took her own measures to ensure I only created this one split, by demanding Gatekeeper to protect the girls from any further splits. I'd made a vow to her and she'd sworn to "make a ruin of me" if I broke it.

She's always had trust issues.

Alters typically have a controller person that can manage them. In our case, the only controller function we foresaw was in upgrading the Gatekeeper program should we think of a loophole. In case I was incapacitated, I needed someone besides myself to know what I had done and why. Yet another of Sage's functions.

Creating alters damages the spirit, no matter the method used. But

I hoped this damage would ultimately heal. I prayed the healed place, much like physical scar tissue, would one day be stronger than the original, undamaged spirit.

I loved these two girls as though they were my own blood—a fact both a hindrance and blessing—but everything I felt could not compare to how Sage loved them. This was many times more painful for her. When she'd finally agreed to it, my mind eased some, that I could believe it truly was right and best.

The last thing I did, after switching back to the full personalities of Ahna and Aiela, was to program in enhanced memory function. I needed to finish their training quickly, and the knowledge they'd have to absorb and commit to memory was extensive. They'd need the boost if we were to accomplish all we needed to in the short time I suspected we had.

"WHAT DID YOU LEARN TODAY?" I kissed the silky, pale top of Ahna's head, the dark pile of braids atop Aiela's, and lingered a moment over a messy white-gold bun crowning my lover. Today she smelled of sweet nutmeg.

The three of them were already digging into the basket of simple supper I'd brought to Squirrel's Nest from the Palace kitchens.

I sensed their tiredness in the comfortable silence around the bamboo table. It glowed of connection, this simple table, centering a lovingly restored common room. Too many eyes and ears in the Palace had convinced Sage to conduct her part of the twin's training out here.

I settled into vibrant, mint green cushions that were trimmed with bright tropical blue, as Ahna began to report.

"We finished up truth serums this morning, after our meditation with the Crystals and started on poisons after lunch. Auntie Sage says we'll spend the next three days on those. Not as exact a science as truth serums, so they won't take as long."

"We could have just *poisoned* the Muta army you know... " Aiela interjected.

"And which poison would you have used for that?" Sage asked, ever the teacher.

Aiela thought for a moment. "The strongest paralytic... synthetic algae toxin. Those work the fastest and require only a drop."

"And how might you have administered it?" Sage set colorful, hand-painted plates in front of each of us, and put sparkling orichalcum serving spoons in large bowls of a mixed grains salad and roasted, herbed root vegetables.

"I'd have put it in their water supply." Aiela replied.

"Oh sure." Ahna jumped in. "That would have been *no problem* since we were discovered and almost shot down, *at night,* from no closer than the air above them."

"I guess the logistics would be riskier." Aiela conceded thoughtfully.

We joined hands and Sage blessed the food. Our eyes met for a moment and I knew she was reading my thoughts; this was the closest we'd get in this lifetime, to having a family together. Waves of gratitude rolled through me. I'd spent the last many decades without family ties and now I had some. I hadn't created these lovely creatures but they was no less mine to care for and enjoy.

"We used truth serums on Auntie Sage this morning." A secretive smile turned Ahna's face mischievous.

"Really? And what did you learn about her?" I perked up, surprised Sage would allow them to question her. She had more secrets than the rest of us combined.

"None of your business." Ahna chirped happily.

"I *can* tell you, our concoctions worked quite well though." Aiela added, smirking at my disappointed look.

They loved knowing things I didn't. It was happening more and more frequently.

"They did very well." Sage confirmed, amused at my intense curiosity. "We prepared little kits of serums and antidotes. They're well-equipped and well-versed in how to create more. Aiela, why don't you tell him what else you discovered?"

"I can gauge what the effects are on a person. My abilities helped me know what Auntie Sage was feeling and where the point of 'greatest truth' was. It's easy to give too much, causing drowsiness. Sometimes a serum just makes the person agreeable, instead of truthful. I could actually feel what she was feeling and adjust accordingly."

Sage raised her eyebrows at me. "Could come in handy with some of your Belial spies."

"She knew exactly which antidote to use too." Ahna was enthusiastic about her sister's ability. "We're putting antidotes in the maze with our emergency stashes and in the Crystal Cathedral. Just in case we end up down there under the influence of some truth serum."

Sage and I shared another look. *They really don't remember a thing about Gatekeeper.*

The three of them were yawning and drooping into their plates by the end of our pleasant supper, so I prepared to go back to the Palace. I longed to stay out here with Sage, but weekly report hall was early in the morning and besides, there was no comfortable place for me to sleep. Someday, the girls and I promised each other, we'd add more rooms to Squirrel's Nest. But that day hadn't yet come.

TAP TAP TAP. I woke quickly and fully, settling a robe on as I went to open the door.

Ahna again. Her glowing hair had flyaway strands sticking up as if electrified, her green eyes both paler and wider than usual.

"Another one?" I pulled her inside and held her slight frame close for a moment. She was tense and the skin on her arms felt icy.

She nodded, rubbing her eyes with delicate fists as though trying to rub away the fright. "I'm sorry to wake you again."

I brushed my hands up and down her bare arms, trying to warm them, and she winced. "Sorry" I muttered. "I forgot." Bruises new and old, along with scratches, cuts and scrapes marked the battles she fought every morning. "I'll get a blanket. Put water on for tea. That'll help."

This was the third night in a row.

Sage had gone home two weeks ago after training the twins thoroughly in poisons, truth serums, and several little known functions of plants outside nutrition and healing.

The girls now spent their mornings training in physical combat, their afternoons learning battle strategies from Atlantis' many wars over the epochs, and their evenings with the Crystals, fiddling with programs.

It was the latter causing Ahna's problem.

She was balled up in a cushion at the table when I returned with the fleecy blanket I'd pulled off my own bed. It still held the warmth of my slumber. She hadn't put any water on to heat.

Tucking the blanket snugly around her, I filled the pot and switched it on before sitting next to her. "Tell me." I said softly, inwardly bracing myself.

"At least they never repeat." She began. A small smile appeared, which was an enormous relief to me. "Aiela has a dream that repeats, but mine are always some new sort of ruin."

I breathed deeply and slowly, knowing she'd subconsciously follow my example.

"This time it was the Second Moon. It crashed. Off our western coast and then tidal waves washed over us—the whole continent. They were... as tall as the sky."

I swallowed. "Where were you?"

Her eyes dilated as she remembered whatever she'd experienced in the dream. "I was in a sort of tunnel system. We were moving things... or people maybe... to another continent through a deep underground tunnel system. You called it the Ark. We were still loading when it happened and I couldn't get the opening sealed fast enough. It flooded. We all drowned."

Two nights ago she'd seen a meteor hit the earth. It had caused massive earthquakes that opened fiery, bottomless splits in the ground, separating her from Aiela, eating buildings whole, and leaving nowhere to run. She'd died, falling into a crevasse that opened right beneath her feet.

Last night it had been Atlantis' many dormant and active volcanoes erupting one by one. She'd been trying to find Aiela in the chaotic Palace, unwilling to board one of the aeros that was taking people away, until she located her sister. She suffocated, with many others, on the smoke and ash before the hot lava ever reached them.

"Is there really a tunnel system to an ark?"

"It's five thousand miles long. Before Atlantis turned negative at the end of the third epoch, the Wise Ones foresaw their own end. They built the tunnels and high speed vehicles to travel through them. They cultivated a land that grew crystals. Seeded it. It was where most of their temple crystals had come from. They hid three of their precious temple crystals in this land and called it the Ark because it would preserve the crystal's until they were needed again."

"Have you been there? Are the tunnels still usable?"

"I have not because it's said to be underwater in our present time. As far as I know the tunnels are still there. The opening is in the middle mountains, not far from Crystal City. It's not a bad idea to send a team, repair them if needed. Perhaps that's the purpose of this dream. To remind us they exist and we could use them if needed."

She shivered. "I'm not going near them."

"Of course not."

I set to making us both tea. Already the stars were fading. First bells would sound soon. "What do you think is happening, really? Why might the Crystals be barraging you with these things?" I had my own idea why, but her mind worked crosswise to mine. She sensed things that didn't occur to me, was more optimistic, perhaps less fatalistic, than I.

When she didn't respond right away I called down to the kitchens to have a light meal sent up for both of us.

"I *hope* they're showing me only random possibilities. *Worst case* possibilities. But I'm scared they're giving me pieces of what is really going to happen." She stood and stretched, my blanket falling away as she worked out the kinks and stiffness of huddling. "I wonder if they show me things that relate to my personal dharma."

"What do you mean exactly?"

"The purpose or purposes I came for."

"Yes, I know what you refer to as dharma, how could seeing these disasters help you with your path or guide the choices you make?"

"Well, when I have visions or dreams—even horrible things—I go over in my mind what I would do if it were real. It prepares me to think of the best possible response or actions instead of being shocked and reacting in my default emotions—which tend to be fear. I run or hide from most things I don't see coming."

"Ah. Well, perhaps then we should start planning. If any of these things are going to happen, we've much to do." I found it easier to be philosophical than emotional—as did Ahna.

She nodded. "As real as the dreams seem, I'd feel better if we prepare. Maybe it'd make them stop."

A knock sounded and I went to fetch the basket of food someone would have left outside my door. "Perhaps you can find Aiela after we break our fast? Cancel your morning lessons and I shall cancel my meetings. It's time I tell you both everything. The Crystals seem to think you are ready."

MONTAUK

9,970 BCE TEMPLE CITY, BELIAL

"... And you, you better run because I'm going to destroy you for what you've taken from me."

— SAMANTHA YOUNG, BLOOD WILL TELL

MARDU

"Send a guard once you know what's inside." Mardu had woken a biology engineer named Montauk.

The man was odd with his red-hued skin and white hair that stood like a flame on his crown, but it was his sharp tongue and even sharper condescension that got him cast out of every lab and temple in Belial.

General Rogan had argued Montauk's brilliance to Mardu, suggesting he become their biological weapon technologist.

So now, in the wake of General Rogan's death, Mardu had sought out the man General Rogan had championed. He'd come to the Dark Tower, a seven-story obelisk of obsidian, hematite and smoky quartz, that rose like a middle finger from a tiny island knuckled with rocks, and no bigger than three acres. Several times a year, the highest tides completely submerged this barren heap to lap against the base of the tower.

Younger than himself, despite the misleading white hair, Montauk insisted on working and living alone. His ideas, experiments and products were valuable enough that Mardu had set him up out here, away from Belial's layers of crowds and corruptions.

Seeing the bag of weapons and the mysterious locked metal box, Montauk had come fully awake, edging rapidly into delight. "Definitely Atlantean—more advanced than ours!" He exclaimed, already prying at the locked box.

At least he was in a good mood. Usually he was sour and bitingly sarcastic, and Mardu hadn't the patience to deal with his obstinance.

"Wait til I'm gone to open that! We've no idea what explosives or viruses it contains!" Mardu barked as though to an ignorant child. "You two stay here." Taking the other four guards he strode towards the narrow winding staircase that led down. Time for food and bed.

But Montauk arrived at Mardu's door not a half hour later.

Mardu was enjoying his favorite late night meal, fried reindeer veal and onions. Mentally, he was turning over the implications of what he now knew; *a Belial border aero was used in Greece—but who did it carry and how did they know about the Mutazio nodes? A young, curly-haired Irishman had likely used the aero and killed the Mutazio, but why? He'd been carrying a bag of Atlantean weapons. Was it proof Atlantis had masterminded the whole plot? Probably.*

Mardu knew the Atlanteans hated him and would find ways to defeat him—even if that meant going against their own laws. *It was a smart move,* he had to concede, *using a foreigner to carry out their illegal work. This way Belial couldn't invoke the violation of blood laws...* Rage shot through him at this, yet another betrayal by the Atlanteans.

They pretended at moral superiority, preached relentless compassion and acceptance, acted like they were better in every way. From where he sat, their kindness was pretense, their revered "Law of One" merely an empty front. A well-disguised method of control.

"I said send a guard." Mardu snarled with irritation when Orja showed Montauk into his library.

Montauk bent in his usual flamboyant bow—a gesture more jeering than respectful. "I didn't think it wise. Your guards are in a peculiar… condition. It's better no one else knows what I've discovered inside that box. You're going to want to see this."

"Well, what is it? Stop speaking riddles."

"It's a stone. There was eye protection alongside it so I put it on before unwrapping the stone. When a defense is provided, best use it aye? The fool guards were crowding around, too curious you know, too good to heed my warning. They fell under its spell instantaneously. By that I mean, they are completely biddable to do anything I ask of them. And I do mean anything… " Montauk's chuckle was secretive.

"How do you mean?" Mardu was on his feet now, supper remnants forgotten, already striding towards the door.

"It's difficult to explain. They are most certainly not themselves. Almost as if asleep, rather blank unless spoken to." Montauk followed him outside. "They respond to questions and anything I say, as a command—that's why I didn't want to send them here. What if they were intercepted, waylaid by what someone else said? It's very noticeable that they are in an altered state."

Mardu stared, the thrill of good fortune shooting through him. "I want you to drop everything you're working on and study this stone. Use other scientists to help if you must. Find a way to replicate it. Then create defenses against it. It's likely the same technology—"

"—as the Second Moon, yes!" Montauk cut Mardu off in his excitement. "It's part of the Second Moon's programs, but hasn't been used since the last epoch."

Mardu grunted. His guards fell in around him as he settled into his aero. "Atlantis claims they would never use such a thing, yet here it is, inside their bag of advanced weapons, carried by a foreign assassin!"

"You truly think Atlantis did this thing? Killed our entire Mutazio army?" Montauk's tone sounded almost approving.

"You don't?" Mardu countered.

"All humans are capable of using what power they can take or make. Everyone has the same desperate need, to be in control. It's the only way to alleviate what we fear."

Mardu eyed this man he barely knew. "So what would you do about it?"

Montauk considered before replying. "I'd strike back with everything we've got." A manic gleam lit his eyes. "I'd punish them for not being who they claim to be. For not following their own beliefs. Better to be who you really are—devil or angel—than lie about it."

Mardu leaned forward. "And what is 'everything that we've got'?"

They had arrived, landing on the only flat spot large enough for Mardu's aero. Often as not, it was covered by water. Tonight the rocks were slick from the last high tide, making the footing treacherous.

"You know my work on biological weapons is advanced. What you don't know, is I've successfully combined as many as six diseases—deadly little Chimeras. Some chimeras I've programmed triggers into, so they can lie dormant until certain conditions are introduced to activate them. We'd have to use a fast-acting one to really cripple them. I'd personally guarantee a thirty percent death rate before they figured out how to treat it—maybe higher. The hardest part would be vaccinating our own people before." Montauk eyed him, waiting.

Mardu shrugged. "Put vaccinations in the water or the food supply."

"Brilliant!" Montauk nodded. "Yes, we'd need vast quantities but that would be the perfect solution. You do have control of all the foods…"

Mardu despised being patronized. This man was an expert at it.

They stepped into a well-ordered laboratory where both guards stood stock-still, staring at a blank stone wall.

Mardu studied their vacant eyes. The guards didn't seem to notice Mardu was there. Slapping one across the face only shifted the guard's eyes to look directly at him. "Bang your head against that wall." Mardu felt a little shocked at these men he knew so well. They seemed in some sort of deep trance state.

The guard immediately began bashing his head against the black-stone blocks, splitting skin each time.

"Stop!" Mardu snapped, as blood welled and began to trickle down the man's face.

Crossing to the other one he asked, "How do you feel?"

"Sleepy." The guard replied.

"What are you thinking about"?

"Nothing."

"Do you know who I am?"

"You are the great and terrible Dominus Mardu."

Even their voices sounded different. No inflections or emotions. This could be very useful. He turned to Montauk. "How long until these effects wear off?"

Montauk shrugged. "I've no idea. I'll want to keep them, study the effects. We've been able to induce a similar state with certain frequencies of sound, but never with an energy field based on sight. This is a trance three times deeper than any I've seen."

"Of course you will study them. I'd expect nothing less" Mardu snapped, walking to the bag of weapons on a counter where the metal box sat open and an object wrapped in felted cloth lay beside it. Seeing the eye shields he put one on.

Montauk put on the other and watched as Mardu unwrapped the cloth, carefully lifting and examining the flattened, diamond-shaped crystal. Milky white, it was veined with faint blue, green and yellow lines.

Together they assembled the wooden rod and screwed a copper wire, formed into a diamond shaped frame, onto the top before setting the crystal within it. Altogether, it stood as tall as he was. A staff topped with a weapon of ultimate power, complete control over the will of another.

Even if they couldn't replicate it—couldn't discover the key to the Second Moon—he'd be able to do much with this.

"How soon could you have a chimera ready to go to High City?"

"Depends on how you want to spread it. Ingestion? Human contact? Airbourne?"

Mardu began disassembling the staff. For the first time since the loss of his Mutazio, hope resurged. This would increase his chances of success. If a plague of unknown illness weakened them first, sneaking the Anubis army into their inner harbor aboard Irish ships would be even easier. Heavily armed, the Anubis could attack at night. He'd let them destroy as much as they could, though it would mean rebuilding. All attention would be on fighting them.

By the time his Belial soldiers arrived—in underwater carriers, not aeros or ships as would be expected—the city should already be decimated. He'd have less people to rule after that high of a death toll, less Atlanteans to shoulder the workload. But he'd have the Second Moon. With its power he could overtake any nation he wanted. No one would stand in his way.

He imagined controlling other armies with the sound eye technology. No bloodshed, no need to take them by force. Everyone would do his bidding without question—or emotion. He just had to get close enough. "What do you suggest?"

Montauk clearly had it worked out in his mind already. "Air. A quick fly over of High City to drop aerosol bombs. They wouldn't even suspect till it was too late. I could program the chimera to activate when the moon was in a certain phase. Ensure everyone's infection before it activates—all at the same time. With everyone sick, who will be able to treat them? Who will be able to discover a cure?"

Mardu raised his chin, allowing a broad smile. Excitement pounded through him, potent as the purest drug. "I will return in the morning to complete our planning. For now, I'll leave you to this work. I trust you keep secrets well?"

"There's a reason I'm your lead weapons technologist... but that reason is a secret—even from you." Montauk winked, then sobered at Mardu's bland look. "Yes Dominus. I'm a veritable stronghold of secrets, shan't breathe a word about our plans. Even those working on our projects won't know what they're working towards."

He bowed lower than ever.

Mardu had just settled into bed. Dawn would demand his arising in just a few hours whether he was rested or not. Though his body felt exhausted, his mind wouldn't cease turning over the possibility of overtaking Atlantis still.

Sleep was finally near when Orja gently shook his shoulder, whispering in the dark, "I'm so sorry Dominus, she is here and demanding to see you. She says it is urgent, imperative, and cannot wait until morning because she must leave again while it's still dark, must return before anyone misses her. She insists she risked much by coming directly to you…"

Mardu dragged his aching body upright and nodded, remembering that Orja wouldn't see his nod. "Send her in." He muttered.

Orja never used this woman's name; a passive aggressive display of disapproval. In Orja's quiet acquiescent language, it meant she despised this person.

Mardu waved on the light just enough that his visitor wouldn't trip in the dark. It had been years since she'd been here in his bedchamber.

Nervous and fluttery as always, Jaydee crept in. She looked old.

"What?" He tried to inject the word with demand and outrage that she'd dare turn up here to disturb his sleep. It came out sounding mildly annoyed, mostly weary.

Falling on her knees before him, she reached tentatively to touch his kneecap. "Atlantis has conspired against you Dominus. I sedu—er drank with a scientist last night and he boasted of making a device that controlled the Belial Mutazio nodes. A whole team of Atlantean scientists worked on it… *for Ruler Ziel.*"

"Don't call him that." Mardu snapped, wide awake now. "You have proof?"

A quick shake of her head. "No. But perhaps I can get some. This man's quite, ah, taken with me."

Mardu was too tired to care about the jealousy she liked to stir up. "What else do you know?"

"It was right before your muta army fell. He said they'd barely finished the devices, hadn't even tested them yet. He was smug about his secret knowledge, that he'd participated in an illegal act against Belial. That's all I know. I didn't want to seem too interested of course. I must hurry back. I will send word once I know more."

She rose without his leave, hovering close for a moment.

He nodded, so tired it was hard to think. "Get proof. Without it, I cannot claim retribution."

She put out a hand as if to touch his face, then thought better of it, quickly stepping back, and bowed. "I will do my best. As I always have." She turned and walked out.

TURNER SAILS AWAY

9,970 BCE HIGH CITY, ATLANTIS

Don't hide your heart but reveal it. So that mine might be revealed, and I might accept what I am capable of.

— RUMI

TURNER

He woke hot and hard in the night, needing her.

Moving closer, spooning his body loosely around hers, he began to touch. Languorously, one rope-roughened palm moved along the erotic ridge of her hip. Crossing the warm, soft, side belly between, his fingertips strummed up each curving rib bone to pause at the hollow of her underarm.

She moved, twisting towards him, hand reaching to fumble sleepily at his head. "Whatsamatter?"

"No' a thing." He whispered, lifting his head to kiss the petal smooth skin below her ear.

"Mmm. 'S nice." She settled again, shoving ripe buttocks back against his erection, wriggling a sleepy little dance.

He sucked at the spot where her cheekbone met the tragus nub of her ear, hand sliding onto her breast, rubbing light circles until the hardening peak tickled his palm. Gathering its mound shape, his fingers wrapped to embrace its fullness.

When she hummed another "Mmmm" he lifted up further. Pressing her shoulder until she lay on her back he took her nipple into his mouth.

This, right here, was what he craved; how her breath quickened, how she pressed her body up to meet his, how her hands slid over his muscles again and again before twining in his rowdy hair.

They'd made love after going to bed tonight, prolonging each other's pleasure, culminating in releases so deep they'd both wept.

Sometimes Aiela would wake him before dawn with a brisk, demanding coupling before she left to bathe and begin her day. This time it was him doing the waking.

He slid a hand very low on her belly, kissing and suckling around the plump edges of her breast. She promptly reached to put his hand between her legs, pushing his fingers where she wanted them, moving against him.

It always made him smile, how she showed him exactly what she wanted.

"I worship the feel o' ya." He whispered to her, fingers moving under hers. "Like nothin' else my hands ever touched—"

She cut him off with a wet kiss that landed on his nostril in the dark before adjusting to his mouth, wriggling under him, wrapping sleep-warm legs around his hips.

He lifted back just enough to whisper "I love ya beyond all reason my dark shiny moon" as she pulled him inside her.

MORNING CAME TOO SOON. He woke at the sound of morning chimes, to find her inches away, watching him solemnly with bottomless blue eyes.

"Hoorrible chimes." He scowled. "At home we do our own wakin' whatever time suits us. An' it's ta the sound o' birds chirpin' an' waves lappin', no' some tin-can tune."

Aiela blinked. "It's not the morning chimes you're upset about. Not really. It's because you have to leave again today. I don't like it either. But at least we get to be together a few days every moon…"

He was tired of this mantra. They used it to convince each other this was the best they could have. "It's no' enough anymore." He softened his grouchy tone with effort. "I want ta build a life wi' ya. Have a home an' wee babes some day. We canna do that in a handful o' days splittin' up weeks and weeks apart. No' well anyway… why are ya starin' at me?"

"I'm memorizing your faces. This is your cross one. Last night was your blissful one—well, first your lusty one and then the blissful. I've already got your happy and satisfied and nostalgic and ashamed—that was on the way back from Belial of course—really? You want to make babies with me?"

His head spun keeping up with her. "Memorizing my… faces? I've only the one, Moon Goddess. A'course I want ta have babes. No' just the makin', the *havin'* and *raisin'*. Little ones that are half me an' half you an' who need us both. Mostly, a home that's ours…"

"Ah. You want to tie me to you. You want predictability."

"Well I do… a'course."

Her eyes softened and she touched his bottom lip. "You don't need anything to tie me to you Turner. I couldn't love you more than I already do. I know only time will prove that, but I'll still say it as much as I need to. It's you I want. You I choose. A home of our own would be nice, but maybe you can think of me as your home. Until we can have those things, until we're in a position to make both our dreams come true, just come home to me—wherever that is."

He felt his eyes prickle and moisten. Hadn't realized how badly he needed to hear her say it.

"As far as predictability though—you're out of luck. Nobody gets that. Doesn't matter how much love or babies or things we make together."

"I know." He pulled her head to his chest, kissing the top of midnight braids. "But a man can dream."

They lay clinging to each other in silence and he wondered what she was thinking about now. Her mind seemed to race through a hundred different subjects while he worked through layers of one. "I want ta marry ya, ya know."

She pulled back to stare at him, again with the solemn expression. "You don't know what our lifemate customs are." Her tone was a bit ominous.

"Canna be all that different than ours."

Her big sapphire eyes widened, as she feigned looking scared. "They'll take us up to the middle mountains. Strip us naked—even in the middle of winter—and send us into the wilds with nothing but each other. If we don't starve, don't die of exposure or snakebite or eating poisonous plants or get hurt and then infected, or sick... or anything else, *and* we both still want to be married after a moon of survival living, then we can wed."

He shrugged. "I can hunt, fish and build—well, I *think* I can build—no' that I've done it much. You're a healer. I doon't know exactly wha' else ya can do, but I look forward ta finding out. I know nothin' about Atlantean plants but I can learn—"

"—oh stop. You know I'm lying." She smacked his chest, giggling softly.

He grinned at her. "It was a *good* lie though. Was it really a custom?"

"Lemurian. I'm sure Atlantis did it too in the beginning. The biggest problem is, we don't have much wilderness left anymore."

"We could do it in Ireland." He wiggled his eyebrows at her. "Just you an' me, *naked*, swimmin' in the lochs, stealin' sheep an' chickens ta butcher together, roamin' the country an' makin' love every night in a big soft fern..." He stopped at the faraway look on her face. "Where are ya now? Yer no' listenin'... "

Her eyes returned to his face. "I was thinking about where we'd do the ceremony... Ireland or here?"

His heart swelled. She was taking him serious. "Sure an' we could do both. Unless all yer people would like ta make a trip ta Ireland? There's joos' too many o' mine. Mam's people would... will all come from Greece. We'd fill up three ships, or more, an' have ta find a place for them all ta stay. What am I sayin'? Da'd never consent ta comin' here. It's ancient tradition ta make vows at our family home."

Their eyes met and stuck. Her luminous blues were solemn again, studying him as if searching for anything hidden.

"You really want to marry me? We've known each other for... not quite seven moons? What if I can't have babies? What if I need to stay here for several years or want to go back to Chiffon? What if you get tired of merchanting... or Atlantis, and decide to go to Greece and make knives and maps? What if we stop loving each other? What if..."

He waited patiently until she ran out. It took a good long while, and a great lot of effort not to laugh at her wilder fears. He didn't interrupt, or deny, or reassure.

Finally she sat quiet, awaiting his response.

"Yes my Moon Goddess. Yes I do want ta make vows ta ya. I'd do it right now. Or tomorrow or any other day ya choose. Yes. I want ta love ya and be wi' ya for the rest o' my life... what's... why are ya cryin'?"

She laughed at him, even with tears in her eyes, and made to get out of bed. "You know you're the only one I can admit my worries to?"

Wrapping a brilliant purple meditation robe around her nakedness, she filled her hot pot. "I tell you every ridiculous fear that goes through my mind." She turned to face him, resting one hand on a hip while her tea water heated. "Doesn't faze ya a bit doos it? No' my stout han'some Irishman, no!"

Smiling at her very accurate mimic of his brogue, Turner rose and pulled his pants on.

Light tapping sounded at the door. Aiela went to open it, inviting Ahna in. "More bad dreams?" She pulled her sister close as if some important communication had happened between them.

Turner was learning to read their body language, could often tell when they communicated without words.

"Ziel wants us to cancel our duties today. Says it's time he tells us everything."

They pulled apart, and Ahna flashed a quick smile at Turner. "Safe journeys to you brother. We'll miss you as always, while you're gone."

"Thank you. Truthfully, I'm no' lookin' forward ta navigating the winter seas…"

"Ruler Kenna won't be happy if I don't show up today." Aiela said, studying her twin's flyaway hair. "He'll need to smooth that over for me."

Her eyes cut to Turner and back. "We'll eat and say our goodbyes. Tell Ziel I'll be there in an hour."

3 5

THE PROPHECY

"Everything is set but everything can be changed."

— *MAHARISHI MAHESH YOGI*

AIELA

*S*he rushed through long curving hallways in Poseidon's Palace towards Ziel's apartment, purple meditation cloak billowing out behind her. Her thoughts still clung to Turner.

She was sick of bidding him farewell. How many times now had she begged him to be careful, to come back to her soon? *I should be grateful we get to be together at all.* It was a mantra she repeated all too often.

This time, he would return to High City only long enough to offload the cargo of crystals delivered from Belial mines. They'd have one night together before he sailed home to Ireland for a visit. He'd stay there for an entire moon, and pick up his next few itineraries from his father. She sighed. Maybe they *should* marry soon like he wanted. Perhaps that would encourage Meihal to schedule Turner for longer stays with her.

Without knocking, she pushed open Ziel's beautifully carved door.

He was deep in discussion with Ahna. "... if Maya knows the southern hemisphere of Merika."

"We'd just need to find someone who knows the northern." Ahna finished, smiling when she saw Aiela. "Oh good, you're here. You want tea?"

Aiela nodded. "Why are we knowing hemispheres?"

"Evacuations." Ahna poured a careful stream of pale ruby tea into one of Ziel's tiny, stone teacups.

Aiela settled onto a plush floor cushion, and reached for the miniature mug, steaming fragrance of rosehip and white sage. Sipping, she forced her mind to let go of Turner and focus on the present. If Ziel had asked them to cancel meetings and trainings, it must be important.

"The Crystal's catastrophic dreams have been about Atlantis ending—one way or another... " Ahna began. She'd bathed, and her hair shone satin as it dried, no longer standing on end.

Aiela frowned, listening to Ahna describe a panoply of dreamt calamities that befell Atlantis.

"... I think these are all possibilities that they want us to prepare for." Ahna finished, eyes fixed on her twin. "What do you think?"

Aiela looked to Ziel but he too waited to hear her reaction.

"It's interesting that you're dreaming instead of visioning... is it just to get your attention?"

"Dreams are longer, more detailed—you know how the visions happen in a split second. It's like the Crystals want to give more complete information than what my mind allows for in a waking vision."

"And you think people will believe this enough to evacuate to another continent?" Aiela addressed both, sounding doubtful.

Ziel smoothed a thick silver eyebrow with a forefinger. "That is the question. There are some who trust me enough to follow my urging. Others will go just because it will seem an adventure, or because their life theme is nobility and patriotism. A few might be receiving their own warnings, or messages, and be relieved to do something about it. Many will scoff and refuse—which is fine. Everyone needs to make their own choices with something this... drastic. We cannot control the response, but we can offer the information, yes?"

"Yes. Alright, so when do we start? And how?" Aiela blew on her tea before sipping.

"I will make a public service announcement as soon as we're ready. Nothing too detailed or dire, just stating the House of Oracles has divined information that suggests a calamity is coming to Atlantis. I will urge everyone to make a plan of evacuation should they need it, and ask for volunteers—groups, entire families—willing to move to other continents to establish colonies, and preserve portions of our libraries of knowledge and culture.

"It is those volunteers I would ultimately like you two to meet with, organize, oversee. It's been done before. Read up on the archives detailing the ends of previous epochs. You'll need a staff of helpers— which I'll give you leave to choose from any of the Houses, once you know how many will be volunteering to go, and how big the project will actually be."

Aiela and Ahna blinked at each other.

"What about our training... and other jobs?" .

"Your training is close to complete... I only have one more item, which we will speak of later. You have made the maze your own— equipped it as you saw fit. You know the Crystal's programming. I'm confidant you're both well-versed in self-defense, mind control and even battle strategy. Aiela, you have learned the makings of a Ruler, how to lead justly with humility. Ahna, you have studied and practiced metaphysics, gained an understanding of your abilities, expanded them."

"It *has* been quite a lot... when you put it like that." Aiela admitted.

"These last two weeks seemed extra intense." Ahna added. "We've absorbed more, and a whole lot faster, than all the other moons. It's odd."

Some emotion or thought flitted across Ziel's face, and Aiela

297

watched his pulsing colors shrink. But he waited, as if they might ask more questions, or have more thoughts on the matter.

"This was what you wanted to tell us? That we're to be in charge of organizing evacuations?" She finally asked into the silence.

"No." He shook his head, attention wandering across the room. "No, there's much more. That's just... our response to Ahna's dreams."

Rising, he crossed the room to open the glass doors enclosing his bookshelves, and removed a large codex with both hands. It looked ancient. Crafted in the style of centuries past with thickly bonded leather covers, it was filled with paper made of wood fibers, instead of the hemp used today. Gilded letters embossed the front, proclaiming in grandly sweeping script; *Atlantis Book of Prophecies, Vol. Six*.

He set it before them with a gentle thump and opened the connected pages to a place marked with a deep blue velvet ribbon.

"Perhaps you would read this? And then I shall explain... " He set about filling the warming pot with fresh water, though the teapot was still full.

Aiela read aloud.

> "Bourne of lightning and fire,
> One shows the way. Mark
> the hour of early birth with
> crimson flower.
> Darkness flayed in breast of men,
> given now the way to mend.
> Heed the two, follow One and
> light prevails before
> end.
>
> One to come and turn
> the tides, clear destruction
> of evil minds.
> Change the course and move
> our race to fearless ground
> on higher plane.
> Be it so on mountains high

midst scouring wind and clouds
that fly.

Courses etched among the stars,
mirrored on earth in blood and flowers.
Salvation wove as dark and light
work together, ignite
a spark of endings to begin.
Birth causes death
and in between,
triumphs of time and sadness wing
to end unholy reign.

-Onus Mark Belial

He was pacing by the time she finished, one fingertip smoothing his eyebrow over and over.

They watched him expectantly, faces swiveling to follow his slow glide, seven steps one way, turn, seven more.

Finally facing them, his hands steepled, fingertips lightly touching under his chin, he spoke. "Rowena, my predecessor and teacher, was a numerologist with spatial sequence synesthesia."

The girls look blankly at him.

"Basically, she saw and experienced everything numerically. Colors, sounds, tastes, words, ideas, anything and everything around her translated to a number, or set of numbers—which held deeper meaning. She saw and understood how everything in the universe was connected mathematically." He resumed the pacing.

"I didn't understand much of what she said, though she tried again and again to explain in mathematical terms why certain things held a greater significance than others, how they fit into an overall pattern or rhythm. I could sense the truth of what she believed and so I carefully documented her most dire concerns."

He veered out of his triangle to tap the page spread open on the table. "This prophecy was at the center of it all. She described it as a triple spiral—universal events, planet earth's evolution, and the fall of souls into humanity—with this writing at the center of all this triple spiral meant for Atlantis."

"*Onus Belial* wrote it?" Ahna had been re-reading while Ziel talked.

He stopped pacing again. "Yes. His full name, the exact date and time he received this, the number of stanzas, and lines within them, even the page number it is written on, all correlates to the importance of this prophecy." The pacing resumed. "Rowena chose me based on the date, time and location of my birth. Even my name was a number that fit her extensive equations. Everyone else thought it was because of my giftedness; a fiction I've kept.

Her synesthesia was known, but how much she relied on it—how extensively it guided her—was not. Most people just thought she was extraordinarily wise." He came to hover by his rosewood table and sip tea gone cold, grimacing at it before continuing.

"She'd studied major events from every epoch and mathematically linked them. From astrological placements, to the inciting events and even the population numbers at the time of each epoch's end, she saw a pattern. The 'overarching pattern of Atlantis', she called it. When she showed it to me, I knew she was onto something. She showed me how it was very much a repeating pattern—though a complex one—and every aspect of the next installment was predictable based on the past. This prophecy, she insisted, was the key. On her deathbed she garbled incoherently about it for hours. Too late, I thought to record her ramblings and only captured the final bits. That partial recording has turned out to be invaluable.

"I've come to believe everything she perceived was indeed a higher form of truth. She'd found a way to mathematically map the future."

Aiela had quietly fixed another pot of tea, a delicate white jasmine sweetened with toasted coconut sugar. She pressed the tiny warm cup she had emptied and refilled into his hands. She'd never seen him this distracted, as though he were miles away while he talked.

"Thank you." He sipped, gazing out his single, long narrow window, the morning light streaming in framing his body in a golden halo.

Aiela resumed her seat to pour fresh tea for herself and Ahna. Sipping, they raised silent eyebrows at each other over their cups.

Finally, we've come to the important part. Silence grew long, as they patiently watched him, instinctively knowing that whatever was coming must come in Ziel's own time.

Finally, he came to stand between them. A bony finger underlined the words he read aloud. *"Bourne of lightning and fire one shows the way...* You'll have heard the story of your birth I am certain. The superstorm wherein lightning decimated Cherry Island while your mother birthed you by the light of a fire. Your *early birth*—an entire moon early I believe—was *marked* with the *crimson flowers* of orchids under cherries ripening on the island's trees—"

"You're saying this prophecy is about *us?!*" Ahna interrupted.

Already, unknown pieces to a puzzle were clicking into place in Aiela's mind, like answers to questions she'd only just begun to form.

At Ziel's nod, Ahna continued, "How can that be? This speaks of One. '*Heed the two, follow One*'... "

"Yes." Ziel's eyes lit as he took his seat. His aura throbbed bright with passion. It told Aiela much.

"See, earth is a *dual* system. Light and Dark, love and fear, fast and slow, male and female, everything here has a mirror opposite. Traditionally, the word 'one' is capitalized when it shows the *completeness* of a duality. So the capitalized One used here, refers to two parts that make the whole. '*Heed the two*' refers to considering two distinct personalities, but it explicitly instructs us to follow the whole, the both. The *One.* That's you two... together."

He paused, and Aiela began to let it sink in. Not that she believed it yet. More that she was considering *his* belief.

"*Darkness flayed in breast of men.* It's clear that greater and greater darkness is being laid bare or opened, particularly in the masculine energies across the globe... twisted sexual excesses, power and control violations and addictions... I believe you incarnated as females to be the counterbalance, or the feminine answer to this masculine imbalance.

"It goes on to speak of a great change in humanity's course. Rowena believed it was an intentional dive into darkness—a fall that goes deeper than anyone imagines. 'Entering the great shadow' she called it. Remember in Crystal City when we spoke of the Order of

Melchizedek? It's the same idea Rowena spoke of. It makes sense that our race cannot overcome fear until we've walked through all that there is to fear. And when that day comes, when fear no longer controls us, we will certainly enter into a higher plane, or dimension.

"The second and third stanzas she believed spoke of future epochs for humanity.

"But I think the third stanza refers again to your birth; *'blood and flowers',* and even your persons; *'light and dark'.* I've long been intrigued as to the *'triumphs of time and sadness'* that can end *'unholy reign'*. What do you imagine would be a triumph of time and sadness?"

Both girls leaned forward, thinking, caught up in the riddles.

"The gift of wisdom." Ahna murmured at the same time Aiela practically shouted "Wisdom!" as the answer rushed in.

He beamed at them. "Yes!" His voice quieted along with his energy colors. "Yes, I believe that's the answer too. With wisdom—the gift only given after completing lessons of time and sadness—the reign of all things unholy, all things unloving, will come to an end. I believe, just as it will take both of you working together to complete your mission, so humanity's ultimate salvation will be a product of both the light and the darkness.

Interesting too; *'the courses set among the stars,'* which I take to be the plans our souls make on the other side, are *'mirrored on earth in blood and flowers'*, or the spiritual plans becoming physical. It touches here on the unending nature of life, the *spark of endings to begin,* and *birth causes death."* He stopped speaking abruptly and leaned back as if placing a physical period at the end of his discourse.

Aiela was filling with rapid questions. Too many to sort out, much less speak aloud. She took a deep long inhale, shaking her head as if that might clear the popcorning thoughts from packing in tighter and tighter. "Obviously, this is why you searched us out when we were little. Why you recruited us, placed us in these positions…"

"… trained us for more than just protecting the Crystals." Ahna finished the thought. "And now you want us to lead the people, tell them where to go and what to do there. You want us to save Atlantis. You think, because of this prophecy, that we *can.*"

Ziel nodded. Such a tiny movement. His eyes flicked back and forth between them.

Aiela realized he'd been worried about telling them. Uncertain how they'd take it, if they'd believe him, or be crushed by the weight of it, or maybe just quit.

"But I thought the future is never set. Probable perhaps—but fluid. Changeable."

"You do understand... " he paused as if deciding whether to continue. Resolve settled in the lines around his eyes. "This is an abrupt change of subject but it relates to the prophecy too. You know Mardu may well retaliate against us. For the Mutazio."

"But he doesn't know who did it. We were careful." Ahna tried to sound confident.

Ziel raised an eyebrow. "He has spies here, just as we do there. If he does find out, I doubt he'll care about the blood laws. He'll decide himself how Atlantis should be punished. I can't help but think he might trigger something... something that causes a disaster like Ahna's dreams. "

"But we stopped him from doing something horrific! It wasn't an attack on Belial, we simply *intervened*. For our *ally*! He can't logically punish Atlantis for that." Aiela protested.

"Ah my girl." Ziel spoke with utmost respect and tenderness. "Evil has no logic. It serves only itself. Its highest goal is more power by which to gain ultimate control. It values pleasure above all else. It is narcissistic to the point where those of that vibration cannot even comprehend another's viewpoint. It has room for only its own experiences, desires, needs."

His face softened to a smile. "You don't have babies yet, but you've heard how a little one wakes its parents repeatedly from their rest. A baby has no capacity to know how its demands affect those around it. The sleepless nights, the fouled diapers, the feeding and holding and endless needs that must be met. This is the same immaturity of consciousness that evil is done from. Very young souls, though inhabiting fully grown adult bodies, have no awareness of the harm they do. They don't care, because they literally cannot comprehend any experience but their own."

"Are you saying we should have *compassion* for Mardu's atrocities?!" Aiela's eye bored into him. He shook his head, leaning in slightly, meeting her gaze fully.

"I'm saying you need to understand how he thinks, so that you know there is *no chance* of compassion stopping him. His or yours."

"Most of Belial are young souls." Ahna realized aloud. "It's why Atlantis can't reason with them, seeks only to contain them."

Ziel's face held regret. "We were never meant to be so separate. Just as all ages of humanity have much to learn from each other, so do soul ages. Yet we've managed to segregate, creating a bubble of utopia on our side, sans the difficulties and hardships that grow us. While on their side it's a horror show, conducted by a million toddlers with adult power and no supervision."

All three of them were silent, holding tea gone cold, sitting with the dark truth of this.

"This might be hard to hear... " Ziel began again.

The girls looked at each other and snickered. "All of that—life-changing revelations and you've something to say that 'might be hard to hear'?" Aiela stretched, standing to work out her stiffness. "Lay it on us then."

"It's about your parents."

This sobered them.

"It's possible Mardu had them killed."

It felt like a bomb of quiet went off. Aiela's mind stopped absorbing and the old numb returned. The nothingness that had padded her from the world after she learned of the avalanche that took her parents away. Nothing on her body seemed to work.

"Wh-what do you mean?" Ahna's words came slow.

Ziel reached to touch her frozen arm. "Sit down Aiela. You're pale. I'll get you something to eat." He went to rummage in his tea cabinet and Aiela sat. She and Ahna reached to link hands, feeling the wound of grief ripped open again, stabilizing each other until Ziel returned with bars of dried fruit and seeds. Her world roared back into focus as she ate.

"Tell us." She demanded.

"There's not much to tell." Ziel sat back down. "I suspected their death wasn't natural but there was no proof, no logical reason to suspect it. Only my intuition. I told myself I was just being paranoid. After you brought me his journal, I understood the why—in light of what Drey knew of the muta nodes. They died around the time Mardu must have been planning the Greece attack using the muta army. But that's still all I have. Suspicions. I only mention it because they're your parents. You deserve to know what I know. It wouldn't be the first time Mardu has assassinated people who posed a problem to him. He's careful and thorough so Belial doesn't lose their land or food rights. We never seem to have proof, but it's happened many many times before."

"I need a break." Ahna announced. "This is... quite a lot."

"Of course. Take as much time as you need. Perhaps a walk would serve. I'll be here with our midday meal when you return."

Aiela's heart hurt. "There's more?" It came out sounding more dejected than she intended, but Ziel only smiled as though he under- stood her overwhelm completely.

"Yes, but it has to do with the Crystals and the Second Moon. No more revelations, involving you, that spans all of time or affects the entirety of humanity."

"Thank every god that will be!" She muttered under her breath, joining Ahna, already waiting at the door. "We'll return... once our minds stop spinning."

THEY HEADED to the top of Holy Mountain. Walking briskly through the Observatory that gleamed like a crystal crown on top of Posei- don's Palace, they followed stone steps that melded into a narrow dirt path.

Winding steeply up, they crossed cascading streams of water again and again as the path spiraled the mountain up, up and up.

Aiela pushed as fast as her laboring lungs would allow. She wanted to run like she used to, trying to outrun the repetitive dreams that haunted her childhood, or the consequences of mistakes she'd made.

But this is neither a dream nor a mistake... is it? Have I done something to bring this enormous weight down upon myself? Perhaps Ziel is just a lunatic, believing that specific prophecy, out of hundreds of thousands the House of Oracles have amassed. Believing the two of us, ordinary girls with no more gifts or intelligence than a million other Atlanteans, will somehow save Atlantis. And from what? The calamities Ahna keeps dreaming? Mardu's revenge? How are we supposed to do that? Convince enough scientists to prepare to somehow combat the fiery temper tantrums of the very Earth? I suppose the military is quite capable of defending against Mardu... and the Rulers can take care of that...

Maybe we have quite a lot of time yet. Perhaps I'm going to become one of the Seven and from that position, and the advancements that will surely have been made scientifically by then, it can be done.

This thought brought so much calm, she clung to it.

Yes, that must be it. There is probably plenty of time yet. And now that we know what may be coming, what our role is to be, we can prepare. Evacuating people, establishing colonies in other places, might actually be how we save Atlantis. Or perhaps we find a way to save some of the land too.

Her thoughts spiraled, mirroring the path they climbed.

Ahna panted behind her, no doubt working through her own thoughts.

"At least we're in this together." She said over her shoulder.

Ahna's reply was simply a rush of gratitude.

At the summit, they flopped down on the grass between the Fingers; columns of sand colored stone which pointed straight up like lumpy antennas or needles fixing to pierce a deeply blue sky.

"This is better." She squinted in bright sunshine, taking in how far High City spread. Halfway out, the great wall circled, cupping the inner city like a crystal goblet treasuring aged wine. Beyond that divider, the outer city sprawled right up to Old Forest, or vast fields, which she could barely see this side of the horizon.

Ahna leaned back against stone and closed her eyes. The panting was gone. She flared her nostrils, inhaling deeply, holding air inside before slowly releasing each spent breath.

Aiela didn't want to meditate. She wanted to go home to Chiffon and Auntie Sage and her animals. She wanted to go back to healing and learning and freedom. She wanted her parents.

"We're not children anymore." Ahna spoke into her mutinous yearnings.

"Then why do I feel so afraid?"

Ahna shrugged, opening her eyes. "I can't answer that for you. *I'm* afraid because there's no way I'm enough... wise enough, strong enough, convincing enough... my list of 'not enoughs' stretches as long as this view. I can't even handle my dreams, much less what Ziel just told us. Only visions and words—yet it's too much. What am I to do when real things happen?" She sighed. "That's why *I'm* afraid."

Aiela pondered this for a moment. Why was she afraid? "Do I die in your dreams?"

"Yes."

"All of them?"

Ahna thought for a moment. Nodded. "Yes."

"Maybe that's why I'm afraid. Since I was about sixteen I started dying in my dreams too. Maybe some part of me has started to believe it. Papa and Mama died while they were still young and it scares me. I don't want to die young. It's like I'm desperate to complete life, to not leave those I love. I want to marry Turner, and have babies and live a long and exciting lifetime with him. I want to see you fall in love and have babies that play with mine and they all grow up loving each other like we do. I want to heal people so they can live too... "

Ahna reached for her hand. "I won't let you die. You're the only reason I have hope. Together, we can do... whatever it is we're supposed to. Without you, I'd probably run and hide, do less than nothing. Besides, the prophecy doesn't say anything about us dying. Ziel's quite certain the two of us together, is what it speaks to."

"I hate fear."

"Yes, but the flip side of it is love, and you don't hate that."

Aiela closed her eyes, tilting her face up to the beaming sun. "So what do you want to do? Believe Ziel? Go along with his plans?"

Ahna puckered her lips and drew her knees up to her chest, wrapping her arms around them like a flower closing against the winter chill. "He may or may not have it *exactly* right. But strange things are happening. I'm fairly certain something is coming and we're already in a position to deal with it, thanks to Ziel's belief in the prophecy… and in us. We might as well go along with it. For now."

"What would Papa and Mama say? Do you think they knew? Does Auntie Sage?"

Ahna smiled. "Add those to the list of questions. He's got a lot of explaining to do. I think… I think Papa and Mama would tell us to do our best and not worry about the Prophecy. In the end, does it really matter? Things will either work out—or they won't."

They walked back down after a time, making plans all the way, excited, now that they'd absorbed a bit, discussing Ziel's startling new assignment.

"We should probably travel to the sites of proposed colonies. Maybe Turner can come along… "

"We'll get to go through all of Atlantis' greatest treasures, decide what's most important to preserve… I want *that* job!"

"Are you going to tell Turner? How we're meant to be great and special *Ones*, fulfilling a prophecy to save our people?" Ahna inflected the words with sarcastic grandiosity.

Aiela laughed. "I don't know. Not yet. I'll have to think about it. It sounds too silly still. I'm not sure I could say it without laughing."

"I'll get right to the point. You eat, I'll talk." Ziel passed a platter of charred plums stuffed with goat cheese and drizzled balsamic.

A plate of smoked sea bass smelling of maple, sat next to the orange and jicama salad Aiela was already spooning onto her plate.

"I want to transfer control of the Second Moon to the Crystal Cathedral. Backup controls, that is, in case the center goes down or the controllers are compromised. It's a relic, but still too powerful of a weapon. We can't completely disarm it—without bringing it down to take out the actual components. The weapon's system could still be controlled from this end, if someone knew what they're doing. I've already had another backup console built, it just has to be installed and tested.

"Day after tomorrow, I've scheduled one of the controllers to train you both on it. It's not difficult, pretty self-explanatory. Once you're comfortable with the console, we'll place it down there and test it."

Aiela talked around her mouthful. "I don't even know what we use it for."

"No, I don't suppose you do. It's been such a fixture, hanging there in the sky since the last epoch, no one even thinks of it. Originally, it was launched with the purpose to magnify and reflect, or distribute power throughout our grid. Our power generators were still small at that time and simple, so the Second Moon more than tripled the output.

"Also, it was the weapon that stopped other nations from constantly attacking us. It's equipped with a laser, capable of decimating an area the size of High City. That threat alone convinced the rest of the world to let us be. Some believe the Moon is responsible for this golden age of prolonged peace.

"Here's what they don't know; its surface slides open to reveal Sound Eye stones, similar to the one I sent with you to Greece. Positioned and programmed correctly, it could take over the will of millions—though only if they connect to the field by looking at it."

"Ah." Ahna said. "That's why they made it so pretty."

"They expected it would be here for millennia so we'd certainly want something attractive. It was meant to stop invasions without bloodshed. We no longer use it to distribute power. Our new Crystals are more than enough. We don't actually need it anymore, but its mere presence seems to deter wars. Besides that, bringing it down would be a major undertaking due to its size, and I imagine our people would riot if we removed it permanently."

"I would." Aiela said indignantly. "It's the icon of our country. It stands for all that we're capable of and all our ancestors accomplished. Without the Second Moon hovering in our sky, we wouldn't even know we were in Atlantis anymore. It'd be like taking away the real moon."

"That may be. But the reality is, it's little more than a massive piece of pretty junk. I'm only concerned it's never used against us."

"You should be more patriotic." Ahna scolded him.

"Patriotism is like romance my dear, designed to bind people together—difficult to sustain while living in reality."

Aiela snorted. "Well then, reality is overrated."

Ziel's boom of laughter rolled around them. "Let's walk to the markets and find dessert when we're done here. We all need a treat, yes?"

"Yes!" They chorused, relieved to be done with revelations.

36

CARVER

"When dark creeps in and eats the light, bury your fears on Sorry Night.
For in the winter's blackest hours, comes the feasting of the Vours.
No one can see it, the life they stole. Your body's here but not your soul... "

— SIMON HOLT, THE DEVOURING

CARVER

Carver woke from another dream of Ahna.

She'd been haunting him more nights than not, ever since the handful of days he'd ruled Belial in his father's stead. Showing up to taunt him or seduce him, she might scream at him, or stand mute and stony while he begged her forgiveness. Always she knew of her Papa's murder.

This time he'd found Mardu standing over her dead body, his hands dripping blood. Mardu had laughed in triumph, expecting Carver to celebrate the dark sticky proof of his victory. Instead, Carver woke with dread clutching his heart like a lead fist.

He got up for water. Tapping his heart center, he whispered to the dark "It's not real. Only a dream... only a dream." Waving the light onto a dim glow, he unstoppered a terracotta jug and drank deeply, hoping to wake enough to forget the dream, rid his heart of this heaviness. Shadows sat in corners of his too-large bedchamber, watching him.

He waved off the lights, returned to sit on the edge of a mattress so big it could sleep six. Darkness was more comfortable. Light only showcased all the things he didn't want to see.

The glare of Temple City ruined the night outside his third story window. He couldn't even tell how long it might be until dawn. Rising again to stand at the window, he strained to see stars, the moon, anything that wasn't Belial built. Anything to remind him there was a better world out there. But he hadn't seen stars since he'd gone to the Belial Mines and met Turner. Before that, it had been Ireland.

Settling back into bed, he let his mind return to that last night on the beach in Scotland. The last night of the Ireland trip where his love for Ahna was sealed, branded permanently into his heart. A crescent moon had shone. Stars blanketed the sky as he and Ahna made love to ceaseless beach music. Even now, the memory of her body made him hard and he groaned. Would it never fade? Would he always be caught in this limbo of memories too precious to let go, her love imprisoning him forever?

His hand moved, releasing at least the physical frustration, his mind transfixed on images: Her delicate outline rocking above him in the moonlight or moaning softly beneath him once he'd found her rhythm. Teasing glimpses of breasts and sex while she dressed in the pink light of morning. If it were a holographic recording he'd have broken it long ago, watching it so often.

SUNLIGHT WOKE him again and he scrambled out of bed. It must be late. Why hadn't Orja woken him earlier?

A servant knocked and entered. "You're expected in your father's library. He's waiting..."

Carver nodded, yanking on clothes. "I know... I'll be there shortly. Where's Orja?"

"Serving the Dominus so he don't get angry at you."

His brothers were lined up in front of the dragon skull desk when Carver arrived. Rarely all together anymore, they still lined up in birth order out of long habit, and he took his place at the end.

Mardu sat eating behind the desk, while Sarim reported on the readiness of the next shipment from the Crystal Mines.

"... hard with only a few Muta workers left, so I've captured a village of natives like you suggested. The Muta trainers are teaching them to—"

"Oh look! Lazy's finally decided to join us." Mardu interrupted, turning all the brother's eyes towards him.

He knew without looking, their faces held contempt, disgust, envy and annoyance.

"You're better than me now, better than them, so you can arrive anytime you please?"

"No. I am very sorry to be late. I have no excuses Dominus. Brothers." He bowed deeply, keeping a blank expression. The line between perceived groveling and defiance was like walking a slack rope over a pit of hungry lions.

"I'd punish you but you're too damn boring to bother with. See it never happens again." Mardu snapped. "Sarim, continue."

Carver's stomach growled as scents of fried pork and eggs with cheese wafted from the platter at his father's elbow.

"The Irish ships are due to arrive by new moon. I've been ready for them since I left to come home." Sarim finished grandly. Carver suspected he was exaggerating.

"I want you to leave within the hour and return there. You will seize the Irish when they arrive. Every crew member, cook and captain. You'll need a secure place to imprison them until I come. Preparing that will take all the time you have between now and then. Treat them well, but give them no information."

Sarim's face was mutinous. No doubt he'd been anticipating a few nights of pleasurable substance-induced haze, long days of naked bodies servicing him before returning to the ugly brutality of empty Muta camps and a mine with too few workers. "May I ask why?"

"You may. The man who killed my Mutazio is a young Irishman with curly hair."

Carver's stomach dropped. *Surely Turner hadn't done it by himself? A young Irishman with curly hair...*

"I intend to kill every one of those vermin if I have to, to get information. Somebody will know who I'm looking for." Mardu spat.

"And... what about the shipment?"

"There won't be a shipment. I have other plans for the fleet. Sit! All of you sit down. You're like stupid hovering vultures. Orja!"

She stepped into the room while the brothers dragged chairs from the library's edges and lined them up, in order, sitting before Mardu's desk.

"Bring food for my sons."

She smiled indulgently at them. "It is already hot. Each of your favorites." Three servants came in, balancing trays loaded with plates and goblets, anticipating the desires of their young masters.

Carver's stomach soured even further. His father was in a good mood. He should have known from not being mercilessly berated, or ridiculed or meted some cruel punishment earlier. And now they'd been invited to sit and join him in a meal. Mardu hated spending time with his offspring. He was only hospitable when excited. And he was only excited when he'd planned some atrocity that brought him more power, more money or more pleasure.

"I'm giving each of you an important task, so listen carefully to the plan. We'll meet with the Generals at noon. Except you Sarim. I expect you to be gone by then. Eat, eat!"

They dug obediently into steaming heaps of food.

Carver would've laughed at the expressions on their faces, if he wasn't so on edge.

All four of them appeared to be hung over. Balek's face was actually green as he took tiny bites and swallowed quickly. No wonder none of them had joined in Mardu's rather gentle reproach, or made suggestions how best to punish his tardiness. No doubt the servants had had to track them down in unsavory places to deliver Mardu's summons last night.

None of them were allowed to bring pleasure girls or even friends home. The times Balek and Ramon had tried to sneak a girl in, Mardu had arranged an accident to cripple one, and sold the other as a pleasure slave. He'd considered it a mild reprimand, assuring the boys next time they'd have to do it themselves. His brothers spent less than three nights a moon in their own beds.

"The time is finally come to take Atlantis."

Every one of them sat suddenly upright.

Carver's was a stiffening near to panic.

"High City was behind the muta assassination and I won't stand for it. Neither will I go groveling to them about blood laws and retribution—though I want them to think I am. Ramon, this is your task. You will meet with the Rulers in High City and demand with your silver tongue more than they will ever give. Charm them, cow them, do what you do best, as long as you distract them from any thoughts of real retribution. You leave in the morning."

Carver almost sighed audibly with relief. The possibility of seeing Ahna again was equally a dream and a dread. He still went back and forth on whether she'd forgive him for all he'd done, or despise him to the depths of his being. Mostly, the latter won out. Who could love a man stuck in his own darkness, and too weak to get out?

"Balek and Carver, you'll go to Anubis, ready their army and bring them to the mines. You'll need to move them fast. They will be the first wave of invasion, using the Irish fleet. Meihal's ships will be allowed to sail right into High City's inner harbor and dock, now that they've twice delivered crystals and are slated to again. Instead, they'll deliver an onslaught of Anubis. Once the Atlantean soldiers are fully engaged with the Anubis, our army will launch a second, much bigger assault and subdue the city. I will take Poseidon's Palace and force the Rulers to surrender. Under the Sound Eye's spell, they'll subdue their own country for me. There may not be many who can even fight by then. They'll be weak and dying long before the Anubis ever arrive." He paused for effect, stretching out the cryptic silence by eating a few bites.

"Norse, you'll stay here and oversee the inoculation of Belials before I release the Bio weapon. We're calling it Chimera." He smiled. "Here's the best part; High City won't even know they've been attacked until it's too late. Crazy Montauk has found a way to program in a trigger. We'll spread Chimera in plenty of time for everyone to breathe it or infect each other, and then the moon will activate it. Chimera is a blend of six diseases, which should make it harder for them to find a cure, before a great many die."

"Why can't *we* attack first? Why let the dogs have all the fun?" Balek started whining and the others clamored for attention with addendums to the plan, or their own assignments.

For once Carver was glad of them. It felt like he'd been kicked in the chest and he couldn't decide whether to fight for breath or fight the little bit of food he'd swallowed from coming back up. He leaned forward, trying to concentrate on keeping his expression blank. Mustn't let the despair show in any way—or the fear.

Breathe in. Breathe out. Get her face out of your head. Breathe, dammit, breathe. Now's not the time for thinking. Time for that later.

Turner's on his way into a trap. Ahna's going to be infected, have to warn her... have to stop it... NO! I can't think of that now. One thing at a time.

Surely High City would have defenses Mardu hadn't thought of. They hadn't sustained five hundred years of peace—a thousand more if you didn't count Onus Belial's uprising—without some very effective defenses. Greece would come to their aid. Especially so soon after the failed attack on them, they'd be rabid for revenge.

"And what of you?" Mardu's voice jerked him back to the present.

At least he could breathe now—and hadn't vomited.

"You have no complaints or demands?" Mardu eyed him suspiciously.

The other boys were leaving, grumbling under their breath.

"Too good for anything I ask them to do! Good for nothing!" Mardu spat loudly after his sons as they left the room.

Carver straightened, squaring his shoulders. *Time to put on a show.* "Only curious why you want me to go with Balek." He left the question hanging.

"Don't play stupid. You know as well as I do, Balek's a danger no matter where I put him. I keep thinking he'll mature at some point... instead he's overly confident and easily distracted. Use him to terrorize if needed, but bring the Anubis to me. I'll make it clear to him you've equal authority."

Carver nodded. "That was my concern. He'll hate having to listen to me."

"He'll hate what I do to him if he doesn't... "

How many times do I have to save them? This can't be happening. You knew it was coming. You knew... The voices were warring in his head now.

"I know you have a soft spot for Atlantis but look at it this way." Mardu stood, draining the last of his morning wine. "There'll be all the sweet little Atlantean girls you could ever want, once we're there." He gave a crude and harsh laugh. " Don't think I haven't noticed you don't care much for Belial cunts. Hey, maybe we can find the twin... which one was it? One of Drey's little bitches, from the Ireland deal— if she doesn't die from Chimera—you could have her every night again. Would you like that?"

Rage lit an inferno deep in his groin. Anger, building since being born into the household of this evil man, unfurled, clearing everything in its path; the panicky thinking, the helplessness, even Ahna's trusting face. The rage forged all of it into a deadly iron calm.

Looking straight into his father's calculating eyes, Carver let the fire fill him completely.

"If we both live through it, I'll make her my own."

~The End~

(to be continued in Book Three)

ACKNOWLEDGMENTS

Many thanks to those long-suffering souls who read early drafts, and helped us make it better.

Many thanks to Jason for his support of Diana's life shifts toward fulfilling a lifelong desire to write. Eternal gratitude to Roy, Logan and Cole for cheerfully excusing Donna from the role of spouse and mom whenever she was on a roll, or needed a writing retreat, or just ignored you because she was lost in the story.

You set us free. And that's true love.

Thank You to Readers

Hands together at the heart, we offer a deep and flourishing bow to each one of you, our beloved readers. Without you falling in love with the heroines and heroes, imagining the splendor of Atlantis, despising the black-hearted villains, and wondering what'll happen next, this story would only be words on a page. Our sincerest gratitude for bringing it all to life.

If you enjoyed this book, please leave us a review on Goodreads, and wherever you purchased it. Your rating and words have a powerful influence on potential readers, and the mysterious algorithms of online marketplaces.

We would love to connect with you. Visit us at www.ddadair.com.

BIBLIOGRAPHY

Though we read every book and article we could find on Atlantis—or any other ancient advanced civilizations that might relate to Atlantis, the following were the most impactful, with data points that repeated. These are the books or articles we'd most recommend.

Andrews, S 2004, *Lemuria and Atlantis; Studying the Past to Survive the Future,* Llewellyn Publications, Woodbury, MN.

Andrews, S 1997, *Atlantis: Insights from a Lost Civilization,* Llewellyn Publications, St. Paul, MN.

Cannon, D 1992, *Jesus and the Essenes.* Gateway Books, Bath, UK

Cannon, D 2001, *The Convoluted Universe: Book One,* Ozark Mountain Publishing Inc., Huntsville, AR.

Cannon, D 2005, *The Convoluted Universe: Book Two,* Ozark Mountain Publishing Inc., Huntsville, AR.

Cannon, D 2008, *The Convoluted Universe: Book Three,* Ozark Mountain Publishing Inc., Huntsville, AR.

Cannon, D 2011, *The Convoluted Universe: Book Four,* Ozark Mountain Publishing Inc., Huntsville, AR.

Cannon, D 2015, *The Convoluted Universe: Book Five,* Ozark Mountain Publishing Inc., Huntsville, AR.

Cannon, D 2014, *The Search for Sacred Hidden Knowledge,* Ozark Mountain Publishing Inc., Huntsville, AR.

Cannon, D 2012, *Keepers of the Garden,* Ozark Mountain Publishing Inc., Huntsville, AR.

Cayce, E 1968, *On Atlantis,* Hawthorne Books, NY, NY.

Donnelly, I 1882, rev. 1976, *Atlantis: The Antediluvian World,* Dover Publications Inc. NY, NY.

Hancock, G 1995, *Fingerprints of the Gods,* Three Rivers Press, NY, NY.

Hancock, G 2015, *Magicians of the Gods,* St. Martin's Press, NY, NY.

Michell, J 2013, *The New View Over Atlantis,* 3rd Edition, Hampton Roads Publishing Company, Charlottesville, VA.

Santesson, H.S. 1972, *Understanding Mu,* 2nd Edition, Coronet Communications, Inc. NY, NY.

Tyberonn, J 2010, *AA Metatron Channel: 'Revisiting Atlantis: The Crystalline Field of 10-10-10',* https://atlara.wordpress.com.

Wilson, C and Flem-Ath, R 2008, *The Atlantis Blueprint: Unlocking the Ancient Mysteries of a Long-Lost Civilization,* Delta Trade Paperbacks,

Wilson, S and Prentis, J 2011 *Atlantis and the New Consciousness,* Ozark Mountain Publishing Inc. Huntsville, AR

ABOUT THE AUTHOR

Author Bio

Sisters Donna (Adair) McMurtry and Diana Adair, were trekking up Colorado mountains or soaking in hot mineral springs while they plotted the Golden Age Series. Atlantis, and other periods of history, have been a long-time obsession and over 10 years of research went into their first series. Luckily, being Quantum Healers who specialize in past life regression hypnotherapy, they can access history first-hand" so there's many more stories to come!

They both live in the wild west. Diana has built her own tiny home in the mountains with her partner and two big hairy dogs. She loves trail-running and climbing fourteeners. Donna writes, hikes, and plays in her own mountain paradise with husband, two nearly grown sons, and two dogs.

Together they're known for hugging trees, constantly plotting future stories, and occasionally podcasting. (thespiralpath.podbean.com)

facebook.com/ddadair

amazon.com/author/ddadair

Continue reading for an excerpt from *"Atlantis Moirai"*.

FESTIVAL OF THE SUN

9,984 BCE High City, Atlantis

"I worship at the temple of the skies." -Albert Einstein

Aiela

Aiela swayed in a sea of thousands to hypnotic chanting, coaxing a new day's sunrise. Standing beside Ahna, as she'd done for nineteen years, she let her mind rest in the present glory of this moment.

> *Come children come, raise the radiant sun.*
> *Up from the dawn, drawn by our song.*

It was a whisper from the lips of the entire nation, though it sounded more like the swish and pull of ocean waves.

I miss Turner. She conjured a favorite image of him; naked on his back staring up at her. She loved how his muscles formed wings behind his ribs and his brown eyes laughed under tight, fire-sparked curls when he looked at her. His expression always held wonder, as if she had bestowed a fairytale kingdom upon him.

Ahna stopped murmuring the chant to cast her a sideways look with raised eyebrows. Her dainty, blonde twin shared such a mind-bond she sometimes saw what Aiela did. Rolling her green eyes at the distraction, she went back to watching brilliant melon colors morph and brighten on the horizon.

She's right. I should be grateful to be in such majesty. Grateful for those I do have.

Festival of the Sun had begun. Celebrated at Spring Equinox, holy and revered since the birth of Lemuria, this longest-held human tradition would rolick for seven days.

Behind her, the entire grounds of Poseidon's Palace were lustrous and festive, adorned with tiny orb lights outlining each corner, curve and cleft of architecture. Solar fabric shrouded windows and doorways, still glowing golden from yesterday's charge.

Eggs of all sizes, along with the seeds of many plants were combined into a dazzling array of artistic creations, from sculptures to paintings and even furniture. A nod to the origins of springtime festivals when they were about the art of sexuality, the magic of procreation.

Far-off clouds colored the eastern sky in vivid swatches, drinking up sacred newborn sun rays. This sunrise marked Spring Equinox morn, perhaps the most holy of holi-days because it honored their physical source of life.

> *Here stand stones and people together*
> *Honoring light, bridging forever.*
> *For stars we were and stars we will be.*
> *Circling through eternity.*

I miss Mama and Papa.

Ahna stopped whisper-chanting again and squeezed her hand. Bubbles of sadness rose between them, glistening as tears when they shared a sad smile.

> *Return to us now, thou most cherished orb,*
> *We reflect your great light. For by you we're reborn.*
> *Rise this new day, never the same.*
> *Nourish us well as we walk on Earth's plane.*

All who could, travelled here to High City for the celebration. Every guesthouse and inn overflowed. Every home hosted relatives and friends, whether hexagonal farm houses dotting fields, orchards and vineyards far outside High City's wall, or neat, closely spaced "outer city" row houses, or elaborate tree houses in OldForest, or high rise apartment buildings in High City proper. Elaborate linen tents erected in parks, gardens, and open spaces, housed the rest. It was estimated a full third of Atlantis' population packed into High City for part or all of Festival of the Sun.

Come children come, raise the radiant sun.

Up from the dawn, drawn by our song.

The whispery swish of the chant grew collectively louder while the sky lightened, until the air itself hummed.

From their spot at the back of the Palace courtyard, Aiela watched performers onstage prepare in a buzz of positioning. Jam-packed with string musicians and vocalists, the eastern Palace stage would lead the hymns. Elevated here, at the foot of Holy Mountain, sunrise would light them first, wafting across Atlantis' capital, borne on tunes of eloquent praise.

Sure enough, before the last refrains of the chant ended, a blinding tip of sunlight reached over the horizon and the stage awoke with song. It was sweet and rhythmic music, rich with harmonies. The choir onstage sang softly so as not to drown out the delicate stringed instruments. Everyone swayed to this new beat, a sea of faces tipped skyward.

Concertos would follow sunbeams as they spread over the city, washing across all the stages, concert halls and bands of musicians in the streets, until reaching the Temple of the Sun where trumpets, flutes, saxophones and tubas would greet it with blasts of joyous symphonies.

Feasts would be served after the sunrise ceremony to break the night's fast. Each day of the week would be filled with classes and lectures, presented by the best High City had to offer—scientists, oracles, healers, artists and priests at the forefront of their respective fields. People came to learn of the newest discoveries, to take home updated tools, skills and ideas.

Aiela's stomach grumbled. She'd usually have broken her fast and had two meetings by this time.

"Back to work. We've only a few hours." Ahna left her side, edging out of the singing, humming crowd. Aiela followed her to a deserted small kitchen inside Poseidon's Palace where they filled a basket with winter citrus fruits, soft-boiled duck eggs and buttery millet muffins.

"To my room?"

Ahna nodded and led the way.

Aiela grabbed a bottle of cream for the rich coffee she favored these days and followed. "You brought the books?"

"Ugh. No. I forgot." Ahna frowned. "I'll go get them. Here." She handed the food basket to Aiela and veered off towards her own room. She seemed a tad grumpy this morning.

Aiela's mind turned to preparations. Ziel would be giving talks twice a day during Festival about the possibility that Atlantis was facing disaster. He'd tell the packed-in crowds about Oracle visions and prophecies, then ask for volunteers who wanted to colonize other continents—just like he'd been doing for several weeks, only now the audience was a hundred times broader. It was Aiela and Ahna's job to organize these volunteers, assigning them destinations, advising on supplies and travel. Of course they had whole teams of people helping to carry out their plans but Aiela was exhausted from trying to keep up with it all.

They'd spent the entire last week researching three new areas where they could send volunteers. Browsing through anything the archives held on the land, the climate, the culture or peoples who inhabited those lands, they'd pinpointed places on maps. Already, expeditions had left to Egypt and Scotland. Families or groups would settle into these areas and send word back on the conditions, their needs, and how many more could be accommodated.

Some were going to distant kin in Greece, taking small libraries with them.

An entire abbey of priests and priestesses had sent word they were relocating to the mountains of Tibet. They had their own portents and prophecies about what was coming and intimated they would establish a spiritual school in their new lands.

Aiela would meet with representatives of other like-minded groups this afternoon to hear and record their plans and provide any needed resources.

Ahna returned, inhaling appreciatively the scent of coffee and warm muffins. "We still don't have many architects or builders. Experienced builders, healers and farmers should be our focus this week. Let's ask Ziel to specifically mention we're in need of those."

Aiela nodded, kicking strewn clothing into a pile. "We've an abundance of educators and scientists though, and those willing to do mundane work— which is good—they'll just need a few leaders."

They worked together, folding Aiela's bed up against the wall, pulling the largest nesting table out and unfolding matching bamboo chairs to sit on either side of it.

"We need more translators too—human ones." Those were the hardest to find. Not many Atlanteans had bothered to learn other languages because they'd always had technology that did it for them. "The groups can't depend on tech to build relationships with the local inhabitants".

Stacking four muffins on a plate beside the fruit, Aiela sweetened coffee for herself, tea for Ahna. "I keep thinking... what if we're wrong? What if a disaster isn't coming for hundreds of years yet? Or never comes? We're sending all these people away from their homes—from everything they know... it could be for nothing."

Ahna had slumped on a chair, silvery blonde head resting on crossed arms. "They're choosing it. Nobody's forcing them. What if we're right and we're not doing enough?" Her tone was rote. They'd said all this before. Both of them worried endlessly—there seemed so much to worry about.

Aiela could feel her twin's disquiet as she set steaming mugs beside the stack of ledgers and notebooks containing their notes, records and plans. "The dreams again?"

"Yes." Ahna lifted her head to gulp green tea, wincing when it burned. "They're stronger than ever. Cycling now, trading details—nothing new."

"Which one... or ones?"

"The earthquake where the ground is falling away and I'm here in the Palace and I can't find you. You're just... gone—which is the worst part because of course I won't leave without you."

"You feel like it's prophetic they've started again or—"

Ahna was shaking her head. "Probably just an outlet for all this worry and busyness. Maybe my fears are bigger than I realize. Maybe the crystals are trying to add urgency." She shrugged. "I suppose I should go down to them. See if there's more they want to show us. It's been awhile... "

"Your colors are off. You should go to the Healing Temple, get help balancing. You've been working too much... " Aiela touched her sister's wrist, feeling immediately the exhaustion and behind that, latent fear.

"You're working just as much! We should *both* go." Ahna reached for a muffin, biting into the comforting warmth.

"It *is* fear, here, I'll—"

"No." Ahna pulled her arm away. "You're doing enough without spending more energy on me. I'll go to the Temple, alright? We could skip supper tonight. It won't be as busy then."

Aiela nodded slowly, understanding the wisdom behind the rejection. "Fine. And you know what else would help?" She let her lips curve in a sly smile, not waiting for an answer. "Sex. You need to find someone. Indulge in a little healthy recreation with him." She wiggled her eyebrows. "It really does raise my energy levels... and lowers stress."

Ahna rolled her eyes but she was smiling. They'd talked about this before too. "When have I had time to get to know anyone that well?"

"It's a vital connection. What about Jai? He adores you."

"Yes, and he's sexually attracted to *men*." Ahna spread jellied rhubarb on her millet cake. "I just—"

"—still miss Carver." Aiela finished, exasperation coloring her tone. "For the sake of every goddess Ahna! You can't go on forever 'saving yourself' for him!" She got up to splash more cream in her mug.

"I'm not saving myself. I've *had* sex since Carver."

"When? With who?" Aiela stopped and turned to stare at her, disbelief plain on her face.

"The night of Winter Solstice. With the Phoenix."

"What? That doesn't make any sense. And why haven't you told me?! Are you making this up so I stop bugging you?"

"It wasn't important... and we've been a little *preoccupied* wouldn't you say?"

Aiela put a hand on her hip, continuing to glare.

Ahna sighed but a mischievous glint crept into her eyes. "He was some friend —or relation maybe—of Jai's lover. I don't remember the exact connection... I'd had a lot of wine. He danced the Phoenix on one of the stages and when we got on a boat after midnight it just... happened." She shrugged.

Aiela waited, knowing she'd fill in more blanks.

"He was lovely—so utterly... graceful. I remember that much. I've no idea who he was really... "

"We'll ask Jai. Maybe you can find this Phoenix again." As if it was settled, Aiela got down to the business of eating, digging out pens for their planning session.

"No! I don't *want* to find him. I don't want random sex with strangers, I want—"

"—love." Aiela finished through a full mouth.

"Yes. I want love. Like you have with Turner."

"Look at you three!" Aiela hugged Nanat and the tiny sleeping baby she cradled, then big handsome Nirka. "So much has changed… it's very good to see you again!"

"You're like a family of golden gods." Ahna took her turn with embraces.

They were on the way into a reunion of those who'd traveled to Ireland together. Because of the festival, most of the students would be here and many of the teachers. It would be the first time they had seen each other since, and excitement ran high. Aiela wished again that Turner wasn't gone, sailing to pick up another crystal cargo. He would have so enjoyed seeing everyone.

"What's his… or her… name?" Ahna touched the dainty hand poking out of blankets.

"Nirka, like his daddy." Nanat had matured but she still looked at her mate the same way she had aboard the sea cruiser bound for Ireland, when she hadn't even known his name yet.

Nirka's smile was proud as he took the baby from Nanat and held him up. "He looks just like me. See?"

The tiny bald head lolled next to Nirka's blonde one. There wasn't much resemblance yet but Aiela still nodded. "He does! He's got a nose, mouth, two eyes even." When Nirka looked disappointed at her humor she added quickly. "You're both enjoying parenthood?"

They gushed, telling every detail of the birth, how much the baby slept, ate and voided, clearly fulfilled with having a new little family.

Inside a meeting room on the Palace's public level, they all greeted Felicia and then Jai. Spotting Helena and Healer Lira across the way, Aiela made her way over, stopping as other friends and acquaintances called to her. She wondered if she'd changed as much as some of them. No longer seeming new adults, many were mated now. All of them were ensconced in apprenticeships across Atlantis.

Finally, after midday meal was served, Aiela found time to speak with Healer Lira. "You've heard of the colonization movement?"

"Only a little. I did hear you and Ahna are organizing it." Lira's reddish brown skin was lighter after the winter moons and her long black hair hung loose and luxurious, unlike when they were traveling and Lira always kept it bound. She seemed somehow younger. Aiela could see the rosy glow of contentment surrounding her.

"I remember our conversations about teaching healing in other places and wondered if you're interested in going?"

Lira nodded slowly. "I might be. Tell me what you have in mind."

"We don't have many Healing Teachers yet. You could of course go anywhere you're interested but there's a place—part of the western continent Merika—that offers what we're looking for. They call is Mayra (current day area of Nevada and Colorado). Sparsely populated with first and second epoch Lemurian and even Atlantean descendants. Our own people really, just a couple epochs apart. Ahna and I both thought of you for leading the expedition there. If you lead it, you'd pick and oversee your team or new community so to speak. We can supply you with people, but ultimately they follow you. We put you in contact with the transportation team, the supplies and resources people. The leader determines the timeline, though we do encourage haste for two reasons: we don't know how soon disaster might strike and we're finding it's better to leave little time for people changing their mind."

Lira's brown eyes lit with interest. "I'll start researching Mayra. I am drawn, still, to establishing a school or schools on other continents but I don't know that I'm interested in *leading* a group. I'm more comfortable focusing on healing and teaching. My mate is a weapons specialist in the military so I'll need to have some conversations with him."

They talked until the others had moved on to other Festival activities. Ahna joined them and Lira agreed to meet them at Temple later that evening. "I will give you both a healing session. It should be pretty empty during supper. We can talk more then."

By suppertime the next evening Aiela and Ahna had recorded triple the number of people willing to leave Atlantis. Ahna yawned, pouring a light soup into mugs on the table, while Aiela

gathered dirty clothing out of the way. "Ziel's only held three lectures so far! At this rate, we'll have a tenth of the population involved by Festival end!" The enthusiasm of so many had breathed new life into their project. She'd hardly thought of Turner at all.

"I'm shocked how many people have received their own warnings." Ahna said, pulling ledgers and knowledge crystals from her pack so they could compare and compile. "A majority that I talked to used the word 'evacuation'. It still seems surreal, but that *is* what we're doing. Evacuating."

Aiela nodded. "I notice quite a few going, have ties to Lemuria. It's almost like their beliefs are stronger that Atlantis really is facing a crisis." She paused to dig out her own record books. "Does it seem like we've become recorders and advisors more than organizers? Everybody I've talked to already has a plan and is putting together their own communities."

Ahna smiled. "Picking their own places too! No more spending weeks researching and trying to guess where might be best. They've thought of things we haven't yet." She looked like a burden had been lifted. "This morning I met with a group leader planning relocation to the Yucatan. He's taking almost his entire village and their conrectus to help with building and farming. Even some warriors for protection. I'd just assumed our people will be welcomed because they bring methods and tools and healing to improve the lives of those they encounter but this man explained that our people could easily be enslaved."

"How quickly we've forgotten the lesson of the islanders in Ireland." Aiela said wryly. "You'll never guess who I talked to today!"

Ahna was busy eating her soup, and shrugged.

"Zan! From home! My old 'still-life tutor'—except now I realize he isn't really that old… "

"You saw Zan? How is he?"

"He caught me up on happenings at home. Auntie Sage sends her love and will come visit once all this 'festival hubbub' is over." They both giggled. Auntie Sage avoided hordes of people if she could. "He's going with a group to the Pyrenees. They have plans to build a temple and educate people on spirituality; the beginnings of humanity, our souls, Source and all that. I guess it's an especially wild and ignorant place and they feel called to bring light there—had already planned a long-term mission. It's just amazing isn't it? We had no idea so many were already feeling the need to move out for different reasons! Zan already has builders and tools and books of sacred teachings. They leave in two days!"

"Huh. Is anyone else we know going?"

"Nate and his whole family, Mira, a few growers and weavers." Aiela named several of their childhood friends, growing nostalgic as she and Ahna shared memories. "Most of the mission group is from the temple where Zan trained…"

"Oh!" Ahna interrupted her, " Before I forget, Ziel wants us both to spend tomorrow morning at the Hall of Records. The Alexandria ship sails with the next tide so they need to load the crates."

They'd spent two days with the Keepers of the Records, selecting precious items and complete histories to contribute to the world Library in Alexandria.

"He wants us to do a sweep of the restricted sections. He's made a list—things he thinks should go just for the sake of preservation—and look," she dangled a ring of keys encoded with crystals, "he gave me his *most secret* keys!"

Aiela's eyebrows shot up. Forgetting her protests, or that she'd already scheduled a morning of meetings, she reached for the keys. "He *would* give these to us when there isn't time to properly snoop!"

"We could skip the evening service tonight…" Ahna lowered her voice conspiratorially and raised an eyebrow.

Sunset services every evening during Festival were as beautiful and varied as the sunsets themselves. Storytellers held the crowds spellbound, making them laugh and cry in turn. Always the stories were imbued with principles teaching the Law of One. Of course there was music and dancing too.

In no way would it compare to this chance to delve into the underground chambers of the Hall of Records where so few were admitted.

"I'm just not sure how we'll get past the Keepers…"

"We have the *most secret* keys…" Aiela replied, with growing excitement, "…and direct orders from Ruler Ziel! What else do we need?"

Made in the USA
Columbia, SC
16 December 2018